PRAISE FOR *THE OPPOSITE OF ME*

"Smart and soulful, Pekkanen explores the place where self and sisterhood intersect." —*REDBOOK*

"Fresh, appealing . . . the story is at turns funny and poignant." —*BOOKLIST*

PRAISE FOR *SKIPPING A BEAT*

"A compelling and satisfying read . . . highly recommended." —*LIBRARY JOURNAL* (starred review)

"Heartbreaking and familiar." —*PEOPLE*

PRAISE FOR *THESE GIRLS*

"At turns bittersweet, laugh-out-loud funny, and painfully real." —JODI PICOULT, #1 *New York Times* bestselling author

"Pekkanen has a knack for making readers care about her characters." —*THE WASHINGTON POST*

W9-AXK-196

The Best of Us

The

Best

of

Us

a novel

SARAH PEKKANEN

WASHINGTON SQUARE PRESS

New York   London   Toronto   Sydney   New Delhi

Washington Square Press
A Division of Simon & Schuster, Inc.
1230 Avenue of the Americas
New York, NY 10020

First Washington Square Press trade paperback edition April 2013

WASHINGTON SQUARE PRESS and colophon are registered trademarks
of Simon & Schuster, Inc.

For information about special discounts for bulk purchases, please
contact Simon & Schuster Special Sales at 1-866-506-1949 or
business@simonandschuster.com.

The Simon & Schuster Speakers Bureau can bring authors to your
live event. For more information or to book an event contact the
Simon & Schuster Speakers Bureau at 1-866-248-3049
or visit our website at www.simonspeakers.com.

Manufactured in the United States of America

10 9 8 7 6 5 4 3 2 1

Library of Congress Cataloging-in-Publication Data

Pekkanen, Sarah.
  The best of us : a novel / Sarah Pekkanen. — 1st Washington Square Press
  trade paperback ed.
      p. cm.
    1. Female friendship—Fiction. 2. Self-realization in women—
Fiction. I. Title.
PS3616.E358B47   2013
813'.6—dc23
                                                    2012036378

ISBN 978-1-4516-7351-7
ISBN 978-1-4516-7352-4 (ebook)

For Greer Hendricks and Victoria Sanders

The Best of Us

Chapter One

The Invitation

TINA ANTONELLI STARED AT the heavy, cream-colored invitation like it was a loose diamond she'd unearthed in the sandbox at the neighborhood playground. No, it was even more valuable than a diamond, she decided as she leaned against her kitchen counter and felt her nightgown-clad hip squish into something. Grape jelly, she thought absently, recalling her early-morning frenzy of sandwich making for school lunches. She reread the first line of calligraphy:

Please join us in celebrating Dwight's 35th birthday!

Dwight Glass. Her old friend. How could he be turning thirty-five when she still pictured him at twenty: thin and awkward as a praying mantis, with a shock of brown hair always falling into his eyes? Dwight had lived in one of the coveted private rooms that encircled the grassy quad at the University of Virginia. While other students tossed around Frisbees or footballs on the sprawling lawn, the guys shirtless in the springtime and the girls wearing bright miniskirts or sundresses, Dwight rarely ventured past the little awning in front of his room. He always seemed to be sitting in a straight-backed chair, wearing an oxford shirt with one too many buttons done up, a thick textbook resting on his lap.

Our plane departs from Dulles International Airport on Sunday, August 18, at 10 a.m. and returns Saturday, August 24, at 5 p.m.

"Our plane," Tina said, the words as airy and sweet in her mouth as a spoonful of chocolate mousse. She'd heard that Dwight had bought his own Gulfstream a few years ago.

We'll stay in a villa in Jamaica that comes with a chef who will fulfill all of our culinary requests. You can choose to surf or snorkel, take a helicopter tour of the island—or do absolutely nothing but relax on a private beach and lift a champagne glass for the birthday toast!

A little moan escaped from Tina's lips. A cook. A private beach. Champagne. She envisioned a whitewashed villa with floor-to-ceiling windows thrown open to reveal a white-sand beach; white couches in the living room—and on the beds, crisp white sheets. Everything could be white because she wouldn't have to worry about four small children and one large dog spilling, shedding, messing, and breaking.

"Mommy!" Or yelling.

"Just a sec, honey," she said.

She imagined herself in a new bathing suit, bronzed like the girls in the Bain de Soleil ads, and mentally erased the pouch of her belly and the crow's-feet framing her eyes. Why not? She was being offered the trip of a lifetime, from a guy she'd kissed once in college (alcohol was involved, of course; lots of alcohol and dim lighting and the bittersweet knowledge that graduation was just around the corner) and who had drifted in and out of her life in the decade and a half since then. Anything was possible.

The telephone rang.

"Did you get it?" Her best friend, Allie's usually low, melodic voice tumbled over the line, containing unfamiliar hints of helium.

"It just arrived," Tina confirmed. "I thought it was a Drugstore.com delivery, so I opened the door in my nightgown to grab the box and I saw this freaking messenger in a tuxedo standing there! How many invitations did Dwight and Pauline send, do you think? It must've cost a fortune to have them hand-delivered!"

"Just three," Allie said. "You and Giovanni, me and Ryan, Savannah and Gary. Pauline called me last week for the addresses."

"And you didn't tell?" Tina squealed.

"And deprive the messenger of seeing you in a nightgown with no makeup?" Allie said. "Come on. I never would've ruined the surprise for you."

"I am too wearing makeup," Tina protested. "It just happens to be left over from yesterday. I fell asleep while putting the kids to bed and woke up in a miniature race car bed at five a.m., looking like a raccoon."

"I heard Angelina Jolie does that every single night, too," Allie teased. "Anyway, Pauline told me she was thinking about having a party for Dwight's thirty-fifth when I talked to them at my birthday party last year. I had no idea it was going to be *this* kind of party, though."

"Or that it would be just us," Tina said. "Doesn't he have any other friends?"

"Come on, Tina." Allie's tone softened the rebuke. "They're inviting you on an amazing trip. And he's a sweetheart. Be nice."

That was Allie: In college, Allie had lived next door to Dwight, although he'd been chosen to receive one of the quad's private rooms because of his academic record, while she'd been awarded one for her leadership qualities. Whenever Dwight had joined their group for pizza and beer or study sessions, it was because Allie had pulled him along—sometimes quite literally by the hand. Back then, she'd read to a blind man once a week at the library, loaned out her class notes to anyone who asked, and smiled at strangers she passed on the street. She was still doing those things—except now she was volunteering at a homeless shelter and baking cookies anytime the PTA asked. The smiling hadn't changed, either.

"Okay, okay, but it's completely insane!" Tina said as she shoved a box of Cheerios into the already crowded pantry. "A weeklong birthday party in Jamaica!"

"It gets better," Allie said. "Pauline e-mailed me photos of the place. There's an infinity pool with a waterfall and a huge hot tub and you won't believe how beautiful the beach is. It's just going to be us and the staff. Can you believe it?"

"The staff," Tina repeated in a mock British accent. "But of course. I take my own miniature-size staff everywhere, too, you know. They even accompany me when I go to the bathroom, unless I race there first and lock the door."

Allie laughed. "Tell you what, I'm about to run to Starbucks. Want me to swing by with lattes?"

"Are you kidding?" Tina said. "First a private jet and butler, now coffee delivery. I think I've stumbled into a Calgon ad."

"Moooooommy!"

"Or not," Tina said.

"See you in twenty," Allie said before hanging up.

"Sorry, honey." Tina hurried into the living room, where Jessica, her four-year-old, was lying on the couch, watching *Dora the Explorer*. A little puddle with an unmistakable smell had formed on the carpet next to her.

"I frowed up." Jessica stated the obvious.

"Oh, baby . . . oh, God, Caesar, no! No! Get away from that! Disgusting!"

Tina lunged and grabbed their big, shaggy mutt by the collar, dragging him through the back door and putting him in the yard. She hurried back into the kitchen, scooping up a roll of paper towels, a spray can of carpet cleaner, and a bucket from the cabinet under the sink. Jessica was the second of their kids to be hit by the stomach bug; Paolo, their eight-year-old, had just gone back to school yesterday after thirty-six hours of retching and moaning.

"I want apple juice," Jessica whimpered. Tina leaned over and touched her lips to her daughter's clammy forehead. She felt a flash of guilt as she remembered arguing when Jessica had protested going to pre-K earlier that morning; she'd thought Jessica's illness was born from the desire for the ginger ale and extra television time she'd seen her big brother receive.

"I'm sorry, honey, we're out. Do you want water?"

"Apple juice." Jessica began to cry, a thin, thready sound. Caesar scratched at the back door, doubtless digging deeper gouges into the wood. Tina thought about the enormous jumble of dirty laundry on the basement floor, the egg-encrusted dishes littering the kitchen sink, the new stain on the rug, which already resembled a Rorschach test. She had an hour and a half before she needed to pick up Sammy, her two-and-a-half-year-old, from preschool, and soon after that, the older kids would filter in, demanding snacks and needing rides to soccer practice and slinging backpacks and lunch boxes and shoes across the living room. She'd meant to start fresh today, to begin an exercise routine, to cull the outgrown clothes from the overflowing closets in their brick rambler, to read the newspaper so she'd have something other than the kids to talk about with Gio tonight. How did she always manage to get so far behind before the day had really begun?

I want my mom, Tina thought, feeling the familiar grief rise in her chest and settle into a hard knot. It had been six years since her mother died from breast cancer, and not a day passed that Tina didn't ache for her. Sometimes, like now, the memories slapped into her like rogue waves at the beach; other times they pulled her deep into a murky undertow that made breathing a struggle.

"Hang on, baby." Tina ran to the basement, got a fresh wash-cloth from the dryer, and rinsed it in warm water before hurrying back to wipe down Jessica's face and lips. "I'm going to get you apple juice," she promised. She found a blanket crumpled on the floor and made an executive decision to ignore the fact that it was covered in dog hair. She shook it out and covered Jessica. "Just wait a minute, honey. Mommy's going to fix everything."

She ran back to the phone and dialed Allie's cell number.

"Can you grab a couple of those little boxes of apple juice from Starbucks?" she asked. "Jessie's sick."

"Oh, my poor goddaughter," Allie said. "Of course. Anything else? A muffin?"

Tina caught a glimpse of herself in the mirror on the dining room wall. Still in her grape-jelly-stained nightgown, her too-long dark curls bouncing wildly around her face, evidence of the four children she'd carried forever imprinted in the roll around her stomach.

"Yes," she said, defying the promises she'd made to herself to begin a diet today—*another* diet. "Can you make it two muffins? Blueberry Streusel for Jess and low-fat bran for me. No, screw it, two blueberry. I'll pay you back."

She put the phone back in its charger, feeling beyond grateful that she and Allie had become best friends in junior high school and had both settled in their original hometown, less than five miles away from each other in Alexandria, Virginia. They'd shared all the milestones in life—first boyfriends, proms, weddings, childbirth, the loss of Tina's mom . . . Their husbands, Giovanni and Ryan, even worked in the same general field, since Gio was a construction manager and Ryan an architect, and they'd become buddies, too. Allie was the only person Tina could imagine inviting over before she'd had a chance to clean up and take a shower.

Tina reached for the invitation and read it one final time, then dropped it into the trash can, feeling a pang as it landed on top of toast crusts and stained paper towels. She thought about what it would be like to sleep as late as she liked, to sit down at a table and savor a gourmet meal—rather than gobble leftover mac-n-cheese—to sink into the soft sand and read an entire book. She used to love reading; when was the last time she'd actually cracked the cover of anything longer than a pamphlet of potty-training tips? She could almost feel the sun's warmth tickling her skin, taste the sweetness of a pineapple-rum drink, smell the coconut suntan lotion . . . They hadn't been on a vacation, other than a few family trips to the shore, since their kids were born. Money was far too tight.

But she hadn't been able to make it to the hairdresser's for three months; it would be impossible to escape to Jamaica for a week.

She'd write a letter to Pauline declining, and send Dwight a little gift. Maybe a bottle of champagne, even though he probably drank far more expensive stuff than she could afford. Allie was right; it was incredibly nice of him to invite them.

She put the carpet cleaner back under the sink, making a mental note to pick up Popsicles when she went to get Sammy at preschool. Poor Jessica would have to come along for the ride; she'd make sure to keep the windows rolled down and bring along a paper bag.

"Mommy!"

How could she and Gio ever go away, when there was no one they could leave their children with?

Allie Reed juggled a tray of lattes and a paper bag filled with muffins and juice boxes as she dug into her jeans pocket for the keys to her blue Honda minivan. She pushed the Unlock button for the door, then arranged everything: drinks in the cup holders, bag on the passenger's side floor, purse on the seat next to her. She glanced at the dashboard clock and made a quick decision. There hadn't been any line at Starbucks, for once, and the grocery store was on the way to Tina's house. She had time.

She pulled out of the parking lot, waving her thanks to the driver of an old pickup truck who slowed to let her go ahead of him, and steered toward the Safeway a half mile away. Because she and Tina talked almost every day, she knew that Tina was running low on milk and just about everything else, that Gio was working long hours, and that her old friend was probably only one more interrupted night's sleep away from becoming ill herself. She'd joked around when Tina mentioned wearing a nightgown and day-old makeup to greet the messenger, but the truth was, she was worried.

Allie's kids were older now—Sasha was nine and Eva was seven, both in school all day long—but she'd never forget the heavy, gray exhaustion that had enveloped her during their early years, when someone always seemed to be teething or wetting the bed or tripping and banging her head against the edge of the coffee table. She'd managed to power through it with the help of a constantly brewing pot of coffee, three-mile, stress-relieving runs when Ryan got home at night, and the oc-casional Saturday when Ryan had gotten up early and snuck out with the girls for pancakes. But the memory of the effort it required to maintain a constant vigil, to anticipate the dangers of bottles of cleaning fluids and speeding cars and exposed light sockets, of all the nights that felt like she'd caught a series of naps rather than a proper sleep, made her feel as if she'd gone through a kind of war.

Right now, though, her life was back in balance, and it felt es-pecially sweet. Allie loved her part-time job as a social worker, and she could fit in clients around the girls' schedules. They weren't rich, but Ryan's commissions as a residential architect, combined with her income, meant money wasn't a concern. She and Ryan were going through a particularly good stretch in their marriage, too. Watching him patiently coach the kids on Sasha's soccer team—who seemed to morph into a giant, thrashing mass of limbs around the ball—or run alongside Eva's two-wheeler, steadying her until she learned to pedal unassisted, conjured in Allie a different kind of love for him, deeper and richer than she'd experienced during the early days of their relationship. More and more lately, she found her eyes seeking out his during little moments, like the time Eva successfully recited a line in a school play, or when Sasha suddenly grasped the basics of multiplication. Seeing his pride and joy made her own multiply.

"Choose your husband well," Allie's mom had once said. "Because you're going to give him the most important job in the world: father of your children."

Allie had chosen exceptionally well. If they had sex a bit less often these days, if all of their activities seemed to revolve around the girls—well, wasn't that to be expected when you had young kids? She was one of the lucky ones, Allie told herself, rapping her knuckles on the dashboard as she pulled into a parking spot at Safeway. She never let herself take it for granted; it was one of the reasons why she served lunch at a homeless shelter every Tuesday and donated counseling sessions to abused women— why she paid into the karma coffers every chance she got. Life had treated her very gently so far. She prayed it would continue to do so, even though she secretly worried that every extra day of good luck was pulling the pendulum back a bit farther, tempting it to swing that much harder in the other direction.

She shook off her superstition as she hurried into the grocery store. "Good morning!" she called as she passed an employee stocking shelves with soup cans.

She began loading a cart: organic 2 percent milk, a large bottle of apple juice, wheat bread for toast, bananas and saltines, two freshly made pizzas from the deli section, and a big green salad. She tossed in a stick of butter, just in case Tina was low, then found the medicine aisle and added a bottle of children's Motrin, bubble gum flavor. That would take care of Jessica as well as dinner tonight. Allie crossed over to another aisle and picked up *People* and *Cosmo*—the good stuff; this was no time for the brain fiber of *Newsweek*. There was just one more thing she needed. She scanned the ice cream cases until she discovered the Häagen-Dazs, and added a pint of chocolate to her cart. She hesitated, feeling as though she'd forgotten something, then picked up a box of the brightly colored Popsicles her girls always wanted when they were sick.

Ten minutes later, she was turning in to Tina's driveway. She walked through the kitchen door, using the key on her chain.

"Coffee delivery!" she sang out. "And apple juice for my sweet goddaughter."

"We're in here." Tina's voice came from the living room. Allie rounded the corner and saw Tina on the couch with Jessica sprawled in her lap. They were both pale and listless; it was hard to say who looked worse.

"Oh, my God, you even remembered the cinnamon sprinkle on the foam," Tina said, closing her eyes as she took her first sip of latte. "I love you."

"You're talking to the coffee, right?" Allie said, fitting a straw into the little hole in the top of a juice box and handing it to Jessica.

"Of course," Tina said. "But you're not half-bad, either."

Allie gave Jessica's fine brown hair a quick stroke. "I have to get something out of the car. Be right back."

She brought in the groceries and filled Tina's refrigerator and freezer, then opened the dishwasher door.

"What's going on in there?" Tina called. "I hope you're not throwing a wild party. Or if you are, that you call me when it's time for the Jell-O shooters."

Allie laughed and finished rinsing and loading the glasses and plates. She wiped down the counters before going back into the living room.

"I'm not working today," she said, picking up Tina's feet so she could sit on the end of the couch, then dropping her friend's feet into her lap. "So I figure that gives me plenty of time to talk you into coming to Jamaica."

"What, and leave all this?" Tina tried to smile, but it didn't reach her eyes.

"Here's your muffin." Allie handed it to her along with a napkin. "Did Gio get home late again last night?"

"Eight," Tina said. "It's this blasted shopping center. Two of the plumbers didn't show yesterday, and they're already behind schedule . . . I shouldn't complain; it's not *that* late. It's just the whole homework-dinner-bathtime routine is so hard to do alone."

She tilted back her head and closed her eyes, but not before Allie caught the sheen of tears in them.

"I know," Allie said. She and Tina could do this; they could flow from jokes to confessions to painful subjects during the course of a single conversation. It was one of the things Allie most valued about their friendship. "It was hard for me with just two kids. I remember once when Eva was around one and I had her in the tub, and then I heard something crash in the kitchen. I ran down and Sasha was standing there with glass all around her. She'd tried to pull a big pitcher of lemonade out of the refrigerator, and of course she'd dropped it. So I picked her up and carried her to the living room and checked to make sure she wasn't bleeding. She wasn't, but, oh, my God, if that pitcher had landed on her head . . . And then it hit me: I couldn't hear anything upstairs. I ran so fast up those steps, I swear my feet didn't touch them. But Eva was just sitting there, filling up her little plastic cups and pouring them out."

"That kind of thing happens to me all the time," Tina said. She lifted her head and looked at Allie again. Her big brown eyes had lines of red running through the whites, like road maps documenting her exhaustion. "Ricocheting from crisis to crisis. Worrying there will be a time when I won't get there fast enough. Just one time."

"Come to Jamaica," Allie said.

"I can't," Tina said. "The kids." She bent her head and kissed the top of Jessica's head, as if in apology, then gave Allie a wry smile. "Unless I bring them along, but somehow I don't think Pauline had that in mind. I have a feeling we'd be asked to leave the first time someone threw up in the hot tub. Or definitely the second."

"My mom and dad are going to watch all the kids," Allie said. She'd set it up with her folks the previous week and had been dying to tell Tina. "They can stay at my house with my kids, and my parents will sleep there."

Tina's eyes grew wide, even as she protested. "No," she said. "That's too much for them."

"My girls are so excited," Allie continued. "They're going to help with the little ones—they're like babysitters in training. I told them we'd pay them twenty bucks each. You know your kids love them. And my mom loves *you*. She really wants to do this."

"I love your mom, too, but it's too much," Tina said again, but Allie kept talking over her.

"Tina, come on. My mom taught second grade for thirty-two years. And she's still got more energy than both of us combined. She'd be insulted if she heard you say that!"

Allie looked at her friend and remembered, as she so often

did, the time when she'd played tennis with her father on a Saturday afternoon a decade earlier. Walking to his car after the game, he'd complained of a feeling of tightness in his left arm. He'd blamed it on a muscle pull and said he was going home to lie down. But something in his face had sent an icy tingle down Allie's spine. Instead of driving home, she'd called Tina, who was just coming off a shift at the hospital where she worked as an ER nurse. Tina had asked quick, crisp questions—Did her dad seem confused? Did he have any other symptoms?—and when Allie had responded yes, come to think of it, he'd walked right past his car, and his face was pale, not at all flushed, like you'd expect after an hour of exercise in the heat, Tina hadn't hesitated.

"I'm turning around and heading to your parents' house. I'll meet you there," she'd said. "It might not be anything, but it's not worth taking a chance."

"Okay," Allie had said, putting her car in drive. "I'm leaving now."

"Allie? Call 911 first."

"Really? Do you think—" Allie had begun, but Tina had cut her off: "Do it right now."

Her father had made it home and was lying on the couch, suffering a massive heart attack, by the time the paramedics arrived. Allie's mother was out running errands. He was alone, and almost certainly would have died had it not been for Tina's intervention.

Now Allie reached over and rested her hand on top of her best friend's. She and her mom had talked about it, and this was a gift they wanted to give to Tina. "There's this terrific seventeen-year-old who sits for us sometimes—Lia. Remember I've mentioned her? She's going to come over every afternoon for a couple hours to give my mom a hand. We can put the kids in day camp, too. It's one week. They'll be fine."

"I can't—" Tina began, but this time she cut herself off. Allie could see tears filling her eyes again.

"You need to," Allie said. "Please. Just come."

"More Dora," Jessica said, nestling against Tina's body. Her eyelids were drooping. "More apple juice."

Allie reached over, grabbed the second apple juice box off the coffee table, and handed it to Jessica as Tina mouthed, "Thank you."

"We'll let them watch *lots* of movies," Allie said. "And order pizza. We can cook some stuff and leave it in the freezer beforehand so my mom won't even have to worry about meals. Doesn't that sound good, Jess?"

"More Dora," Jessica repeated, her voice almost robotic-sounding.

"And they say TV doesn't kill brain cells," Tina joked. Allie could see something come into her friend's eyes, something she hadn't seen in a while. A brightness.

"I may love you just as much as I love coffee," Tina said. "And that's saying something. Do you think when Pauline says we can get everything we want at the villa, that includes liposuction?"

"Oh, sure," Allie said. "We'll squeeze it in before the champagne and caviar and after the deep-tissue massages."

Tina tilted her head back against the cushion, and a huge smile spread across her face. Allie held her breath.

"I'm in," Tina finally said.

"This house has amazing bones," Savannah McGrivey said, being careful to keep her voice enthusiastic but not cross the line into gushing. No one trusted a gushing real estate agent.

She led the way through the living room and into the dining room. "The crown molding is original, and so is the wainscoting."

She stepped back and let the fortyish, prosperous-looking couple take in the space in silence. They'd pulled up in a BMW convertible twenty minutes into her open house, after she'd lit an orange-blossom-scented candle and put bouquets of blue and yellow wildflowers in the powder room and decluttered and scrubbed the kitchen counters. You'd think the owners would've listened to her suggestions to move out some of the furniture to make the rooms seem bigger, to replace the paisley wallpaper in the dining room with a fresh coat of neutral paint, to tear up the worn runner on the stairs. Savannah had even e-mailed them the name of a reasonably priced contractor, but they'd acted almost offended.

Isn't our house good enough? the husband had asked as Savannah considered the dated family photos in ugly gold frames lining the wall above the staircase banister. She'd turned to him with a smile, mentally accepting the fact that the portraits of their bucktoothed, turtleneck-wearing kids would stay.

"Of course it is," she'd said.

She hadn't been lying. But couldn't they see that good enough wouldn't cut it—that a little extra effort could mean the difference between a sale and a future spent languishing on the market?

She had an innate sense of how far she could push clients, and she knew it was time to let it go. But she began to question her decision as she saw her potential buyers notice the peeling edges of the wallpaper, the wife's manicured fingernail tracing a seam like it was a scar.

"What year was it built?" the husband asked. His potbelly strained against his blue golf shirt, and he rubbed it like he was trying to conjure good luck from a Buddha. He was probably hungry. Damn. She should've gone with freshly baked cookies instead of a scented candle.

"Nineteen eighty-five," Savannah said. *Smile,* she reminded

herself, making sure to include the wife in her gaze. When Savannah had first opened the door, the wife had looked her up
and down, then reached for her husband's arm. Wives tended
to react that way to Savannah.

"Needs a little work," the husband—Don? Dan? Did it
matter?—said. "If you tore down this wall, opened up the
kitchen . . . maybe bumped it out in back."

His wife yawned. She'd said they had young twin daughters;
no way would they want to take on the hassle of a renovation
along with a move. It all boiled down to maintenance, Savannah had learned. Forget houses with character and potential
and quirky charm—people were too busy these days to act on
a romantic fantasy of buying a fixer-upper. They wanted something pretty and pleasing, with no major flaws.

"Honey, we've got that other place to look at," the wife said.

"Would you like to leave your e-mail address so I can keep
you apprised of new homes that come on the market?" Savannah
offered.

"That's okay," the wife said, and ten seconds later, they were
gone.

Savannah closed the door behind them and leaned back
against it, rolling her head in circles to get the kinks out of her
neck as she kicked off her three-inch heels. She'd woken up
too early this morning, again. She'd known it the instant she
saw the weak gray light seeping in around the edges of the window blinds, and the anxiety that gripped her had immediately
chased away the possibility of falling back asleep.

For the first thirty-five years of her life, she'd been a world-
class sleeper. Nine, ten—even eleven a.m. on the weekends was
her routine. On the rare occasions when she did wake early,
she'd roll over and spoon against her husband, Gary's back,
soaking in his warmth, until she dozed again.

But for the past two months, their queen-size bed had seemed too big, and the sheets were always cold against her skin.

At some point Savannah would come face-to-face with her husband again to sign divorce papers. Gary had indicated he wouldn't balk at a fair division of their assets, which surprised her, given how few scruples he'd shown recently. But apparently the selective memory that had caused him to forget the fact that he wore a wedding ring had kicked back in, because he hadn't objected when Savannah's lawyer demanded compensation for the years Savannah had spent supporting Gary. She'd been so proud when he could officially add the initials "M.D." after his name, feeling as though it was their shared triumph. How ironic that an anesthesiologist had caused her the most pain she'd ever felt in her entire life.

But at least she'd be able to keep their pretty home, with its wide front porch and soaking bathtub and kitchen skylights on an eighth-acre of land in Charlotte, North Carolina. Gary would pay monthly alimony that would cover half the mortgage payment plus a thousand for expenses, just as he'd been doing ever since he'd cleared out his closet, packed up the expensive electronics, and taken the barbells he almost never used. She thought of those thousand-dollar checks as her screw-you money. She never spent them on car repairs or the electricity bill. Instead, she treated herself to massages and yoga classes, lacy push-up bras and pedicures, and an injection of Botox for the frown lines that had deepened since she stumbled across those messages on Gary's BlackBerry.

So she tore through his money, watching her hair become glossier, her clothes nicer, her body fitter. It didn't help as much as she'd thought it would. Still, Savannah knew she'd never looked better. She'd always been striking, with her hourglass shape and long, wavy hair with streaks of red and gold, and the

sort of full lips most women had to purchase from plastic sur-
geons. But she'd lost ten pounds after the separation—adultery
accomplishing what the Atkins diet and regular kickboxing sessions couldn't—and now her stomach was almost completely
flat, and her already strong jawline seemed more pronounced.

Savannah walked into the living room and flopped down on
a couch—upholstered in a client-repelling old-lady floral, of
course—and pulled her laptop out of her shoulder bag. She'd
kill time until the doorbell rang again by buying flannel sheets
online, then she needed to book an eyebrow and bikini-line
waxing.

She also had to make a decision about Dwight's invitation.
Dwight, she thought, as a smile played on her lips. He was such
an adorable geek. She was pretty sure he'd had a crush on her in
college, since he'd been pathetically eager to help her through
her math classes, but she'd never minded the attention. What
was the harm in teasing him a little, in leaning over the table
to let him glimpse her cleavage, in gently raking her fingernails
through his hair as he turned bright red and tried to keep his
mind on his stuttered explanations of variables and exponents?
She was just giving him a little ammunition for his nocturnal
fantasies; it was a form of charity, like dropping a few dollars
into the church collection basket.

They'd all known Dwight would become a millionaire—that
was as clear as the fact that Tina and Gio would get married
right out of college, and that Allie would find the perfect husband, produce two perfect kids, and stay as perfectly adorable
as she'd been her freshman year. Savannah wondered if the others had seen her own future as clearly as she'd predicted theirs.
Was it obvious that Gary was a user, that he'd unimaginatively
dump Savannah for a young, blond nurse, trading up as so
many of her real estate clients did?

Savannah had never truly cheated on Gary, but not for the lack of opportunity. She'd flirted with plenty of guys, though, and even kissed a few. But it never went any further than a few hot moments in the darkened basement at a party while everyone else chatted upstairs, or a lingering glance with a stranger at a bar that led to a quick tryst in the hallway outside the bathroom . . . What was the harm in a few kisses, a quick pressing up against an intoxicatingly new man? Flirting made her feel sexy, and when she came home, lifting the covers and whispering, "Wake up, honey," while she ran a finger under the waistband of Gary's pajama bottoms, she knew he was the one benefiting from it.

If Gary wanted to have a bit of fun with The Nurse, Savannah would've been furious, but she would've understood on some level. Guys were like farmers; they felt the need to spread around their seed. She would've made Gary sleep on the couch for a few weeks. But then she would have put on his favorite garter belt and black, silky stockings, and strolled into the den to invite him back into their bed. Her message would have been clear: This was what he'd miss if he strayed again.

But Gary hadn't apologized when she confronted him. He didn't beg for her forgiveness, or send roses. Instead, he moved in with The Nurse—who wasn't even that pretty! But she was young; Savannah would give her that. Try to hold on to him for another ten years, though, sweetheart, she thought as she felt her eyes narrow. In another decade, Gary would be richer and more established and he'd still look good. He was tall and lean, and his hair was just starting to turn silver around the temples, which suited him. But The Nurse wouldn't fare so well; she had the sort of thin, pale skin that would wrinkle quickly and severely, and her pear-shaped figure—which no doubt had been the catalyst for their relationship, since Gary was an ass man—would eventually lose its battle against gravity.

Savannah wondered if The Nurse wanted kids. Savannah most definitely didn't; it didn't even feel like a choice. It was more of a . . . *certainty,* like the fact that she had blue eyes and was highly allergic to shrimp. Gary hadn't wanted kids, either—at least, the Gary she'd once known hadn't. He was a stranger now, this man who hummed every time he shaved, who pretended he didn't read her *People* magazines in the bathroom, who had naturally broad shoulders that she used to love resting her head against.

Savannah forced away the memories and began to search the Internet for new sheets. She was considering a chocolate brown set trimmed in hot pink satin when an e-mail popped into her in-box. Allie.

Have you gotten any special deliveries recently?

Savannah typed back: *Yes, my new vibrator arrived this week. How did you know?*

She grinned as she hit Send. Allie was such a good girl; Savannah could almost hear her squeal.

Ha ha!

The messenger came yesterday, Savannah typed. *Unbelievable!*

Are you guys coming? Can Gary get off work?

Savannah's fingers paused over the keyboard. It would've been better if the invitation had come last year, when she and Gary were still together. Or next year, when Savannah could show up with a suitcase full of bikinis and a hot new boyfriend. She'd told her friends in North Carolina, but no one in the group from college knew because for some reason, saying the words—*I'm separated*—seemed almost as hard as actually going through a separation.

Screw it, she thought as she exhaled loudly. She'd pick up a new sarong and get a spray tan with Gary's next check, and she'd go to Jamaica. She'd dance barefoot to steel drum music on the beach and take a few windsurfing lessons, and fool around with the instructor, if he was as hot as Savannah imagined a windsurfing instructor was constitutionally required to be. She'd even give Dwight a few free glimpses of cleavage, for old times' sake.

Wouldn't miss it, Savannah typed.

She couldn't tell Allie about the looming divorce, not now. Allie would immediately phone, asking sympathetic questions in her gentle social worker's voice, and Savannah would probably do something ridiculous, like burst into tears. And then a good prospect would walk in the door and size everything up—ugly picture frames, bucktoothed children, peeling wallpaper, sobbing real estate agent—and flee.

She'd call Allie later, when she had a glass of good scotch in hand—the expensive, aged scotch Gary splurged on and adored, which Savannah had relocated to under the sink on his moving day.

Yippee! Allie wrote back.

Savannah could almost see her leaping into the air like the high school cheerleader she'd been. Savannah pictured Allie with her reddish brown hair pulled back in a ponytail, her big blue eyes bright, her perfect teeth displayed in a big smile. Since Allie went running almost every day, she'd probably be wearing spandex—but nothing too tight or revealing, which was a shame, because Allie had a cute little body, even if she was flat-chested. Why not show it off while she still could? For that matter, why not just buy a set of better boobs?

I can't wait! Allie wrote. *Hugs!*

Savannah smiled. Allie's relentless optimism could grate at times, but maybe it would be contagious on this trip, and Savannah could use a little infusion of joy. Sure, it might feel odd to be the only single one, but Savannah had always felt comfortable around Gio and Ryan. She'd kicked back with them on the couch many times, shouting orders at the football players on TV and drinking Sam Adams from the bottle, leaving Allie and Tina to gossip in the kitchen. In fact, *Gary* was the one who hadn't fit in with them; he had no interest in sports.

See you soon, babe, Savannah typed.

She needed to get used to doing things alone. She needed to feel desirable again. This trip would be a good start.

You could divide the ten women sitting around the big rectangular table into two equal-size groups, Pauline mused as she reached for the silver coffee service and freshened her cup of French roast.

Group A was composed of the high achievers: the well-connected women who brokered seven- and eight-figure deals and jetted to Tokyo for a day. They wore plain business suits and expensive watches, had short hair—Pauline imagined their schedules were too busy to accommodate blowouts—and frowned while their fingers flew across their BlackBerrys.

Then there was Group B, the ones like her. The spouses.

Pauline had already figured out that the high achievers had joined the board of Children's Hospital to balance the gritty realities of their day jobs, during which they screwed over employees and fattened the bottom lines of environment-polluting companies. They could tell themselves that they were doing some good—plus, it was a networking opportunity.

The spouses, on the other hand, did it to fill time, because the alternative was to shop, or take another exercise class, or look around for a room to redecorate.

The pot of coffee felt light in Pauline's hand, and as if he'd sensed her thoughts, Caleb, the house manager, turned to look at her. She glanced pointedly at the server, and he came over, relieved her of it, and replaced it with a fresh one.

"Anything else, Ms. Glass?" he whispered.

She shook her head, and he stepped back, his movements so smooth and discreet that he seemingly melted away.

Pauline hid a small, satisfied smile. Soon after she and Dwight had gotten married, eighteen months earlier, they'd moved into a home with a library big enough to seat twenty people. She oversaw a staff composed of Caleb, a maid, a gardener, and a part-time driver. Their two-story garage held five cars, including a classic Karmann Ghia, as well as Dwight's collection of vintage arcade games.

Pauline had grown up with some money—her great-grandfather was one of the founding members of the stock market—but the perception, carefully cultivated by her mother, was that the family was wealthier than they actually were. There was a big difference between founding the stock market and buying a lot of early shares, and while her grandfather had been a genius, he'd lacked common sense. Still, her trust fund had covered a top boarding school in Massachusetts and her degree from Vassar.

Pauline was about to turn twenty-seven and was working at an art gallery in Georgetown, on one of D.C.'s most exclusive streets, when she answered the phone call that would forever change her quiet, comfortable life. On the other end of the line was Val, her old boarding school roommate, who'd suggested a blind date with her husband's boss.

"He's kind of shy, very rich, and brilliant," Val had said, reeling off Dwight's attributes as efficiently as a police officer detailing a suspect's vitals. "He created a dot-com company right after he got out of college and took it public, then he sold most of his shares just before the Internet bubble burst. Now he's got

his fingers in a lot of different ventures. He's thirty-one. Not bad looking. I was seated next to him at a dinner last night, and I asked if he was dating anyone. He said no and asked if I knew anyone . . . so I thought of you. What do you think?"

"Sure," Pauline had said, a little too quickly. Why had Val picked her, especially since they didn't talk all that often? she'd wondered. Maybe all of Val's other friends were already taken.

She'd cringed, glad that the gallery was empty of customers and that Val couldn't see her face. Pauline certainly wasn't in old maid territory yet, but she'd long carried the expectation that she'd marry, and marry well. It was unspoken but understood, as clear as the rule in some families that only a union within the same religious faith would be acceptable. Pauline sometimes wondered if things would be different if her older sister—her only sibling—hadn't been born with congenital birth defects that required round-the-clock care. Therese was unable to speak and had the mental capacity of an infant, yet was fully grown. Her parents had entrusted her to a private institution, but Pauline knew insurance covered only some of the costs. And shortly after Pauline had graduated from college, her father had passed away from a brain aneurysm, leaving only a small portfolio and a smaller insurance policy.

As Pauline had traveled through her twenties, she'd begun noticing the changes: Her mother had suddenly professed an interest in taking over the gardening that had always been left to professionals; and she'd stopped traveling, complaining that planes were too crowded to make the experience enjoyable. Then the small warnings had erupted into larger ones: Her mother began talking about downsizing to an apartment—"All these stairs are so rough on my knees!" And Pauline had noticed a cherished heirloom diamond ring was missing from its usual place on her mother's right hand. She hadn't been able to bring herself to ask why.

Pauline had tried to slip her mother money, but her mother always refused to take it. "Buy yourself a pretty new dress," she'd say, but that seemingly carefree comment would be followed by a question with tension underlying it: "Meet anyone interesting lately?"

One night shortly before Val's unexpected phone call, Pauline had been unable to sleep and was flipping through television channels when she'd paused on a poker tournament being broadcast live from Vegas. The camera had zoomed in on a guy who looked like he was barely out of his teens. He wore a black hoodie and sunglasses and had spent a long time studying the five cards in his hand.

"I'm all in," he'd finally said, pushing his pile of chips forward.

The poker player and Pauline's mother were different genders, races, and ages, but in that moment, they could've been the same person. Her mother was going all in on Pauline, and while some daughters might've chafed under the weight of the implied responsibility, Pauline never did. She had the exact same goals for herself—or maybe she'd unconsciously absorbed her mother's so long ago that they'd become part of her.

Kind of shy. Pauline had repeated Val's words as she'd gotten dressed for her blind date, choosing a taupe silk sleeveless wrap dress. *Very rich.* She'd pulled her blond-streaked hair back into a chignon, applied brownish black mascara, and dotted the insides of her wrists with a delicate floral perfume. *Thirty-one.* She'd taken a final, appraising look in the mirror after she inserted her two-carat diamond teardrop earrings—fakes, but good ones—into her lobes. From a distance, she was classically beautiful. Closer up, one saw past the tricks of makeup and noticed that her eyes were set a fraction too close together, her mouth was a shade too small, and her nose was too narrow, as if someone had placed two strong hands on the sides of her features and squeezed.

Still, she'd once read that the three things women needed to be gorgeous were great hair, teeth, and skin. Those she had; those could be bought.

When she'd first glimpsed Dwight, what she'd felt more than anything was disappointment. The doorman had phoned to let her know Dwight was in the lobby of her apartment, and she'd picked up her clutch purse, counted off sixty seconds in her head, then gone to meet him.

Not bad looking, Val had said, but Pauline thought the assessment was overly generous. Dwight was as skinny as some of the women in her Pilates classes, wore a brown jacket with oddly large lapels, and had an angry red zit on his chin.

But she'd smiled, and reached for his hand, and spoken his name in a soft voice. And then he'd led her to his Mercedes, and whisked her off to one of those restaurants that was so exclusive it had no name on the door. Or maybe it was a club? She'd had no idea.

Don't screw this up, she'd warned herself as she sipped a glass of crisp Sancerre and perused the menu. One of her most embarrassing secrets was that she hated expensive food. Escargots, foie gras, and lobster tasted like slime and lard to her. What she really adored was comfort food: If she was on death row and being granted a final meal, she'd order mashed potatoes with gravy, roast chicken, and hot, yeasty buttered rolls—the kind that came out of a refrigerated cardboard tube.

Of course, that night in the restaurant—club?—she'd ordered the escargots and lobster, and she'd smiled through every bite. To this day Dwight thought she loved them. He had no idea that when he was out of town, she snuck down to the kitchen and made a piece of cinnamon toast for dinner, layering the sweet cream butter on thick and sprinkling on a perfect combination of cinnamon and sugar before carrying it to her room on a tray to savor slowly.

Now she put down her cup of coffee and tuned back in to the board meeting—or as she'd once referred to it in an e-mail, the "bored meeting." Luckily she'd caught that Freudian slip before blasting the message to the group.

"So we have venue and entertainment taken care of for the auction," Delores Debonis, the chairwoman, was saying. She was in Group B, the spouses, but you'd never know it by the way she obsessively checked her iPhone. She tapped her pen against the table. "Flowers. Who wants to handle flowers?"

"I will," Pauline said, just as another woman at the end of the table spoke the identical words.

The other woman deferred to Pauline with a gracious nod. "Please. I'll find something else."

"Thank you." Pauline smiled back, just as graciously, and swallowed a yawn.

"Food," Delores Debonis said loudly, and Pauline started, thinking for a second that Delores was demanding a snack. "We've received bids from three catering companies with proposed menus for passed hors d'oeuvres and the seated meal. I've made copies for everyone."

Delores reached for the papers in front of her and handed them out.

"Aren't stuffed mushroom caps kind of . . . I don't know . . . nineteen nineties?" someone said, wrinkling her nose as if one of the unfashionable fungi had materialized in front of her.

"I agree," another woman added. "It shows a lack of creativity. The first caterer isn't impressing me."

A third woman cleared her throat. "I'm worried we won't have enough passed hors d'oeuvres. Six selections for two hundred people isn't much variety. And what about the vegetarians? I only see two non-meat or seafood options."

Pauline allowed her mind to drift again, as she did so often during these meetings. She began to think about what would happen the day after the auction, when they'd leave for Dwight's birthday trip to Jamaica along with his college friends—people Pauline barely knew and probably had nothing in common with.

She'd made a massive mistake.

What had come over her? Why had she blurted out the idea the moment it popped into her head, without even sleeping on it first? Now it was far too late to cancel the trip; the invitations had been delivered, and everyone had sent back gushing acceptances. She was going to be stuck spending an entire week with these people.

"So no mushroom caps," Delores was saying. Tap, tap, tap went her pen. "Are we in agreement about the goat cheese—Pauline?"

She hadn't realized she'd stood up until she heard Delores speak her name.

"Are you unwell?" Delores asked as every head swiveled to look at Pauline. "You're so pale."

"It's nothing," Pauline said. She pressed her hands together to camouflage their sudden trembling. "Excuse me a moment."

She walked down the hallway to a bathroom, locked the door behind her, and studied her reflection in the large oval mirror. Delores was right; she did look even paler than usual.

She might as well get this over with, she thought as she slipped her skirt down over her hips and sat on the toilet. And there it was again: a streak of red on her panty liner. She stared at it, wondering how much longer she could blame it on Dwight's traveling, on bad timing, on it being harder for a woman to get pregnant after she turned thirty.

Dwight wanted children. It wasn't something they'd discussed at length, but an older woman who'd been friends with Dwight's mother had asked about it at their wedding reception, and he'd said, "Of course." As if it was such a given that his response had required no thought at all. Dwight and the woman had turned to look at her, and she'd smiled. "One or two, definitely," she'd said. "Or three or four," Dwight had said, and the old woman had laughed and said, "You'd better get started!"

To her surprise, Pauline had discovered she liked the idea of a little girl in a dress with a wide silk sash, throwing a tea party for her dolls. Pauline had trouble envisioning a baby, but she could see a daughter at age five or six—after the mess of diapers and formulas and spit-up was over.

Did Dwight wonder why it was taking so long, too? Maybe he was beginning to suspect that Pauline had a problem, that a life with her wouldn't be the one he was counting on.

The natural thing to do would be to go to a fertility doctor. But she couldn't. She knew there would be questions she couldn't risk Dwight ever learning the answers to. She covered her mouth with her hand, feeling nausea rise up through her throat.

The irony didn't escape her that she was feeling ill for a reason that was the precise opposite of the one she'd hoped.

Her nausea passed and she stood up, flushed the toilet, and washed her hands. Then she walked back into the boardroom. People were waiting for her.

"What did I miss?" she asked, forcing a smile as she slipped into her seat.

Chapter Two

The Night Before

"WHERE'S MY LIST?" TINA asked as she dumped a pile of warm laundry on the bed.

Gio didn't look away from the television. "Which one? You've got a hundred."

"Four," Tina corrected, picking up one of his legs, peering under it, and letting it flop roughly back onto the bed. "One with everything I need to pack for us. One with everything I need to pack for the kids. One with the kids' schedules and all the emergency numbers to give to Allie's mom. And one with everything I need to do before we leave. And that's the one I can't—"

She snatched a piece of paper from under Gio's other leg and smoothed it out.

"I've got to give a spare key to what's-his-name," she said. "We've lost all the spares. We'll have to take it off my key chain."

"Who's what's-his-name?" Gio asked.

"The kid down the street who's going to walk Caesar and get our mail," Tina said. "The one with the pierced eyebrow." She was jotting something on a piece of paper as she talked.

"Tell me you're not writing another list," Gio said. "And a pierced eyebrow? He'll drink all my beer the first night."

Tina looked at him, sprawled on top of the bedspread, one arm bent behind his head. Her husband was so sexy, with his black hair, heavy eyebrows, and tan skin—genetic gifts from his Italian ancestors. He was only five-foot-seven, but perfectly proportioned, with the shoulders and chest of a weight lifter, a benefit of his very physical job. Six years ago, she would've caught one glimpse of him lying there in his faded Levi's and launched herself on top of him like a nimble Russian gymnast.

But right now, annoyance dueled with her desire. Why couldn't Gio understand that watching him unload the dishwasher was as big an aphrodisiac as watching him flex his washboard abs?

"You know what would really help me? If *you* helped," she said. "C'mon, fold this laundry so I can get the kids packed."

"Jesus, baby, I just got home from work," Gio said. "Can't I relax for ten minutes?"

Tina exhaled slowly. Gio knew those words were a trigger for her; did he think she *didn't* work all day long?

"You've been relaxing for almost an hour," she said, working hard to keep her voice level. "Let's just get this all done so we can both relax."

"After this show," Gio said, turning up the volume.

Tina snatched the remote out of his hand and hit the Mute button.

"What's your prob——" Gio began, but Tina shushed him.

"Did you hear that?" she asked.

He shook his head.

"I think Sammy was coughing. Oh, God, I hope he's not getting sick."

"Baby, he's fine," Gio said. He reclaimed the clicker and turned the television back up.

Tina felt a knot in her stomach as she moved closer to the door. She'd definitely heard a cough. Could Sammy be coming down with something? He had allergies, which made even a slight cold problematic. She'd planned to pack his nebulizer just in case, and she'd asked Louise, Allie's mom, to be sure that Sammy took a shower every night and washed his hair, to remove the ragweed pollen that always plagued him in late summer. But Louise was going to have six kids underfoot—she might forget.

Her hands reached for the laundry piled on her side of the bed and automatically began to sort the shirts and shorts and pajamas into four neat stacks. Gio accused her of being overly alarmist sometimes, and she knew it was true, but what she didn't know was how to change this particular dynamic in their marriage. His flat-out refusal to worry made her anxieties all the more intense, as if they kept needing to move to opposite extremes in order to create the middle ground of a reasonable reaction.

She'd keep her cell phone on, she reminded herself. And Dwight had a private jet, for goodness' sake. She could always fly home if Sammy really was becoming ill.

She reached for one of Sammy's tiny shirts with a smiling Elmo on the front and felt unexpected tears form. Seven days without her children seemed like an endless stretch of time, and while it had been so enticing in theory, now that the vacation was upon her, she felt almost panicked.

Did other women feel torn in two when they left their children? she wondered as she placed the Elmo T-shirt into Sammy's pile of clean clothes. Maybe not; it could all be the result of her old job as a nurse. There were two kids who stood out in her mind from all those shifts in the ER; two faces that rose above the blur of swallowed coins and sudden cases of croup and leg-breaking falls from playground structures. A little boy, aged six, who was riding in the backseat of a car that was slammed by a truck whose driver hadn't noticed the stoplight turn red. Tina had been closest to the emergency room doors when the EMTs brought him in. She could see only one of his brown eyes through the mass of red, but it had looked straight at her. She'd reached out to hold his hand as they rushed him into surgery, running alongside the gurney. He hadn't made it through.

The other child Tina still saw vividly was a tiny girl—she didn't know her age but thought she'd been two or so—who had found a bottle of flavored medicine that hadn't been properly closed and had swallowed most of the contents. Tina didn't know if the little girl had survived; she couldn't bear to ask. Because by then Tina was six months pregnant. And the previous weekend she'd gone shopping and had bought a few onesies, some blankets, and a soft-looking teddy bear that she'd tucked into a corner of the crib. That bear was too similar to one the desperately ill girl held as she was carried out of the ambulance.

Tina's job had demonstrated over and over how easily the life of a parent could shatter. How simply turning your head at the wrong time, or answering a doorbell, could invite catastrophe. That was why she couldn't entrust her kids to anyone, why she'd chosen to stay at home instead of hiring a nanny.

But a private villa! she reminded herself. A *chef*! She'd be forced to relax; she'd have no other choice. She and Allie had spent hours on the phone in the weeks since the invitation had arrived, oohing and aahing over the pictures Pauline had e-mailed of the villa called Summer Escape, the enormous rooftop patio with a pool and hot tub, and the views of the glass-green Caribbean Sea.

"Okay, that's done," Tina said as she finished sorting the laundry and nestled each pile into a small bag. The kids had T-shirts and shorts, bathing suits and pajamas, stuffed animals and books, toothbrushes and one sweatshirt apiece, even though it was August, just in case the nights turned chilly. She'd filled a separate bag with Sammy's nebulizer, some basic medicines, and the list of emergency numbers. She glanced at the clock. It was nine-thirty and she hadn't packed a single thing for herself, guaranteeing she'd forget something crucial. She glanced at her to-do list again. She had to make sure the timers she'd bought for the living room lights were set, and she needed to water the plants, and she should really put Caesar's dog food on the counter so their beer-swilling dog walker could find it . . . Oh, God, the key for what's-his-name! Was it too late to drop it off?

"Gio, I need you to run the key down the street," she said as she shoved a bright red Miraclesuit bathing suit into her suitcase. She'd ordered it online after it promised to erase ten pounds from her frame. Ten pounds wasn't enough—she should've bought two so she could wear them both, one over the other.

"Gio?"

She looked over and saw that he'd fallen asleep, clutching the remote against his chest like a little kid with a security blanket.

There were so many things she loved about her husband: his deep voice, the way he smelled after he worked up a sweat on the job; how he could diagnose any problem in the house or car, from a leaky pipe to a dying carburetor. Even the things she pretended to roll her eyes at—like the fact that he refused ever to dance or to cook anything more complex than a toaster waffle—fit into his deliciously macho image.

She knew his job was stressful. Gio worked on sweltering sites during the summer and unheated ones in the winter, and was usually the first one at the job in the morning and the last one to leave at night. He was under tremendous pressure to come in on time and at budget for this particular project, especially since the company he worked for had already let go a half dozen employees this year because of the poor economy. Gio was working so hard to spare himself—and his family—from the same fate.

Tina leaned over, untied her husband's yellow work boots, and slid them off. He must have been too tired to bother removing them.

She watched him sleep, feeling anger mingle with sympathy while she held a boot that was scuffed at the toe and still contained some of Gio's warmth. She wondered if all marriages were this complicated.

It was four a.m., and Allie was conceding defeat.

She slipped out of bed and into her terry-cloth robe, then crept down the stairs, her feet soundless against the soft carpet. Last night she and Ryan had opened a bottle of chardonnay and watched an old episode of *The Office,* and while an extra glass of wine and the comedy had helped her drift off, she'd known it wouldn't last. She hadn't slept through the night in weeks.

Ever since that phone call with a woman she barely knew but was inexorably tied to, Allie felt as if she'd been split into two people. One Allie chatted with the post office clerk and wrote knock-knock jokes on slips of paper to tuck into the girls' lunch boxes and set aside the sports page for Ryan. The other Allie looked up at the clock to see an entire hour had mysteriously passed, and wandered around her house in the middle of the night, running her fingertip over the family photos on the mantel.

Now she passed the suitcases stacked by the front door and headed for the kitchen, where a small light above the stove cast a gentle glow. It resembled a stage set—a lonely room waiting for dishes to clatter into the sink and bacon to sizzle in a pan and people to talk in bright morning voices.

Allie kept the lights off but switched on the coffeemaker and put in a scoop of French roast, then opened a window to allow the August morning's soft air to filter into the house. In a few hours, she'd cook a special breakfast of cinnamon-sprinkled French toast and fill glasses with orange juice, then drive the girls to her mother's house. She'd hug them tight and say good-bye, secure in the knowledge that her mom would care for them well. And then she'd step onto a private plane and drink Savannah's Sex on the Beach shooters—how like Savannah to bring not just any old drinks but ones with suggestive names—and she'd spend the next week sunbathing, jogging on the beach, eating, and drinking.

But most of all, not thinking. That was the private deal she'd made with herself: She'd get one more week, then she'd face whatever her future held. She stood there, gripping the handle of the coffeepot even after it gave a final gurgle. She wondered if she'd be able to pull it off. Surely Ryan would notice something was wrong, and the others might, too, since they were going to spend so much time together. Maybe she should have an excuse handy in case . . . Allie yanked her mind away from that train of thought as swiftly as if she were pulling away her hand from a hot stove top. *Jamaica,* she told herself, summoning the iron discipline that had her reaching for her running shoes even on cold, rain-soaked days. *Think about the vacation.*

It would be a strange week, Allie conceded as she began moving again and filled up her favorite mug, a chunky purple piece of glazed pottery she'd bought from a local artist at a farmers' market. Pauline was basically a stranger, and while Allie and Dwight saw each other a couple of times a year for lunch, Dwight wasn't in regular touch with the rest of the group. Allie couldn't imagine two more different women than Pauline and Savannah, and Gary had never meshed with the other husbands. But surely everyone would be on their best behavior in such an idyllic setting.

At first Allie had balked at the idea of accepting. But Pauline had insisted: "Dwight really wants to do this," she'd said. "It's the only thing he truly hopes for on his birthday."

Allie had sensed Pauline was telling the truth, which was why she'd finally said yes, even though she still wasn't entirely comfortable with Dwight footing the bill. She'd spent a long time searching for a gift for him, and had finally decided on two small ones: a basket full of the vintage candy he'd once told her he'd adored as a child and still craved—Smarties, Pop Rocks, Hot Tamales, Razzles, FireBalls, and Reese's Pieces. She was also going to take photographs during the trip and compile them into a Snapfish album, along with all the old pictures of them from college that she could find. Dwight wasn't in many of them, but she'd managed to locate a few. It seemed like such a small thing to do, but what could she possibly buy the man that he didn't already own?

She lightened her coffee with a splash of cream, then carried her mug to the big, soft couch in the living room and sat down, tucking her legs underneath her. Her eyes roamed around the familiar contours of the room—the denim-covered chairs with striped accent pillows, Sasha's pink ballet slipper half-hidden under the coffee table, the vase of sunflowers whose edges were just beginning to turn brown.

In a week, she'd be preparing to reverse her journey, stacking her suitcases by the door of the Jamaican villa and hugging her friends good-bye. And then, when she stepped out of the fantasy and came home . . . She gulped air and dropped her head into her hands.

"Mommy?"

Allie looked up and saw her seven-year-old daughter, Eva, padding down the stairs in pink footie pajamas. She quickly wiped her eyes with the sleeve of her robe.

"Hey, baby girl," Allie said, opening her arms. "Why aren't you sleeping?"

"I thought it was morning," Eva said. "But it's still dark out."

"The sun is getting ready to come up, though," Allie said. She smoothed Eva's auburn hair, a perfect match for her own, relishing the way her daughter's warm, soft body felt in her arms. "Try to go back to sleep if you can."

"Tell me a story," Eva said. It was their nighttime ritual, but rather than reading from books about girl detectives or talking animals, Allie always recounted family stories from her own memories: the time Eva climbed into the fireplace and climbed out covered in cold ashes; the day Sasha crawled over to the DVD player, decided it looked hungry, and tried to feed a piece of toast through its slot; and Allie's disastrous first date with Ryan, when he'd taken them to a restaurant that had shut down the previous week, then had gotten a flat tire as he pulled out of the empty parking lot. Instead of becoming angry or embarrassed, he'd burst into laughter—then he'd made Allie laugh, too, by joking that he'd lined the parking lot with sharp nails so he could woo her with his macho tire-changing skills.

"Which story would you like?" Allie asked. "The day you were born?"

"The day *you* were born," Eva said.

"Okay," Allie said. She took a deep breath. "The day I was born. Well, I grew in another woman's tummy, not Grandma Louise's, because Grandma Louise couldn't grow babies. And there I was, growing bigger and bigger, and Grandma Louise and Grandpa Bucky were getting all ready for me."

"They painted your room," Eva prompted, snuggling closer.

"They did," Allie confirmed. "They painted it yellow, just like Daddy and I painted your room before you were born."

"But they didn't know it was you who was coming," Eva said.

"That's true," Allie said. "They wanted a baby so badly, but they didn't know which one was meant to belong to them. And then I decided I was tired of being squished in a tummy, so I wiggled my way out and gave a great big yell. And Grandma Louise swears she somehow felt that yell in her bones and knew I was trying to tell her to come get me."

"And then she and Grandpa came to get you," Eva said.

"They rushed right to the hospital," Allie confirmed. "They fed me a bottle of milk and changed my diaper, and as soon as the doctors said I could leave, Grandma and Grandpa dressed me in a little pink outfit and brought me home. And then we were a family."

"What about the lady whose tummy you lived in? Was she your family, too?"

Allie's hand froze on her daughter's head. Could Eva have overheard something—a snippet of conversation from the phone call she'd tried to keep private? Kids were so intuitive; maybe she'd just absorbed something from the very air.

Allie needed to choose her words carefully. "That lady was named Debby, and she wasn't really my family," she finally said. "She just took care of me until my real family could get me. She was more of a . . . friend."

"Oh," Eva said in a small voice.

"Honey?" Allie asked. "Is there anything bothering you?"

Eva shook her head, and Allie had no idea whether to push her to talk. So she just held her little girl, whispering more stories as the sky turned from black to gray to blue. Even after Allie felt Eva's body relax into sleep, she kept talking softly, telling of the day Eva was born, and Sasha—the best days of her life. The days that made her realize that everything else she'd experienced—college, meeting Ryan, even her wedding day—had just been dress rehearsals for the pivotal chapter of her life: motherhood.

Allie had told Eva the truth about her birth mother, Debby. Ever since Debby had reached out to her through the adoption agency after Allie turned eighteen and Allie had agreed to a meeting, they'd fallen into a casually friendly relationship. But they weren't close, and witnessing the tumult of Debby's life— she was constantly fighting with her third husband, and always short of money—made Allie grateful for that.

She didn't talk to Debby often, maybe every four or five months. But a few weeks after Dwight's invitation had been delivered, Debby had called.

"Hank died," she'd said. No preamble, just those stark words. Allie had felt tears gathering in her eyes, even though she'd never met her biological father, who'd gotten Debby pregnant when they were both teenagers. Allie had been standing at the counter, sorting through the day's mail while Ryan was giving the girls a bath upstairs. Her legs had suddenly felt weak, and she'd sunk into a chair.

"How?" she'd asked, the possibilities racing through her mind. She knew, through Debby, that he'd been a heavy drinker and smoker.

"Lou Gehrig's disease," Debby had said. "It happened a couple weeks ago. I didn't know until I saw some stuff about the funeral on the Facebook page for our old high school."

Debby didn't sound upset—she and Hank had broken up before Allie had even been born. Hank had been furious that Debby decided against an abortion, Debby had said, in one of her breathtakingly thoughtless remarks that made Allie all the more grateful for her true parents.

Allie had talked to Debby awhile longer, listening to her lament her current husband's job troubles. Then, just as she'd begun to ease off the phone, Debby had said, "It happened to Hank's father, too, you know. I remember when I went to his house once, in the tenth grade. He could barely move. It

really creeped me out. He had to blink his eyes to communicate."

"*What?*" Allie had asked.

"Yeah, he had it, too. Lou Gehrig's disease."

"So my biological father and grandfather had the same disease?" Allie had asked. "It isn't . . . genetic, is it?"

Debby had paused to take another drag of her cigarette.
"Huh. Never thought of that."

"I've got to go," Allie had blurted, unable to listen to Debby's raspy voice for another minute. She'd hung up and raced
into the living room, then back into the kitchen. Then she'd
abruptly stopped, her heart thudding in her chest.

It was probably nothing, she'd told herself as she grabbed a
sponge and began violently scrubbing a pan she'd left soaking
in the sink. The fact that two of her relatives had the same fatal
illness was a fluke. Was ALS even inherited? She'd thought it
was a random disease that struck as swiftly and irrevocably as
a bolt of lightning, impossible to predict where it would touch
down. Besides, Debby wasn't the most reliable source; Allie had
caught her in a half dozen untruths before. Or maybe she'd gotten confused about Hank's father's diagnosis. He could have had
a stroke, or . . . or been paralyzed in an accident.

Allie had abandoned the pan and then, despite the warning shrieking in her brain that she shouldn't do it, that she'd
forever regret it, she'd opened her laptop and begun searching
the Internet.

"No," she'd whispered a moment later, just before she slammed
her laptop shut. The death notices she'd found confirmed that
Hank and his father had both died of ALS, an always fatal illness
that causes complete paralysis before death.

But that didn't mean she had the same mutated gene, Allie
reminded herself now, as she shifted Eva into a more comfortable position on her lap. Her birth father had never given her

anything—not his name, not a college graduation card, not a single stinking phone call. He wouldn't give her this legacy, either. She wouldn't let him!

She looked through the window and saw the sun begin its ascent. A beautiful day awaited them: It was a good omen. Allie leaned down to smell her daughter's hair, remembering how small her soapy head had felt the previous night when Allie cradled it in her hands, massaging in baby shampoo. Eva was so little; she still believed in the Tooth Fairy.

A sob formed in Allie's throat, but she forced it down.

The pendulum wouldn't swing, not now. It couldn't.

"So you're a chef?" Savannah asked, crossing her legs and taking a gulp of her vodka tonic. She'd already forgotten the name of the guy seated across from her.

He smiled, revealing more gums than seemed normal. "No. I own a courier company. You didn't confuse me with someone else, did you?"

"Of course not," Savannah said, even as she thought: *You're on Match.com, asshole. You think yours is the only picture I looked at?*

And speaking of pictures, when was his taken? Probably ten years ago, when he was vaguely acquainted with the concept of a treadmill. Because the doughy-looking guy sitting on the stool across from hers bore no resemblance to that photo. She'd almost walked out of the bar after scanning it and seeing only a few losers watching TV and tossing back drinks. And then one of them had put down his draft beer and walked over to her, not hiding the fact that he was assessing her body and approving of it.

Glad I'm good enough for you, Savannah had thought, already counting down the minutes until she could escape. One drink. That was her safety mechanism, the secret trapdoor designed to maneuver her out of situations exactly like this one. She never agreed to a meal or a movie with a guy she hadn't seen in person, especially not after the six dates she'd gone on in the past three weeks. She regretted every single one of them. The worst was a fix-up from a fellow real estate agent who'd sent Savannah out with an oily-looking guy who sucked the salt off his fingers after eating a handful of bar nuts and checked out every woman who walked by. As if that was the best Savannah could hope for, just because most men in her age range were married. She'd lasted half a drink before walking out, and told off her friend—make that ex-friend—the next morning. She'd never be that desperate.

"Interested in dinner after this?" the guy was asking. *What was that smell?* Savannah wondered. *Eww—was it* him? "I know a great little Italian place."

What, Domino's Pizza? Savannah thought, hiding a smirk. She took another long sip of her vodka tonic before realizing he was looking at her, a question in his eyes. She mentally replayed the last bit of conversation and realized she hadn't answered him.

"Sorry, but I'm going out of town tomorrow," she said. "Still haven't packed."

"Sure," the guy said. Savannah could see hurt flare in his dark eyes, but she didn't care. He'd deceived her and wasted her time; he didn't deserve kindness. His chinos were too short, revealing thick white athletic socks, and his face was moon-shaped. He kept staring at her cleavage. And that was definitely the scent of stale sweat coming off him. He was awful. Did he even own a courier company? That was probably another lie; he looked like the sort of man who lived with his mother.

Two more big sips and she'd be done. She knew she should've stayed home tonight and taken a bubble bath and finished packing, especially since she had an eight a.m. flight from North Carolina to D.C., but she'd thought . . . well, she'd thought it would be easier to show up in Jamaica with the promise of a relationship back at home. She couldn't believe she hadn't told Allie or Tina about the separation yet. She'd meant to, but the timing was never right. Or maybe she just couldn't figure out which words to choose. She'd told Pauline that Gary couldn't come, but she hadn't revealed the reason why.

She dreaded having to explain; the thought of it made Savannah itchy. She didn't want sympathy. She wanted to move on—but first she needed to move away from this loser.

"This has been great," she lied, not bothering to inject enthusiasm into her tone. "But I need to get going."

"Mind if I catch a ride with you?" the guy asked. "I'm only a mile away."

Savannah put her empty glass on the bar and turned to look at him. "You don't have a car?" she asked. This dude just got more and more desirable.

"It's in the shop," he said. "I've been cabbing it, but it's raining out and I'll probably have to wait awhile . . ."

"Kind of funny that you own a courier service and don't have a ride," she said.

"Bike couriers," he said, shrugging. "I can't exactly hop on the back of one of those."

Uh-huh. Savannah picked up her purse. "Sorry, but I need to run a few errands and I'm heading out of town really early in the morning."

"No worries," he said. "I wouldn't let a stranger in my car, either."

So why'd you ask? she thought, but all she said was "Bye."

She stood up, smoothing her skirt and walking away. She stopped in the bathroom to pee and checked her watch while she was washing her hands; it was only seven-thirty. She could still take that bubble bath after all, she thought as she pulled open the heavy wooden back door, unfurled her umbrella, and walked through the parking lot. In the backseat of her Miata were two shopping bags filled with new clothes she'd bought for the trip: a coral strapless sundress, two bikinis, cutoff jean shorts to toss on over her bathing suits, a tight white T-shirt, and a black sheath with a slit up the leg in case she felt like dressing for dinner one night. Maybe she'd make a quick stop at the bookstore to pick up a few novels for the beach, she thought as she clicked the button on her key chain to unlock the car.

Someone grabbed her arm.

She spun around, a scream rising in her throat, knowing it was him before she saw the round moon face.

"You bitch. You think you're too good for me?"

What was wrong with her voice? She couldn't yell, couldn't make a sound. Her fingers searched for the panic button on her keys, but they slipped out of her grasp and clattered on the asphalt.

"You didn't even pay for your drink," he said. Rain streamed down, flattening his hair against his face. His eyes were so dark she couldn't see his pupils. "You come in with your tits hanging out like a whore and I still treated you nice. And you don't appreciate it."

He was insane. He was so close she could feel his hot breath on her face. Why couldn't she scream? She made herself look into his eyes and tried to smile, but her lips felt frozen.

"Wait," she whispered. "It was a misunderstanding."

Kick him in the balls, she thought. But her legs refused to obey, and anyway, he was too close.

"Bitch!" he hissed again. His grip on her arm tightened, his fingers biting into her flesh. He pressed his body up against hers. She couldn't move back; the car trapped her from behind. "Don't try to be all fake now. You think I'm stupid?"

She'd always imagined she'd fight in a situation like this—yell and kick and claw her attacker's eyes. But every bit of strength seemed to have drained out of her body. Any second now, he was going to pull out a shining butcher's knife and slide it into her, and she'd be left to die here, her blood mingling with the rain in the parking lot of this crappy little bar.

"Hey, lady, are you okay?"

Savannah looked over her attacker's shoulder and saw the bartender, holding a full bag of trash. He dropped the bag and stepped out from under the awning, toward them.

The guy didn't say another word; he just let go of Savannah's arm and walked away, toward the street.

Her knees gave way, and she slid down the side of her Miata, not caring that she landed on her bottom in a muddy puddle. She couldn't stop shaking—deep, violent shudders that felt like convulsions.

"Do you want me to call the cops?" the bartender asked. He picked up her umbrella and knelt beside her, covering her with it.

She shook her head. Her throat was so constricted that she still couldn't speak.

"Are you sure? My cell phone is inside," he said. He stood up again and scanned their surroundings, turning around a full 360 degrees. "He's gone. I could run and get it."

"I'm okay," she croaked. "Just . . . stay here for a minute?"

She leaned her head back against her car, letting the tears finally come. What would that psycho have done to her if the bartender hadn't appeared? Thirty seconds later and he could have had her in her car in the darkness, his hands around her throat, her skirt hiked up . . . She sobbed harder, not caring that the bartender was watching.

She'd never kidded herself that she and Gary had a perfect marriage: They fought over her sloppiness and his rigidity, and they didn't share the kinds of inside jokes that other couples

48 Sarah Pekkanen

seemed to. But they'd wanted the exact same things in life. They both liked nice cars, traveling, fine restaurants, and good wine. Savannah had remained attracted to him throughout the seven years of their marriage, probably because they led somewhat independent lives, not feeling as though they had to check in incessantly with phone calls and e-mails. When Gary was on call, he'd sleep at the hospital and she wouldn't see him for thirty-six hours, or even longer. She'd go out for dinner with her girlfriends, get a massage, hit her favorite shops—and she thoroughly enjoyed every moment of it.

She and Gary were partners, not soul mates, and that had suited her just fine.

So why, when she'd thought she was about to be raped and killed, had one word stuck in her throat like a cork, preventing any sounds from escaping?

Gary. When she'd desperately needed rescuing, his was the name she'd tried to yell.

"Fabulous job." Delores Debonis swept across the room and leaned forward, kissing each of Pauline's cheeks in turn. "The flowers are to die for!"

"Oh, but the appetizers are exquisite," Pauline said. "That caviar . . . and I can't stop eating the goat cheese crostinis!"

That was only a half lie, she told herself. She'd heard the goat cheese was good, but she'd never been able to abide the sour taste of it, personally.

"Cheers," Delores said, clinking her champagne glass against Pauline's and emitting a schoolgirl's giggle that was at odds with her matronly figure. "We pulled it off!"

Pauline glanced around the room. In one corner a string quartet played Bach, and waiters circled with trays of wine and champagne. The flowers Pauline had selected—elegant purple orchids—adorned the two dozen large round tables, which were all about to be filled by well-heeled guests. In a few moments the auctioneer would stand up and press people to buy the donated prizes: a spin around a racetrack with Danica Patrick, a helicopter tour of New York followed by four backstage passes to a Broadway show of the winner's choice, a luxury trip to Thailand . . .

They'd raise a nice amount for the hospital—at least six figures—but it didn't escape Pauline's notice that it would've been much easier for her and the other board members to each write a check directly to the hospital. They were the ones donating prizes—Dwight and Pauline had given the trip to Thailand—and their friends were the ones filling the tables. It was like the old three-card monte game, with the money being shuffled around until its original origin was camouflaged. What was the point, really?

Delores gave a squeal and hurried off to greet another board member. "Are you okay, darling?" Pauline asked Dwight. "Can I get you another Coke? Or maybe a glass of wine?"

"N-no, I'm good," he said. Dwight sometimes stuttered when he got nervous, and large gatherings like this one made him anxious. Pauline placed a hand on his arm and smiled at him.

He gave a little tug to his bow tie, and she moved to straighten it, wishing it could cover his prominent Adam's apple. Still, she loved seeing her husband in a tuxedo with his hair gelled back. When they'd first met, Dwight had dressed like a much older man—one who lacked even a passing acquaintanceship with fashion. There had also been an unfortunate incident—Pauline still shuddered to think of it—involving an afternoon pool party, Dwight, and a Speedo. Right after they married, Pauline had begun shopping for him, replacing his plaid shorts, leather sandals, and sweater vests with clothing that straddled the line between classic and hip: perfectly plain black T-shirts made of the finest cotton, gray pants that fit his trim hips correctly, and—her crowning achievement—bathing suits that almost reached his knees.

"You look so handsome," she said and was rewarded with a smile. "I see former Senator Dodd across the room. Remember, you met him in the Hamptons last summer. He's the CEO of the Motion Picture Association now. We should go say hello."

Dwight nodded, and they began to weave their way toward him, Pauline leading slightly and casting bright smiles at acquaintances she passed.

"What time do you think this will wrap up?" Dwight asked. She started to cringe but reflexively hid it. His question had been loud enough for those around them to hear.

"Surely by ten," she said, her voice low and concerned. She stopped walking. "Are you tired? Because you could go on ahead, and send the car back for me . . ."

He squeezed her hand. "Of course not. Just wanted to make sure we'll be ready for tomorrow."

"It's a big day," Pauline said, smiling at him.

"M-maybe I should check the weather again," Dwight said, pulling out his iPhone. "The long-range forecast shows a storm heading that way . . ."

"Sweetie, everything's going to be wonderful. It's supposed to be bright and sunny for the first part of the week, and if it rains one day, there will be lots to do. Remember, I can set up a wine tasting. And the house is stocked with books and movies and games. Plus I've got a few other surprises up my sleeve. So I don't want you to worry about a thing. Your friends are going to have the time of their lives, and so will we."

Pauline could see gratitude fill his eyes. How strange—especially since he didn't see them regularly—that Dwight cared more about what these old college friends thought than about networking at the event tonight. He was so brilliant about some things, and so clueless about others.

Pauline still couldn't quite believe this trip was going to happen, even if it had been her idea. At least they had Caleb to ease the burden of traveling. He would walk and feed their two Irish setters, collect and sort the mail, and answer the phone. He'd make sure that the maids came in on time, and that the gardens were watered. Any unexpected emergency—say, a broken pipe—would be dealt with swiftly and expertly. The refrigerator would be stocked the afternoon of their return, and their suitcases would be whisked away moments after they stepped through the front door, so the contents could be laundered and dry-cleaned.

Still, she couldn't help wishing the seven days were already behind them. She resumed walking toward Senator Dodd and thought back to how it had all started, when an invitation had arrived at their home a few months earlier. She'd turned over the envelope, reading the return address, then opened it as she walked into Dwight's study.

"Who's Allie?" she'd asked.

Dwight was tapping away on one of his three computers. "Hmmm . . . What? Why?"

"She just invited us to her thirty-fifth birthday," Pauline had said, handing him the card. It was one of those preprinted ones with open spaces to write in the date and time of the event.

"An old friend from college," Dwight had said, grinning as he looked at the invitation. "You've met her a few times . . . she came to our wedding."

Pauline had nodded, even though that day had been a blur of other people's faces, her mother's happy tears, and her own nerves.

"I'll let her know we're coming," Dwight had continued, putting the card down next to his keyboard and turning back to his work.

Pauline had been too surprised to say anything other than "Okay." She and Dwight received a lot of invitations, but there was always a catch—someone wanting money or access. This Allie—who, come to think of it, Pauline did vaguely recall; she was a peppy, smiling sort—had written "Absolutely no gifts!" at the bottom of the invitation and underlined it twice. She truly just wanted their company?

Pauline had guessed correctly to dress in jeans and leather boots and a thin-knit sweater, and when she'd walked into Allie's house, she'd noticed the sweet-sharp smell of chili bubbling on the stove, the sound of laughter, and the trays of corn bread spread out on kitchen counters to cool. It was a pleasant, modern home, with one room spilling into the next, all connected by gleaming blond wood floors and high ceilings. Kids' artwork decorated the walls, but the scribbles and streaks of paint were displayed in creative, whimsical frames that actually made them look interesting.

Allie had spotted Dwight and run across the room to give him a hug, then she'd turned to Pauline to do the same. After a surprised moment, Pauline had patted Allie's back twice.

"It's so good to see you!" Allie had cried. Her face was open and lightly freckled, and smile lines creased the skin around her eyes. "Pauline, I've heard so much about you, but we've never had a chance to talk."

You've heard about me? Pauline had almost asked. *From who?*

But she'd just said thanks, because she was too embarrassed to admit she hadn't realized that Dwight had any real friends from college. Pauline had never thought it was odd because she'd never felt the need for many friends, either. Sometimes she thought it was one of the reasons why she and Dwight felt so well-matched; why theirs seemed like a perfectly arranged marriage. She was his escort at dinners and galas, where she remembered names and made small talk to cover Dwight's shyness; they had sex three or four times a month; and they never fought. She'd never had an orgasm with Dwight, either, and had never been consumed by a rush of love when she walked into a room and unexpectedly discovered him there. But she admired Dwight's mind and his innate sense of fairness, and was amused by his interest in comic books and computer games. Her manchild, she sometimes thought of him. If she had to pick one word to describe her emotions about their marriage, it would be *contentment:* This was the life she'd expected, the one she'd yearned for. She believed Dwight felt the same way.

But during Allie's party, she'd seen another side of her husband emerge. She'd watched as a woman named Tina burst through the door, dark curls cascading down her back, a handsome man at her side and a gaggle of kids hanging on her like ornaments dangling from a human Christmas tree.

"Sitter canceled," Tina had gasped, and Allie had flapped her hand toward the basement door. "Bring the kids down there," she'd said. "I'll put on a movie and bring down a bowl of potato chips. *You* go get a drink."

She'd watched as Tina had spotted Dwight on her way to the bar set up on the kitchen counter, and how she'd hugged him, too, and had offered him a shot of tequila, teasing him about a party in which they'd both tossed back four straight shots. Dwight had turned bright red, leading Pauline to think there was more to the story than that. But he'd accepted the shot, and clinked glasses with Tina.

"To college," she'd said. "We had no idea how good we had it back then, did we?"

"You, ah, still look every bit as pretty," Dwight had said, a flush lingering on his cheeks.

Was he flirting? Pauline wondered, more amused than jealous. She couldn't imagine Tina would be his type, with her huge breasts spilling out of her V-neck sweater and jeans that looked like they were about to split at the knees.

Pauline had been intrigued by the other college friend who came to the party, a tall redhead named Savannah, who'd dipped a finger into the chocolate frosting on the cake and slowly sucked her fingertip, not caring if anyone noticed. Now if *she* tried to flirt with Dwight, Pauline wouldn't be quite so amused.

"Where's Gary?" someone had asked.

"Working, as usual," Savannah had tossed back. Then her eyes had widened.

"Dwight Glass! I haven't seen you in ten years!"

"A-actually, fourteen and a half," he'd corrected her, but she'd covered his mouth with her hand, laughing. "Stop it! You're making me feel old!"

Pauline had promptly wandered over to join them, and Savannah had embraced her as warmly as Allie had.

"Never would've gotten through math classes without your husband," Savannah had said. She'd seemed to be a little tipsy—she was leaning heavily against Pauline, and speaking too loudly—and Pauline had shifted away on the pretext of covering a cough. She'd listened as Savannah reminisced about a pancake house where they'd gone on Sunday mornings, where bottomless cups of coffee and heaping plates of carbs had cured their hangovers.

"So you spent a lot of time together in college?" Pauline had interjected.

"With Dwighty?" Savannah had laughed instead of answering. "He's always been a sweetheart. And he's looking good! Are you working out, Dwight?" Savannah had squeezed Dwight's biceps—Pauline had felt herself stiffen—but then Allie's husband, Ryan, had clinked a glass, quieting the room for his toast.

"To my wife," he'd begun.

"Which one?" a prankster had hooted from the back of the room.

"The one who made the chili you're eating!" Allie had shot back, but she was smiling.

"To my wife!" Ryan had repeated as two young girls carried out a birthday cake. "Our family's Superwoman. Happy thirty-fifth, honey. I love you."

"Awww," Savannah had called as Allie took a deep breath to blow out the candles. Pauline had looked around the room at the colorful paper streamers, the smiles, the raised glasses of beer and wine. Then she saw the look on Dwight's face. It was as if he'd been illuminated from within; she'd never before witnessed such a pure expression of joy on his face. On *anyone's* face. It was as if he'd finally been chosen to play kickball after a lifetime of watching from the sidelines, as if he'd come down the stairs on Christmas morning to see Santa himself filling the stocking by the hearth.

He really liked these people, she'd realized. Her shy, sweet husband loved being part of a group.

That was when her idea was born.

She wanted to do something for him, something spectacular— to make him realize she could make him that happy, too. No, it was more than a want. She *needed* to. She'd filled her wineglass again as she began plotting the details. By the time they left the party, the foundation of her plan was in place.

Dwight had been tipsy by then, all loose-limbed and clumsy, and after they slid into the backseat of their Town Car, she'd hit the button to raise the tinted partition, separating them from their driver.

"Lean your head back," she'd whispered, her voice low and husky, and then she'd scooted across the seat. She'd bent down and unzipped his pants, taking him in her hand and feeling him grow instantly hard.

"Pauline . . ." he'd said, but it wasn't a protest.

She'd run her tongue up and down his length, then slowly circled the tip, teasing him before taking him into her mouth with quick, firm movements, not letting up on the pressure for a moment. He hadn't lasted long, which had pleased her. He wouldn't want sex for another week or so, which meant there would be a plausible excuse for why she wouldn't get pregnant this month.

She'd found a handkerchief in her purse and wiped her mouth. His head was lolling back, and she knew he'd drift off before they arrived home. She'd taken a deep breath and put her lips close to his ear.

"Honey? I've got a great idea for your birthday . . ."

Chapter Three

Sunday Morning, Dulles International Airport

"WOO-HOOOOO!"

The whoop cut through the thick, humid air as Savannah flung open the airport's private exit door, stepped onto the tarmac, and spotted the rest of the group.

Holy cow, what happened to her? Tina wondered, lifting up her sunglasses for a better look. Savannah's hair appeared lighter, and it flowed down past her shoulder blades. She wore a wisp of an emerald-green, silky dress that showcased her toned, tan legs. She seemed taller, somehow—or maybe she'd just lost a few pounds in all the right places—and her skin glowed.

"Girlfriends!" Savannah threw her arms around Tina and Allie. "Are we going to have an amazing time or what?"

"Hey, gorgeous!" Allie said, hugging Savannah back. "How do you keep on getting prettier?"

"Clearly she's a witch," Tina joked. But her laugh sounded forced, and she suddenly felt frumpy as she watched Savannah greet Gio and Ryan. Tina knew her own thighs were sausaged into her tight white capris, and her blue tunic wasn't fooling anyone—it had clearly been chosen to camouflage her muffin top.

"Okay, enough chitchat," Savannah ordered, turning back to Tina and Allie as she held up a silver thermos. "Who wants a Sex on the Beach shooter? I didn't bring cups, but it'll be more fun to pass it around. Just like at the football games in college, right?"

"Oh, I don't know . . ." Tina began. She'd been up past midnight packing and organizing the house, and Jessica had woken her at three a.m. by climbing into her bed. She'd finally dozed off again, but Angela, their six-year-old, had fallen asleep too early, and was raring to go at a little after five-thirty. Tina was so tired she'd probably pass out if she had a shot. Plus she couldn't stop thinking about the way little Sammy's eyes had filled with tears as she'd said good-bye. He'd tried to be brave, but he was going to miss her so much . . .

"I'll take that as a hell, yes," Savannah said, pressing the thermos into her hands. "Drink up." Tina shrugged, unscrewed the top, and took a little sip. It tasted like summertime—fruity and sweet, with a strong kick of rum. Her mood instantly lifted. Suddenly she remembered how Sammy had been expertly distracted by Allie's mom, who'd swooped in with promises of cookie making and new tins of Play-Doh.

"That was totally wimpy. Unworthy of a UVa girl. More!" Savannah ordered, and Tina took another sip, a bigger one this time. The sky was a brilliant blue, the sun was shining, and she was about to go to Jamaica! Who cared if Savannah looked like a Victoria's Secret model while she looked like an elementary school class's room mother on a field trip to the zoo? Gio loved *her,* and even though they fought too often these days, and never had time to talk anymore, their sex life had always been good. Occasionally it was even great. She knew her husband was attracted to her, belly roll and all. Gio was Italian—he liked a little meat on his women.

"Thanks, Van," Tina said, surprised that Savannah had been

the one to make her feel better. Usually Allie took on that role. Tina licked a drop of alcohol from her lips and passed the thermos to Ryan.

"So where's Gary?" Allie asked, craning her head to look back at the door Savannah had just emerged from.

Tina couldn't see Savannah's eyes behind her oversize sunglasses, but her smile stayed bright. "Oh, the big jerk is working," she said. "We'll have more fun without him."

"Gary's not coming?" Tina asked, feeling her eyebrows lift. She didn't know if she'd be comfortable going away on a vacation with three other couples without Gio. No, scratch that, she definitely wouldn't be comfortable. And yet Savannah acted as if it were the most natural thing in the world.

There was an awkward silence, then Allie broke it. "Well, we're glad you made it, anyway!"

"I'm dying to get a look at this plane!" Savannah said. "Have any of you ever been on a private jet? We need to have a code for the bathroom in case you guys decide to join the mile-high club. Maybe a scarf around the handle means come back in ten minutes."

"Savannah!" Allie said, laughing.

"Sorry, fifteen minutes?" Savannah asked sweetly. "I wasn't implying anything about Ryan."

Allie swatted her on the rear and blushed as Tina glanced around at the half dozen private planes resting on the tarmac around them. "So which one is ours?"

As if on cue, the engines turned on in the jet closest to them—a snow-white machine with a long, pointy nose and lines of black and red running down its sides. Stairs unfolded out of the side of the plane, and Dwight and Pauline appeared at the top of them.

"That's their jet?" Tina asked. It was the biggest—and most expensive-looking—one in the area.

"Oh, I likee," Savannah said. "I likee very much."

"Welcome!" Pauline shouted, waving for them to come aboard.

"They look like a royal couple," Allie breathed. Tina realized Allie was right; even Dwight appeared handsome from this angle. He had on a white linen shirt, baggy khaki shorts, and a Washington Nationals cap. Of course, Quasimodo would probably look hot, too, if he was standing next to his personal plane.

Gio and Ryan began reaching for the bags, but Pauline called, "Just leave your luggage. The steward will carry it all on board."

"Amen to that," Tina murmured as she walked toward the steps. "Gio, can you believe it?"

"Eh. Not bad," he said, and she elbowed him in the ribs. A moment later, she reached the top of the steps and stopped walking, almost causing Gio to crash into her. Instead of too-small seats covered in itchy fabric and crammed into narrow rows, the interior of Dwight's plane featured twelve black leather club chairs in groupings around low coffee tables. The carpet was white with black and red streaks—matching the color scheme of the plane's exterior—and the walls were paneled in wood. A man in a crisp navy blue uniform stood by with a tray of drinks, smiling.

"Would you like a Bellini?" he offered Tina. "Or Perrier? Or would you prefer something else?"

"Um . . . could I have a Bellini? I've never tried one."

"Of course you can!" Pauline, who had been standing back with Dwight to let everyone enter the plane, hurried forward and kissed Tina's cheek. "We're so thrilled you could come!"

"No, trust me, I'm the one who's thrilled," Tina said. She turned to Dwight. "This is so great. It's your birthday, but you're the one giving a present to all of us."

Dwight smiled and started to say something, but then Savannah launched herself at him, squealing, and Allie and Gio and Ryan were crowding onto the plane, and suddenly everyone was hugging and laughing and slapping high fives.

"This is so gorgeous!" Allie said, running a hand over the soft leather of a seat. "Dwight, I can't believe it. You actually own a plane!"

"Nice, man," Gio said. He plopped down in a seat and looked around. "Yeah, I could get used to this."

"Remind me to buy you one for your next birthday," Ryan said and grinned.

"There's beer and vodka tonics if you don't like Bellinis," Pauline was saying. "And of course we'll have a bite to eat after takeoff."

"We're a little bit ahead of you on the cocktails," Savannah said, gesturing with her thermos. "Here's to Jamaica!" As everyone cheered she took a guzzle and passed the thermos to Gio.

Did Pauline's smile slip just the slightest bit? Tina wondered, glancing at the tray of already prepared beverages. Maybe Pauline had wanted to be the one to make things festive, to offer a toast.

Savannah didn't notice—she was too busy exploring. "The bathroom is *marble*!" she shouted, peering inside a door at the back of the plane. "Ooh, and there's a shower!"

"What time is takeoff?" Allie asked as she plopped down in a seat with a sigh. "Ah, cashmere blankets!"

"Whenever we want," Pauline said.

Tina chose the seat next to Allie's and slowly leaned back and shut her eyes. She took a deep breath and felt herself exhale for what felt like the first time in years. *Whenever we want.* Those three words seemed to capture the essence of this trip: Tina would do whatever she wanted, whenever she wanted, during these seven precious days. She'd drink Bellinis and get tipsy and maybe she'd even see if that bathroom sink would hold her up, after all. Gio would love it . . . Tina glanced at Pauline, who was wearing an immaculate cream-colored sleeveless dress and crisply telling the pilot they'd be ready to take off in five minutes. Well, maybe not.

But she and Gio were going to fool around on the beach, under the moonlight, at least once. She reached back and yanked the elastic out of her hair, letting it spill down around her shoulders. She'd managed to squeeze in a haircut last week, and her skin was already brown from splashing around in the neighborhood pool with the kids on sunny afternoons. Plus she had her new red bathing suit. Her kids would be fine; Sammy hadn't coughed once this morning, and Allie's mom had promised to call her if he became ill.

She felt, quite suddenly, as if she'd been working an endless shift in a hot, busy restaurant and had just been told to go off duty. It was almost unsettling—she kept expecting to need to leap into action.

Could she really relax?

"Your Bellini, madam," the steward said, placing a tall, frosted glass on the table in front of Tina. "And would you care for shrimp cocktail or a selection of assorted tropical fruits once we're airborne? Or perhaps both?"

Tina laughed out loud. She felt twenty-one years old again, vibrant and hopeful.

"Both, please," she said.

She'd have to keep an eye on Savannah, Pauline thought as she stood up from her seat next to Dwight and went to make a phone call at the front of the plane. An extra single woman always upended a group's dynamics—especially when the woman acted like Savannah. Didn't she realize her skirt was too short, and that whenever she crossed her legs, she revealed far too much skin?

Of course she did. And it certainly hadn't escaped the notice of any of the guys on the plane, either—even the steward, and Pauline was fairly certain he was gay.

Pauline touched a button on her cell phone, and after just one ring, her call was answered.

"Caleb? We're in the air."

"Everything's ready," he said. "I'll alert the house's staff that you've taken off."

"And the drivers at the airport," she said, keeping her voice low. "They should be there at least a half hour early."

"Of course."

Pauline glanced back and saw that Savannah had moved into the seat Pauline had just vacated and was leaning over to talk to Dwight.

". . . so drunk that when we first met, I thought his name was Wright," Savannah was saying with a giggle. "Remember how confused you were when I kept asking if you were related to the inventor brothers?"

Pauline let out a measured breath. She'd tried to anticipate every detail of this trip, but she suddenly realized she'd forgotten one: College was the lone common denominator linking this group. Would they talk about anything else all week?

"Ms. Glass? Is that all?"

"No," she said. She closed her eyes and mentally reviewed the layout of the house. She'd never seen it firsthand, but she'd viewed the photos so many times that she could diagram it from memory.

She cupped her hand over her mouth and turned her back on the others. "I'd like to assign bedrooms. Please instruct the maid to put our bags into these rooms when we arrive: Dwight and I will stay in the master suite upstairs, and Allie and Ryan will take the room next to us. Tina and Gio will have the large en suite downstairs, and Savannah will be in the smaller room next to them."

"Certainly." Caleb's voice didn't betray a hint of surprise or curiosity, and he didn't ask why one guest was being assigned to the small bedroom when there was a third, much larger one, upstairs. Pauline wouldn't expect anything less of him.

"Thank you, Caleb."

She hung up and glanced out the window. It was a perfect day, with no cumulus clouds to jostle the plane and unsettle any nervous fliers. The steward was preparing the appetizers and mixing another round of Bellinis—the first batch had been a hit—and Pauline knew that when everyone stepped into the villa, they'd be completely overwhelmed, just as they'd been by the plane. Their reactions were kind of sweet, really: They hadn't pretended to be sophisticated or blasé, and Pauline was glad. She wanted Dwight to feel their gratitude and excitement.

Savannah was still in the seat next to Dwight. Pauline considered what to do: walk back over and stand next to Savannah to see if she'd offer to relinquish it? No, Pauline decided. She didn't want to appear insecure. She'd take the empty seat across from Allie and chat with her for the duration of the flight. Maybe she'd put Allie or Ryan by her side at dinner, too; from what she remembered from Allie's party, they were both easygoing, quick to smile or lighten a conversation with a joke. They even looked a bit alike, with their blue eyes and fair skin and even features, Pauline realized. Had they always resembled each other, or did they grow to, like some happily married couples were said to do?

Pauline looked at Allie more closely. The others were all leaning toward one another and talking, but Allie seemed set apart. She was staring out the window, her face blank.

Then someone cracked a joke, and sharp laughter erupted. Allie started and turned back to the others, her face suddenly bright, laughing as hard as anyone. But Pauline would've sworn she hadn't even heard the joke—she'd been a million miles away.

"Ms. Glass? There's one shrimp allergy, just so you know," the steward said quietly as he arranged the crustaceans on a silver platter along with fresh lemon wedges and little dishes of cocktail sauce.

"Who?" she asked.

He indicated Savannah. "The lady in green."

Pauline nodded and tapped her index finger against her bottom lip. She'd planned a classic clambake on the beach for one of the dinners, so she'd have to remember to tell the chef to eliminate shrimp from the menu. And, to be safe, she'd ask the butler to buy a bottle of Benadryl for the house. She didn't want anything to go wrong on this trip.

"Guys, do you remember that lit professor with the bushy gray hair?" Savannah was saying in a voice so loud it easily carried the length of the plane. "I swear he was drunk half the time. Dwight should've taught that class—didn't you always jump up to correct him when he wrote the wrong information on the board? Of course, I was usually asleep in the back row, so I was the only one who didn't get totally confused in that class."

Did Savannah rub anyone else the wrong way, too? Pauline wondered. Maybe because she was so pretty and vivacious, everyone was content to let her dominate the conversation. Things had probably been that way ever since she'd been a girl, so maybe it had never occurred to Savannah to share the spotlight.

Pauline glanced at the serving tray as the steward finished slicing fresh mango, pineapple, and native Jamaican Ugli fruit. Everything looked perfect. There was only one nagging worry in the back of Pauline's mind—the storm that was building in the center of the Atlantic was looking more troublesome, and although the brunt of it would miss them, they might get hit by heavy winds toward the end of the week. Pauline made a mental note to check that the house had plenty of alcohol, candles, and a few boogie boards in case the guys wanted to catch the big waves.

She smiled and walked down the aisle. Just as she'd expected, Savannah didn't move, and Pauline slipped into a new seat.

Savannah hadn't explained why Gary wasn't coming, and Pauline would never be rude enough to ask. But wasn't it obvious?

Savannah's ring finger was bare.

Chapter Four

Jamaica

THEY'D ENTERED PARADISE.

All one could see from the great stone rooftop patio was denim-blue sky, turquoise water, acres of tropical trees, and an explosion of coral, pink, and purple flowers. Their villa sat on a bluff overlooking the Caribbean, and wooden steps led to a pristine white-sand beach with a fire pit, lounge chairs arranged under blue-and-white-striped umbrellas, and a floating wooden pier. Two woven hammocks swung between trees, right by the charming little tiki bar. At one end of the patio was an infinity pool that seemed to drop off into the sea, at the other end, a hot tub.

And that was just the outside.

A smiling maid in a khaki uniform took them on a tour of the house, pointing out the chef's kitchen trimmed in rose granite that flowed into an enormous, open-air living room. Just a few pillars separated the house from the outdoors, but heavy, retractable awnings could be pulled down to form walls in case of bad weather.

The dining room furniture was crafted using native bamboo, the maid explained, and the lower level held a gym, a steam room, and what the guys clearly considered the crown jewel of the house: a game room with a huge sectional couch and leather recliners, pinball machines, pool and Ping-Pong tables, and a Wii attached to a flat-screen TV. There was also a closet full of games—everything from Twister to Pictionary—and a bookshelf stocked with novels and current issues of a dozen glossy magazines.

"Uh . . . *wow*," Ryan said.

"I'm glad you like it," Dwight said.

"Like?" Ryan repeated. "Dude, I *like* Cool Ranch Doritos. This place . . ." He shook his head.

"Dwight, it's perfect!" Allie cried. "Something out of a dream."

"I can smell the salt water, even from here," Tina said. She closed her eyes and inhaled. "Doesn't it smell like summertime?"

"Our bags should be in our rooms by now," Pauline said. "Ryan and Allie, you'll be upstairs next to us, and everyone else is down here. Sheila"—she smiled at the maid—"will show you the way."

"I need to change into my bathing suit," Savannah said. "The beach is calling my name!"

"How do outdoor massages sound?" Pauline offered. "The ladies can also have mani-pedis if they choose."

"Oh, my God," Tina said. She put a hand over her heart. "Stop it. You're kidding me."

"Tina should go first," Allie said. "She needs it the most! Oh, I'm sorry, Dwight—it's your birthday week. You take the first one."

"We've got two masseuses coming," Pauline said. "You can both go first. They'll be here in thirty minutes, and— Tina? Are you okay?"

"I'm sorry," Tina said. She wiped the corners of her eyes and sniffled. "I'm just so happy right now."

Allie laughed and put her arm around Tina's shoulder. "She

really needed this trip," she said. "You have no idea how badly." Allie caught Dwight's eye and noticed his cheeks were flushed. She winked at him. "You did good, old friend."

Dwight held Allie's gaze for a moment, and she let go of Tina and reached for the Nikon slung around her neck. "Don't move," she said, raising it to her eye. "I want to capture you just like this. You know what, Dwight? You don't look a day over twenty-five!"

"We should hate him for that," Savannah said. "But we'll forgive him because of the villa. If he'd booked us into a Motel 6, though, it'd be all over."

"Okay, crazy episode over," Tina said. "The beach! Massages! I'm ready!"

"Allie and Ryan, do you want to follow me upstairs and I'll show you your suite?" Pauline suggested.

Allie sighed when Pauline opened a door, revealing an enormous bed, bright woven rugs scattered across hardwood floors, and a wide, wooden balcony overlooking the sea. A bathroom twice the size of the master one in Allie's home revealed double sinks, a separate glassed-in shower with a dozen wall jets, and a Jacuzzi tub for two.

Their bags were already set on stands by the closet. Allie meant to dig out her bathing suit, but instead she kicked off her shoes and flopped on the bed, still slightly tipsy from the two drinks she'd consumed on the plane.

"Hey, beautiful," Ryan said, lying down next to her and rolling her toward him.

"Hey, you," Allie said, looking into his eyes. The first time she'd seen him was in a bar in Ocean City beach in Maryland, two summers after she'd graduated from college. She wasn't looking for a boyfriend—she'd just broken up with a guy she'd been dating for a year—but his eyes were so kind that she couldn't turn him down when he asked her to dance. She'd planned to slip away after a song or two, pretending she had to use the restroom. But then Ryan had started goofing around, striking *Saturday Night Fever* poses and picking up Allie by her waist and swinging her around, and she couldn't stop laughing. Her friends all went back to the hotel when the bar closed, but Allie had ended up sitting on the edge of a picnic table at an outdoor pizza place, sharing a pineapple-and-red-pepper pie with Ryan. Much later, he admitted he'd picked off the pineapple and tossed it under the table when Allie wasn't looking. "Putting fruit on pizza is sacrilegious," he'd joked.

"Why didn't you tell me you hated it?" she'd asked.

"Are you kidding?" he'd said. "And risk you running away with another guy who likes your weird pizza toppings?"

Now his sandy blond hair was receding and he'd put on a little weight, but his blue eyes hadn't changed. And their inherent promise had held up through the years: Ryan was kind to her mother, rarely lost his temper, and was content to stay home and watch TV on Saturday nights or gather with friends at a restaurant—whichever Allie preferred. She could count the times they'd fought on one hand, and even then, they'd always made up within a day.

"Not used to drinking in the daytime," Ryan was saying. "I need a nap." He stretched his arms over his head, and Allie heard his back crack.

"Sounds like you need a massage, too," she said. "I can't believe Pauline arranged all this."

"Why do you think they're doing it?" he asked.

His tone was mild, but Allie felt an old, familiar flare of protectiveness for Dwight. Few people had understood him in college or realized that his awkward exterior hid such a gentle heart. He had told her once that his parents had been older— Dwight was born when they were in their late forties, which was highly unusual back then—and he had no siblings. Instantly

Allie's imagination had filled in the rest: His father had probably never tossed around a football with Dwight, or wrestled with him on the living room rug. His mother wouldn't have had any friends with young kids, so he wouldn't have had playdates. It was a shame, because Dwight was the kind of boy who needed a nudge from his parents to invite a friend over for a game of tag or Monopoly. He could've used someone to give him tips on how to approach girls for dates—but his parents wouldn't have known how to guide him; things were completely different for their generation. Now Dwight was starting to come into his own, but it was no wonder he'd struggled to fit in while growing up.

"Dwight's a nice guy, that's why he's doing it!" she snapped.

"Whoa, Mike Tyson," Ryan said, brushing a strand of hair away from her face. "No one's criticizing him."

"Sorry," she said. She snuggled against him and put her head on his shoulder. "I guess I feel a little . . . I don't know, guilty about it. I want to make sure Dwight has fun, too. And Pauline, of course."

"What do you think of her?" he said.

Allie considered the question. "I don't know," she said finally. "She's a little cold . . . or maybe *cold*'s not the right word. Just, controlled. She acts older than all of us, even though she's younger. But she seems like a good person. I mean, she organized this whole trip just to make Dwight happy on his birthday. She doesn't even know any of us. And she's certainly beautiful, don't you think?"

"I guess," Ryan said. "She's not my type, though."

He kissed her hair. "I like redheads."

She knew he was referring to her, but Allie couldn't help but think about Savannah sitting on the plane, her skirt slit up the side of her leg, her laugh drawing the eyes of everyone on board.

"Savannah's looking good," she said.

"Yeah," Ryan agreed. Maybe a little too quickly?

Allie gave herself a mental shake. Ryan was the best husband anyone could ask for, and she was acting like an idiot. She'd noticed how pretty Savannah looked; why shouldn't Ryan have, too? She trusted him completely. Those two cocktails had affected her more than she'd thought. She needed a nap on the beach, then a long jog to clear her mind.

She looked into Ryan's eyes again, and he blinked three times: *I. Love. You.* It was the special signal they'd arranged with the girls, a way to connect secretly when they dropped them off at school or at a friend's for a sleepover.

But now Allie's heart went into a free fall. She saw her paternal grandfather, a man she'd never met, sitting in a wheelchair in a small, gray room, blinking to communicate while his body slowly shut down.

"Allie?"

"Sorry," she said.

But her eyes flitted to her bag just a few feet away, which contained a slip of paper with the phone number for a genetic counselor. She hadn't made the call yet. But she'd found the number on the Internet, and even though she'd vowed to give herself another week, something had made her tuck it into her toiletries case. She wondered now if bringing it had been a mistake. She felt incredibly aware of the scrap of paper, as if it was a gun or bomb she was hiding from Ryan.

How easy it had been to keep this secret from her husband, creating a space between them where none had existed before, she thought with a wisp of sadness. But she would never ruin this vacation for him, especially since after her initial panic, she'd begun to develop the sense, deep in her gut, that she was going to be fine. Wouldn't she be able to feel it if something was so very wrong with her? Of course she would.

"Should we hit the beach?" she asked as Ryan covered a yawn. "Or do you want to take a ten-minute siesta first?"

"Whatever," he said. "I could go either way."

"The beach," she decided.

She sprang out of bed and reached for her suitcase. Her hands were trembling, and it took two tries to unzip it. She hung up a few dresses, then found her swimsuit. "Race you there."

Chapter Five

The Beach

"MMMM," SAVANNAH SAID, FEELING the masseuse's strong fingers dig into her neck. "That's the spot."

Dwight and Tina had already gotten massages—Pauline had turned down the others' urging to go first, saying she'd just had one the previous week—and now Savannah and Gio were lying side by side on woven mats in the warm sunshine.

"Have you and your husband been to Jamaica before?" the massage therapist asked.

"Oh, he's not my husband," Savannah said. Gio's face was smushed against the mat next to hers, but his one visible eye opened and it looked amused.

"Sorry," the massage therapist said.

Why are you apologizing? Savannah wanted to ask, but she just closed her eyes and let her mind drift. She had a husband—or at least she'd have one for a few more months. But if she'd known how things were going to turn out, she never would have sauntered up to Gary at a bar eight years ago. He'd been drinking a single malt scotch and reading the newspaper after a long exam during his third year of medical school. She didn't know he was in med school then, but Savannah had felt certain he was the type of guy who'd be successful. She'd liked the look of him: tall and lean and elegant, and sitting upright on his stool instead of slumping over like other men. She'd also liked the way he didn't glance up from his newspaper as she slid onto the seat beside him.

"Hi," she'd said. "I'm Savannah."

He'd finally looked up, and blinked twice, then he'd folded his paper and put it down on the bar. He'd never finished the article he'd been reading.

After they'd dated for a year or so, he'd suggested going to the movies—but after picking her up, Gary had kept driving out of the city, on and off the highway, and through streets that grew progressively narrower and bumpier, while she'd laughed from the passenger's seat and demanded to know what was going on. Then she'd looked up and seen a beautiful little winery with an attached café come into view. A private table on a wooden deck awaited them. They'd sampled wines, Brie with fig spread on a crusty French bread, olives and cured salamis, and then he'd reached into his pocket, and pulled out a small velvet box . . .

"Is this spot tender?" the massage therapist asked, jolting her back to reality.

"What?" Savannah said.

"You were tensing up."

"I'm fine," Savannah said, but she didn't close her eyes again.

It was always interesting to see people's bodies under their clothes, she mused as she glanced at her friends. They could appear so different, as if they'd suddenly revealed a staggering talent, like the ability to play the piano by ear—or a major flaw, like a gold membership in Yanni's fan club.

Ryan was a bit of a disappointment. His broad shoulders hid a multitude of sins in clothes, but without his shirt, he looked soft and flabby, as if he hadn't worked out in years. Dwight, on the other hand, had definitely improved since college. He was still too thin, but at least he had some definition in his arms and stomach. But Gio was a revelation: the guy was ripped. With his black hair slicked back from the water and his blue trunks riding low on his slim hips, he was by far the best looking of the bunch.

As for the women, Pauline was predictably trim—maybe verging on too thin—and Allie was sleekly fit, with muscular calves and not an ounce of flab, but she was wearing a sensible one-piece instead of a cute bikini. Couldn't she get Ryan to run with her? Savannah wondered. She would, if he were her husband. Tina, though, was the biggest surprise: She'd probably put on fifteen or twenty pounds since college. Bearing all those kids really wreaked havoc on the figure; you could see her stomach muscles had long ago given up the effort to hold things in check, even though Tina had tied a little sarong around her waist to hide it.

Savannah stretched her back, feeling pleased that she'd been working out more rigorously than ever. At thirty-five, she was fitter than she'd been in her early twenties, and her newly upgraded tits were as perky as a teenager's.

"Is this spot tender, too?" the massage therapist asked again, and Savannah realized the therapist was working on her left arm, the one the asshole had gripped last night in the parking lot. There were little bruises shaped like fingertips around her biceps, which she'd tried to cover with makeup.

"It's fine," Savannah said. "But do you mind moving on to the other arm?"

The therapist obeyed without a word. She probably thought Savannah was in an abusive relationship.

"Oh, yeah, that's great," Gio said, and Savannah looked over at him. His masseuse was rubbing his calves, and she suddenly wondered if that was the kind of sound he made during sex. Lucky, lucky Tina.

Almost as if she'd read Savannah's mind, Tina carried over her towel and spread it out next to Gio a moment later.

"I brought you a Red Stripe beer, honey," she said, digging the bottom of the can into the sand by his hand.

"Thanks," he said.

"Come for a swim with me after this?" she asked. "The water's so warm!"

"Definitely, babe." Gio's hand reached out for Tina's.

Unexpected tears stung Savannah's eyes. She blinked, hard, and cleared her throat. The therapist finished working on Savannah's arm and moved to her legs. "What's the plan for tonight?" Savannah asked.

"Pauline said something about dinner at the house," Tina said. "Apparently she's chartered a sailboat for tomorrow morning to take anyone who wants to go snorkeling."

A chartered sailboat . . . now that sounded promising. Savannah knew she'd have to tell Allie and Tina about the separation soon, and they'd want to know all the details. She'd seen the surprise that had come into Allie's eyes when she learned Gary wasn't coming, and she was certain Tina had swallowed a question. She probably didn't want to put Savannah on the spot in front of the whole group, but the moment they were alone, she'd bring it up. Savannah couldn't blame her; she would, too, if their situations were reversed. Even if she tried to keep things light, she'd probably give away the existence of The Nurse, and the fact that Gary had moved out months ago.

It would be easier for everyone if Savannah had the distraction of a handsome young sailboat captain, so she could prove that she'd moved on. That she barely ever thought about Gary anymore.

*   *   *

"Come in with me," Dwight said, reaching a wet hand out of the shower to grab Pauline. "It would be fun to make a baby in Jamaica."

"Oh, honey," she said, slipping free from his grasp as she fumbled for an excuse. "I need to check to make sure the chef has dinner under control."

Besides, she'd just spent half an hour coaxing her hair into simple waves that tumbled over her shoulders. *Men,* she thought. They had no idea how much work went into making something look effortless. Take dinner tonight—she knew that Allie was the lone vegetarian in the group, which complicated things. She could hardly serve spareribs to everyone else and leave Allie picking at the side dishes. Luckily, Allie ate seafood, which meant Pauline had instructed the cook to make fresh-caught snapper with saffron rice for the main course.

"How about I bring back two glasses of wine for us to enjoy while you get ready?" Pauline suggested.

"That's not much of a consolation prize, but I guess I'll take it," he said as he closed the glass door.

Pauline fastened her earrings—real diamonds that had replaced her fake pair soon after she and Dwight got married—and studied herself in the mirror. She needed another shot of Botox, she realized. The faint lines between her eyebrows were beginning to show again. And should she get just the slightest injection of Restylane in her lips? They were on the thin side, and this would only become more apparent as Pauline grew older. Better to make a preventive strike now.

She'd book both appointments after they returned from Jamaica. She might as well spend a full day at the spa—she'd need it. Everyone else viewed this week as the ultimate relaxing getaway, but not Pauline. She was constantly monitoring things, making sure to hand sunscreen to Ryan when his nose began to turn pink, offering a bottle of water to Savannah after she'd tossed back her third cocktail on the beach, and double-checking to ensure the snorkeling trip was still booked for the following morning.

The only way this vacation would be a roaring success was if she remained vigilant.

She smoothed the skirt of her hot pink slip dress and stepped into her simple silver sandals, then left the suite and walked downstairs, inhaling the smells of sizzling garlic and roasting vegetables.

"Everything looks wonderful, Chef," she said as she surveyed the half dozen copper pans steaming up the kitchen. "We'll start with a soup?"

"Lobster bisque," he confirmed. He was a middle-aged man, slightly plump, wearing a white jacket over black trousers and a tall, poufy hat. The hat was a good sign, as was the extra weight, Pauline decided. Who trusted a skinny chef?

"I make it with just a splash of cream and sherry, and chunks of the lobster I selected at the market this morning," the chef continued.

He reached for a tasting spoon and offered her a bit. She rolled her eyes in a show of delight. She was sure most people would consider it delicious, but the fishy taste revolted her.

"Perfection. Just to double-check, there's no shrimp in it, is there?"

"No," he said.

"Good. I know I mentioned it, but one of our guests is allergic."

"Yes, madam." The chef turned to stir a pot while she opened the double-wide refrigerator, noting a dozen bottles of white wine were already chilling on the bottom shelf.

"Are you planning to serve a different wine with each course?" she asked.

"Of course," he said. "And a Madeira with dessert."

"Which is?"

"Warm chocolate puddle cakes with raspberries and blood-orange sorbet."

"Wonderful." Pauline smiled as she uncorked a bottle of Pinot Grigio and filled two goblets. She'd approved the menu a week ago, and it was good to know the chef wasn't straying from it.

She'd booked a waiter from a nearby resort to serve their dinners, with the exception of the clambake, which would be more casual. She wanted to make sure glasses stayed full and plates were cleared at the right time between courses, and she wasn't sure the maid was experienced enough to gauge the rhythms of a fine dinner. It wasn't just that things needed to be perfect for Dwight's birthday; she wanted everyone to be blown away. To praise Dwight—to *admire* him for providing all of this. And, okay, to admire her as well, and to recognize that Dwight, the man who could've had almost anyone, had picked a wonderful wife. Even if she hadn't become pregnant yet.

"Is the waiter here yet?" Pauline asked the chef as she glanced at her watch and noted the time: seven-fifty.

"He's on his way," the chef said, and she nodded her approval.

"Ooh, something smells good!" Savannah came into the kitchen, her hair still wet from the shower. Her feet were bare, and she wore a coral-colored sundress that, against all reason, worked with her hair. Pauline looked down at her own dress. It was similar to Savannah's, but contained about twice as much material.

"We'll eat at eight-thirty," Pauline said. "I hope you're hungry."

"Starving," Savannah said. "Oh, are you pouring drinks?"

Pauline handed Savannah the wineglass she'd intended for herself and reached for another one.

"Mmm." Savannah took a sip. "I feel like we've been here a week already."

"Jamaica is magical that way," Pauline said, as the chef sliced a few pieces of cheese and placed them on a white china plate along with crackers and three fat red strawberries.

"A little nibble, for the starving lady," he said, putting the plate next to Savannah.

"You must be a mind reader!" she squealed. "This is just what I needed. I think I'll take this and go sit outside by the pool for a bit."

Pauline smiled. She didn't want to be rude and walk away from Savannah, but she'd promised Dwight. By the time she returned to their suite, he'd already put on a dark blue T-shirt and white shorts. He was standing next to the bed, typing away on his BlackBerry.

"Room service," she said.

"Thanks," he said. He tucked his BlackBerry in his pocket and took a sip from the glass she handed him. "It's good."

"It's a 2008 Chassagne-Montrachet. One of your favorites," she reminded him.

"Are the others still getting ready?" he asked.

"I think so," she said, her mind sliding past the image of Savannah sitting alone by the pool. "Shall we finish these on the balcony?"

He agreed, and they sat together for fifteen minutes while she chatted easily, telling him about the snorkeling trip the next morning, and letting him know about the meal the chef was preparing. A quick late-afternoon shower had left the air clean and sweet, and the wine felt deliciously crisp on her tongue.

"Everyone's having fun, aren't they?" Dwight asked, and Pauline tamped down on the irritation that suddenly swelled inside her. Why *wouldn't* they be? she wanted to ask. She was working her behind off to make sure of it.

But she just reached for his hand. "Everyone is having an amazing time," she said. "And it's just going to get better and better."

He smiled then and finished his wine. "Shall we go to dinner?"

"The first course," the waiter announced as he placed a white china bowl in front of Tina, "is a lobster bisque."

"Oh, my gosh, I haven't had lobster in forever!" she practically shouted. She knew she sounded like a rube—they were in such an elegant setting—but she didn't care. This had been one of the best days in her entire life, and she didn't feel like pretending to be someone she wasn't. She'd been massaged on the beach, then she and Gio had swum together. Tina had always loved open water, had relished how sensual and languid she felt as she glided into its heavy, silent depths. But ever since she'd had kids, her relationship with water had shifted, because now it represented danger: She had to scan the neighborhood pool constantly to see the heads of her children, since she was pretty sure the teenage lifeguards were dozing behind their sunglasses. And the beach? Forget it; she couldn't relax for a second.

Today, though, she'd felt like a mermaid as she dove and splashed and kicked. She'd squealed in surprise as Gio caught her by the waist and pulled her underwater for a long kiss. Then she and Gio had come back to the beach and collapsed onto lounge chairs and the massage therapist had offered her a mani-pedi, which she'd desperately needed. She'd fallen asleep somewhere between the base and second coat of bright pink polish. When she'd woken up, she'd had a dry mouth and a headache, but there was a fully stocked medicine cabinet in their suite, and two Advils had chased away the throbbing in her temples.

She and Gio had showered together—they'd had sex, too, which was surprisingly comfortable thanks to the bench built into the shower—and then Tina had taken her time with her makeup.

Now here she was, with a pink- and violet-streaked sunset visible from her seat, Bob Marley's infectious voice on the sound system, and crystal goblets glowing like fireflies on the table. Bliss.

"Oh, no!" Tina said suddenly, putting down her spoon with a clank. Everyone turned to look at her. "I forgot to call the children to say good night! I promised I would!"

Gio threw back his head and laughed. "Man, give her a day away from the kids, and she forgets all about them."

"They're probably putting your photo on a milk carton, Tina," Savannah cracked.

Tina glared at Savannah and punched Gio in the arm. "Stop it!"

This wasn't the slightest bit funny. She'd only thought about her kids in tiny glimpses today. Guilt flooded her. What kind of a mother was she?

"Do you want to go call them now?" Allie asked quietly. "If it would make you feel better . . ."

Tina glanced at her watch and shook her head. "They probably just fell asleep, and the phone might wake them again . . . Your mom would've called if they were upset, right? If they'd wanted to talk to me?"

"Of course she would've," Allie said.

"Did I tell you I bought *Marmaduke* for them to watch tonight?" Ryan said.

"You did? My kids go crazy for any show with dogs in it!" Tina said.

"Yeah, I figured, since the last time I was at your house they tried to put a leash on me and make me bark," Ryan said. "I thought it would make their first night away easier." He topped off her wineglass, even though it was half-full. Tina smiled at him, recognizing it as a gesture of support, and the tension in her stomach uncoiled.

"Wow, Ryan, I thought that was just a little trick you did for Allie when you two were alone," Savannah said, but Tina didn't join in the laughter.

Tina didn't expect Savannah to understand—Savannah had never hidden the fact that she thought children were life's most highly overrated and overpriced joy—but Gio should've taken up for her the way Allie and Ryan had. Come to think of it, why hadn't *he* remembered to call their kids?

She opened her mouth to say something to him, then closed it. *Breathe,* she reminded herself. She took another spoonful of soup, forcing herself to focus on its velvety texture. She'd finally achieved a state of relaxation today, and she needed to hang on to it, or the vacation would be ruined. Gio adored their kids; he just had a different parenting style.

"Someone stop me from swan-diving into my soup," Savannah said. "I want to rip off my clothes and bathe in it. It's just incredible!"

"I'll be sure to let the chef know you enjoyed it," Pauline said in a neutral voice.

There was a brief pause, then Allie said, "So catch us up on what's going on at work, Van." Allie turned to Pauline. "Did you know Savannah's a real estate agent?"

Typical Allie, always taking care of everyone, Tina thought, feeling a surge of affection for her old friend. First Allie had assuaged Tina's fears, and now she was making sure Pauline felt included in the conversation. Plus she was letting Savannah talk about herself, which would keep Savannah happy.

"There's this one house that is killing me," Savannah said with a dramatic sigh. "Just fucking killing me. I've had it on the market for months. The owner has the ugliest kids imaginable, and he refuses to take down their photos. They're like a hex on this house. The photos send prospective buyers running away screaming."

Tina scraped the last spoonful of bisque from her bowl, then sat back as the waiter cleared away her dishes. She listened to Savannah's chatter, laughing in all the right places as Savannah kept talking: "Seriously, these clients I had last year looked like apple-cheeked grandparents. You'd think all they did was play canasta and eat early-bird specials. And fur-lined handcuffs fell out of their bedroom closet when I opened the door to show it to a young couple! And then as we all stood there, gaping down at the handcuffs, the guy goes, 'We'll take it!'"

A loaf of warm bread was set out on the table, along with individual ramekins of herbed butter. The waiter served the fish, then filled up the second wineglass at Tina's place.

"A French chardonnay," he said quietly, since Savannah was in the middle of another story. "The light citrus notes go beautifully with the snapper. And would you care for green salad with roasted garlic dressing?"

"Thank you," Tina said, smiling at him. A rush of contentment flooded her body, making her limbs feel as rich and loose as honey. What she'd been craving hadn't just been sleep or a break from the high, demanding voices in her home, she realized. It was the chance to be taken care of, in the way she was always taking care of others. In the way she hadn't been since her mother died.

"You okay?" Gio whispered in her ear. She felt his foot find hers under the table, and he rubbed his leg against hers.

Interesting, she thought. Normally, their exchange of a few minutes earlier would've led to a fight. She would've gotten increasingly stressed, Gio would've snapped at her to relax, and she would've reacted angrily. But because she'd let it go—

mostly because there were witnesses around—*Gio* was the one trying to make up.

She gave him a fleeting smile, suddenly wanting to keep him off guard for a while longer, then glanced at Savannah and wondered, for the dozenth time, exactly what was going on with Gary. Clearly Van didn't want to talk about it, but Tina knew the fact that he wasn't along on the trip—not even for a few days—wasn't good. No one was that busy.

Dwight wasn't talking much, but that was typical, since he was always a little shy in a group, Allie thought as she brought a forkful of tender fish to her mouth. He looked like he was having fun, which was the most important thing.

She glanced around the table, taking in the faces of her dear friends: Savannah was gesturing with her fork, her white teeth flashing as she talked, while Gio took a bite of the snapper and rolled his eyes in appreciation. Ryan was throwing back his head and laughing at Savannah's outrageous stories, and Tina looked so relaxed, with her cheeks glowing pink from the sun and the worry lines erased from her forehead. Pauline was buttering a slice of bread, and Dwight turned to meet Allie's gaze. She lifted her wineglass to him in a quick, private toast, and they drank together.

Their group wasn't perfect, of course. Allie sensed Savannah grated on Pauline; little clues—like Pauline's overly formal response to Savannah's compliment about the soup—were seeping out. But Pauline hid it well. The others might not have even seen the annoyance that had briefly flashed in Pauline's eyes.

Savannah finally wrapped up a story about a brother and sister who'd squabbled nonstop during the sale of their parents' home, before breaking down and sobbing on the day the final papers were signed, delaying the proceedings by nearly an hour as they apologized for all their transgressions against each other, down to the time the brother had falsely blamed the sister for knocking over the family Christmas tree when they were five years old.

"Do you have any siblings, Pauline?" Allie broke in when Savannah paused to take a sip of chardonnay.

Pauline dabbed her lips with her napkin before answering. "Just one," she said. "An older sister."

"Are you close?" Allie asked.

"Not particularly," Pauline said.

It seemed like a perfectly normal question, but had she overstepped? Allie wondered. Pauline's voice had seemed . . . strained.

"How about you, Allie? Any siblings?" Pauline asked.

"No," Allie said. She must've been imagining things; Pauline sounded perfectly normal now. "I'm adopted, and my parents wanted another child, but it never worked out. We live just a few minutes away from them."

"Which is nice, because we have built-in babysitters," Ryan said. He winked. "They don't even charge us that much."

"Are they taking care of the kids while you're on this trip?" Pauline asked.

"Yep," Ryan said.

"They've got my kids, too," Tina said. "I hope it's not too overwhelm——— No! You know what? I'm not going to feel guilty. Not tonight."

Savannah lifted her glass. "Good for you! To shameless self-absorption!"

Tina laughed and clinked her glass against Savannah's. "To over-the-top indulgence!"

"To gluttony!" Ryan shouted, getting into it.

"To—to . . ." Dwight began, then he stopped and silence filled the room.

"To . . . d-debauchery and hedonism!" he finally shouted, and everyone cheered.

The waiter cleared the plates and brought in dessert. When Allie's fork broke the crust of her little cake, molten chocolate ran out. She speared one of the raspberries rimming her plate and swirled it in the chocolate, then almost moaned in delight as the flavors exploded on her tongue.

"So after we finish massacring this meal," Savannah said, "would anyone be up for a moonlight swim? Or maybe a soak in the hot tub?"

"Me!" Tina shouted.

"Who else?" Savannah asked. "Dwight? You in?"

"Sure," he said.

"What a perfect way to end the night," Pauline said.

"Oh, it's only nine-thirty," Savannah said. "The night's just beginning."

Allie hid a yawn. True, it was relatively early—but they'd traveled half the day, including the bumpy Jeep ride to the villa in Negril, and they'd been drinking since morning. Plus so much time in the sun and water, combined with the sleepless nights of the past few weeks, had made her feel so drowsy she wanted to drop her head onto the table and drift off.

"C'mon, guys, we're in Jamaica, not on a seniors' cruise," Savannah said, looking around the table.

"She's right," Gio said. "Strap one on, people."

"That's the spirit," Savannah said. "I'm thinking a game of pool, a dip in the hot tub, maybe a visit to that tiki bar on the beach . . . Oh, and I brought this for you, Dwight."

She reached under her chair and held out a small square package wrapped in green foil.

"It's just a little gift," she said. "Something I thought we might enjoy this week."

Dwight tore open the paper, revealing a homemade CD.

"I burned the songs. They're all from the nineties," Savannah said. "College music."

"That was really nice of you," Allie said.

"I couldn't risk leaving the music to chance," Savannah said. "If this house was stocked with inadequate tunes, I'd have trouble dancing. And you know how much I love to dance."

"'Closing Time' . . . 'Baby Got Back'!" Dwight read. "'Then the Morning Comes' . . . How does that one go again?"

"The Smash Mouth song? . . . 'Paint the town, take a bow. Thank everybody, you're gonna do it again. You are the few, the proud, you are the antibody . . .'" Ryan sang.

"Hey, our boy can sing!" Savannah said. "Do we have a karaoke machine in the house?"

"We could get one," Pauline said. "I'll have it delivered tomorrow."

"A woman of action!" Savannah cried. "That's what I like to see!"

Allie thanked the waiter as he refilled her wineglass. Unlike people who loved to debate buttery notes and subtle finishes, she'd never appreciated wine, but she knew one thing: This stuff was good. It tasted so different from the chardonnay she bought at the grocery store and kept in the fridge.

She closed her eyes and took another sip, trying to tease out the hint of lime and the peppery notes the waiter had described, but instead her mind again fluttered to an image of the piece of paper hidden in her toiletries case. Suddenly she was wide awake.

"'I Don't Want to Miss a Thing' by Aerosmith . . ." Dwight read. "Thanks, Van."

"Can't have a reunion without a sound track," Savannah said. "And speaking of not missing a thing—sleep can wait. Who's ready for a little ass kicking in a game of pool?"

"Me, me, me!" Tina shouted. "I want to play!"

"Wait, Tina, I'm confused," Ryan cracked. "Are you in or not?"

"Champagne, everyone?" Pauline offered, as the waiter stood by, ready to uncork a bottle of Cristal. "It's from 1978, the year Dwight was born."

Savannah was right, Allie decided, holding out her glass. They should stay up. The last thing she wanted right now was to close her eyes in the darkness.

Chapter Six

Monday

THE DAY WAS ALMOST surreal in its perfection, Savannah thought. The tropical storm was carrying rain and wind ever closer to them, but it seemed hard to believe now. The sky was an endless swath of blue, and sunlight glinted against the water, creating countless, tiny reflections so bright they almost hurt the eye.

Savannah's skin felt warm, but not uncomfortably so, because the catamaran caught a breeze as it cut through the Caribbean Sea. She leaned back against the fiberglass hull, her eyes shielded by dark sunglasses as she watched a twentysomething crewman let out a sail. He wore nothing but bright red bathing trunks. The muscles in his back flexed as he tugged on the ropes, and his dark skin gleamed from the spray of seawater.

He'll do, she thought as she took a sip of her pineapple spritzer. *He'll do quite nicely.*

She'd set a goal for herself this morning: She needed to have sex on this trip. She'd been intimate with only one guy since Gary—a clichéd fling with her personal trainer, who could've used some of the endurance he was always preaching about to his clients—and she was horny. And didn't women hit their sexual peaks in their midthirties? That settled it; she wasn't going to get back on Dwight's plane again until she'd rolled around in the sand with a hot guy.

Allie was leaning back, snapping pictures of Dwight as he stared out at the water. Savannah glanced over at Tina and Gio, sprawled a few feet away. Tina's eyes were closed against the sun, but she seemed to sense Savannah's gaze and opened them. Savannah raised her sunglasses, glanced pointedly at Dwight, then stuck out her tongue and wiggled it.

When she looked back, Tina was glaring at her.

Stop it! Tina mouthed.

Savannah winked, then dropped her sunglasses back down. She still couldn't believe what Tina had revealed this morning. It made one look at Dwight in a whole new light. She closed her eyes, feeling drowsy from the sun and the effects of last night's alcohol, as she recalled the conversation:

Savannah had been asleep when Tina knocked on her door.

"Go away," Savannah had muttered, burying her head under her pillow.

"Wake up, Little Miss Sunshine," Tina had said, bustling right in. She'd opened the blinds, and light had flooded the room.

"Jesus, Tina, I'm not one of your fourteen children," Savannah had said, but there was a smile in her voice. "What time is it, you sadist?"

"Nine," Tina had said. "And we're going snorkeling in an hour."

Savannah had lifted her head up and rolled over. Images of the previous night had drifted back to her: There was a game of pool, girls versus guys. Maybe two games? And they'd blared Dwight's CD . . . more champagne had been brought out. Had someone dumped a bit on Dwight's head, like they did in locker rooms after a winning football game? Oh, right, that was her . . . There had been dancing, lots of dancing on the patio by the pool. Ryan had fallen in at one point, but he'd managed to hold up his beer and hadn't spilled a drop, which made everyone cheer . . . Oh, and she'd tried to teach Dwight to salsa, but they both kept laughing too hard. Luckily, Pauline had gone to bed by then; somehow Savannah knew she wouldn't have approved.

"Are you feeling okay?" Tina was asking.

Savannah had slowly sat up, wincing. "Why is a heavy-metal drummer practicing on my temples? And is everyone else up?"

Tina had nodded. "Allie went for a jog."

"Now there's a shocker."

"And the boys are devouring breakfast. The chef is doing individual omelets."

"Pigs. I'm still full from last night," Savannah had said. She'd stretched her arms over her head. "Okay, okay, I'm getting up. Just tell me they have coffee ready."

"Cappuccinos and lattes," Tina had confirmed. "Plus fresh-squeezed juice."

"I knew I should've married Dwight when I had the chance," Savannah had cracked.

"Hey, *I'm* the one that made out with him," Tina had said.

"Oh, my God, I'd totally forgotten about that!" Savannah had said. She'd winced and massaged her forehead with her thumb and index finger. "Remind me again. What happened, exactly?"

Tina had glanced toward the open door, then she'd moved closer, to sit on the edge of Savannah's bed. "It was at that Pi Kappa Phi party right before graduation. Allie brought Dwight along, and Gio and I were fighting about something stupid. We were taking a little break."

"Oh, sure, try and justify it," Savannah had teased. This sounded juicier than she'd remembered.

"I started drinking tequila shots, which for the record, you should never do when you're pissed off at your boyfriend," Tina had said. "I was in a crappy mood, and everyone else was dancing and having fun, and then Dwight came over to the bar to hang out with me. I poured him a shot."

"The plot thickens," Savannah had said as she mock-leered.

"I got really drunk—"

"Ah, the old tequila goggles excuse."

"—and Dwight walked me home. He came into my room . . . Allie was still at the party. And he was so sweet. He took off my shoes."

"What about your panties?" Savannah had asked, and Tina had thrown a pillow at her.

"Van! Shhh! Anyway, suddenly I realized I hadn't kissed that many guys in my life. I mean, my high school boyfriend, and two boys in college before I met Gio. But that was it. And I felt like I was, I don't know, maybe missing out. So I just grabbed Dwight and went for it."

"Was it like kissing your brother?" Savannah had asked, wrinkling her nose. "I love Dwight, but the sex appeal bus completely passed his stop."

"Actually . . ." Tina had said, drawing out the word. "His lips were really soft."

"Seriously?" Savannah had felt her eyebrows lift toward the ceiling. She couldn't believe she'd never grilled Tina about this before.

"Uh-huh. And he was so gentle. He kissed me really slowly."

"I figured he'd be so eager he'd be all tongue and slobber," Savannah had said.

"Van!" Tina had chastised her. "Not at all. He was a good kisser!"

"Well, well," Savannah had said. "You know, he does have nice lips, come to think of it. Full."

"I'm telling you," Tina had said. Was she blushing? Savannah had considered her: Tina had been a fun girl in college, but lately she'd seemed as worn-out as an old-time photo. Even her voice had changed—had become more reedy and anxious since she'd started popping out kids. Since they lived a few states apart, they didn't see each other all that often, but every time they did, Tina had slipped a bit more. Comfort had long ago beaten the crap out of style when it came to her clothes, and her hair was always a mess.

But Tina looked different now. She wore a peach-colored cover-up with a V-neck that complimented her deep tan. Her eyes were bright, and she couldn't stop giggling. Sure, she had a few more lines around her eyes and pounds around her middle, but it was as if the old Tina—or make that the young Tina—was finally back.

"Did you do anything else? Lunge for his package?"

Tina had laughed. "I wasn't a hussy like you back then. We just kissed."

"You're blushing," Savannah had said.

"I am not," Tina had said as she turned redder. "It's sunburn!"

"Who knew you had it in you, Tina Antonelli? You've got a smoking hot hubby and you made out with our millionaire host. It must be your fertile loins."

Tina was holding her stomach and laughing so hard she almost fell off the bed. But then a sound had made her jerk upright: a knock on the open door.

"I figured you might need a cappuccino," Pauline had said, bringing one into the room on a silver tray. "It was a late night."

Savannah had sat up straighter. "How'd you know that's just what I was craving? Thank you, Pauline."

She'd glanced at Tina, who was displaying an intense interest in the fringe on a throw pillow.

"I'll leave it on the nightstand," Pauline had said. "Meet you in the dining room whenever you're ready."

Tina had kept her head down until the door clicked shut behind Pauline. "Oh, my God . . . that was bad. She heard, didn't she?"

"No way," Savannah had said, even though she wasn't sure. Pauline hadn't looked at Tina when she entered the room, not once. And the door had closed a tad sharply.

"The door was open! She was standing right there! She totally heard," Tina had moaned. She'd flopped backward on the bed and covered her eyes with her arm. "She thinks I'm going to make a play for her husband. Do you think she'll say something to Dwight?"

"Oh, come on," Savannah had said. "She was probably flattered. *I'd* be."

"You know, I never told Gio," Tina had said. "I mean, we were on a break! And it was just kissing. Shit, what if she says something?"

Savannah had rolled her eyes. "Come on, you think Gio would really be upset about a kiss from fifteen years ago?"

"He can be a little jealous," Tina had said. "Not that he has any reason to be. Things between us are great, really."

Savannah had reached for her cappuccino and taken a long sip, already a little bored with the new direction of this conversation. She could taste the Splenda; how did Pauline know it was her preferred sweetener? She must've asked Allie, or maybe she'd just intuited it. That woman could send Martha Stewart into intensive therapy for feelings of domestic inadequacy.

"Savannah? What do you think I should do?" Tina was nibbling on a fingernail.

"Stop it," Savannah had said, batting Tina's hand out of her mouth. "You just got a manicure, for Christ's sake. Look, it's no big deal. Pauline didn't hear, and if she did, it'll probably give her a giggle. It's already over. Now let's throw on bathing suits and go hit that boat."

She'd known her voice sounded brusque, but it was ridiculous, really. Tina thought this was an actual problem? She'd just said it herself: Things with her gorgeous husband were great. And it wasn't as if Savannah hadn't noticed the way Gio had pulled Tina onto his lap in the hot tub, and the look they'd given each other as they left "to get another drink," before they'd returned ten minutes later.

Remembering it now, Savannah glanced back over at Tina and Gio beside her on the boat. His hand was resting on her bare thigh. That man was a stallion; how come she'd never noticed that before, either? Or maybe she was just so horny that every guy around looked good to her now. She lifted her arms over her head and stretched her midsection toward the sky, feeling a satisfying little pop in her spine. Did she imagine it, or had the young crewman done a double take?

She had five more days to get laid, she reminded herself. Not a lot of time, but then, she'd always liked a challenge.

The crewman pulled in the sail in preparation to slow the boat before they dropped anchor while Pauline pointed out the snorkeling equipment and told everyone a beautiful tropical reef lay just ahead of them. All she needed was a red umbrella and she'd be the perfect tour guide, Savannah thought.

Savannah was the first one to grab a mask, slip on fins, and drop into the sea. For a few minutes, she floated on her back, letting the cool water bubble up over her shoulders as thoughts flitted through her mind like silverfish.

In another few months, she'd meet her divorce lawyer to sign the final papers. Gary would be there, too, of course, with his attorney by his side. Would he marry The Nurse as soon as he was free? What would it feel like to see him again? Savannah wondered if there would be a last gesture, like a final overpriced latte, a good-bye cocktail, or a farewell fuck. Whatever it was, she decided, Gary would pay for it—in one way or another. She wouldn't consider sleeping with him, except she loved the idea of Gary going back to The Nurse with Savannah's perfume all over him.

And then . . . and then she'd figure out what to do with the rest of her life. Maybe she should sell her house—downsize to a cute condo closer to the heart of the city. One thing for sure: She wasn't going to join a knitting club or start baking bread. She'd take up something sexy, like snowboarding. Maybe she should plan a winter trip to Vail.

Someone splashed into the water next to Savannah, and she glanced over. It was the young crewman. A wide smile broke apart his face and revealed a dimple in his right cheek. His teeth were white and perfectly straight.

"I'll lead you to the reef, if you'd like," he said, a light Jamaican accent lending an uptilt to his words.

Savannah held his eyes for a long moment. "Oh, I'd like," she finally said.

It had been another flawless day, Pauline reflected as she glanced at the platters of hors d'oeuvres the chef was preparing: pan-seared baby crab cakes, mini London broil sandwiches on sourdough croutons with spicy mustard, tropical fruit skewers, and a trio of tapenades—olive, eggplant, and red pepper—with garlicky crostini for dipping.

They'd come back from the snorkeling trip two hours earlier, and the rest of the group had immediately collapsed onto cushioned lounge chairs by the pool. Everyone seemed relaxed and cheerful, Pauline noted with approval. And although Savannah had embarrassed herself on the boat, at least she was behaving now. In fact, Pauline thought, peering out the window to check, she seemed to be asleep. All that flirting must've worn her out.

Pauline held back a snort, remembering how Savannah had

asked the crewman, who looked like he was barely out of high school, to rub sunscreen on her back.

Even Gio had noticed, teasing Savannah when the crewman moved away. "Stella? You trying to get your groove back?"

Instead of being embarrassed, Savannah had thrown back her head and laughed. She was completely shameless, and the worst part was, she seemed to revel in it. Even her bikini was over the top—it was a metallic gold with slim chains linking the tiny triangles of fabric. Compared to what the other women were wearing, it seemed like a cry for attention. No, *cry* was too subtle—that bathing suit was an air-raid siren.

"You've outdone yourself, Chef," Pauline said, turning back to the food. "Shall we serve these poolside, maybe with a few pitchers of water with sliced lemon in case people are feeling dehydrated? There are plenty of tables, and everyone looks so comfortable there now . . ."

"My pleasure." He smiled and began to carry out the platters.

Pauline glanced down at her iPhone and noticed a new call had come in, from her mother. She hadn't left a message, though. Pauline couldn't remember if she'd told her mother they'd be away this week or not. She'd return the call later, she decided.

Pauline felt pleasure mingle with pride as she thought about her mother's life now: The gardeners were back, the house had been redecorated, and her mother had just flown with two friends to Monte Carlo. Pauline had also taken over all the bills related to her sister Therese's care, of course.

She thought about how her mother's face had transformed when Pauline and Dwight had returned from their honeymoon to Tokyo and Pauline had handed her mother a plain white envelope. Sweet Dwight, who'd gotten so excited about the anime cartoons and sumo wrestling match they'd seen on their trip, had never asked for a prenup. Of course Pauline hadn't brought up the subject, either. During their engagement, she'd slipped into handling their finances as naturally as she'd taken over everything else in their lives.

When she'd mentioned to Dwight that she wanted to help her mother, he hadn't hesitated. "Of course," he'd said. "Whatever she needs."

"You're so good to me," Pauline had said, meaning every word. Some of the wealthy people she knew from her work in the art world were unbelievably stingy, seeming to feel that they needed to hold on to their money lest someone try to wrench it out of their hands. But not Dwight. For a man worth so much, he cared surprisingly little about his bank account.

Inside the envelope Pauline gave her mother was a blank check. Her mother didn't open the envelope then, but she knew. Pauline would never forget how her mother's face had become ten years younger in the space of an instant. She'd tucked the envelope into her purse; then she'd turned to Pauline and studied her for a long moment.

"Are you . . . happy?" she'd finally asked. She'd nibbled her lower lip while she waited for Pauline's answer—which was strange, since Pauline had had the same nervous habit as a girl. Her mother had been the one to train her to stop doing it.

But Pauline had merely answered the question. "Of course. Blissfully."

Her mother had nodded. "I always worried . . . I just thought, with your father gone, and Therese needing so much . . . Well, I knew it would take a special man to accept that kind of responsibility."

Pauline didn't tell her mother that she hadn't been completely honest with Dwight about Therese. He knew she had an older sister with birth defects, but he didn't know the severity. *Sort of like Down syndrome,* Pauline had murmured when she first brought up Therese. *But why is she in an institution?* Dwight had asked. *A lot of people with Down syndrome live independent lives.*

Pauline had been unable to meet his eyes then. *It's . . . well, she also can't easily walk, or talk much.*

The lie had caused a lump to form in Pauline's throat, and her voice had roughened around it. Dwight hadn't pressed her for any more details, not then. He'd just looked at her for a long moment and nodded. She'd been vague about Therese's location, too, implying that she was in a facility much farther away—"up North," she'd said, which was technically true, even if Therese was twenty miles away instead of three states. It seemed simpler to keep the parts of her life revolving around her husband and her sister completely separate.

"Mom." Pauline had started to reach for her mother's hand, but she and her mother touched so rarely that the gesture felt unnatural, and she'd stilled her arm. "Everything is okay. Really."

"Wonderful," her mother had said, and then the complicated swirl of emotions that had washed over her face—relief, joy, and was that a bit of regret, too?—was gone. "I could use a cup of tea," she'd said. "Will you have one with me?"

Now Pauline glanced back down at her phone and read the weather forecast. The tropical storm was still heading in their general direction, but it looked like it would miss them by a hundred miles. Still, they'd probably get rain on Thursday and maybe Friday, too—heavy rain, not like the light afternoon showers that routinely refreshed Negril.

She clicked through her mental inventory of indoor activities: They had the game room, of course, and she'd arranged for delivery of some first-run DVD movies. Plus she could have the sommelier come to the house for a wine tasting. No one knew it yet, but she'd instructed him to monitor everyone's preferences. When they returned home, her guests would discover they'd each been delivered a case of their favorite wine, as a way of commemorating their week together.

Still, she'd need to stay on top of the weather. Storms were notoriously unpredictable; this one's direction could shift at any moment. She'd need to create a backup plan for that, too—they couldn't stay on the water if things became dangerous. Jamaica was in the hurricane belt, after all. She'd find the name of the best hotel in town and book a block of rooms, just in case they had to leave quickly.

"Everything all right, Ms. Glass?"

Pauline glanced up to see the chef watching her as he hefted the final platter.

"Yes," she said, smiling. She tucked her iPhone back into her purse. "We're in Jamaica. How could it not be?"

"You are kidding me!" Allie shouted. "Really?"

"I've never been on a helicopter in my life!" Tina squealed.

"Jamaica is at its most beautiful at sunset," Pauline said. "A spin around the island, then a late dinner at home. How does that sound? Of course, if you'd rather stay here and rest, that's completely fine, too. Everyone should do exactly what they want."

"No way am I turning down a helicopter ride," Ryan said, as everyone added their assent.

"They'll be touching down within the hour," Pauline said. "We'll need two helicopters for all of us."

"I'm going to hop in the shower and wash off the salt water," Tina said as she stood up.

"I'm right behind you," Savannah said, yawning.

"Me, too," Allie said. She reflexively reached for her dirty plate, but Pauline shook her head.

"Oh, no, please leave that. It'll be cleared away. You girls just go take your time getting ready."

"Ryan? You coming?" Allie asked.

"Yeah, buddy, don't you need to go primp?" Gio said, leaning over to elbow Ryan in the ribs.

"Forget that," Ryan said. "The only primping I'm doing is diving in the pool."

"My man," Gio said, holding up his beer to clink against Ryan's. "Gives us more time to toss back a few."

"Hoo-yeah!" Ryan shouted.

Allie rolled her eyes. She loved Gio, but whenever Ryan was around him, her husband acted like he'd just gotten a shot of testosterone.

She glanced over and noticed that since Tina had gotten up, there was an empty lounge chair separating Dwight from the other guys. He wasn't excluded from their conversation, exactly, but the distance would make it harder for him to participate in it.

Move over, she thought, but he didn't.

"Dwight?" Allie asked. "Do you need a cold one as long as I'm up?"

"Sure," he said. "Thanks."

She reached into the poolside cooler, then walked over and handed him a Red Stripe.

"So, Dwight, you guys travel like this all the time?" Gio was asking in a loud voice.

Allie smiled and began to go inside, but then Gio continued and she paused on the landing.

"Must be nice. I mean, private planes, helicopters. You going to buy a train next? Just so you can cover every mode of transportation?"

Something in Gio's tone marred what should've been light banter. Was he drunk? Allie wondered, studying him. He was leaning back, one arm folded behind his head, his legs crossed at the ankles. His position was relaxed, but the way he was staring at Dwight . . .

A memory popped into Allie's mind: Gio pushing a guy up

against the wall at a college bar, a blue vein in his neck bulging as his forearm pressed against the guy's throat, cutting off his air while a girl screamed and Tina pulled on his arm, yelling, "Gio! Stop!" The guy had pinched Tina's behind, Allie remembered. And Gio would've really hurt him—Allie was certain of that—if the bouncers hadn't broken his grip and thrown him out of the bar.

Gio hadn't seemed to be putting away too many beers today, but maybe she just hadn't noticed. She *had* seen Savannah drinking a lot, though. Allie paused under the pretext of pouring herself a glass of water from the pitcher on one of the outdoor tables and kept listening.

"A train. Yeah," Dwight said. There was a little pause, then Dwight laughed, but he was the only one who did so.

"So, Gio, buddy, how the hell do helicopters stay up in the air?" Ryan said. "It can't all be in the propeller."

"Same basic principle as an airplane," Gio said. He broke his stare at Dwight and turned to look at Ryan, and when he spoke again the tension had left his voice. "Seriously, man, you don't know this? They get lift and thrust from the main rotor . . ."

Allie exhaled and went inside. She should have known Ryan would defuse the tension; he was good at that. But Gio's comments stayed with her while she showered and applied mascara and cherry ChapStick, and slipped on a long flowered skirt and white tank top. Finally she went downstairs and knocked on Tina's door.

"Come in!" Tina called, and Allie opened the door. Tina was on the phone, having either an imaginary conversation with George Clooney or a real one with her children, judging from all the "I love you"s and kissing sounds. Allie sat down in an oversize chair to wait. The French doors were open to the breeze, and an arrangement of delicate purple orchids in a vase sat atop the dresser across from the bed.

"Ice cream sundaes after dinner?" Tina was saying. "You're so lucky! Yup, just a little while longer . . . Okay, sweetie . . ."

Allie smiled. She'd talked to her mom right after the snorkeling trip, and although she had sounded a little tired, her mother had insisted everything was fine. The teenage babysitter was a big help, and all the kids were getting along beautifully so far.

"Oh, do I love your mother," Tina said as she put down her cell phone. "My kids sounded happy!"

"Of course they are," Allie said. "Just like you are, right?"

"I think I'm a little too happy right now," Tina said. "I can't believe we only have five days left."

"Don't think about that," Allie said. "Just concentrate on the now. That's what Buddhists say is the key to joy anyway."

"You're right. So what do you think is really going on with Savannah and Gary?" Tina asked as she reached for a comb and began to untangle her mass of wet curls. "I tried to ask her today on the boat, but she kind of brushed me off. She's not wearing her rings, but sometimes she doesn't. She once told me she takes them off when she plays golf or works out and never remembers to put them back on."

"I started to ask, too, but then Pauline walked up to us, and I didn't want to bring it up in front of her," Allie said. "Do you think he really had to work this whole week?"

"Even a doctor gets time off," Tina said. "Especially for a free trip to Jamaica. I mean, unless he got offended because Dwight was paying for everything and he didn't want to come because it was an insult to his male ego. Lotion, lotion, where'd I put that bottle of lotion? No, something else is going on between the two of them."

Allie reached for the Lubriderm on the table next to her and handed it to her friend. "Tina? Does Gio feel weird about that, too? I mean, about Dwight paying for everything?"

Tina stopped moving. "Why do you ask? Does Ryan?"

Allie shook her head. "No. I mean, not that I know of. He understands it's a gift Dwight really wants to give us."

Tina finished moisturizing her legs before she answered. "Things are . . . really tight for us right now," she said. "Gio's worried he might lose his job."

"But he's so good at it!" Allie protested.

"Yeah, but so were the guys who got laid off last winter," Tina said. "And if his company doesn't land another big project soon, it won't matter how good he is. And you know he wants our kids to go to private Catholic school, and it's ridiculously expensive. So we decided they can't, and I think on some level Gio feels like God is going to be angry with him. You know how old-fashioned Gio is. It's just how he was raised."

"So he feels like he's not providing well enough?" Allie asked. "Even though you have a nice home and you're raising four kids?"

"I don't think he feels that way all the time," Tina said. "It's . . . well, seeing everything Dwight has, especially right now . . . I mean, Dwight was just this shy little twerp in college, and now he's this hotshot. And the crazy thing is, Dwight didn't even work that hard to get his money! It all came from an idea!"

"It was more than that," Allie corrected. "He started a great dot-com company. Everyone thought it was going to be the new UPS."

"I know," Tina said. "And I agree, the idea was brilliant. I mean, who wouldn't want to be able to click a computer button and have anything from Chinese food to wine to DVDs—or all three—delivered within thirty minutes?"

"So that bothers Gio, too? That he feels like Dwight got lucky?" Allie asked. "Because no one knew the dot-com bubble would burst."

"Seemed like Dwight did," Tina said. "He cashed out a lot of his stock right before it happened."

"See? It was more than luck," Allie said. "Maybe he sensed it was coming. And it's not like he doesn't work. He's always dabbling in new things! He started that company to develop new apps, and he's got some rental properties in Breckenridge . . ."

"I don't know, Al, we haven't even really talked about it." Tina sighed. "Gio said something last night, a little jab about Dwight's prissy gold Rolex. It wasn't hard to figure out where it was coming from."

"What did you say?"

Tina shrugged. "I ignored it. Why? Do you think it's a big deal?"

"I don't know," Allie said, choosing her words carefully. She didn't want to stress Tina out, not now, when she was finally getting to relax. "But you might want to reassure Gio about how well he's doing, if it's a sensitive point. Everyone has different emotional triggers, and even if they don't make sense to the rest of us, it's important to respect them. I'd just hate for Gio to feel even a little bit badly when this trip is supposed to be a fun vacation for you two."

Tina crossed the room and gave Allie a hug. "You know why I love you? Because you care so much about everyone else. Now let's go grab a glass of wine and jump aboard that helicopter."

Allie stood up, feeling as if she hadn't conveyed the urgency she was sensing about Gio's feelings.

"Let me just throw some gel in my hair. I'm going to let the wind dry it," Tina was saying. "And how about tonight we dance on the beach? I feel like dancing again! That was so much fun last night!"

Allie forced herself to tuck away her worries, and she reached for the bottle of lotion Tina had left on the nightstand, intending to smooth a little on her hands. But it slid out of her grasp and bounced off the floor.

"Butterfingers," Tina joked.

Allie stared down at the bottle, stricken. Was it slippery, or had something inside of her begun to misfire?

"Allie?" Tina scooped up the bottle and handed it to her. "You okay?"

The bottle *was* slippery—a sheen of lotion, probably left over from Tina's fingertips, clung to its surface.

Just concentrate on the now, Allie thought again. Those five words would be her mantra this week.

Allie took a slow, deep breath, focusing on it like she'd learned to do in a meditation class. "I'm great," she said.

She linked arms with Tina, and they walked through the house to the pool. The guys were no longer there, and the dirty plates and glasses and damp towels had been cleared away and magically replaced with a table full of fruity rum drinks in hollowed-out pineapples.

"Don't you feel as if we stepped into a fantasy?" Allie said, handing Tina a pineapple. "Or maybe a movie set."

"All we need is Ryan Gosling to rise, dripping wet, out of the pool," Tina said.

"Did someone say a naked Ryan Gosling?" a voice called. "I think Pauline can probably arrange that."

They turned and saw Savannah. The warm late-afternoon light hit her as she crossed the patio toward them, illuminating the red and gold in her hair. She wore a white dress with navy blue trim that clung to her slim hips, and her lightly tanned skin was flawless. *She has never looked more beautiful,* Allie thought.

"Van! We didn't say naked!" Allie protested, laughing.

"Ah, but you were thinking it. Don't you love those flowers?" Savannah asked, pointing to a trellis covered in white-blue and purple blooms. "They're passionflowers, the butler told me. Native to Jamaica."

"Gorgeous," Allie said.

Savannah picked up a pineapple drink. "Cheers, girlfriends. To passion."

"I'm so glad we're here together," Allie said. "I've missed you, Van. I feel like we haven't really talked in a while."

Savannah nodded. "I know. Things have been . . ." Her voice trailed off, and she took another sip of her drink. "Look, I know you guys have been tiptoeing around the subject, so just let me say this fast, okay? Gary and I are splitting up."

Savannah lifted her chin, and Allie could see a defiant gleam in her eyes. It didn't fool Allie, not one bit.

"I'm so sorry," Tina said.

Savannah nodded again.

"Whenever you want to talk, I'm here. *We're* here," Allie said.

"I know that. Just—not now, okay? I really want to have fun tonight."

"Then we better go tell Pauline about our Ryan Gosling request," Tina said. She squeezed Savannah's arm. "Do you think we should order him lightly oiled?"

"Definitely," Savannah said. She looked up again and took in a deep breath that made a shuddery sound at the end. "A light application of oil, a little bit of bronzing . . ."

"Are you girls talking about food *again*?"

Gio paused in the doorway, looking back and forth at them. "What's so funny?"

Savannah picked up a pineapple and walked over to give it to him. "Yes, Gio, we're talking about something we're all absolutely ravenous for," she said, prompting squeals of laughter from Tina and Allie.

"Whatever." Gio rolled his eyes. "Van, what are you doing giving me a girlie drink? I'm sticking to beer."

"Sorry, macho man," Savannah said, nudging him in the shoulder. "Did you want to slaughter a woolly mammoth to go with your beer? Because we can find you a club."

"Me like club," Gio said. He wiggled his eyebrows. "Me use it on my wife, later, to bring her into cave."

Poor Van, Allie thought, watching her joke around with Gio. *How brave of her to come on this trip alone.*

"So where is everyone else?" Allie asked.

"Ryan and I just finished a game of pinball," Gio said. "I think he went to use the john."

A thumping sound made them all glance up. Two silver helicopters were cutting through the sky, heading their way.

"Perfect timing," Pauline said, walking up to the group with Dwight and Ryan a few steps behind her.

"Shall we head to the beach?" Pauline suggested. "That's where they'll touch down."

"Let me just grab my camera," Allie said, scooping her Nikon case up off a chair.

"Conga line!" Savannah shouted. "Everyone get behind me!"

Whooping and dancing, they made their way down the steps to the waiting helicopters.

Tina hadn't planned to say it. But when everyone began to divide up to climb aboard the copters, in couples as usual, she suddenly shouted, "Let's mix it up, people!"

"What do you mean?" Pauline asked, turning to look at her.

"Oh, I thought it would be fun if we went without spouses for this ride," she said, realizing how strange she must sound. "Just, um, for a change of pace." She caught Savannah's gaze— was it obvious she was doing this for Savannah's benefit?—and then Gio looked at her, too.

"Seriously?" he asked.

She remembered how she'd caught him off guard at dinner last night, when she hadn't reacted to his teasing about not calling the kids, and she smiled in what she hoped was a mysterious way. Let Gio wonder a little bit; it would be good for him.

"Why not?" she said. "Maybe you'll miss me."

And so Pauline, Gio, and Ryan were aboard one helicopter that was already climbing into the air. And Allie, Savannah, Dwight, and Tina were about to take off in the other. It was interesting that the spontaneous division had caused the smaller, core group from college to split off from the others, Tina thought. She and Allie had been roommates freshman year at UVa, of course, and they'd met Savannah during orientation week. Savannah had been struggling to carry her belongings down the dorm's hallway, dropping sweatshirts and Madonna CDs in her wake, and they'd jumped in to help her unload her blue Pinto. Tina had always thought it strange that Savannah had come to college alone, while Allie's and Tina's mothers had made their beds and lined their bureaus with flowered contact paper and, along with their fathers, had taken them out for a nice lunch. None of them had been able to hold back tears while saying good-bye.

There was something cool about driving yourself to college—not to mention having a car, even if it was a beat-up old Pinto—but Tina knew she wouldn't have wanted that, even if Savannah didn't seem to mind. If it hadn't been for Allie, so close by that they could lie in their twin beds and stretch out their arms and touch each other's fingertips, Tina probably would have cried herself to sleep the whole first week of school.

Tina knew Allie felt the same sympathy for their new dorm mate; they'd talked about it that very first night, then they'd walked down to Savannah's room and knocked on the open door. Savannah had been lounging on her bed, flipping through a celebrity gossip magazine.

"We're going to grab a piece of pizza. Want to come?" Allie had asked.

"Sure," Savannah had said, sliding her feet into a pair of flip-flops by the door and slicking on red lip gloss. And just like that, their new friendship was born. Tina had never felt as close to Savannah as she did to Allie—it wasn't just geography or the comparative longevity of the relationship; there was something about Savannah's character that kept their friendship from deepening. Probably her blazing streak of selfishness: Savannah would leave you at a party without saying good-bye if she met a guy who interested her, and she'd borrow your favorite jeans, delay returning them for a week even if you asked, then drop them off unwashed. She was funny and vivacious and outrageous—and both aware of and unapologetic about her flaws—which took away some of their sting.

But Savannah also had a good heart, Tina reminded herself, and she'd stick up for you if you needed her. She didn't gossip or backstab, either, which was another mixed blessing—she'd tell you exactly what she thought, to your face.

Tina also knew Savannah's selfishness was a form of self-preservation, because no one else was looking out for her. Her parents had split up when she was five, and they'd both started new families. Once during junior year, just before UVa's holiday break, Tina had noticed a Christmas card featuring a photo of a family—a man and wife in red shirts and two boys in matching green ones—on Savannah's desk.

"My stepmonster and Dad and their kids," Savannah had said when she'd seen Tina looking at the picture.

You're not in the family photo? Tina had almost asked, but something in Savannah's face had stopped her from releasing the question.

Savannah had also confided that her mother and stepfather both worked long hours and had twins, and Savannah was always expected to babysit when she stayed with them. It was, Savannah claimed, what had cured her of ever wanting children.

"I changed a green diaper once," she'd said, shuddering. "Bright green! Isn't that some sort of crime?"

"Against who?" Tina had asked.

"All of humanity?" Savannah had said.

But Savannah never seemed to pity herself. They'd had a lot of fun together in college during their first three years. Then Allie had won the private room on the quad and become friendly with Dwight, and Tina had moved into an apartment off campus with a group of girls from her sorority. And just before Thanksgiving break, she'd met Gio.

Tina had known who Gio was, of course. She'd lusted after him from across campus, and they'd crossed paths at parties dozens of times. He'd even handed her a drink once—although Tina couldn't find anything remotely romantic about a gesture involving slightly flat Bud Light and a plastic cup, no matter how hard she tried. On that November night, though, when she left the library, she'd heard footsteps behind her. It was already dark out, but plenty of students were around. Still, Tina had quickened her step. Then the heavy footsteps had sped up, too. Instead of looking back, Tina had walked even faster.

"Tanya? Tori?" A voice had shouted behind her. "Umm . . . Terry?"

She'd smiled then, and stopped. She'd recognized the voice.

"I'm not going to turn around until you get my name right," she'd said.

"Hang on, let me catch my breath. Were you power-walking or something?" he'd said. "Okay, okay, I know it starts with a *T*."

"You can do better than that," she'd said.

"Tiny?" he'd guessed, and she'd doubled over in laughter.

"Do you really think I'd go by the name Tiny?" she'd asked. "Do you think *anyone* would?"

"I think some old Hollywood star did," he'd said. "A long time ago. Come on, tell me your name."

She'd shaken her head, feeling her curls bounce against her cheeks, grateful she'd deep-conditioned them the night before.

"Then at least look at me," he'd said, and she'd slowly turned around, knowing she'd remember this moment for the rest of her life and wanting to draw it out. And just as her eyes had met his, he'd smiled, his perfect teeth standing out against his five o'clock shadow. "Tina," he'd said. "That's your name."

She'd nodded and he'd moved closer. "Did I scare you?" he'd asked. She could see the outlines of his muscular biceps and shoulders beneath his black T-shirt. All the other guys in college looked like boys, she'd thought, but Gio was a man already. "I just wondered . . . I was leaving the library and I saw you on the stairs ahead of me and I thought . . . well, do you want to go grab a beer?"

She'd nodded once more—at that point she wasn't sure if she'd ever speak again—and he'd reached out to carry her books. They'd fought some during that year—broken up a few times, too—but Tina had known, deep in her bones, even before she finished drinking her first beer, that Gio was the guy for her.

Allie had become better friends with Dwight then, and probably with Savannah, too, Tina mused. Neither of them was dating anyone seriously at the time; Allie wouldn't meet Ryan until a couple years after college, and the same for Savannah and Gary. By now Ryan was so woven into their group that they sometimes forgot he hadn't gone to UVa, but Tina had never felt that way about Gary. He'd always been . . . aloof. That was the most polite word she could muster.

"YS Falls," the pilot was shouting. "One of Jamaica's national treasures." Tina could barely make out the words over the air being whipped around them. She glanced down as the copter swooped lower, and an involuntary sigh escaped from her lips. The sun was just beginning to set, and the contrast of the rose- and orange-streaked sky, tumbling blue water, and surrounding flowers was one of the most beautiful sights she could imagine.

She leaned closer to the open window and drank in the view for a long moment, then turned to Savannah in the next seat over. Savannah was holding back her hair with one hand, and when Tina caught her eye, she grinned.

"Allie? Dwight? Can you guys believe this?" Tina twisted around to glance toward the second row of seats. Her eyes widened: Allie was bent over with her head between her knees, and Dwight was patting her back.

"She's okay," Dwight shouted. "Just feeling a little sick. Can you tell the pilot to head back right now?"

"Of course," Tina said. "Allie? Honey?"

Dwight spoke again, and Tina was surprised at the authority in his voice. "Tina, I changed my mind. Tell the pilot to touch down as soon as he can find a spot."

Tina leaned forward and spoke to the pilot, who nodded, then she turned back to Allie. Now Dwight was speaking in her ear and holding her hand. What was he saying?

Tina strained to hear: "Visualize a box. Now trace a vertical line of the box as you breathe in for two. Okay, good. Now trace a horizontal line and breathe out for two. Go to the next line and breathe in, nice and slow . . . one . . . two."

Allie lifted her head. Her face was so pale! All of her freckles stood out as sharply as if they'd been freshly painted on a stark white canvas.

"What's going on?" Savannah shouted.

"Allie's airsick," Tina shouted back. She felt the copter jerk and dip as they descended, and she hoped Allie wouldn't vomit.

Minutes later, they were on a beach, and everyone moved aside quickly so Allie could climb off first.

"Are you okay?" Tina asked as she jumped down onto the sand. She moved closer and put her hand on her friend's arm. Allie nodded and gulped air.

"Here," Dwight said as he twisted the lid off a bottle of water and handed it to Allie. "Try to drink a little."

"I don't know . . . what happened," Allie said. She took a small sip, and a little water dribbled down her chin, but she didn't wipe it off; she didn't even appear to notice. Her hands were shaking, Tina realized.

"You're okay now," Dwight said. "Listen, Tina and Van, you guys go on. The other helicopter is going to a beach a few miles ahead. Pauline arranged to have champagne there. I'm going to call a cab. Allie and I will meet you at the house."

"No, no," Tina said. "We'll all take a cab back."

"Absolutely not," Allie said. "I'll be really mad if you miss out on this because of me. Besides, I'm feeling better."

A bit of color was coming back into Allie's face, Tina noticed. But she was clutching that bottle of water so tightly it was crumpling like an accordion.

"I'm staying with her, Tina," Dwight said. "I'll take care of her."

Tina looked at him; she'd never seen this take-charge side of Dwight before. His occasional stutter was gone, and his face was so intent. Was this what he was like at work? No wonder he was so successful.

"Are you sure?" Tina hesitated. "Because, Allie, I don't mind at all . . ."

"I insist." Allie smiled, but it looked more like a grimace. "Beat it, you two."

"C'mon, Tina," Savannah said. "She looks okay now."

"Okay." Tina climbed into the helicopter and stared down as it lurched into the sky again, watching the figures of Allie and Dwight on the beach grow smaller as the colors of the sunset intensified around them.

"I don't know what happened," Allie said. "I've never . . . Nothing like that has ever . . ."

"Let's sit down," Dwight said. He took off his T-shirt and spread it on the sand. "Here."

"Oh, Dwight," Allie said. "Thank you."

She was still holding the water bottle, her fingers compulsively pleating the plastic.

"I know you don't feel like sitting down," Dwight said, taking her hand and guiding her to a seat anyway. "You probably want to run screaming down the beach, don't you?"

Allie turned to him. "How do you *know*?"

"I'm pretty sure you had a panic attack," he said. "I figured it out when you told me you had to get off the helicopter, plus you were shaking. Which means adrenaline is coursing through your body like . . . like . . . wild horses. I've had them, too."

"You have?" she said. She was still wrapping her mind around what had happened: She had been staring out the window, watching the ground drop away. Then her heart had sped up, and her hands had grown icy. It felt like her skin was shrinking. She'd thought she was just airsick, but suddenly her mind had seized in panic and her heart had tried to throw itself out of her chest.

"Maybe we should do the box again," Dwight was saying.

"Dwight, what's happening to me?" she whispered.

He put an arm around her. "It's pretty common, believe it or not. I used to get them a lot."

"I feel like I'm going crazy," Allie said. She could feel tears running down her cheeks, and she leaned back against Dwight's shoulder. His skin felt so warm.

"I know," he said. "But you're not."

"Do you still get them?" Allie asked.

"Not often," he said. "It's been a year or two. And I can usually stop them when I feel them coming on now."

"Can you teach me?" Allie asked. "Because I never want to go through that again."

"Yeah, sure," he said.

The tension had left Allie's body, but now weakness was replacing it. And she deeply regretted that pineapple drink and the crab cake appetizers by the pool; her stomach was in knots.

"Is there anything . . . worrying you?" he asked after a minute.

She felt her heart speed up again. "What do you mean?" she asked.

"For me, the attacks began when I was under a ton of stress at work, trying to get my company started. They got worse when my parents died," he said.

"I don't know," she whispered. "I can't—" Her chest felt tight.

"It's okay. Hey, look at the sunset."

Allie could feel Dwight's chest rise and fall, and she tried to match her breaths to his slow, steady inhalations.

"This may be the prettiest sunset I've ever seen," he was saying. "I like sunsets better than sunrises, I think . . . not that I'm ever up early enough to watch sunrises. Remember back in college when you used to pound on my wall to wake me up during finals?"

He chatted for another few minutes, and Allie knew he was trying to distract her from her fear. This was the sweet, sensitive side of Dwight that the others didn't know. Her Dwight.

"I'm so tired all of a sudden," she said.

"You've been through a workout," he said. "Why don't I call a cab now? You can go to bed when we get home if you feel like it."

She shook her head. "I don't want to be alone."

"Okay," he said. "Whatever you want."

"Could we just stay here a little longer?" she whispered.

"Sure," he said.

Allie slowly became aware of the sound of the water crashing against the shore, the grit of the sand between her toes, and the heat draining out of the day as the sun sank lower. She sighed and turned her head slightly, so her cheek was resting against Dwight's chest.

"You know I was adopted, right? I just found out that my biological father and grandfather both had ALS," she said. "Lou Gehrig's disease. It turns out there's something called familial ALS. I read about it on the Internet. Sometimes it runs in families, Dwight."

His arm tightened around her, and then his other arm came forward to wrap around her, too.

"I'm scared," she whispered. She began to shake, but his arms stayed steady around her.

"You don't have it," he said.

"I can't leave my girls, Dwight. I can't."

"You won't," he said.

"I know," she said. "I just . . . I can't help thinking, what if? Ryan can't raise the kids alone; he works long hours and I don't even know if our medical insurance is all that good. We've never needed it for anything big before, and—"

"Allie." Dwight's voice cut her off. He sounded almost stern. "You're not going to get sick. But I don't want you to worry. If anything ever happens to you, I'll take care of everything."

She tilted her head up to look at him. "What do you mean?"

"I mean, I'll take care of everything for you," he repeated.

"I'd give Ryan enough money so he could stay at home full-time. I'd—I'd get you the best treatment. I'd pay for your kids' college . . . anything."

She stared at him. His eyes told her he was completely serious.

"Why?" was all she could think to say.

By way of an answer, he bent his head and kissed her.

Chapter Seven

Monday Night

"THERE'S A BIT OF news," Pauline said.

The others looked up. The waiter had just served a late dinner of burgers and fries—with a twist. Everybody but Allie was given a Kobe burger with sautéed sweet Vidalia onions; Allie's version was made from grains and portobello mushroom. The fries were hand-cut and crisp, and the chef had set out dishes of homemade ketchup, lemony mayonnaise, and other fixings. It was, Gio had declared after the first bite, the best burger he'd had in his entire life.

"Is everything okay?" Tina asked.

"Of course," Pauline said. "But it looks like bad weather is heading our way."

"The tropical storm?" Ryan asked, and Pauline nodded. She hadn't expected the others not to know, of course—despite how isolated they were out here, everyone had iPhones and BlackBerrys. "They're expected to issue a tropical storm warning for our area," she said. "Not for a few days, though."

"Do you think it might turn into a hurricane?" Tina asked, and Pauline drew in her breath. This was exactly what she didn't want: for people to worry.

"No, and it's not expected to come that close," she said. "But we will get some rain. So, let's soak up the sun while we can."

"Fine with me," Savannah said. "I could nap on the beach all day tomorrow."

"I saw a badminton set in the games closet," Allie said. "We could set it up and have a tournament!"

"What part of 'nap on the beach all day' don't you understand?" Savannah asked, but she was smiling.

Pauline sat back and nibbled a salty fry while the others made plans, their voices overlapping as they talked about bringing Frisbees and snorkeling equipment to the beach. The storm had shifted course, just a bit. But it was probably going to come a lot closer to Jamaica than had been originally expected, unless it shifted again. She knew it wasn't her fault, but a sense of failure tinged the evening for her. She'd hoped the weather would be flawless this week. Who liked a rainy beach vacation?

On a table across the room, a cell phone rang.

"Whose is that?" Tina asked, reflexively checking her pockets. "I hope the kids are okay . . ."

"It's mine. I'm sorry," Pauline said. "I should have shut it off during dinner."

"Why?" Savannah asked. "I never turn mine off. Well, maybe just during sex. But that really depends on the guy."

Ryan and Gio hooted, and Savannah laughed. That settled it Pauline decided; she officially hated Savannah. But Pauline made sure her voice was soft when she replied, "I don't want to interrupt our meal."

Her phone rang a second time, then went to voice mail.

"Are you sure you don't want to check it?" Dwight asked. He looked at his watch. "It's after nine o'clock. Who would be calling you?"

"Maybe it's something I'm planning for your birthday," Pauline said, smiling at him. *Who could be calling?* she thought.

"When is the actual day?" Ryan asked.

"Thursday," Allie and Pauline responded in unison.

Allie quickly bent her head to take another bite of her veggie burger, and her hair swung forward, hiding her face.

"Are you feeling better, Allie?" Pauline asked, turning to look at her. "We missed you and Dwight on the beach earlier."

Allie reached for her wine. She took a sip, then cleared her throat.

"I'm much better," she said. "Just a little airsickness. I'm only sorry we couldn't finish the ride."

"It wasn't the same without you two," Pauline said, smiling at Dwight.

"The helicopter pilot was kind of hot," Savannah said, biting off the end of a French fry. "Didn't you think?"

"Which one?" Ryan asked.

"Yours," Savannah said. "Ours was, like, sixty."

Which is probably a more appropriate age for you than the crewman you were flirting with today, Pauline refrained from saying.

"I have to confess I didn't exactly notice," Gio said with a smirk.

"I have to confess I'm kind of relieved about that," Tina joked.

"Think a young Harrison Ford," Savannah said. "Great shoulders, too."

"In any case, how about a clambake on the beach tomorrow night?" Pauline suggested. "I was going to do it later in the week, but maybe with the weather . . ."

"Yummy!" Tina said. "We'll just have a lazy day."

"So what's the plan for tonight?" Savannah asked. "Should we start with drinks by the pool?"

"Sounds good to me," Gio said.

"Shall we have dessert out there, too?" Pauline suggested. "It's such a lovely night."

When everyone assented, she stood up. "I'll let the chef know."

She scooped up her phone on the way to the kitchen. But before she swung open the door, she could hear someone coughing.

"Chef?" She swung open the door and found him next to the sink. Luckily a handkerchief was pressed to his mouth.

"I'm sorry, madam," he said when he could speak. "I think I'm coming down with the flu."

Perfect, Pauline thought. They'd racked up two disasters—the storm and now this—and they were barely two days into the trip.

"You need to stay home tomorrow," she said, suppressing a shudder. She hoped his germs hadn't made it into the food. "I'm going to get a replacement."

He nodded, put his handkerchief into his pocket, and began scrubbing his hands at the sink while Pauline searched her iPhone for the name of the company that had rented the bungalow. Luckily the company was prepared for contingencies like this, as well they should have been, considering what they charged. Moments after Pauline wrote an e-mail outlining the problem and hit Send, a response pinged into her in-box: *Our apologies. A replacement chef will be there tomorrow morning.*

"Why don't you go home now?" Pauline suggested to the chef. "The waiter can handle serving dessert and cleanup."

He nodded. "Thank you, miss."

Pauline almost felt sorry for him; he looked so miserable, with his sweaty brow and glazed eyes. But a moment later, as she glanced down at her iPhone again, her pity was replaced with a twinge of anxiety: There were three new messages within the past couple of hours, all from her mother. She must've missed the first two calls over the noise of the helicopters. Pauline stepped outside, by the pool, so she could speak privately. Her mother answered on the first ring.

"Pauline?"

There was no other word for it; her mother's voice was shattered.

"What's wrong?" Pauline's mind was leaping ahead to make plans even before her mother responded. If it was cancer, they'd get the best doctors. She'd move her mother into the guest suite at the house. She'd—

"It's Therese."

Pauline's mind went blank.

"She caught pneumonia a few days ago. They moved her to a hospital this morning . . . She was so frail anyway; no one even expected her to live this long. They don't . . . think—"

Her mother's sentence ended on a sob.

Pauline opened her mouth to speak, but her voice had been erased. Therese had been such a constant in her life, but an intangible one. She hadn't even known about her sister's existence until she was six or seven, when her parents had sat her down in the living room to reveal it. Pauline's first reaction was relief: She'd thought from the expressions on their faces that she was in serious trouble for an unknown offense. They'd explained that Pauline had a sister, older by two years, who was ill. That was the word they'd used, *ill*, even though Therese wasn't. She'd been born with a genetic deformity. She was a fully grown adult with an infant's brain—a grotesque, sad paradox. Pauline hadn't thought about her much, save for those brief, chilling moments when she wondered how close the genetic mutation had come to touching her own strands of DNA. But sometimes Therese had entered Pauline's mind at odd moments, like when Pauline got her first period. Did Therese menstruate, too? Pauline knew she could never ask the question; her parents would've been bewildered and shocked, and maybe angry, too.

She hadn't visited her sister much growing up—mostly on holidays, and on Therese's birthday, when everyone but Therese sang and ate cake—but after college, Pauline had made an effort to go with her mother every couple of months. She never stayed long, though, and usually filled the time by cutting the stems off the flowers she'd brought and arranging them one by one in a vase. Therese was small, just shy of four foot ten, with sparse blond hair and a round face. Her light blue eyes seemed vacant. Visiting her, Pauline felt the exact same way she had when she'd seen her grandfather in the hospital during his losing battle with lung cancer: claustrophobic, nervous, and eager to leave. She didn't feel any connection to Therese, and once when she was in the room, she smelled something sharp and vaguely antiseptic and realized that Therese had wet her diaper. Pauline was ashamed of it, but she felt more revulsion than pity for her sister.

After Pauline married Dwight and her life became so much busier, her visits grew less frequent—the spaces between them stretching to three months, and sometimes even four. Pauline tried to reassure herself that her sister didn't even seem to know when she was there. Therese didn't seem to respond to anyone except her regular nurses, and even then, the most she might do was smile.

Pauline could hear her mother's shuddery inhalation on the phone, and it spurred her to find her voice: "How long?"

At her mother's answer—"Any time now"—she squeezed her eyes shut.

"Okay," she said. "Okay." She tried to focus. "Are you at home?"

"I'm at the hospital," her mother said. "I'm not going to leave, until . . ."

Tension roiled Pauline's stomach. "Are you alone?"

"Yes," her mother said.

For one of the few times in her life, Pauline had no idea what to do. She couldn't leave the vacation, not now. But how could she forsake her mother?

Finally she said: "We're in Jamaica . . . but do you want me to come home?"

Her mother paused for what seemed like a long time, and Pauline squeezed her eyes shut. "If you can, I would be . . . grateful. Wouldn't Dwight understand?" her mother asked.

Pauline dropped onto a lounge chair and massaged her forehead with one hand.

"I don't know," she whispered. "He . . . doesn't know everything about Therese. How bad off she is."

"I see." Silence filled the phone line again, and Pauline suspected her mother was doing the exact same calculation Pauline had, before the wedding: Would her sister's condition have scared off Dwight, made him think they might have an abnormal child? Maybe he would've married her anyway, but Pauline didn't want to take that chance—to alter the dynamic of their relationship. What she brought to their marriage was a kind of ease and grace; she smoothed problems out of Dwight's way so that his burdens were lessened and he could focus on business. Maybe it was an outdated model for a relationship—the equivalent of a fifties housewife bringing slippers and a pipe to her husband the moment he arrived home—but she didn't care. It worked for both of them.

"It's all right," her mother finally said. "You should be with your husband."

But even as those words traveled over the line, Pauline knew: She had to go, that very night.

"Well, that was weird," Savannah said as she flicked the switch on the margarita machine and watched the ice and tequila mixture churn into a minicyclone.

"She seemed so upset," Tina said.

"I know," Savannah said. "It's only a broken hip."

"I bet it's more than that," Allie said, and Savannah looked up. She'd had the exact same thought. "When things like this happen to a parent, it's a symbol of their mortality. I bet Pauline's realizing that her mother is getting older . . ."

Savannah tuned out the psychobabble as she poured the frothy margaritas into salt-rimmed glasses. Sometimes she thought Allie had missed her true calling; she could've given Dr. Phil a run for his money.

"To your health," Tina said, lifting a glass.

"We need a better toast than that," Savannah said, leaning back against the big granite island. "How about: 'One drink is good, two at the most, three I'm under the table, four I'm under the host'?"

"Savannah!" Allie shrieked.

Savannah grinned. "I'm paraphrasing Dorothy Parker. But, you know, give me a few more of these . . ."

"You would not," Tina said, but her voice was laced with a thrill.

"Oh, I don't know, Tina. It's kind of your fault, actually. After hearing you talk about what a great kisser Dwight was, he's looking awfully tempting," Savannah said.

At the shock on Allie's face, she added, "I'm not going to throw myself at Dwight while his wife's away. But I might have some fun dancing with him again tonight."

Allie drew in an audible breath. "I think that's really disrespectful," she said. "Pauline worked hard to give us this nice trip. And now you're talking about hitting on her husband while she's away taking care of her injured mother?"

"Whoa, girl, settle down," Savannah said. What the hell was wrong with Allie? Her cheeks and ears were turning red, and she was almost shouting. It was one of the few times Savannah could recall seeing Allie mad.

"Allie? What's going on?" Tina said, putting a hand on Allie's shoulder. "You know what Savannah's like. She was just kidding around."

Allie looked back and forth at the two of them, and then it was as if a switch had been flipped inside of her—all of the anger drained out of her face. "Sorry," she said. "I just . . . I don't know what got into me."

Savannah shrugged. "It's forgotten." She meant it; she'd never believed in holding grudges over small infractions. "But Tina's right, you should know what I'm like by now." She winked at Tina. "Demure and shy, right? Isn't that what you meant?"

Tina's and Allie's laughter chased the remaining tension out of the room.

"Dwight seems to really love Pauline," Tina said. "And she's certainly devoted to him."

"To each his own," Savannah said. "I mean, yeah, I appreciate the trip and everything. Don't get all riled up again, Al. I'm not being bitchy. But she's kind of . . . stiff. Usually I like things that are stiff, but that's not a compliment."

Tina rolled her eyes at Savannah. "I think she must come from a lot of money. I just get that feeling."

"And I love it that we're being so pampered here," Savannah said. "But it would be fun to just kick back and play quarters like we used to and act like idiots, instead of having everything be so fancy. When Gio burped last night, you should've seen the look on her face."

"Well, she said she wouldn't be back until tomorrow night at the earliest. The staff is gone, too," Tina said. "And I used to be really good at quarters."

"Is that a challenge, Ms. Antonelli?" Savannah asked.

"No, this is: I'm going to kick your ass in quarters."

Savannah laughed and took another sip of margarita. She was already a little buzzed from the pineapple drink by the pool and all the wine with dinner, but she'd always had a high tolerance. Lately she'd been anesthetizing herself with a couple of drinks at the end of the day, but she was confident it was a temporary routine: If having your husband dump you for a big-assed, jailbait nurse wasn't enough to justify tossing back a few, then what was?

"Let's get the guys," Savannah said. "Where are they, anyway?"

"The game room, probably," Allie said.

"Someone go get a quarter," Savannah said as she poured the rest of the margaritas into a pitcher and Tina scurried off to find her purse. "It's party time, ladies."

Downstairs, they found Gio bent over the pinball machine, hitting the flippers with more force than was necessary.

"Damn it," he said, smacking the side of the machine with an open hand.

"You okay, honey?" Tina asked.

"Crap!" Gio jerked away from the machine. He didn't answer Tina. "You're up, D-man."

He reached for his beer and swigged while Dwight took his place at the game's controls. The machine pinged and lit up and shook as the numbers rolled forward: 3,450; 5,200; 8,500 . . .

Savannah glanced at Gio's score: 1,250.

Men, she thought. Gio was getting all pouty, crossing his arms and glaring as Dwight trounced him in a ridiculous game meant for junior high school boys, and Ryan looked half-asleep as he watched a baseball game on the big-screen TV. This wouldn't do at all.

She reached over and flicked on the iPod attached to speakers. Dwight had already downloaded the CD she'd made him onto the iPod, and she blasted the first song: Sir Mix-A-Lot's "Baby Got Back."

"Hey," Ryan shouted as she reached past him and grabbed the clicker. "Be careful with that man-tool!" She ignored him and turned off the television, then hid the clicker behind a sofa cushion.

"Dwight, that's your last ball," Savannah shouted. "It's time for quarters!"

She saw Tina approach Gio, put a hand on his arm, and whisper something in his ear. He pulled away and shook his head.

Somebody give that big baby a pacifier, Savannah thought. At least Ryan was getting up off the couch and Dwight was clearing the glasses off the bamboo bar.

"Here are the rules, in case you old fogies forgot," Savannah said, sharply clapping her hands so everyone would listen. "The quarter has to bounce once before landing in the cup. The cup starts half-full of beer, and we add an inch every time someone misses."

"Who's first?" Tina asked.

"You're holding the quarter, so you are, hot mama," Savannah said.

Tina missed the cup completely, as did Allie. Dwight tapped the rim on his turn, but the quarter fell back onto the table. By now the cup was almost completely full of foamy beer.

"Not off to the best start." Savannah flicked the quarter against the table, and it splashed into the beer. "Allie," she said.

"Me!" Allie squealed. "Why are you picking on me?"

"You just seemed a little tense earlier in the kitchen, like you needed a drink." Savannah winked.

"You mean other than the margarita I'm holding?" Allie laughed, but she still picked up the cup and chugged.

"That's my girl," Savannah said. She took aim as Allie refilled the cup, and the quarter plopped in again.

"Christ," Ryan said. "I think she's a ringer."

"Sorry, Ry, I didn't catch that. Did you say you were thirsty?" Savannah asked, handing him the cup.

Savannah glanced at Gio, who was leaning against the back of the couch, watching the game. He was still smoldering as intently as if he was posing for a Calvin Klein ad. Why had Tina let him get away with dismissing her? Savannah wondered. She wouldn't have put a meek little hand on his arm. Guys like Gio didn't respond to that sort of thing. How come Tina didn't know that, after all those years of being with Gio?

She took aim at the cup a third time, but she made sure to look up at Gio just before she released the quarter. She heard the gentle plop that told her the coin had landed in liquid, and she reached for the beer, still holding Gio's gaze.

"Let's see . . ." she said. "I think a caveman type might need a drink. I wonder where I can find one?"

A smile tugged at the corner of Gio's mouth.

Savannah danced across the room until she was directly in front of Gio. "You must be parched," she said, handing him the cup.

He made her wait a few seconds, then he took the cup and swallowed the beer in one gulp.

"Now get your ass over here," Savannah told him. "These amateurs are boring me. You're the only one of this group who could ever play quarters."

Gio shrugged and followed her back to the bar. But instead of walking around it to stand next to Tina, he squeezed in next to Savannah.

"Hurry up and miss," he said. "It's my turn next, and I think you're about three drinks behind everyone else."

"Oh, I'll catch up." Savannah laughed.

"Go ahead, Van," Tina said. "It's your turn."

This time Savannah missed, but Gio didn't. Not the next

two times, either. And all three times, he made Savannah drink.

"Remind me again why I made you join us?" Savannah said as she reached for the cup again. She swallowed the beer—she'd never really liked the taste of it, so she always drank as quickly as possible—and felt warmth spread throughout her body. Screw Gary. She was having an amazing week, and she'd managed to make plans with the crewman from the catamaran, whose name she couldn't remember. He was going away on a chartered trip, but when he got back on Wednesday night, they were going to meet on the beach. She might not even say a single word to him. Maybe she'd just reach for his red bathing suit—she imagined he'd be wearing it, and absolutely nothing else—and slowly tug it down over that brown, muscular stomach . . .

Ryan made his shot and handed the cup to Tina, who gulped it down, then Dwight got one in and made Allie drink.

The iPod changed to a new song—"3 AM" by Matchbox Twenty—and Savannah began dancing to the music. Tina came around from the other side of the bar and joined her.

"Not bad, Ms. Antonelli," Savannah said. At first they were just swaying back and forth, but Tina began getting into it, shaking her hips and dropping to the floor, then swiveling back up.

"You took one of those pole-dancing exercise classes, didn't you?" Savannah asked.

Tina shook her head. "Video," she gasped. "I only did it once, though."

"Nice!" Savannah said. "I took the class. Want to see the Fireman?"

Without waiting for an answer, she wrapped her hands around an imaginary pole and mimicked sliding down it. She could feel her dress hiking up as she tossed back her hair. None of the guys were playing quarters anymore.

"Show me that move!" Tina shouted.

"It's all in the hips, baby," Savannah said. "Watch me."

Tina tried to twist around the imaginary pole and promptly fell over. "Oh, God," she said. "I'm drunk. I haven't been drunk in forever! I love being drunk!"

Savannah reached down to help her up. "That's because you've been either pregnant or nursing for the past fifty years."

"True," Tina gasped. "Once I was pregnant *and* nursing. Can we dance on the beach? Please?"

"Sure," Savannah said. "Who's up for it?"

"Everyone grab a drink or three," Gio said, "and let's go."

"Let's make another round of margaritas first," Savannah said. "Is there any more mix under the bar? We finished off the one we had in the kitchen."

Gio opened a cabinet and peered inside. "Yup." He tucked two bottles under his arms and handed the third to Savannah. "Let's hit it, Red. Follow me to the kitchen."

"Meet you on the beach!" Allie called.

Savannah could hear Allie and Tina giggling as they stumbled past the kitchen to the outdoor stairs leading down to the water, with Dwight and Ryan right behind them. "God, I hope the girls don't fall," Savannah said. "It's a long way down."

"They probably wouldn't even feel it," Gio said. He pulled the ice maker's bucket out of the freezer and dumped the cubes into the blender while Savannah added the tequila mix.

"I'm sure Pauline has a doctor on standby anyway, circling the house just in case she summons," Savannah said.

"You're wicked," Gio said with a laugh. He flicked the switch on the margarita machine as Savannah hoisted herself up to sit on a counter. She caught Gio glancing at her and realized the strap of her dress had slipped off one shoulder. She didn't fix it; she wanted to feel his eyes on her. She'd never do anything with a friend's husband—well, technically she'd kissed the spouse of one at a party, but she hadn't known that woman nearly as well as she knew Tina. But a little flirting with Gio was definitely allowable. It wasn't as if it was the first time; she'd sensed a little heat between them in the past.

Her eyelids felt heavy from the alcohol and the sexual tension suddenly infusing the room. She gazed at Gio, watching the muscles flex in his arms as he turned off the machine and reached for her glass. Their fingertips brushed as she handed it to him.

He filled their glasses and reached out a hand to help her down from the counter.

"Gary has no idea what he's missing," he said all of a sudden, still holding her hand. Savannah looked at him out of the corner of her eye. What did he mean? That Gary was missing out on Jamaica . . . or missing out on *her*?

"Tina told you everything, didn't she?" Savannah said.

Gio shrugged and released her hand. "He's a fucking moron."

Somehow, those rough words made her feel better than any soft expression of sympathy ever could.

"He's already in my rearview mirror," she said.

"Just don't put your car in reverse," Gio told her. "Actually, do it. I never liked that prissy little fucker."

Savannah laughed, even though she felt a little twinge in her chest: She'd always suspected Gio and Ryan weren't fans of Gary, but hearing it aloud didn't feel like vindication.

"Haven't we talked about him long enough?" Savannah said. She took a sip of margarita and slowly licked the residue from her lips. "Ready for the beach?"

"You going to do the Fireman again?" Gio asked, grinning.

"Maybe," Savannah said. She walked out of the room, adding a little sway to her step, knowing his eyes were fixed on her ass.

The others were already clustered around the fire pit, and

Dwight was lighting the logs by the time Savannah descended the stairs.

"Who makes a fire when it's eighty degrees out?" Ryan asked.

"Who cares!" Tina shouted. "I want to run through the flames and dive in the waves!"

"Oh, jeez," Allie said. "Tina, take this bottle of water. Come on, give me your margarita."

"Nope!" Tina ran away and promptly tripped over her own feet. She lay in the sand, giggling. "You can't take my drunk away. It's mine!"

"If you can't beat 'em . . ." Savannah said, reaching for the fresh pitcher of drinks that Gio was holding and filling up Allie's glass. She blinked to clear her vision, which suddenly seemed blurry. "Dwight? You empty?"

He drained his glass and held it up. "Look at that! I am!"

Savannah stared at the leaping gold and blue flames. The air was moist and heavy, and the cool water beckoned. She felt a little dizzy, and it had been an effort not to slur Dwight's name. What sorts of idiots named a kid Dwight anyway? She extended a middle finger toward the sky.

"What are you doing?" Tina asked. She'd crawled forward to fill up her glass again.

"Flipping off Dwight's parents," Savannah said.

"Oh," Tina said. "They're not here, are they?"

"What?" Savannah blinked. "Who?"

"Never mind," Tina said. "What were we talking about?"

"I feel like swimming," Savannah said.

"Oh, no!" Tina looked at her with big eyes. She was trying so hard to seem serious but was undercut by the fact that she had a big patch of sand covering her right cheek and had developed a lisp. "There aren't any lifeguards. You could drown!"

"Na-nuh. Na-nuh." Ryan chanted the theme from *Jaws*.

"Screw all of you," Savannah said. "I'm going in."

She walked to the end of the floating dock. There were enough tiki torches to bathe the beach area in a soft light—not enough for everyone to see her clearly, but they could probably glimpse the outline of her body. She lifted her dress over her head. She was wearing a lacy lavender thong and matching bra underneath. She paused, keeping her back to the rest of the group, then slowly descended the steps into the water.

"Oh, this feels *good!*" she shouted. "Who's joining me?"

She treaded water as she watched Gio take off his shirt and shorts. He wore those hybrid briefs that were like formfitting boxers, which Savannah happened to be a fan of. He ran to the end of the dock and cannonballed in, making a huge splash.

"Van? Gio? I can barely see you!"

It was Allie, who'd come to the end of the dock. The others were following her. Savannah felt a surge of disappointment; she'd have liked to be alone with Gio in the water, brushing up against each other and teasing. Or wait—no! Gio was Tina's husband. What was she thinking?

If only he wasn't so hot. If only she wasn't so horny.

At the sound of another splash, she jerked her head around. Tina had been standing by the corner of the dock a moment earlier, but now that space was empty.

"Tina? Was that you?"

Suddenly Allie jumped into the water, fully clothed. "Oh, my God! Where is she?"

"I'm fine!" Tina surfaced. "I meant to do that! Well, sort of."

"You scared me," Allie scolded, pushing her wet hair off her face.

"You know, most people take off their clothes first," Savannah said, paddling over to them.

"I'm a little drunk," Tina revealed.

"You?" Savannah mock-gasped.

"And I lost my shoes. But they were just from Target. Don't

you guys love Target? You can get everything there. I bet I could live there for a year, without ever leaving. Wanna dare me?"

Allie took Tina's hand and put it on the metal steps attached to the dock. "You hold on to this, okay? Don't let go."

Savannah looked up as Gio climbed out of the water. A second later, there were two more splashes—he'd pushed in Dwight and Ryan.

"Aw, shit, man," Gio said, peering down at them as they bobbed back up. "I forgot about your watch. Did I ruin it?"

Dwight unclasped it and reached up to put it on the dock. "Doesn't matter."

"Must be nice," Gio said. He shook his head.

"Mine's waterproof," Ryan said. He pumped his fist in the air. "The Timex trumps the Rolex again!"

"Come back in, Gio!" Allie called.

"Yeah, Gio," Savannah said. She reached up, grabbed his ankle, and yanked. He almost fell in but caught his balance at the last moment and pulled away.

"You are so going to pay for that," he said. He jumped in and disappeared beneath the inky surface.

Savannah stared at the ripples he'd created, waiting for his head to pop back up.

"Where'd he go?" Allie asked. She looked around. "He's been under at least thirty seconds."

"More like fifteen," Savannah said, but she wasn't sure. When had she crossed the line from tipsy into drunk? Maybe between the second and third beers she'd chugged. Her brain felt thick and dull.

"Check out the moon," Ryan said, floating on his back. "It's huge."

"Gio!" Allie called.

"I don't feel so good," Tina said and hiccuped.

"Oh, God. Can you climb up the steps and sit on the dock?" Allie asked. "If you have to get sick, lean over the water."

"Don't puke on Pauline's dock," Savannah said. "It won't go with the decor."

She was surprised when Dwight laughed along with the others.

"I don't think I can climb those steps," Tina said. "There are too many."

"Keep holding that railing," Allie said. "Has Gio come up yet? What if he hit his head on something?"

"Let me look around." Ryan dove under the water and came up a few seconds later. "I didn't see him. But the water's so dark . . ."

Worry cut through the haze surrounding Savannah. Gio had been under at least a minute. Suddenly she felt something brush by her leg, and she screamed. Then hands encircled her ankle, yanking her under the surface. She knew it was Gio, but it was still scary to feel herself being pulled deeper into the darkness as her lungs grew tight. And then Gio let go and she began kicking her way back up.

"You asshole," she sputtered.

"You say that like it's a bad thing, babe," Gio said. Savannah splashed him in the face, and he retaliated by splashing back.

"Giovanni!" Tina called. Her voice was sharp. "I don't feel so good!"

"Come on, honey," Allie said. "I'll help you up the steps."

Savannah watched as the two of them made slow progress, with Tina nearly slipping off the steps and falling back in.

"I just wanna rest awhile," Tina said. "A little nap. Then I'm coming back to dance."

"Of course you are," Allie said. "You're going to show Jennifer Lopez a thing or two." She draped Tina's arms over her shoulder, half-carrying her as if she was a wounded athlete needing assistance off the field. "Another few steps . . . come on, Tina, keep walking . . ."

"How much did your wife have to drink?" Savannah asked Gio.

"I wasn't counting," he said. "But it couldn't have been more than the rest of us."

Allie was easing Tina into a cushion-covered lounge chair and covering her with towels. "I think we need to get something nonalcoholic into your system," she said, her voice carrying easily over the water. "Maybe some Evian now, and a few crackers in a bit."

Savannah tuned out and began to wonder if Gio would go to bed at the same time as Tina, or if he'd stay up. She didn't feel like going to sleep, not now. It wasn't even midnight!

She glanced up as Dwight pulled himself onto the dock. He and Gio were complete opposites, she thought as she treaded water and considered them. Dwight was the guy who'd bring you flowers and open your car door on your dates. Gio was the bad boy with the motorcycle and tattoos who'd drop you off on your doorstep and roar away without waiting to see if you'd gotten in safely.

She'd always thought Gio was devoted to Tina, but tonight she'd definitely picked up signals from him. They were the only two in the water now. What would happen if she glided closer to him, maybe giving him a peek at her breasts through the transparent veil of water?

An unexpected image of Gary and The Nurse, together in bed, floated into her mind. Those visions had tortured her during the first few weeks after Gary left. She'd been unable to sleep some nights, wondering if he and The Nurse were having sex as she lay there, alone.

Maybe they were having sex at this very moment! Gary could be pulling that slut into a supply closet at work, flashing his perfect teeth in a smile as he lifted up her white skirt and she squealed a protest that wasn't truly a protest . . . Damn it, he was still officially her husband!

Since her husband was screwing someone else, shouldn't Savannah be allowed to flirt with someone else's husband? She blinked as she tried to think through the logic. It seemed flawed, but she wasn't sure how.

She knew what she should do. She should get out of the water and help Tina into the house and maybe have some water and a few of those crackers herself.

But she didn't want to.

Chapter Eight

Tuesday

WHERE WAS GIO?

Tina rolled over in bed and groaned. The digital clock reported that it was just after three a.m. Her head throbbed, and her mouth felt stuffed with cotton. She forced herself to sit up and, clutching the edge of the mattress for balance, swung her legs over the edge. She had to pee so desperately it was painful.

She stumbled toward the bathroom, sat down on the toilet, and felt instantaneous relief in at least one part of her body. But a moment later, she realized her teeth and tongue felt vile. She cupped her hands under the sink's tap and gulped water, then reached for her toothbrush. Had she gotten sick last night? Yes, she remembered. Allie had held back her hair while she'd vomited into the toilet.

The thought of it made Tina's stomach lurch again, but she took a deep breath, rinsed out a washcloth in cold water, and rubbed it across her face until the nausea passed.

She'd forgotten how awful a hangover felt. Her hands were shaking, and even her eye sockets felt sore. She brushed her teeth, then started to get back into bed before remembering it was empty. Gio hadn't come to their room last night. Something was bothering her, something that had happened while they were all in the water. She fished through hazy fragments of memories until it came to her: Gio had called Savannah "babe." Maybe it wasn't the most creative term of affection, but it was Gio's private nickname for Tina.

Jealousy flared in Tina, and she suddenly felt wide awake. She remembered how the two of them had flirted in the water—she couldn't remember the details, but she recalled feeling angry at a distance. Last night the alcohol had put up a barrier against the full force of her feelings, but now her rage surged. Where the hell was her husband?

She flung open the door of their bedroom and walked down the hall, to Savannah's room. The door was shut. Tina didn't bother to knock—she tore it open. But the bed was empty.

Where were they? They couldn't be down at the beach, could they?

She rushed into the living room and found them.

Gio was on one couch and Savannah was sprawled on another. Half-full margarita glasses littered the coffee table. They were both sound asleep.

"Get up," Tina said, nudging Gio's shoulder. He opened his eyes but didn't seem to see her.

"What are you doing out here?" Tina demanded.

"Sleeping." His eyes closed again.

"Oh, no you're not," Tina said. "Get up and come back to our bed!"

Gio groaned, but he stood up and followed her down the hall. He flopped on their bed, still fully clothed.

"What in the fuck happened between you two?" Tina asked.

Gio rolled over and looked at her. "Babe?"

"Don't you dare call me that!" Tina's anger hit a fever pitch. She'd devoted herself to raising their family—sacrificing part of herself in the process—and Gio was flirting with her friend while she lay in bed, sick. What did he do on the job all day? Were there women there, too—interior designers who tottered around in short skirts and high heels to survey the property? Or maybe some of the construction workers were women—fit, strong chicks who cracked jokes and clinked beers with the guys at the end of the day. Did Gio take off his shirt in the heat, strutting around like a rooster while she scrubbed toilets and cared for their children?

"Nothing happened," Gio said. His face wore a wounded expression. "I can't believe you'd think that."

"You were flirting with her all night!" Tina said. She knew her voice was bordering on a yell, but she didn't care who could hear. She was still half-drunk, and all she could see was Gio calling Savannah "babe" and— Wait, another image was coming back to her. Savannah pulling off her dress and jumping in the water, and Gio following her.

"I could kill you," Tina hissed. "This was supposed to be our vacation. Ours!"

"It *is* our vacation," Gio said. "Come here. Do you honestly think I'd do anything with Savannah? You were the one who told me to be nice to her! You said I should talk to her!"

"Don't touch me," Tina said, but her voice wasn't as angry as before. She *had* said that to Gio, after telling him about the separation.

"You weren't being nice," she finally said. "Nice is holding out her chair at dinner, Giovanni. Not naked wrestling in the water."

"Look, babe—" Gio began, but Tina cut him off.

"Don't ever call me that again! You called *her* that!"

Gio exhaled and began again. "Tina," he said. "Nothing happened. We didn't wrestle, and I wasn't naked. Sure, I paid some extra attention to Savannah because you told me she's going through a tough time. I like her; she's a fun girl. But that's it. I wouldn't touch her."

Tina studied him. Should she believe him? She knew how religious Gio was; adultery was a big sin, and she'd never suspected he'd cross that line. But damn it, he'd gone too far. Or had the alcohol addled her perception of the night? Her head felt thick, and her throat was dry; she was too confused to continue the conversation.

"Don't be nice to her anymore," Tina finally said. "Treat her like everyone else. No—leave her alone, okay? Don't go near her."

"Okay," Gio said. "Whatever you want. Will you come to bed now?"

Tina shook her head. "I'm getting some juice."

She left the room and walked through the house to the kitchen, passing Savannah's form on the couch. Savannah must be cold in nothing but her skimpy—no, make that slutty—dress, but Tina didn't bother to cover her up with the throw from the back of the couch. Let her get sick. Maybe her nose would become all red and runny and disgusting.

She made her way into the kitchen, filled a tall glass with lemonade, and drank it down quickly. There were some chocolate-chip cookies on a plate, and she gobbled one to help settle her stomach.

Then she started to wander back into the living room, but something—a faint noise, or maybe just instinct—made her turn in the opposite direction. She stepped through the darkness until she was at the edge of the room and looked out toward the pool.

She could barely make out two figures sitting close together on the lounge chairs. They weren't touching, but they were leaning toward each other, talking intently.

As her eyes adjusted to the darkness, she realized it was Allie and Dwight.

What the hell was going on in this house?

"I think I'll get a cup of coffee," Pauline said to her mother. "Would you like one?"

She'd arrived at the hospital a few hours earlier, after taking a cab from the airport to the house to pick up her car. She'd checked in at the reception desk and had been directed to a small waiting room. She found her mother there, sitting on a couch. The first thing Pauline noticed was that her mother wore a navy suit with a string of pearls and low heels, and her posture was perfectly straight. Change her surroundings, and she could be at a country club for a ladies' lunch.

But as she drew closer, Pauline realized her mother's face betrayed her turmoil; she was pale, and her rose-colored lipstick had rubbed off. Most of her lips' natural color had been worn away, too, by age, leaving her looking unexpectedly vulnerable. Pauline had always borne a strong resemblance to her mother, and she realized with a start that she was looking into a mirror of herself in the future. She became aware that her own hand was moving up to touch her mouth, and she stilled it.

"No, thank you," her mother said. "I better not have any more caffeine."

"Be back in a minute," Pauline said.

She stood up and glanced at her slim Chopard watch as she moved down the quiet hallway: a few minutes before seven a.m. Therese's condition hadn't worsened since Pauline arrived, and a nurse had said she'd inform them of any changes. A doctor would also come by around eight to check on Therese and answer any questions Pauline had. She could think of only one, but she knew the doctor wouldn't be able to answer it: *How much longer, exactly?*

She didn't want to be away from Jamaica for another night. Such an absence would only raise questions from Dwight and the others, but more important, she'd been feeling a strange undercurrent forming at the villa. It was the same sense she always picked up at parties: You felt it when the wine was flowing, when the food was good and abundant, when conversations were clicking and a buzz of energy was building in the room. And you knew when things were falling flat, even if all the right elements seemed to be in place. Sometimes it took just one spark to set things down either course—an outrageously funny comment to turn around a dull conversation or, conversely, a few yawns that became as contagious as the flu.

The source of magnetic energy in Jamaica, she suspected, was Savannah. And it wasn't completely positive.

Pauline hadn't been able to turn on her iPhone in the main part of the hospital, but as the elevator doors opened into the lobby, she switched it on. No new calls. She thought of texting Dwight to say good morning, but she didn't want to wake him.

She blinked against the bright morning light flooding in through the hospital's big windows as she walked to the kiosk by the front doors. The lobby was almost empty at this time of day, with just two women working behind the front desk and a guy flipping through a well-worn *Reader's Digest* in the waiting area.

"A large latte, please," Pauline said to the middle-aged woman behind the kiosk's counter.

"Anything else?" the woman asked. Her blond hair was pulled back into a ballerina's bun, and her hands were slim and elegant—not what you'd expect from a barista who spent all day around steam and heat. Maybe it was a new job for the woman; she could be a recent divorcée who'd had to go back to work to make ends meet. How sobering to think that one bad choice could change the entire course of your life. Pauline said a silent prayer of gratitude for Dwight.

"Sorry," Pauline said to explain the pause. "Just thinking . . . A cup of herbal tea with honey, too."

"The honey's by the napkins," the barista said as she accepted the twenty Pauline held out and made change. Pauline tucked a five-dollar bill in the tip jar, then doctored the drinks and carried them back to the little waiting room. Her mother didn't seem to have moved.

"I brought tea, just in case you changed your mind," Pauline said, setting it on the table in front of her mother and sitting back down.

"Thank you," her mother said, but she didn't touch it. She cleared her throat. "We should go in to see Therese in a bit. Maybe after the doctor comes."

"Of course," Pauline said, even as her heart sped up. She'd been following her mother's cues, and although she'd wondered why they hadn't gone into Therese's room yet, she didn't want to ask why. She didn't want it to come across as an accusation. And then there was the fact that being so close to death frightened Pauline. Her father had been healthy up until the day the brain aneurysm instantly killed him. His casket had been closed at the funeral, so Pauline's final memory of him was a vision of him standing on his front steps, waving good-bye as she climbed into her car after joining her parents for a Sunday dinner.

Would they be there at the moment Therese passed away? she wondered. Probably, she decided. She wondered if she had any Valium in her purse.

She took a sip of coffee and tried to think of something to say. Her resemblance to her mother was more than skin-deep; neither of them felt comfortable with emotional talks or gushy physical displays. But that didn't mean they didn't love each other; love was what had made Pauline run for the plane as soon as she'd heard the news.

"I thought maybe you'd like to come stay with us for a bit . . . afterward," Pauline said. "Or maybe you and I could take a little trip. Just somewhere for a few days together."

"I'd like that," her mother said. "Yes, getting away would be good."

They sat quietly again, the silence broken only when Pauline finished her coffee and set the empty paper cup on the table.

"Have you thought about arrangements?" she finally asked. Bringing it up felt almost unseemly in this small, sterile room just steps away from where Therese lay, still breathing. But Pauline felt compelled to ask; she needed to give her mind something to focus on. Because in the silences, she was beginning to picture her sister. Had she changed much in the months since Pauline had seen her? Was her hair still blond? Would her blue eyes be open when they went into her room?

"I thought just a very small service," her mother said. "Family and Therese's caretakers only."

Pauline nodded. She knew there would be no death notice in the paper, no sympathy cards from acquaintances. There would be only a gray gravestone and a wreath of flowers. What would Therese like? she wondered. Not roses. Something soft and pretty, with no thorns. Daisies, maybe.

She'd have to tell Dwight about Therese's death, but she wouldn't tell him that it had happened during his birthday trip, and that she'd been in the room. She could say it was sudden; maybe she'd pretend Therese had died on the day they were scheduled to leave. She didn't like lying to him again but couldn't see any other way to avoid putting a big damper on the vacation.

A man in a white coat lightly rapped on the open door of the waiting room. "I'm Dr. Klavin."

Pauline and her mother both stood up.

"Is she . . ." her mother began.

"I just checked on Therese," the doctor said. He was short and balding, with big brown eyes, and Pauline was struck by the thought that he looked more like a plumber than a doctor. "No real change."

"I see," her mother said.

"How much longer, do you think?" Pauline blurted. She almost gasped from the shock of releasing the question that had been lurking in her mind.

"I don't think it will be more than a day or so," the doctor said. He didn't seem to think the question was unusual. Maybe, Pauline realized with a hot rush of shame, it was because he thought she was dreading the event and wanted to steel herself.

She ducked her head, not wanting to meet anyone's eyes.

"I'll be back in a few hours," the doctor said.

Pauline forced herself to nod before he walked away.

"We'll go see her now," her mother said. She took a deep breath.

Pauline swallowed. "Do you mind if I just use the ladies' room first?"

"Of course," her mother said. "I'll wait here for you."

Pauline hurried down the hallway and found a small bathroom. She set her purse on the counter by the sink and fumbled into the zippered inside compartment, but she'd taken her last Valium on the plane the previous night, so she could get some sleep.

"Damn," she whispered.

She turned on the taps and washed her hands, because she couldn't think of what else to do. She ran them under the air from the hand dryer, welcoming the heat. Then she twisted the door handle and walked back out, toward Therese, the woman who both was and wasn't her sister.

*   *   *

They'd needed this lazy day, Savannah reflected. Without Pauline flitting about, organizing activities and checking on everyone, the mood at the villa had become much more relaxed—or maybe it just seemed that way to Savannah. The strong sun was tempered by a delicious breeze, and everyone had wandered down to the beach after a late breakfast. They'd carried books and magazines, and Allie had dug out that badminton set. A few people had played a game or two, and the guys had tossed around a Nerf football in the shallows, but mostly everyone had just lain on the sand, lulled by the crash of the waves that had gained in strength since the previous day.

No one felt like a big lunch—they'd been gorging themselves for the past two days—so they'd requested sandwiches from the new chef who'd arrived that morning. He was just as talented as the old chef, as evidenced by the spread he'd laid out: turkey, avocado, and bacon; grilled eggplant and roasted red peppers with baked goat cheese; and melted cheddar and tomato on thickly sliced bread. Served alongside the sandwiches were strawberries, raspberries, and blueberries mixed together and spiked with mint, and golden homemade potato chips. Everyone had eaten on the beach, still in bathing suits.

"Might as well get in our time in the sun while we can," Allie had said as she refilled her glass of iced tea. "The rain's going to come soon."

"Don't be a pessimist, Al," Savannah had said. She'd almost reached for another of the addictive chips but stopped herself; she'd probably gained a pound already on the trip. "It's not going to rain, is it, Tina?"

Tina had just shrugged. Savannah hadn't been able to see her eyes behind her sunglasses, but Tina wasn't smiling. That had settled it: Tina was mad. Savannah's question had been a kind of test. Tina had seemed to be avoiding her this morning; she'd stretched out her towel far away from Savannah's, and when Savannah had wandered over to ask if Tina had the *People* magazine, Tina had handed it to her without a word.

Why didn't people just tell you when they were angry, rather than sulking? Savannah wondered. It was as obvious as if Tina had grabbed a stick and dug giant words into the sand. And judging by how Gio was acting today—he'd been avoiding Savannah, too—he'd been chastised by his wife and was falling in line. That was surprising; Savannah would have thought Gio was the kind of guy who'd stand up for himself. But Tina clearly called the shots when it came to big things in their relationship.

Savannah was a little hungover, so she'd napped on the dock for an hour, dangling her fingertips in the salty water while the late-afternoon sun painted freckles on her shoulders. The gentle tapping of raindrops had woken her, and she'd realized everyone else had gone inside. She'd sat up and wrapped her towel around her shoulders, suddenly cold, looking around the deserted beach.

She'd gone to her room to take a long, warm shower, then she'd slipped into cutoff jean shorts and a gauzy white shirt.

Now she wandered into the living room, thinking the others might be gathered for cocktails. But the room was empty. She checked the game room, but no one was there, either. Maybe the other couples were having sex, she thought. She'd noticed Tina and Gio's bedroom door was closed as she passed by. And Dwight was probably checking in with his wife.

Savannah wondered if Pauline was planning to come back that night. Her neighbor had broken a hip the previous year, tripping off a curb in front of her own house, and had spent less than twenty-four hours in the hospital. Surely Pauline wouldn't miss the rest of the trip to care for her mother.

Savannah didn't know what else to do, so she went back into her room. She'd already applied a coat of mascara and dotted her lips with a shade of gloss called Sangria, but now she reached for her bronzer, adding to the glow the sun had given her face. She looked in the full-length mirror, twisting from side to side, and frowned. Was that cellulite on her upper thighs, or a trick of the light?

A trick of the light. It had to be. She'd been working out so hard!

She flopped down on the bed and clicked through the television channels, but there wasn't anything on she wanted to see. She checked the urge to glance down at her thighs to see how they looked from this angle. Her legs were perfect; she had another five years before she needed to start worrying about sagging skin or cellulite. Ten, if she severely limited carbs.

She opened the book on her nightstand, but she didn't want to read. She only knew she didn't want to be alone. She'd never been any good at that; in college, she'd always left the door to her room open, so anyone passing by could call out a hello, or pop in to visit.

Savannah finally went into the kitchen, where the new chef, Patrick, was gathering plates and napkins and putting them in a wicker basket in preparation for the clambake on the beach.

"Mind if I open a bottle of wine?" she asked.

"Allow me," he said, uncorking a Riesling and pouring her a generous serving.

"Perfect," she said. "If the others are looking for me, I'm going to head down now."

"I'll let them know," he said. "I'll bring down the food as soon as everyone's ready."

She walked down the steps to the beach, feeling unsettled and restless. Had she overdone it with Gio the night before? Maybe Allie was angry with her, too; Allie had been on the quiet side today as well. Savannah cast back in her memory for details of the night: She remembered making margaritas, and splashing Gio in the water . . . They'd talked for a while, too, in the living room, before they passed out. But Ryan had been there most of the time. At least, she thought he had . . . She descended the final steps and conceded the fact that her memory of the previous night contained holes. It wasn't the first time it had happened to her—lately there had been a few mornings when she'd woken up on the couch, fully dressed, with an empty wine bottle on the table and the television blaring. And once she'd met a friend for martinis and had no recollection of driving home, even though her car was parked in the driveway.

Nothing had happened with Gio, though, she thought as she lay down in a hammock and pushed off against the sand with her toes to set it swinging. She'd remember it if they'd kissed. Surely she would have stopped it! No, they'd talked, then passed out, and Savannah had found herself on the couch around five a.m., freezing cold and alone, just like when she'd woken up on the beach after her afternoon nap. She'd stumbled to her bedroom, putting on sweatpants and a long-sleeved T-shirt and crawling under the covers. It had taken her a long time to fall back asleep.

Savannah glanced up at the sound of voices; everyone was coming down the stairs, carrying blankets and coolers and the picnic basket. The chef brought up the rear, carrying an enormous silver pot that must weigh a ton, judging by the strained look on his face.

"Hey, Van," Ryan said, shaking out a blue blanket on the sand.

"Hi," she said. She swung her legs over the side of the hammock and stood up. "I like your dress, Tina."

"Thanks," Tina said in a clipped voice.

Oh, for God's sakes, were they still in high school? Savannah wondered. This was getting ridiculous.

Patrick finished setting out plates and began to ladle food onto a giant serving platter—bright red lobsters, cherrystone clams, mussels, steaming corn on the cob, tender new potatoes . . .

"Ooh, let me get a picture of this," Allie said, snapping away with her camera. "I want to remember this feast."

Savannah adored cherrystone clams, and she hadn't had one in forever. She reached over and snagged one, then slid the meat and juice into her mouth. "Sorry," she said. "I couldn't wait."

"Help yourself," Tina said, under her breath but loud enough for Savannah to hear. "You always take whatever you want anyway."

Allie cleared her throat. "Tina, would you help me get some more drinks?" she said. "I think I forgot to bring down the rest of the wine."

Savannah's eyes tracked the two women as they left. Suddenly, she hurried over to the stairs to follow them. Tina and Allie had already entered the kitchen by the time Savannah walked into the house, but she could clearly hear their conversation as she approached the swinging door.

"I know her life is falling apart, but that doesn't mean she gets to hit on my husband."

"I don't think she was hitting on him. I mean, you're right, she was a little over the top, but she was just flirting. You saw how she was dancing with Dwight the other night, too." That would be Allie, trying to smooth things over, Savannah thought. Why bother? Why not just have it out and be done with it?

Savannah swung open the door and popped in her head. "Talking about me, girls?" She smiled brightly.

"Oh!" Allie looked so flustered it was almost comical. "We were just—"

Savannah entered the room and met Tina's eyes. "Look, you're pissed at me. That's obvious."

"You're right," Tina said. She lifted her chin. "I am."

"I can't believe you accused me of hitting on Gio," Savannah said.

"What the hell do you think you were doing, taking off your dress and showing your pole dancing moves?" Tina asked.

"Come on, Tina," Savannah said. "I've known him forever. He's practically my brother."

"He's not your brother!" Tina said. "He's my husband."

"You were pole dancing, too!" Savannah said.

"Not the way you were," Tina said. She crossed her arms over her chest. "And you were wrapped around Dwight the other night when you were pretending to teach him how to salsa."

"So now I'm trying to steal your husband *and* Dwight?" Savannah said. "My bed isn't that big. You're being stupid."

"Why don't you just apologize? You can never admit it when you're wrong!" Tina cried. "That's always bugged me about you."

"Because I'm *not* wrong," Savannah said. "We were having a good time. Which is something you used to know how to do."

"Look, I really think we should—" Allie began.

"What is that supposed to mean?" Tina narrowed her eyes.

"It means you need to lighten up," Savannah said.

"Fuck you," Tina said.

"Oh, no," Allie said. "Let's all take a deep breath and—"

"Lighten up? You have no idea what my life is like, because you're so selfish you never think about anyone except yourself!" Tina shouted.

"Don't hold back, Tina," Savannah said. She tried to smirk, but her lips wouldn't obey. "Say what you really think."

"Okay, I will," Tina said. "There's a code among girlfriends. We don't hit on each other's husbands. Do you even care, or are you that desperate for attention?"

"Desperate?" Savannah rolled her eyes, even as she felt the truth of the words stab into her. "I get plenty of attention, Tina.

Maybe if you got out a little more you'd get some attention, too, and you wouldn't be so anal about me joking around with Gio. What's wrong with you? You're acting like a prissy old lady. You used to be *fun*."

Tina's voice was so flat it took a moment for her words to sink in. "Is that why Gary left? Because you're so fun?"

Silence filled the room, then Tina clapped a hand over her mouth.

"Oh, shit," she whispered. "I'm sorry, Van. You know I didn't mean it. It's just . . ." She shook her head and looked down. "Everything you said is true. I know I should get out more! Don't you think I want to?" Her lower lip began to tremble. "I want to be more fun! I want to go to restaurants, and flirt a little, and laugh . . . But I can't!" Her shoulders began to shake, and she dropped her face into her hands.

Savannah walked over and flung her arms around Tina. Her own throat felt tight, too, as if Tina's tears were contagious. "Look, you're right. I was flirting with Gio because my husband left me for a nurse who's practically in high school. I'm a bitch."

"It's not that," Tina said. She lifted her head and sniffed. "Yeah, I mean, you are a bitch. But so am I."

"I'm a selfish bitch, though, so I'm worse," Savannah said. This time her smile was genuine. She let go of Tina and handed her the glass of Riesling.

"A nurse?" Tina asked. "I'm really sorry, Van. On behalf of my profession."

Savannah shrugged. "Yeah" was all she said. Her throat still felt strange, but her eyes were dry.

Allie looked back and forth, as if she was a medic staring at two injured people, unsure of who to treat first. "Are you okay, Tina?" she finally asked.

Tina nodded and took another sip of wine, then handed it back to Savannah. "You need this as much as I do," she said. "I don't know, it's just being here, getting to sleep late and relax and eat good food . . . the contrast with my normal life is so extreme. You guys, it hit me this morning: I'm scared to go back home."

Her voice dropped to a whisper. "I don't think I *want* to go back. I mean, I will, of course, but I'm dreading it. What kind of mother am I, that I don't want to see my own kids?"

"The best mother I know," Allie said firmly, but the words didn't seem to register.

"You know why I was so mean to you, Savannah?" Tina said. The words began tumbling out of her, and her voice grew uneven again. "Because you're sexy and gorgeous and sometimes I wish I could be you. Or just look like you for a day. I've gained weight and my clothes are awful and if I manage to shower in the morning it's a banner day. All I do is clean and nag and drive and cook and break up fights and . . . and . . . I don't know how to change things! Gio works late and on weekends he's so tired. I can't just leave him with four kids . . ."

"Why not?" Savannah asked. "I mean, not for the whole weekend, but why not for a few hours so you can go grab a glass of wine and a nice meal? Maybe even spend the night in a hotel by yourself?"

"Do you have any idea of how tired I am by seven p.m.?" Tina asked. "I'm in my pajamas by then. I'd never have the energy to go out. Not counting this trip, I've only slept through the night a few times in the past six years."

"Seriously?" Savannah said.

"Want to know the first thought that pops into my mind almost every morning after opening my eyes? I start anticipating being able to go to bed at night. I'm just so tired all the time."

Savannah hid a shudder. She couldn't imagine living like that. The thought of it made her literally itchy.

"Wow," Savannah said. She scraped her nails down her left

arm. Was she being attacked by a bug? There was a raised blotch on the inside of her elbow. "That kind of . . . sucks."

"Yeah," Tina said. She took another sip of wine. Her face was still red, but her voice had evened out. "I love my kids more than anything in the world. And I wish they came with a Pause button, so I could get caught up and relax, and then go back to them sometime in the future. Like in a year or two."

"I think every mother in the world feels that way," Allie said.

"*You* never did," Tina said.

"Are you kidding me? Of course I did," Allie said. "Why does everyone think my life is so perfect? Because it *isn't,* Tina. No one's is."

"Amen to that, girlfriend," Savannah said.

Tina nodded. "Okay," she finally said. She looked at Savannah, and her face softened. "I'm really sorry about . . . Well, Gary's an asshole."

"Is there anything we can do, Van?" Allie asked.

Savannah shrugged again. "Nah. I've got a good lawyer. And I'm going after Gary for every cent I can get."

"Will you stay in the house?" Tina asked.

"Probably, for a while," Savannah said. "I've kind of put decision making on hold for now, but—"

"Is your arm okay?" Tina interrupted, moving closer to look at it.

"Bug bite," Savannah said, pulling her sleeve back down to cover it. "Hey, maybe the three of us should hang out alone tonight. We'll let the boys do boy things after dinner."

"Look, you don't have to avoid Gio," Tina said. "Just keep your clothes on, okay?"

"Who?" Savannah asked, scrunching up her nose. "Is he the short, hairy one? He's not even my type."

Tina stared at her a moment, then burst into laughter. Savannah laughed, too, and then Allie joined in, throwing her arms around both of them.

"You thought you were going to have to jump in between us and break up a fight, didn't you?" Tina asked Allie.

"Kind of," Allie admitted. "I think this kitchen has a hex on it. We always seem to be fighting in here."

"There's a moral to that," Savannah said. "Women should stay out of"—she coughed—"the kitchen." She put a hand against her chest, hurried over to the sink, and filled a glass with water.

"Are you really okay?" Allie said. "I know it must be hard. You and Gary were together for so many years . . ."

Savannah shook her head. Her eyes were huge.

She hadn't experienced the sensation in years, but now she recognized it. Her heart was pounding and it was difficult to breathe. And she itched everywhere—even the soles of her feet.

"Shrimp," she gasped. "Allergic."

Allie froze. But Tina, the former nurse, sprang into action.

"Find some Benadryl or Claritin!" she shouted at Allie. "Search all the medicine cabinets. Savannah, do you have an EpiPen?"

Savannah nodded as Allie hurried off.

"Where?" Tina asked.

"My room . . . I don't know exactly . . ."

"Can you walk?" Tina asked. "Come with me. I can't let you out of my sight."

Breathe, Savannah told herself as she nodded again and reached for Tina's extended hand. *Don't panic—that'll make it worse.* She had the EpiPen somewhere—did she put it in her medicine cabinet? Or maybe it was in her cosmetics bag. It was hard to think; she felt almost drunk, even though she'd had only a few sips of wine. She lay down on her bed, listening to Tina tear through the bathroom. Something crashed to the floor and shattered.

"It's not here," Tina said. She tore open the dresser drawers and began rifling through them, flinging clothes around.

"My suitcase," Savannah gasped. It was hard to swallow. She was so dizzy . . .

Tina hurried to the closet, yanked open the door, and bent down. "Got it." She hurried to Savannah's side, unbuttoned her jean shorts, pulled them down, and jabbed her upper thigh with the EpiPen.

"One . . . two . . ." Tina slowly counted to ten, then withdrew the pen. "Just lie there for a minute. I found your prescription steroids, too. I'm going to give you four of them. Let them dissolve on your tongue, okay?"

Savannah nodded. She was already feeling better; it was as if she'd been stuffed up with the world's worst cold and then inhaled Vicks VapoRub. She swallowed, just to make sure she could. *Thank God*, she thought.

"Good girl," Tina said. She fed Savannah the steroids one at a time.

"Now I know you've forgiven me," Savannah whispered. "You'd have let me die if you were still mad."

Tina shook her head. "Only you," she said. "How can you joke at a time like this?"

Savannah closed her eyes and focused on the newly sweet sensation of breathing as Tina went to toss the EpiPen in the bathroom's trash can. What would have happened if she'd stayed on the beach? Would the guys have even known what to do?

Her allergy was so strange: She'd been able to eat as much shrimp as she wanted until her late twenties, when suddenly, she developed hives on her arms during a night out at a sushi restaurant. An allergist had tested her and warned her to avoid shrimp, but one night a year or so later she'd unknowingly consumed some in a quiche. This time, her reaction was even quicker and more severe: angry red hives covered her body within minutes. One had even sprouted on her lower lip.

"The next reaction could be life-threatening," the allergist had told Savannah as he prescribed an EpiPen and dissolvable steroids for her to carry around. And she'd been careful, always asking waiters in restaurants to make sure her meals didn't include shrimp or any cross-contaminated ingredients. But Pauline had known about the allergy, and had told Savannah not to worry—that no shrimp would be served this week. So why was there shrimp in the clambake?

"Do you want some water?" Tina was asking.

"I'm okay," Savannah said. She swallowed again. "I actually feel pretty good."

"You need to go to the hospital to get checked out," Tina said.

"That's the last thing I want to do," Savannah said. She pulled her shorts back up and buttoned them. "Come on, I've got my own personal nurse here."

"But what if you start reacting again?" Tina asked.

Savannah stood up and walked over to her bag. "I've got another EpiPen," she said, holding it up. "They come two to a package, so I threw them both in."

"I found the Benadryl!"

Allie burst into the room, holding the bottle aloft. She looked at Savannah, then at Tina. "She's okay?"

"Tina just pulled down my pants, but aside from that awkward moment, everything is groovy," Savannah said.

Tina rolled her eyes. "As you can see, she's back to normal. I want you to take twenty-five milligrams of this, though. Just in case."

"Fine," Savannah said as Allie unscrewed the lid and filled the little measuring cup to the right line. She swallowed it down in one gulp, grateful her throat seemed to be completely open now.

"Also, stay close to me tonight," Tina said. "I want to come along even when you go to the bathroom, okay?"

"Wow, let a girl see your hoochie and suddenly she thinks you're a couple," Savannah said. "Come on, let's go back to the beach. The guys must be wondering what we're doing." She still felt anxious, but the giant hive on her arm was already disappearing. She wanted to put this episode behind her, fast.

"Sure," Tina said. "We better grab something else for you to eat, though. And you can't drink any more tonight."

"Okay, okay," Savannah said, even though she was already plotting how to pour wine into a water bottle to fake Tina out. She started to exit the room, then turned back around.

"Tina?" Savannah waited until Tina's eyes met hers. "Thanks, girl."

Tina reached for Savannah's hand and squeezed it.

Chapter Nine

Wednesday

ALLIE WOKE UP AND slowly stretched her arms toward the ceiling. She took a moment to orient herself: It was Wednesday morning, almost halfway through the vacation. She could tell by the faint light in the room that it was dawn, but she wasn't the slightest bit tired. Everyone had gone to bed relatively early last night, around midnight.

She slipped out of bed and pulled on a sports bra and nylon shorts, then laced up her red Nikes. She opened the bedroom door quietly so she wouldn't wake Ryan, then went into the gym and reached for one of the colorful resistance bands heaped by the free weights. She sat down, hooked the end of the band around one foot, and leaned back, relishing the gentle stretch in her hamstring. She finished warming up, then stepped outside. The sun was the color of fire as it hovered over the water, and the surrounding clouds looked like tufts of cotton candy.

It was the kind of morning that cried out for a run.

She set off for the beach, finding the perfect length of sand a few feet away from where the waves were breaking—firm enough that she didn't slip, but soft enough so that her muscles felt the effort. She logged a slow, easy half mile, then picked up speed, feeling sweat dot her brow. She knew exactly how far she could push herself; her steps were as steady and reliable as a metronome. Though she wasn't wearing a watch, she knew she was running a nine-minute-mile pace—she'd logged so many of them through the years that her rhythm was instinctual.

She took steady inhalations through her nose and breathed out through her mouth, feeling her arms churn up and down in perfect synchrony with her legs. Her body felt strong and clean, like a beautifully maintained machine.

What if it suddenly failed her? she wondered as her feet beat against the sand. What if her strong legs refuse to move? How could her arms—which used to carry both of her children at once when she crossed a busy road—suddenly turn limp and useless at her sides? It seemed incomprehensible.

Allie turned back toward the house, tasting salt in her mouth. She reached up with her forearm to wipe away her tears and sweat. When she'd first learned about familial ALS, she'd wondered, fleetingly, if her girls could have copies of the damaged gene. But she'd immediately stricken the impossible thought from her mind. They'd find a cure for ALS long before it ever had a chance to hurt her daughters. There was no other option.

When she finally unfurled that strip of paper in her cosmetics bag and called the genetic counselor, she might be reassured. Maybe she'd learn that she could be tested to see if she carried a gene with a kind of typo in it. That's what an ALS website had called it—a typo. Allie had almost laughed, it was so ridiculous. A typo was a misplaced apostrophe; it was scream in your coffee instead of cream. It wasn't the difference between life and death.

Allie imagined going in for a test, then sitting across a desk and waiting for the counselor to give her the results. She ran faster, feeling her heart pound. She knew that if she learned she had the mutated gene, it would be impossible to live with that kind of sentence hanging over her head. It was a recipe for insanity.

I don't know what to do! Allie wanted to scream. *I don't know what I want anymore—except to have my old life back!*

It was so unfair. Allie had never taken her body for granted; she'd always treated it well. Cherished it, even. She'd been a vegetarian since college, and she went to the doctor every year for a physical exam and Pap smear. She did monthly breast checks in the shower. She took a multivitamin!

How could her body turn on her? Why did idiots who abused drugs and ate nothing but McDonald's get to live long lives, while her own might be cut in half?

She reached the bottom of the steps leading to the villa and took them two at a time, hoping that by exhausting her body, she'd quiet her mind. It helped, but not as much as she'd hoped. Instead of going inside, she walked over to the pool so she could have a little more time alone.

She felt as if she'd been wearing a mask since that call from her birth mother—that her reactions were subdued, her smile less bright. But no one had noticed, not even Ryan.

Especially not Ryan.

She'd always thought their connection was strong as steel. So why hadn't he sensed her terror, or noticed how alone she felt?

She leaned against a lounge chair to stretch her calves, then realized it was the same one she'd chosen two nights ago, when she and Dwight had sat up talking for hours.

She took off her sneakers and curled up in the chair, wondering for the dozenth time what the kiss on the beach had meant. It hadn't lasted long—ten or fifteen seconds—but it was a gesture of love. She thought about how she'd hugged Van and Tina in the kitchen after their fight, and about visiting Tina in the hospital after Tina had given birth to Sammy. Tina's feet had looked so tired and swollen that Allie, without a word, had pulled up a chair and massaged them for an hour. Those were all loving, physical gestures, too.

Oh, who was she kidding? Dwight hadn't given her a friendly peck—he'd kissed her. Really kissed her. And she'd kissed him back. She'd wound her hand around the back of his neck and held him tight.

"Thank you," she'd whispered as they drew apart. Whether for his promise of taking care of her and her family, or for the kiss, she didn't know. Maybe for both.

They'd sat together in silence for a little while, then they'd silently reached for each other's hands as they'd walked to the road to wait for the cab Dwight had called. They hadn't let go until the cab was pulling into the driveway of the house.

After meeting Ryan, Allie had never kissed another man—she hadn't really even looked at one that way. Not until this trip. Her husband was a kind, easygoing guy, and she'd always admired those qualities in him. She'd see other couples squabbling in the grocery store over whether to buy steak or pasta for dinner, and once at a cocktail party she'd watched, aghast, as a wife and husband began shouting at each other when the subject of summer camp for their kids came up (the husband wanted to send them to sleepaway camp, the wife was dead set against it). At those times, Allie felt grateful for the calm waters of her marriage.

But the possibility of ALS was making her scrutinize everything anew: her body, her friendship with Dwight, and yes, even her relationship with Ryan. She'd never before realized how much he leaned on her to keep their lives running seamlessly. Allie was the one who made the kids' dentist appointments and noticed when they were outgrowing their clothes. She cut their toenails and scheduled the gutter cleaners and planned birthday parties and paid the bills. She held their household together with her checklists and checkbook and calendar. If she suddenly . . . disappeared, could Ryan handle everything? He wasn't a weak man, but he'd never been proactive. It hadn't bothered her until now.

Even on this trip, on the very first day, he'd left the choice of whether to take a nap or go to the beach to her. She frowned, thinking about clues that had been there all along—clues she'd never needed before. He hadn't even spoken up to say he hated pineapple pizza on the night they first met.

Allie felt chilled: Had she been mistaking her husband's passivity for agreeableness all these years?

Ryan wasn't good around illness, either. His mother had died of pancreatic cancer when he was a teenager, and Allie knew being near sickness conjured a great unease in him. If one of the girls spiked a fever, his default reaction was to call out "Allie?" then stand back while she rushed in and took over. Sure, he'd run to the store to pick up children's Tylenol and juice, but Allie was the one who would administer it.

Allie pressed her fingertips against her temples, feeling as if her head might explode from the intensity of her thoughts. Every one of her long-held truths was shattering. Maybe those squabbling couples in the grocery store—the ones Allie had pitied!—would be by each other's sides in a crisis, steadfast until the end. Meanwhile Allie and Ryan, the seemingly perfect couple, would fall apart as soon as a crisis hit. After all, they'd never been tested before.

Ryan's fear of illness meant she might not be able to depend on him if she desperately needed him. Would he sit by her side, feeding her with a spoon when her arms failed her; would he clean her after she went to the bathroom? She pictured his face, and the expression she saw was fear mingled with revulsion.

She wanted—needed—Ryan to become a different kind of man, someone who would challenge the doctors and research alternative therapies and fight like hell to save her. But instead, it was Dwight who seemed to have transformed. He'd known she was having a panic attack, then he'd encouraged her to talk about the reason why. He'd sensed something was wrong, whereas Ryan hadn't even noticed that Allie had been pacing the house in the middle of the night in the weeks before the trip. He'd just slept on, blissfully unaware.

Allie stood up and began to turn slow circles around the pool. She'd always loved Dwight. Not in a romantic way, but she'd understood him and knew she was one of the few people who did. Hearing Savannah joke about hooking up with him had ignited a jealousy in Allie that she'd never felt about Ryan. Dwight was *hers*!

The other night, when everyone had gotten so drunk and Tina had passed out early, Allie had come out here to the pool to get some fresh air, feeling woozy from the game of quarters. Savannah, Ryan, and Gio were all in the living room, still drinking, and the sound of their laughter easily carried outside. Dwight had followed her out, as she'd known he would.

They'd talked until the sun came up.

"What can I do?" Dwight had asked.

"I'm feeling so out of control and scared right now," she'd said. They were on separate lounge chairs, but their heads were close together. "Maybe if I focus on things I can control, it'll help."

"Okay. So let's think about that," he'd said, and she'd grown warm inside at his use of the word *let's*.

They'd come up with good ideas, like keeping a running list of things she did for the kids: foods they liked, how candlelit bubble baths soothed them when they were upset, books they loved to listen to . . .

"It's not that I expect anything to . . . to happen to you," he'd said. "It won't. But if this helps . . ."

"It really does," she'd said, and she'd inched a bit closer to him. They were a team now.

"So we'll write this down," Dwight had said, nodding. "And I can keep a copy in my desk, too, if you want."

She'd almost wept at his words.

It had been dark outside, but the pool lights had cast a golden glow around them. She'd heard Ryan laughing a bit too heartily at one of Gio's dirty jokes, and she'd felt a flash of scorn: Why did Ryan act like someone he wasn't around Gio? Why hadn't *he* come out here to check on her?

His joking around while she sat planning for her own death felt like a staggering betrayal. She would've been so lonely, if it hadn't been for Dwight.

The sound of the raucous laughter had also conjured a memory in her: She'd been in her senior year of college, walking down the quad at UVa, heading to her room after her last class of the day. It had been one of those afternoons that seemed to straddle summer and fall: warm when the sun beamed down on you, chilly when it ducked behind a cloud. Dwight had been fifty or so yards ahead of her, and Allie had been about to yell out a greeting when he tripped on something—a rock or uneven patch of sidewalk or maybe just his own feet. He'd sprawled out, papers and books flying everywhere, and a gaggle of bitchy girls had stood by and laughed instead of helping him.

Allie had hurried over, picked up a notebook, and handed it to Dwight, who'd looked like he was about to cry.

"Thanks," he'd said. He was still crouched down, jamming papers into a three-ring binder that had split open. One of his palms was bleeding slightly.

"Want to come over and study for a while?" she'd asked, bending down next to him. She didn't know Dwight well— they'd lived next to each other for only a few weeks—but she knew that he didn't have a lot of friends. His room was always quiet.

"Sh-sh-sure," he'd said. And then he'd stood up and she'd noticed the back cuff of one of his pants legs had gotten stuck in the elastic band of one of his socks, making him look especially dorky and vulnerable. She'd had to swallow a lump in her throat.

They'd studied together for a few hours, in a companionable silence, and she'd made them both hot cocoa before he left her room. His face had lit up like a little boy's when she'd added mini-marshmallows to their mugs.

"This was nice," he'd said.

"Let's do it again sometime soon," she'd responded.

"I'd, ah, like that," he'd said, looking down. But she could see him smiling. He had a wonderful smile.

Later that night, as she lay in bed, she'd realized he was just inches away on the other side of the wall, and she'd sent out a little prayer for him, that life would begin to treat him more kindly.

Once Dwight felt completely safe around Allie, he rarely stuttered or hesitated when they talked. She liked the way he listened carefully to everything she said, and spoke only when he had something to say in return, not to fill the silence.

Now, fifteen years after they'd first met, Allie appreciated those qualities in him even more. As a social worker, she listened to people's problems for a living. Just *being* with someone was so relaxing and rare.

But that night by the pool, after Dwight had helped Allie figure out ways to feel in control, their conversation had turned—gone deeper than it ever had before. By then Ryan had poked his head outside and announced he was going to bed, and Allie had promised to come in soon. But she hadn't. Something about the late hour, and the dark, and the deep timbre of Dwight's voice, made it impossible for her to leave her chair. To leave him.

"Do you want kids, Dwight?" she'd asked at one point.

"Yeah," he'd said. "Definitely."

"You'll be a great dad," she'd said.

"We've been trying for . . . well, a while. Pretty much since we got married."

"So almost two years?" Allie said. "Have you guys talked to a specialist? There's nothing to be ashamed of, you know."

"I'll mention it to Pauline," he'd said.

Allie had swallowed a surprised *You haven't yet?*

How could Dwight fail to discuss something so important with his wife? she wondered, then immediately felt a rush of recognition. She'd done the exact same thing to Ryan. Instead of confiding in her husband, she'd taken her deepest worries to another man.

When she and Dwight had finally risen from their chairs by the pool, the house was completely silent and the sky had turned a shade or two lighter. She'd reached out her arms and they'd hugged for a long time. It had felt even more intimate than their kiss on the beach.

Now Allie continued walking around the pool, thinking about how she could get Dwight alone, to tell him she needed him by her side when she finally called the genetic counselor. Maybe he could take off work for a day when they got back home, and he could come over and hold her while she dialed the number. She could do it, if Dwight was there with her.

Why couldn't she stop thinking about that kiss?

Allie picked up her jogging shoes and was about to go into the house when she heard a car coming down the road, spitting up gravel as it turned in to the driveway. She watched as a gleaming black sedan stopped and Pauline stepped out. The

driver hurried to open the trunk and handed Pauline her overnight case, which she took without a word.

Pauline looked . . . different, Allie thought. Her blond hair
was up in a ponytail, with some pieces trailing out to the side in
a way that looked sloppy instead of artful. She wore jeans and
a simple cotton shirt.

Allie watched Pauline pay the driver. But instead of going
into the house, Pauline walked toward the pool as Allie shrank
behind a pillar. Allie felt as if she should look away—as if she
was witnessing something private—but she couldn't.

She kept watching as Pauline sank into the chair Allie had
just vacated, and stared into space. A moment later, something
strange happened: Rain began pouring down, even though the
sky was still mostly clear. It rained hard for about two minutes,
then it stopped abruptly and the sun burst into view again.
If it hadn't been for the fact that Allie could see Pauline's wet
hair and damp clothes, Allie might have worried she'd imagined it all—the abrupt turn in the weather, the sudden absence
of light, and the thin blond woman making no effort to shield
herself against the downpour.

"So, we had a little excitement last night," Savannah said, leaning back in her chair at the dining room table toward the end of
lunch. "There was shrimp in the clambake."

Pauline looked at Savannah, but her expression didn't change.

"Remember, I'm allergic to shrimp?" Savannah prompted.
"We talked about it on the plane?"

"Oh, yes," Pauline said.

Clearly Savannah had expected a different reaction—a
shocked exclamation, maybe, followed by an effusive apology.
But Pauline just kept looking at her. It seemed to throw Savannah, who sat up straighter.

"Luckily Tina found my EpiPen before my throat completely closed up," she said, a note of pique running through her voice.

"The old chef must've forgotten to tell the new chef about your allergy." Pauline lifted a shoulder, as if dismissing the incident. "But you're obviously okay now."

"Well, yes, but only because Tina's a nurse and she knew what to do!" Savannah said.

There was another pause, the perfect space for Pauline to apologize. But she simply took an unhurried sip of her coffee. Tina studied her from across the table, wondering if Pauline was trying to get under Savannah's skin. But it seemed as if Pauline was truly out of it—almost as if she'd heard Savannah's words without understanding their meaning. Tina hid a little smile; Savannah loved being the center of attention, and it was kind of funny to see her denied that role, especially since she actually deserved it in this case.

"Are you sure you don't want anything to eat, Pauline?" Tina asked after a moment. "A little pasta salad, maybe?"

Pauline turned to look at Tina. "I'm fine," she said.

Maybe that was how she stayed so skinny, Tina thought as she spooned another helping of the salad onto her plate. Nothing had passed Pauline's lips during this meal but three or four cups of coffee. You'd expect her to be jittery, but the caffeine seemed to be having the opposite effect on her. Her movements were a beat slower than normal, as if she were underwater.

Tina sighed and closed her lips around tender farfalle, mixed with grilled asparagus, feta, and toasted pine nuts. She didn't feel the slightest bit guilty because she knew it was real fuel for her body, not like the empty calories she usually consumed. The problem was, she was so busy at home that she tended to gobble anything that could be held in one hand—usually peanut butter and jelly sandwiches or, shamefully, a sleeve of cookies on some days. Sometimes she even ate off a paper towel when she couldn't bear the thought of creating more dirty dishes.

She used to love to cook, though. She'd enjoyed layering meat and cheese in perfect proportions into a lasagna, baking it until it was golden and just the slightest bit crusty on top. She'd liked to simmer a stew and let the aroma fill the entire house, sneaking a taste now and then to determine if it needed another dash of pepper or thyme. But everything had changed when her second child had arrived, squalling and delicate of stomach and equipped with the world's pickiest taste buds. Angela hated everything but the blandest dishes—mac and cheese, rice, pizza with no toppings, toast and bananas. Present the kid with a burrito and she'd recoil as if it were a tarantula.

Paolo, Tina's oldest, liked pretty much everything—but he was the only kid in America who refused to eat rice. As an added bonus, he was allergic to dairy. And so it became easier for Tina to find the lowest common denominator, to cook the simplest foods that would please everyone. She usually made something like a roasted chicken and a bowl of mac and cheese for dinner, and tossed it on the table alongside fruit and bread and maybe a tray of baby carrots and cut-up cucumbers, if she were feeling especially guilty about her family's dysfunctional relationship with the food pyramid.

And of course she always went straight for the mac and cheese. It was easy and soothing and filling, something she could shovel in between leaping up to fill water glasses and admonishing the kids to use their napkins instead of their shirts. Sometimes she was gripped with a passion to change things— to wait until Gio came home to eat a proper meal with him, something involving candles and a nice salad with grilled fish. But invariably, by the time she finished baths and homework supervision and bedtime stories, she was too wiped out to do anything but cover a plate of leftovers in Saran Wrap and leave it on the counter for him. It made her feel like a failure in both wife and mother categories.

Tina felt unexpected tears prick her eyes. Going on a vacation was supposed to relax you, not make you realize how stressful your life had become.

"So what's the plan for today, Pauline?" Savannah was saying.

Tina glanced up when their hostess didn't answer immediately.

"We can watch a movie, or . . . read on the beach," Pauline finally said. She sounded as if she couldn't have cared less.

"That sounds good," Allie said. "I think an afternoon of reading is just what I need."

"Great," Tina said. She was feeling a little low, and a few hours of lighthearted fiction did sound nice. She took a closer look at Pauline. She had dark shadows under her eyes, and despite all the time in the sun, her skin looked even paler than usual. Could she be coming down with something?

"Would you excuse me?" Pauline asked.

She stood up without waiting for an answer and walked in the direction of her bedroom. Everyone at the table watched her go.

"Well, that was odd," Savannah said. "She doesn't have anything lined up for the afternoon? Not that I'm complaining; she just had so much planned for the beginning of the trip."

"She's probably tired," Allie said. "All that flying . . ."

"I'll bring her a cup of tea," Dwight said, standing. "She loves tea."

"I feel like a little bodysurfing," Gio said as Dwight left. "The waves are getting really good."

"I'm in," Ryan said. "Allie? How about you?"

She shook her head. "I'm just going to hang out by the pool. I might come down to the beach later."

"Me, too," Tina said. "The weather's kind of weird anyway. It keeps raining for a few minutes, then stopping."

"It's weather bands from the approaching storm," Gio said. "But there's still plenty of sun. I saw a bunch of boogie boards by the tiki bar, so let's hit it. Tell Dwight to meet us down at the water if he wants."

Everyone got up and split in different directions, with Tina heading into her room and shutting the door behind her. She was glad Gio was going down to the beach with the guys. She was suddenly craving solitude and felt desperate to try to stock-pile it while she had the chance. She'd choose a book from the shelf downstairs and curl up and read, then drift off into a nap. Her belly was full of good, rich food, and her bed was so com-fortable—she'd been right when she imagined the sheets and comforters would be snowy white.

She sighed in relief as she unsnapped her shorts, which had been a bit tight even before lunch. She slipped off her clothes, then put on the soft terry bathrobe that was hanging on the back of their bathroom door. Maybe she'd take a long soak in the Jacuzzi before napping, she thought.

But first she reached for her cell phone and dialed a familiar number.

"Hi, Louise," she said when Allie's mom answered. "I thought I'd check in . . ."

"Oh, Tina! Funny you called just now."

Tina caught her breath. "Is everything okay?"

"Fine, fine," Louise said. "It's just that Sammy came down with a little bug this morning. His stomach hurts, so I was going to run him to the doctor."

"Does he have a fever?" Tina asked.

"Not really," Louise said. "It's a touch above normal. But mostly it's the stomach pain he's complaining about."

"Which side of his stomach? Is the pain coming from below his belly button?"

"I'm not sure," Louise said. "Should I ask him?"

"Um . . . actually, can you put him on?" Tina asked.

"Sure," Louise said.

She could hear voices in the background, then the sound of heavy breathing into the phone.

"Sammy?"

"Mama?"

She bit her lower lip as her eyes grew wet. Her baby was sick, and she was hundreds of miles away.

"Hi, little bunny," she said. "Louise told me your tummy hurts."

"Mmn-hmm," Sammy said.

"Below your belly button, Sammy? Is that where it hurts?"

"Yeah," he said.

Please don't let it be his appendix, Tina thought.

"Is it above your belly button, too?"

"Yeah," he said. "And my feet."

She should've known better than to try to diagnose a two-and-a-half-year-old over the phone. She glanced out the window and saw the weather had turned again; the rain was coming down, hard.

"I miss you," she said. "But Louise is going to take good care of you."

"Come home, Mama," he said. His voice was small.

"Oh, baby," she whispered. She squeezed her eyes shut. "I'm coming soon . . ."

"Now?" he asked.

Tina pictured Sammy standing there, holding the phone to his ear with his chubby little hands, his poor sore belly sticking out from the bottom of his T-shirt, wanting a hug from his mama. She felt horrible.

Then a traitorous thought wormed into her mind: *Damn it, don't I deserve a break for once?*

For just a moment, she felt angry at Sammy. Not at Sammy, she told herself, feeling ashamed. What kind of mother would be mad at her child for getting sick? She was angry at the situation, that was all.

"I can't come home now," she said, keeping her voice light. "Louise is going to take you to the doctor. Remember you get stickers every time you go? You can pick a Thomas the Train sticker if you want. And then you can call me right afterward, okay?"

More heavy breathing, then Louise picked up again.

"Tina? I'm afraid we have to go . . . the doctor's squeezing us in."

"Can you make sure the doctor checks his appendix?" Tina blurted.

"Of course," Louise said, her voice reassuring. "But I'm sure it's just a stomachache. That's why I didn't call you . . ."

"I know," Tina said, holding back a sigh. She'd specifically asked Louise to call her if any of the kids became sick. Maybe Louise was waiting for the official report from the doctor, but Tina still wished she'd phoned earlier.

"Could you call me after you see the doctor?" Tina asked.

"It's a deal," Louise said. "But don't let it ruin your day . . . There's no sense in you worrying. I'll call you as soon as we get back."

"Okay," Tina said. "And thanks for taking care of him."

She hung up and plopped down heavily on the bed. Sammy was fine; he'd had tummy aches before. Every kid in the world got them. He'd take a bit of medicine and watch some TV and he'd be all better by morning.

Still, reading a book held no appeal now; she knew she

wouldn't be able to concentrate. And she no longer felt like being alone.

She glanced at the clock on the nightstand. It would take at least an hour for Louise to get to the doctor, have Sammy checked out, and arrive home. In the meantime, Tina was going to force herself to enjoy Jamaica.

She almost laughed, realizing how ridiculous that thought sounded. "You can do it," she said aloud, giving herself a mock pep talk. "Make yourself lie down by the private pool. Try to choke down a gourmet dinner. Then work your way up to sleeping in!"

She looked out the window and saw the weather was still freaky; the rain had abruptly stopped—not just tapered off but halted so suddenly it was as if the drops had evaporated between the clouds and the ground. The sun was edging back out.

Tina stood up and flung open the door. "Allie? Van? Where is everybody?"

Chapter Ten

Therese

EVERY TIME PAULINE CLOSED her eyes, she was back in the hospital.

When she walked through the door of Therese's room, her gaze was instantly drawn to the small figure lying on a bed. Therese was dressed in a thin cotton gown, and a blue blanket covered her lower body. Her eyes were shut.

Okay, Pauline thought. *I can do this.*

There were two chairs by Therese's bed, and Pauline took the one farther away. The room was stark white and sterile, as hospital rooms tended to be, but there was something different about this one. After a moment Pauline realized what it was. Every other time she'd visited a patient, they'd been surrounded by personal belongings: family photographs, a pretty bathrobe draped on the end of the bed, greeting cards. Therese wasn't.

She forced herself to look at her sister's face, scanning her wide forehead, her full cheeks, and her small nose. With a start, Pauline realized Therese had a few tiny lines around her eyes. How strange that her body's aging process had continued to march relentlessly ahead while her mind had remained locked in its earliest stage.

Pauline shifted in her chair. She wondered what was happening in Jamaica. Maybe everyone was getting ready to head to the beach . . .

She stole another glance at Therese. Her sister was slightly pudgy—no, that was the wrong word. She looked . . . soft. Her skin was a creamy white, and her hands were almost dainty. Pauline blinked and looked again.

Someone had painted Therese's nails. They'd been filed into smooth ovals and covered with a light pink polish.

It must've been one of her aides, Pauline thought, leaning forward in her chair to get a better view. Care had been taken to coat Therese's nails smoothly and evenly. To make them look pretty. It wasn't the sort of job that would be required, and Pauline wondered why someone had done it.

A sudden, awful sound made her flinch: Therese coughing. Her lungs seemed to be losing the battle to suck in enough air.

Pauline leapt to her feet to get help, but before she could reach the door, a middle-aged nurse hurried into the room. "You can give her some oxygen," the nurse said, reaching for a clear mask that was attached to a machine by thin tubes. She demonstrated how to hold the mask an inch or two away from Therese's face, and soon the raspy-sounding coughing ceased.

"Thank you," Pauline's mother said, reaching for the mask. "Should we hold it all the time? Or just when she needs it?"

"When she needs it," the nurse said. Her expression was compassionate, but her manner was rushed. "And she'll begin to require it more frequently." She checked one of the machines near Therese—there weren't as many as Pauline had expected; just two, including the one supplying oxygen—then left the room.

Pauline and her mother sat together in silence for a while. Now and then, Therese coughed, but the oxygen always eased her breathing.

After a while, someone knocked on the door. Pauline and her mother looked at each other.

"Come in," Pauline finally called.

A man who looked to be in his midfifties stepped in. He wore jeans and a dark blue sweatshirt with white sneakers.

"I'm Carlos," he said, extending his hand.

Pauline's mother rose and reached out to clasp his hand with her own. "Of course," she said. "We met last month, I believe. Thank you for coming."

"I'm Therese's aide," the man said to Pauline. She nodded a greeting and hid her surprise. Her mother hadn't mentioned going to visit Therese last month. She would've gone, too, if she'd known, but she'd been so busy with the charity auction, and planning the vacation . . .

Carlos moved closer to Therese. He was standing on the other side of the bed, and Pauline could see his face clearly. He stared down at Therese for a moment, then closed his eyes. His lips moved, but he didn't make any sound.

He was praying, Pauline realized. She wished she could hear him.

Carlos opened his eyes again and reached down to adjust Therese's blanket, the gesture as natural as if he'd done it dozens of times before. He probably had, Pauline realized with a start.

Then Carlos lifted Therese's right hand and held it between his own. Her eyes stayed closed, and her hand was limp in his much bigger one.

"Would you mind if I sang to her?" he asked.

"Sang?" Pauline's mother asked. "No, I don't mind . . . of course not."

Carlos nodded.

" 'You are my sunshine, my only sunshine,' " he began. His

voice was off-key, but deep and gentle. " 'You make me happy, when skies are gray . . .' "

Pauline didn't realize she was crying until a tear splashed onto her lap.

Carlos finished the song. "It's one of her favorites," he said. "This and 'Twinkle, Twinkle Little Star.' "

Pauline stared at him. "It is?" she whispered. "She has a favorite song? How do you know?"

"She always looks happy when I sing it," Carlos said simply. "She smiles sometimes."

Pauline stood up and fumbled to put her purse's strap over her shoulder. "I'll—I'll be right back," she said.

"Pauline?" her mother called.

But Pauline was already running down the hallway. She tore down three flights of stairs and kept running, past the blond woman at the coffee kiosk in the lobby, through the automatic sliding doors, and down the sidewalk toward the parking garage where she'd left her car just hours ago. A lifetime ago.

Savannah was in the middle of a delicious fantasy about the crewman from the catamaran when her iPhone rang. She sighed and began to roll over in her lounge chair, thinking that maybe a buyer had finally made an offer on the house with the ugly family photos and peeling wallpaper. She'd try to keep her voice professional, even though she was hot, horny, and half-asleep.

Then she recognized the ring tone: Carrie Underwood singing, *"I dug my key into the side of his pretty little souped up four wheel drive, carved my name into his leather seat . . . Maybe next time he'll think before he cheats."*

She stared at the phone for a second before answering with a terse "Yes?"

"Savannah?"

She inhaled quickly, feeling her body tense. She hadn't heard his voice in months.

"What do you want?"

"I'd like to talk."

How typically Gary. No apology, no chitchat—just a simple, declarative sentence. She used to love his directness.

"Really?" She purred, stretching out the word even as her heart began to pound. "And what exactly would you like to talk about, Gary?"

"Savannah, I know I screwed up."

She squeezed her eyes shut. She'd wanted to hear those words so desperately in the weeks after he left. But now? She was too numb to feel vindicated.

"Actually, you screwed your way down," she said. "I know what your girlfriend looks like."

Maybe she shouldn't have given away that particular detail. Gary didn't need to know that she'd lurked by the elevator in the hospital's employee parking lot, waiting to see The Nurse exit after her shift one evening. This, of course, after she'd called the hospital to verify that The Nurse was working (speaking her name aloud was so awful that Savannah had vowed never to do it again). Of course, Savannah had also Googled her and found a few photos on Facebook to confirm she'd be viewing the right woman. She was proud of her investigative prowess, actually.

She could hear Gary sigh. "She's not my girlfriend," he said. "Not anymore."

"Really?" Savannah said. "Now why doesn't that surprise me?"

She couldn't believe how cool she was playing it. Thank God they were talking on the phone and not in person—she knew the expression on her face didn't match her casual tone.

"Please. Can I see you?" he asked. "Just to talk."

"Well, that might be a little difficult," she said. "Since I'm in Jamaica."

"Jamaica?" Gary asked. He paused, and she could almost see him tapping his chin with his index finger as he formulated a Plan B. Gary always could come up with a Plan B, whether they'd gotten lost on the way to a party or been overcharged by a repairman. "Okay, when will you be back? I can come over then."

No. She wasn't going to let him control things. He'd given up that right the day he walked out.

"You really want to talk?" she asked. "Okay, then. I'm available tonight at ten o'clock. I'm afraid that's the only opening I have in my schedule for the foreseeable future."

"Sure," Gary said, sounding puzzled. "I wanted to do it in person, but I guess I could call you back."

"Nope," Savannah said. This was actually fun. Gary had gutted her emotionally, and now she relished the chance to torture him a bit. "If you truly want to talk, you'll be here at ten o'clock."

"In *Jamaica*?"

"We're at a private villa in Negril. It's called Summer Escape."

"But . . . that's in seven hours. I can't get there in seven hours."

"Technically you can," Savannah said. "Unless it's not important enough to you."

"Savannah, look—" Gary began, but she pressed a button to cut off the call.

She lay there for a moment, not believing what had just happened. Then she glanced to her left, where Tina and Allie were sitting bolt upright on their lounge chairs, staring at her.

"No way did you just do that," Tina said.

"Yup," Savannah said.

"You told Gary to come here? Tonight?"

"It appears so," Savannah said. She gave a little laugh.

She couldn't believe how good she felt. When Gary left,

her confidence had been deeply shaken. She knew he was the one with the character flaw, but she couldn't help questioning whether she was smart enough, interesting enough, knowledgeable enough. Gary was brilliant—he could converse about national politics as easily as he could about chemistry or the stock market. But while Savannah had always been savvy and quick, she'd never been a particularly good student. She'd barely squeaked into UVa, and she knew it was only because admissions officials went easier on students who lived in state. Even so, she'd been wait-listed at first. She hated reading the newspaper, other than the gossip columns, and she'd once been deeply embarrassed while playing some silly game at a party when she couldn't point to Ohio on the U.S. map.

But now she was the one with power. Gary wanted her back.

"Savannah, what are you going to *do*?" Allie asked.

"I haven't exactly figured that part out yet," Savannah said.

She was meeting the crewman at ten o'clock, which was probably why she'd blurted out that precise time. She had no idea if Gary would show up or not—he'd have to scramble to get coverage at work, plus find a flight and locate the villa—but she certainly wasn't going to wait around to see if he managed it.

"Um, Savannah?" Tina was saying. "Do you really think Gary's going to come here?"

Savannah smiled and put on her sunglasses. Tina and Allie were freaking out, but for some reason she felt calmer than she'd been in a long time. "We'll just have to wait and see."

Allie stood outside Pauline's room, debating what to do.

The door was cracked, but she couldn't hear any noise from inside. She started to turn away, then Pauline called out, "Is someone there?"

"It's just me. Allie."

"Come in," Pauline said.

Allie pushed open the door, but she didn't step inside.

"Hi," she said. "I'm sorry to bother you. Savannah went down to the beach to tell the guys, but I thought you should know, too, since you're our hostess. There's a chance her husband, Gary, might join us here after all."

Pauline was sitting all the way across the expansive room, in a chair by the open doors to the balcony. She stared at Allie, not responding, and Allie grew so nervous she began to ramble. "It's kind of unclear. He might come tonight . . . but he might not show up, too. I know that sounds sort of nutty . . . Anyway, that's all I wanted to tell you . . ."

Pauline still didn't say anything, and Allie was suddenly seized by an awful thought: *She knows Dwight kissed me.*

Finally, Pauline said, "Okay."

Relief washed over Allie, and she turned to go, but then Pauline called out her name.

"Can you come in for a minute?" Pauline asked. "And close the door behind you."

Uh-oh, Allie thought, but she obeyed. She felt as if she was walking a plank as she took slow steps from the door to the chair opposite Pauline's. Her feet were bare, and the wood underneath them felt cold and unforgiving. She tried to think of an excuse to exit the room, but her mind seemed frozen.

"How's your mom doing?" she blurted, trying to steer the conversation into a safe direction, but Pauline ignored her.

"Can I ask you something?" Pauline said in a voice that was close to a whisper. "Have you ever kept something from your husband? Something big?"

Allie's knees buckled, and she dropped into the matching chair opposite Pauline's. Her mouth was dry.

Luckily, Pauline didn't wait for an answer. "I have." She inhaled and glanced out toward the water. "It's such a beautiful day, isn't it?"

Allie nodded. She was completely confused, but here, at last, was a question she could answer. "It is. It's really beautiful."

"I don't know why I'm telling you this," Pauline said. "But you seem . . . kindhearted. And you're a social worker. So people must tell you their problems all the time."

"They do," Allie said carefully. "But usually they're clients, and there's a kind of structure to it . . . I try to link them with other resources to help them. I'm not like a psychiatrist."

She couldn't remember when she'd felt so intensely uncomfortable. She didn't want to hear Pauline's secret. She didn't even want to be alone with Dwight's wife!

"Still," Pauline said. "You know that everyone is flawed. And that sometimes we do things that hurt others, even if we don't mean to."

"That's true," Allie said quickly. "Most of the time we don't mean to."

"So I think you'd understand," Pauline said.

Allie braced herself—oh, the irony if Pauline confessed an infidelity to her!—but Pauline just asked another of her cryptic questions. "Do you think most people are forgiving?"

"Yes," Allie said. Maybe it was the optimist in her, but she believed that most personal grudges were born out of hurt, not innate hatred, and that many could be resolved.

"I do, too," Pauline said. "At least, I hope so."

Pauline looked older than she had a few days ago, Allie thought suddenly. She'd changed—or something had changed her. She was such a small woman. Her bones were fine and her shoulders were narrow. For a woman with presence, she took up so little physical space.

"I had an abortion," Pauline said. "I was twenty years old. It was during my junior year in college."

Allie nodded and kept her face neutral, even though abortion conjured strong feelings in her. She believed in the importance of allowing women a choice—and yet, she wouldn't exist if her birth mother had listened to the advice of everyone around her. Allie supported a woman's right to choose on a philosophical and legal level, but not on a raw, emotional one.

"Does Dwight know?" she asked.

"No," Pauline said. "I never told him."

They're having trouble getting pregnant, Allie thought suddenly. But Dwight didn't know that Pauline *could* get pregnant—was that why she hadn't brought up going to a fertility specialist? Allie couldn't reveal she knew that highly personal fact, of course. She shifted uncomfortably in her chair.

"Do you think I should tell him?" Pauline said.

"You're the only person who can decide that," Allie said. No way was she getting in the middle of this.

"It's . . . weighing on me," Pauline said. "The secrets we keep from each other. We all have them, you know. Do your best friends know everything about you? Does your husband? I think sometimes we even keep our deepest secrets from ourselves."

She glanced at Allie, and something changed in her eyes. It was almost as if she was surprised to see Allie sitting there. Allie had experienced that before with clients—sometimes, they seemed to feel she was a blank slate to project their thoughts and feelings onto. They didn't always see her as a person.

"I'm sorry," Pauline said. "I don't mean to make you uncomfortable. This is your vacation, after all." She tried to laugh, but the sound was weak and forced.

"Allie?" Tina's voice floated through the hallway, sounding slightly muffled from traveling through the closed door. She must have been checking Allie and Ryan's room next door. "Are you up here?"

"Right here," Allie called loudly. "I'm with Pauline in her room."

Thank God, she thought when she heard a knock a moment later.

"Oh, hi!" Tina said, poking in her head. "Sorry to interrupt . . . I just wanted to let you know the guys are back from the beach and everyone's having happy hour on the patio."

"That sounds great," Allie said as she stood up. She wiped her damp palms on her shorts. "Pauline? Will you come with us?"

Disappointment flitted across Pauline's face, but it disappeared quickly. "Of course," she said. "I'll be there in a minute. Go on ahead."

A tiny part of Allie felt guilty as she hurried out of the room. Pauline was clearly yearning for a heart-to-heart—a chance to spill her secrets and feel the absolution that a confession carried. Allie usually didn't mind the fact that people with problems seemed drawn to her, but right now, she couldn't spare the compassion.

For the first time in her life, she was tired of helping others.

Chapter Eleven

The Attack

MEN WERE IDIOTS, TINA thought as she watched Dwight and Gio slam into each other.

They *could* be relaxing in the hot tub, sipping Kahlúa-spiked mudslides and feeling strong jets untangle the knots that always seemed to form between shoulder blades. But instead, they were grunting and sweating and cursing as they tried, mostly unsuccessfully, to throw a ball through a hoop.

"Barbarians," Savannah said, and Tina grinned.

Ever since their fight, Savannah had been casually friendly with Gio, but she hadn't crossed the line into flirting. That must've been a challenge for Savannah, who could flirt with a rock, Tina mused. And Gio was being extra solicitous, too, keeping his hand on Tina's knee during lunch and bringing her a mudslide while she sat in the hot tub. He'd barely even looked at Savannah. They were forgiven, both of them, Tina decided. Just as long as nothing like it ever happened again.

But the incident had made Tina realize how long it had been since she'd had a harmless little crush on anyone. When she and Gio were first married and she was working at Children's Hospital, there was a physical therapist named Steven whom

Tina loved talking to—he was funny and energetic and kept her spirits high whenever she bumped into him during a rough shift. They'd eat lunch together every few weeks, and Steven would talk about the various women he was dating. The tingle of attraction was never mentioned—until the holiday party when Steven had too much to drink.

"No!" she'd said, putting a hand on his chest to push him away when he tried to kiss her.

Tina didn't want to make out with him—she just enjoyed knowing someone other than her husband found her attractive. Oh, how she missed that sensation! But these days, the only males she came into contact with were pimply teenage baggers at the grocery store who committed the ultimate offense of calling her "ma'am." Even her UPS delivery person was a woman, which seemed completely unfair, considering the TV ads that all but promised hot guys with good legs.

She took another sip of her mudslide and sighed as she sank deeper into the bubbling water, feeling the last bit of tension seep out of her limbs. The doctor had diagnosed Sammy with a minor stomach flu, and Allie's mom reported that after a lime Popsicle and a few viewings of *Sesame Street*, he seemed to be rallying. Everything was fine. Better than fine.

Except . . . her eyes flitted toward the basketball court again, and she frowned. Gio was bumping Dwight repeatedly with his chest, harder than seemed necessary. Dwight's body rocked backward with each blow. But Dwight was about six inches taller than Gio, and he managed to shoot the ball through the air, just out of reach of Gio's straining fingertips.

"Damn!" Gio said as the ball swished through the hoop.

"What's the score? Eight–four?" Dwight asked.

"Rub it in," Gio said.

"Your macho man doesn't like to lose," Savannah observed.

"Tell me about it," Tina said, keeping her voice light. But the conversation she'd had with Allie came back to her: Was Gio resentful that Dwight could afford trips like this one, while Gio could barely manage to take his family to a cheap motel at the shore every summer?

She took another sip of her drink and kept her eyes on the basketball court. Ryan had left his shirt down on the beach and had gone to get it. He seemed to be taking a really long time. She wished he'd get back and join the game.

"That makes eleven," Dwight said as he shot another basket.

"Ten!" Gio argued. "You were nowhere near the three-point line!"

"Yes I was!" Dwight said.

"Whatever," Gio said. "You want to play that way? Fine."

Tina set down her drink on the hot tub's ledge and sat up straighter.

On the next play, Gio crashed into Dwight, knocking him to the ground, then went in under the basket for a layup.

"Eleven–six," Gio said, grinning.

Dwight got up without a word, moving slowly and rubbing his knee, and Gio bounced the ball to him. Dwight moved in to make a shot, and Gio smashed him again, landing on top of Dwight as Dwight fell to the ground.

"Stop fouling him!"

Everyone turned to look at Allie, who was standing up in the hot tub. Her fists were clenched at her sides, and water dripped off her body.

"Gio, you're acting like a big bully!" she yelled. "Just knock it off!"

"A bully?" Gio said. He was still pinning Dwight to the ground.

"Get *off* him!" Allie shouted.

Gio looked down, seeming almost surprised to find Dwight underneath him. He stood and extended a hand, helping Dwight up.

"Why don't we take a break for a while," Gio said to Dwight. He reached out his palm and slapped Dwight's, which was the closest Gio would get to an apology, Tina knew. Her husband had a temper, and yes, he could be immature at times. But he was also deeply sensitive to criticism, and she knew Allie's words had wounded him, especially since Allie was usually the peacemaker in the group.

Gio walked over to the cooler to grab a beer while Dwight pulled off his shirt and dove into the pool.

"Allie Cat, you've gotten feisty lately, haven't you?" Savannah observed.

Allie sat back down. "I guess so," she said. "It just bugged me, seeing that. Dwight's being really nice by having us all here and it was just a stupid game and Gio was . . . well, he was act-ing like an idiot just then. Sorry, Tina."

Tina smiled at her. "It's okay. He does get a little worked up sometimes. I was about to say something, too."

Dwight pulled himself out of the pool and sat on the edge, kicking his feet in the water. Tina looked back and forth from Allie to Dwight, but she didn't say anything more.

"Are you guys up for karaoke later?" Savannah asked. "We've barely used Pauline's machine."

"Sure," Tina said. "But don't forget you invited a guest for tonight."

"Have you heard back from him?" Allie asked.

Savannah shook her head. "Nope. Either he shows up, or he doesn't. I'll find out soon enough."

"What if he begs you to take him back?" Allie asked. "Would you?"

"Hell no," Savannah said.

"Good," Tina said. "I think it would be impossible to trust him again."

"So what's your plan if he does show up?" Allie asked.

"I'll hear what he has to say," Savannah said. "Then I'll smile and tell him to leave."

"It's kind of mean, making him come all this way just for that," Tina said. "I love it."

"He deserves it," Savannah said. "I saw something on Facebook about a woman who took out a billboard in New York City to publicly chew out her cheating husband and let everyone know he wasn't exactly well-endowed—*and* she put it on his credit card."

"Wow," Allie said. "Gary's getting off easy."

Allie seemed back to herself now, Tina noticed. Her brief episode of anger toward Gio had passed. Gio was lounging on a chair a few feet away from the hot tub, sneaking occasional glances at the women. Clearly he had been shocked by Allie's outburst, and he was acting chastised. It was strange that Allie was ignoring him. She knew Gio well, and understood that he had a great heart beneath his tough exterior.

Funny, Tina mused as she took another sip of the cold, sweet mudslide, but Allie—the most even-keeled woman in the universe—had gotten seriously angry twice on this trip, and both times it had revolved around Dwight.

"Don't you wish we could stay here forever?" Allie was asking, tilting her head back and letting the tips of her hair dip into the hot tub's water as she looked up at the sky. The sun was braiding crimson into the blue as it set.

"Stay forever with two other chicks in a hot tub? Not that I don't love you guys, but I'd only do it if one of you morphed into a lightly oiled Ryan Gosling," Savannah said. "Wasn't Pauline working on arranging that, by the way?"

Allie splashed her. "You know what I mean, silly. We're all together, and this trip is so amazing. I don't want it to end."

"Amen to that, sister," Tina said.

"So let's do it every year," Savannah said. "I mean, not like *this,* of course. But we could get together for a long weekend in South Carolina or something. Maybe rent a house in Hilton Head."

"I'd love it," Tina said. Maybe in another year, when the kids were older, it would be easier to get away. She could try to figure out a way to save money, maybe put aside a little bit every week.

"No, let's promise to do it," Allie said. She reached out and gripped Tina's and Savannah's hands. "It's too easy to let good intentions slip by . . . look at how many years have already passed since college! Before we know it, it'll be too late . . . We have to vow that we're going to make it happen."

"Okay," Savannah said. "I'm in."

"Tina?" Allie turned to look at her. "Please?"

"Of course," Tina said. She frowned. "Allie? You're kind of hurting my hand. Is everything okay?"

But before Allie could answer, Ryan came up the steps from the beach. His shirt was torn and he was breathing hard.

He stared at them, his eyes wide. "I just got mugged," he said.

Chapter Twelve

Waiting

AFTER PAULINE HAD RUN out of Therese's hospital room, she'd found her Mercedes and pulled out of the parking lot, tossing a twenty-dollar bill at the attendant and speeding off without her change.

There was a big store with a silly name that she'd passed dozens of times on Rockville Pike, and she needed to get there now . . . it wasn't far from Sibley Hospital.

It wasn't quite ten a.m., late enough that rush hour had passed and the streets were relatively quiet. Pauline pulled up at a red light, looked around for incoming traffic and cops, then ran it.

She made it to the store moments before it opened and stood by the big glass doors while a sleepy-looking employee, a young guy with long dreadlocks, unlocked them. She stepped inside and looked around, blinking in the fluorescent lights, then grabbed a cart and began to load it, piling in tiny washcloths shaped like ducks and lavender-scented lotion. A CD player and a few CDs. Soft blankets in pink and yellow patterns. A mobile with brightly painted wooden animals dangling from its wires.

Everything was so clean and bright in here. The store seemed to promise that if you just bought this gadget or that outfit, you'd be guaranteed a perfect child. Pauline wondered if her mother had shopped at a place like this before Therese was born, dreaming about playing peekaboo with the child she was carrying. Maybe she'd bought one of those baby books with pages to document each accomplishment: the first time Baby crawled, the first words, the first steps . . . If so, all the pages must have remained blank.

More customers were in the store now—obviously pregnant women along with a few husbands—and Pauline veered past them as she raced through more aisles, filling her cart, then hurried to the blessedly empty checkout line and began unloading everything onto the counter.

"Sorry, but do you mind if I ask . . . ?"

Pauline turned to look at a woman standing in line behind her. The woman was dark-haired, probably in her midforties, and very slim. She wore jeans and a white oxford shirt and a tentative smile.

"Are you adopting, too?"

"Adopting?" Pauline repeated, as if she'd never heard the word.

The woman took a step back. "I'm sorry. I'm adopting a little girl from China. We're going there next month. I just thought . . . Every other time I've been in here, all the other women seem to be pregnant and you're buying everything . . ." Her cheeks were turning pink.

Pauline turned back around without a word and continued unloading her cart. She knew the woman meant no harm, but she didn't have time to talk. She swiped her Visa card and accepted two bags from the cashier, then ran to her car and threw the bags into the backseat.

As she sped toward the hospital, she glanced at her watch: She'd been gone for only twenty minutes.

Wait a little longer, Therese, she thought. *Please wait for me.*

"There were two of them," Ryan said. He took a long sip of Red Stripe beer and settled back in his chair.

"There wasn't anyone else around, which is why I decided to walk down the beach in the first place," he continued. "Just kinda spur of the moment, because it was so nice out. I'd gotten about a half mile away, to that little bend in the coastline, you know? As I come around it, I see these guys leaning over and looking at something in the sand. They're kind of far off, but they keep gesturing and acting all excited, and I decide to go see what's so interesting."

Ryan paused while the waiter removed his dinner plate.

"So I get closer, and one of the guys calls out to me, 'Come look at this!' And I walk up to them."

"Guess you found out what was so interesting to them," Gio said. "A rich tourist."

"One of them had a knife," Ryan said. "I didn't even see it until the other one grabbed me from behind."

"Jesus." Allie closed her eyes, as if to shut out the image.

"They wanted my wallet, but I wasn't carrying it. So I took off my watch to distract them, because they looked really pissed off. But instead of handing it to the guy with the knife, I tossed it a few feet to his left, like it was a bad throw."

"That was so smart! What made you think to do that?" Tina asked. Her eyes were fixed on Ryan, even though it was the third time she'd heard the story. Ryan had recounted it by the hot tub, but he'd rushed through the telling. He'd called the police, too, and had answered their questions over the phone. They were

coming by to take a report later, but Ryan said they didn't seem
in any hurry once they'd ascertained that no one had been hurt.
Now that his shock had passed, he seemed to be relishing drawing out the story.

"My natural superhero instincts," he said. "Okay, so I saw
someone do it on TV once. This cop show. Anyway, both guys
went to reach down for the watch, and that was when I jerked
away. One of them grabbed hold of my shirt, but it tore and I
got away. Man, did I fly down that beach. Usain Bolt couldn't
have caught me."

"Did they chase you?" Tina asked.

"Nah," Ryan said. "I turned back to look, but they were already gone."

"Well, I'm glad you're safe," Tina said. "It's so scary to think
something like that could happen!"

The waiter had finished circling the table, refilling everyone's
glasses, and now he brought out a pie for dessert.

"Lemon-raspberry," he said as he set down the generous
slices. "Served warm, with homemade vanilla bean ice cream."

"Pouf! And there goes the hour I spent on the StairMaster in
the gym this morning," Savannah said.

"Oh, my God . . ." Tina moaned around a mouthful. "I could
write a poem about this crust!"

"Really?" Savannah said. "The only poem I know by heart is
about the guy from Nantucket. Is yours along the same lines?"

Ryan snorted. "Come on, Tina! Now you've gotta tell us your
poem," he said.

But it was Savannah who spoke up: "There once was a pie
from Nantucket." She grinned and held up her fork. "It was so
good on my fork I could suck it . . ."

Dwight's voice cut into everyone's laughter. "How did those
guys know you'd be coming down the beach alone right at that
precise time?" he asked. "You said they were already looking at

something when you came around the bend into view, right?"

Everyone turned to look at him.

"I never thought of that," Allie said. "It's almost like they were . . . waiting for you."

"Oh, my God," Tina breathed. Her fork clattered onto her plate. "You don't think they were watching the house, do you?"

"No," Dwight said, shaking his head. "That part of the beach is public. Anyone could be walking on it. More likely, they had a lookout hiding behind a palm tree who signaled them . . . or maybe they saw you walking that way and they ran ahead."

"Maybe," Ryan said. He frowned. "I didn't think of it until just now, but there was something on the sand near them. A pair of binoculars. Funny the things you notice at times like that."

"Ah," Dwight said. "That explains it. They could see you long before you saw them."

Savannah savored one final forkful of dessert, then forced herself to push away her plate. She could've eaten the entire pie, but she'd hate herself in the morning. For dinner, the chef had served seared sea diver scallops so tender her fork cut through them like butter, along with a sweet potato soufflé garnished with caramelized onions. But the bread was what was killing her—tonight's was a crusty, fragrant rosemary spiked with sea salt. Served still warm from the oven, it was irresistible.

At least she'd work off some of the calories with the young crewman, she thought, glancing at her watch. She was surprised to note that it was later than she'd expected—a few minutes before nine. They'd settled into a European rhythm on this vacation; a slow start to the morning, siesta in the early afternoon, a late dinner . . .

Savannah drained her wineglass.

"That was fabulous," she said. "I need to go freshen up, but I can't bring myself to move."

"This should help energize you," Tina said, laughing as she refilled Savannah's wineglass.

"Women sure do a lot of freshening up," Ryan observed.

"It must be because they're more naturally stinky than men," Gio said, and Tina swatted him with her napkin.

Savannah was a little nervous about walking alone after what had happened to Ryan, but she'd be safe, she told herself. Mr. Red Bathing Suit would be waiting for her. Still, maybe she should let Allie and Tina know where she was going, just in case. And she'd bring her cell phone. Her Match.com date's psycho eyes floated into her mind, and she shuddered.

Unless . . . Savannah frowned. What if the crewman blew her off? He was young and gorgeous and probably had women fighting over him. Maybe he'd met some teenage nymph in the last couple days and had decided to spend tonight with her instead.

Savannah dismissed the notion. Gary must've done a bigger number on her than she'd thought if she was doubting herself this way. Mr. Red Bathing Suit *was* interested—it couldn't have been more obvious on the boat.

"You know what? I wonder if your watch is still there," Gio was saying.

"You think?" Ryan asked.

"They wanted a wallet stuffed with cash; they wouldn't carry around a watch you could identify in case the cops stopped them. And they had to have known you would've phoned in a description of them within minutes of getting away," Gio said. "They were pros."

"Yeah, I can see that," Ryan said. "So you think they just tossed it?"

"It was that waterproof watch you've been wearing all week, right?" Gio said. "Those things are a dime a dozen, especially

on an island. Now if it had been a"—he gestured to Dwight—
"Rolex, they would've kept it. Worth the risk."

Savannah looked back and forth at Dwight and Gio, compar-
ing them, just as she had on that drunken night when they'd
all gone swimming in their underwear. Their minds worked so
differently, she thought. Dwight was drawn to the almost academic problem of how the crime had been executed, while Gio
was interested in the practical aftermath of how to minimize
the damage.

"We should go check," Gio said.

"No," Tina said. "It's not safe."

"Three of us guys, two of them," Gio said. "Besides, they're
long gone."

"So you and Dwight and Ryan think you're going to take
on knife-wielding thugs to get back a cheap watch?" Allie said.
"Forget it."

"You probably wouldn't be able to find the watch in the dark,
even if it was there," Tina said.

"And no one else is going to find it tonight, either," Allie said.
"Going would be foolish."

"Do you think maybe the wives don't want us to go?" Ryan
asked. "Just a hunch."

"Call me a psychic, but I'm kind of getting that vague sense,"
Gio said.

Tina rolled her eyes. "What's the plan for tonight? Savannah?"

"Why are you looking at me?" Savannah asked. "I'm just sitting here not talking about going after the watch."

"Because you're the one who's usually after us to party at
night," Tina said. "And you're the one who may or may not have
a surprise visitor."

"If Gary shows up, do you want some time alone with him?"
Allie asked. "Or should we all sit around and glare at him?"

"Come on, he's not going to show up," Savannah said. "Even if he's not working tonight, it'd be really hard to get a flight on such short notice."

"I bet he comes," Tina said.

"Nah, he's too chicken to face all of us after what he did," Gio said.

"Oh, he'll be here," Ryan said. "Tail between his legs."

Savannah flinched—did Allie and Tina have to tell their husbands *all* the details behind her separation?—but she recovered quickly.

"So two yeses and one no," she said.

"I'm with Gio," Allie said. "I doubt he'll come. Not because you aren't worth it, but I bet he thinks that if you're willing to talk to him here, you'll be willing to do it at home. So I think he'll wait."

"Dwight? Want to cast the tie-breaking vote?" Savannah asked. "Or Pauline?"

Weird; she'd almost forgotten Pauline was there. Their hostess had barely said anything the entire night. It seemed like the others had forgotten her presence, too; everyone suddenly turned to look at Pauline. But she didn't answer Savannah's question.

Tina's brow wrinkled. "Pauline? Is everything okay with your mom?"

Pauline looked up and met Tina's eyes. "She's fine," Pauline said. "A little . . . tired, but that's to be expected."

"Are you sure?" Tina pressed. "Because I can tell you're still worried. And if there's one thing I learned working in the hospital, it's that our instincts can warn us when something is wrong."

"Should we send someone to check on her?" Dwight asked. "A visiting nurse? Or I could get a doctor there. Tonight, even."

Pauline was looking down at her plate and blinking. "No, no," she said. "But . . . thank you."

"You sure?" Dwight said softly, but Pauline just shook her head.

There was a brief pause, then Allie changed the subject. "What were we talking about? Oh, right. Dwight, what's your guess—is Gary coming?"

"I think the better question is, Does Savannah want him to come?" Dwight asked.

"Ah," Savannah said. Since when had Dwight gotten so sensitive? she wondered. The stutter that had plagued him during college seemed to have mostly disappeared, too. Maybe all of his success had cured it.

"Well, yes, I'd like for him to come," Savannah said in a soft voice, looking down. She pretended to wipe away a tear. Then she looked up and flashed a wicked grin. "So I can send his ass back home. But Gio and Allie are right. He won't come."

She wasn't going to sit around anticipating his arrival. She wouldn't even be back from the beach when he showed up.

If he showed up, she reminded herself, hating the way her heart betrayed her and sped up at the thought of walking in the door to find Gary here. But of course she had complicated feelings about him. They'd been married for seven years. Maybe seeing him one last time would be what she needed to finally wipe away the thoughts of him for good.

Chapter Thirteen

Passion

"WHERE DID EVERYONE GO?" Allie asked. "It seems like the house emptied out all of a sudden."

"Well, Tina's right there," Dwight said, motioning to a sofa in the living room. Tina was curled up, her head resting on a cushion and her long curls covering most of her face. She was snoring softly. Allie and Dwight exchanged a smile.

Poor Tina, Allie thought as she walked over to remove her friend's shoes and cover her with the chenille throw from the back of the couch. Tina might be mad that she'd missed out on the night's fun, but she needed to catch up on her sleep.

"And Savannah has . . . other plans for the next hour or so," Allie said.

She could hardly believe that Savannah was meeting the guy from the catamaran on the beach, but Allie certainly wasn't in a position to judge. At least Savannah and the guy were both single. "She said she'd be back by eleven or so. But Ryan and Gio . . . where are they, anyway? In the game room?"

Dwight shook his head. "They went down to the beach. To look for Ryan's watch."

Fury enveloped Allie. Her husband had lied to her. She'd

told Ryan not to go, and he'd acted like he wouldn't! He was a fool; he was risking his life to save face with Gio. He made such horrible choices—how could he ever handle taking care of the girls alone if it came to that? She felt so distant from her husband. He kept failing her, again and again.

"Pauline's resting in our room," Dwight was saying.

"Is she okay?" Allie asked. "She's acting strange."

"I don't know," Dwight said. "I'm not sure if she's going to come back out tonight."

"Should we go out to the pool again? We can talk more there," Allie said.

She and Dwight stepped outside and, as if by unspoken agreement, walked around to the far side of the patio. The little waterfall at the edge of the pool made enough noise to cover the sound of their voices, and although the stars shone brightly in the clear sky, it was dark enough that Allie and Dwight couldn't be easily seen from the house unless someone knew they were there.

"I'm not sure what's wrong with Pauline," Dwight said.

"You don't think she knows about . . . what happened between us on the beach, do you?" Allie asked.

"No," Dwight shook his head. "That's impossible." But he frowned.

"Have you asked her what's wrong?" Allie asked.

"About ten times. She keeps saying she has a headache." He looked away from Allie, toward the door. "Maybe I should go check again . . ."

Jealousy twisted Allie's stomach so sharply she almost felt ill. "I'm sure she's sleeping," she said quickly. "I bet she's completely drained. I saw her rubbing her temples earlier. Sleep would be the best thing for her. You shouldn't bother her."

"You're probably right," Dwight said, but his voice still held doubt.

Who was she becoming? Allie wondered with more awe than alarm. She hadn't seen Pauline rubbing her temples; she'd lied about that to manipulate Dwight. To keep him with her, so she wouldn't have to be alone with the terrifying thoughts she found harder and harder to keep at bay.

Allie looked back up at Dwight. He was glancing toward the house again, and she couldn't see the expression in his eyes. She didn't want Dwight thinking about his wife. She needed him more.

"Follow me," she said. She stood up and walked to the edge of the patio, then stepped into the yard. There was a cluster of palm trees ahead, past the spotlights that illuminated the flowers surrounding the patio. Passionflowers, Allie remembered Savannah calling them.

Allie looked around once, to make sure that no one was coming up the steps from the beach and that Tina and Pauline were still inside. Then she moved behind a tree and pulled Dwight closer to her. She reached up and wound her arms around his neck, sighing as his warm mouth moved down to cover hers, and everything else finally, blessedly, disappeared.

Tap . . . tap . . . tap.

One of the kids was jabbing her in the shoulder, trying to wake her up, but Tina didn't move. After all, sometimes playing dead worked for possums when predators targeted them.

Tap. *Oh, leave me alone!* she thought. She was so tired.

Tap. God, this was like Chinese water torture. "Come on in," she murmured, lifting up one edge of her covers and waiting for the kid to snuggle up.

"Tina?"

She felt as if the voice was pulling her out of a deep, dark well. She blinked a few times, then yawned. She was completely disoriented until she remembered she was in Jamaica instead of in her queen-size bed at home.

"Is Savannah here?"

Suddenly Tina was wide awake.

"I won the bet," she said.

Gary peered down at her, and she almost laughed. He looked so ridiculous, in his fancy gray suit and white shirt and red tie, like he was a politician off to woo voters at a rally. Actually, that wasn't too far from the truth, she realized. He was definitely going after a second term.

"What time is it?" Tina asked.

"Ten-fifteen," Gary said without looking at his watch.

She'd been asleep for only a half hour or so. It had felt much longer.

"Impressive," Tina said, sitting up and running a hand through her hair. "You really made it here."

"It wasn't easy," Gary said. He lifted a shoulder. "Or cheap."

"Did you check her room?" Tina asked.

"I don't know which one is hers," Gary said.

"Right," Tina said. She stood up. "Follow me."

She smoothed her skirt and ran her index fingers under her eyes to swipe away any wayward traces of mascara. Being around Gary made her feel a bit frumpy—he was one of those guys who always had creases in his slacks, and she suspected he even had his eyebrows waxed. They'd been much bushier when she first met him, verging into unibrow territory.

"Here we go," Tina said, gesturing to Savannah's door, which was open.

Gary poked his head into the room. "Van?" he called, but there was no answer. The bathroom door was open, but the light was off. It was clear the space was empty.

Tina's eyes were drawn toward the bed, where a few pairs of

lacy panties and a black sheer teddy were laid out, as if Savannah had been debating which to wear.

Was Savannah putting on sexy lingerie for *Gary's* benefit? Tina wondered, remembering her friend's tough talk about sending her ex back home.

"Where else could she be?" Gary asked, a touch of impatience in his voice, and Tina suddenly was reminded of why she'd never liked him. Tina knew doctors had a reputation for being arrogant, but the ones she'd worked with rarely hewed to that stereotype. Most of them were busy, sleep-deprived, and had to turn off their emotions in order to do their jobs effectively. But Gary was an ass, out of the operating room and in it, too, she suspected.

"I have no idea," she said sweetly. "I was asleep, remember?"

"I guess I'll put my bag here," Gary said, setting his overnight case on the floor by the bedroom door.

Ruh-roh, Tina thought. That would definitely piss off Savannah. "Great idea," she said, hiding a smile.

She turned around and walked back to the living room as Gary silently followed. Dwight was now sitting in a chair adjoining the couch where she'd been napping.

"Have you been studying at Hogwarts?" she asked. "I swear you weren't here ninety seconds ago. You must have apparated."

Dwight just blinked at her.

"Hi," Gary said, crossing the room in a few long strides and sticking out his hand. "I'm Gary McGrivey. Savannah's husband."

Tina turned her laugh into a cough. Gary truly had no idea what he was in for if he thought one extravagant gesture could erase the months of pain he'd caused Savannah and he could just go back to being her husband.

"Dwight Glass," Dwight said, standing up. The two men were almost the exact same height. "We've met a few times."

"Of course, I remember," Gary said.

Liar, thought Tina.

"So where is everyone else?" she asked.

Allie came through the door from the kitchen, exhibiting the perfect timing of an actress waiting for her cue. "Hey, guys," she said, "would you mind coming in here for a second? The chef wants to talk to us . . . Oh, my gosh! Gary! When did you get here? I didn't even hear a car pull up."

Something was off in Allie's reaction, Tina thought. She seemed to be trying too hard to convey surprise. But there was no way she could have known Gary was coming. Tina shook her head to clear it; Allie was probably just worried that Gary's presence might mar the trip for everyone and her voice was revealing her strain.

"I just got in a couple minutes ago," Gary said. "I took a cab from the airport. Nice to see you again."

"You, too," Allie said, then she blushed, as if the words had escaped without her permission.

"Wow, this is some place," Gary said, glancing around.

"What were you saying about the chef?" Tina asked.

"He's worried about the storm," Allie said. "He's been through a few hurricanes before . . ."

"Wait, it's a *hurricane* now?" Tina asked.

Allie nodded. "They upgraded it from a tropical storm a couple hours ago. They still don't expect it to hit us, but—"

"No one can predict this stuff," Gary interrupted. "It could swing around at the last second."

"Crap," Tina breathed. "When is it due?"

"Not for at least twenty-four hours," Allie said. "Patrick has the Weather Channel on in the kitchen."

Gary turned and strode into the kitchen and, after catching Allie's eyes and rolling her own in Gary's direction, Tina followed.

The chef had clearly been prepping for breakfast the next morning: an empty egg carton, a gallon of milk, and small bowls of cheeses and herbs were scattered on the counters.

"This is no good," he said, shaking his head.

"It looks like the wind is going to carry it north of us," Dwight said, watching the swirling colors on the television screen. The bright reds and blues made the image seem like something a preschooler might've finger-painted.

"I have a family," Patrick said as he began to untie his apron. "Three kids. I need to go to them. I quit."

"You're leaving?" Gary asked. "Seriously?"

Allie frowned at him and stepped forward to put her hand on the chef's shoulder. "It's okay," she said. "Go take care of your family. And don't worry—we won't tell your boss you left. It's only a few more meals, and we can easily cook them."

Patrick nodded. "Thank you. Get somewhere safe, okay?"

"If the hurricane changes course, we will," Allie said. "But I think we'll be fine."

"Check the house for plywood," he said. "You need to board up the windows and secure the awnings if you're going to try to stay here."

"Seriously?" Gary asked again.

"Better be safe," Patrick said. By now he'd taken off his apron, neatly folded it, and removed his poufy hat. Without it, he looked younger than Allie had thought. "Go inland, is my advice. We lost so many in Hurricane Gilbert. One of my uncles was among them. He was standing on a cliff and the storm surge swept him away."

"We'll move away from the water if it starts to get bad," Allie said.

Patrick began to reply, then glanced out the window over the sink. "My wife is here to bring me home," he said. "Goodbye."

There was silence in the kitchen after he left. Allie finally broke it.

"I'm sorry, Dwight," she said. "It wasn't my place to tell him that he could go . . . It's just . . ."

"He has children and you knew he was worried about them," Dwight finished for her. "It's okay. You were right to tell him to go take care of them."

Allie smiled at Dwight, then looked at the mess on the counter.

"You know what?" she said. "This is the most beautiful kitchen I've ever seen, and I feel like cooking. Who wants to help?"

"Sure," Tina said. She reached into a bowl of herbs and took out a pinch. "Parsley," she said, sniffing. "I can't remember the last time I cooked with fresh parsley. Looks like all we need is a loaf of bread and we can assemble these suckers."

"You know what he was going to make?" Dwight asked, wrinkling his forehead.

"Breakfast casseroles," Tina said, sniffing the contents of another bowl. "Mmm . . . dried mustard. You layer in the ingredients, and let them blend together overnight. My mom used to make them every Christmas. Dwight, do you want to beat the eggs?"

"Um, sure?" Dwight said. He opened a few drawers, finally finding the one containing teaspoons. Tina stifled a smile, removed the teaspoon from his hand, and replaced it with a whisk. Allie began greasing the casserole pans with butter as Tina soaked the bread in a mixture of milk and eggs.

"Oh, I miss cooking." Tina sighed. "After this I'll rummage through the fridge and see what I can put together for dinner tomorrow night."

"I'll help," Allie said. "It's Dwight's birthday. We'll make him something delicious."

"That's right!" Tina said. "I make an awesome birthday cake. Well, if you like Batman themes."

Dwight laughed. "I've never had a superhero cake, but I always secretly wanted one."

"Just for that, you might get Robin on your cake, too," Tina said. "I only do that trick for special occasions. I'll just need extra icing, but we can make that. This kitchen seems to be stocked with everything."

"Mind if I grab a glass of wine?" Gary asked, selecting a bottle of red from the counter and examining the label.

"Why don't you pour us all a glass?" Tina asked. She watched as Gary lifted the wine bottle with his long, thin fingers and suddenly felt grateful for Gio. She got annoyed with her husband so often lately, but she loved him deeply. She loved the way he wrestled with the kids and put a blanket over his head and chased them through the house, pretending to be a monster. She loved the way his eyes told her she was beautiful, even when she had baby spit-up on her shirt. The way he always wanted her.

This vacation had given her the gift of a glimpse into their shared future: lazy mornings when she and Gio would linger in bed; evenings when they'd finally sit down together to a real dinner, times when they'd watch the sunset and realize their hands had found each other's.

If they could just make it through the next few years, she thought as she blended the spices into the egg mixture. When Sammy was in full-day kindergarten, she could go back to work. The wonderful thing about nursing was that she could do three twelve-hour shifts a week—maybe even overnight shifts, from seven p.m. to seven a.m.—and it would count as full-time. The extra income would be such a relief. And, thought Tina, so would it be to get to talk to adults again, to engage her brain, to wear work clothes. She and Gio just had to keep scrambling until then, and try to avoid murdering each other in the process.

"So where is Savannah?" Gary asked. "Does anyone know?"

"I, ah, think she's down on the beach with the guys," Allie said. "Ryan and Gio were going to take a walk. She probably joined them."

"Maybe I should go look for them," Gary said.

Tina looked down at his shiny wingtips. "Might want to change your shoes first."

"Oh, she'll probably be back any minute," Allie said. "And I don't know which way they went . . . You might miss her."

Gary shrugged and poured another inch of wine into his glass. "She told me to be here at ten, so . . ."

And you vowed to her that you wouldn't screw other women, Tina thought. *So you both made oopsies!*

". . . knew we'd find it . . . right where I thought . . ." Gio's muted voice filtered into the room.

"Guys?" Tina called out. "We're in the kitchen!"

The door swung open a moment later, and Gio and Ryan came in. Ryan was holding something aloft in his right hand.

"We got the watch!" he said. "They just left it there on the sand, right where I threw it."

"Well, congratulations," Allie said in a tight voice, but her comment was almost lost in the guys' exclamations of surprise upon spotting Gary.

"Hey!" Gio almost shouted, just as Ryan said, "You made it."

Gary nodded. "That I did," he said. "It only took two flights and a thousand bucks."

"Can I give you a tip?" Tina said. "You probably shouldn't complain about that to Savannah."

Gary looked taken aback, and Tina felt a little thrill of victory. As angry as she'd been at Savannah earlier this week, their bond had only gotten stronger since then. Savannah had made her laugh, had gotten her to dance, and encouraged her to feel young again. It would have been a different trip without her— not as much fun.

"Is she coming?" Gary asked, looking at Gio.

"Are you asking me?" Gio replied, a furrow forming between his eyebrows.

"Wait, I'm confused . . . wasn't she with you?"

"Nope."

"But I thought you said . . ." Gary looked at Allie, who suddenly seemed very busy examining the contents of her wineglass.

"Gary, why don't you pour the guys a drink?" Tina said. "Allie, can you come here for a second?"

She pulled Allie into the living room. "What the hell's going on?" she hissed.

"Savannah's having sex with that guy from the catamaran right now," Allie whispered.

"*What?*" Tina stared at her, then burst into laughter. "When did she tell you she was going to do that?"

"Right before she left," Allie said. "You were asleep."

"So what should we do with Gary?" Tina asked.

"I guess just let him wait for her," Allie said.

"Okay," Tina said. "So . . . we'll go finish making breakfast. Oh, and congrats on not bursting into laughter when Gary asked if Savannah was coming."

"Tina!" Allie squealed and whacked her friend on the bottom.

"This is going to be good," Tina said, heading back into the kitchen. She looked at Allie and smiled. "And to think the Weather Channel said we weren't going to get a hurricane here."

Chapter Fourteen

Good-byes

AFTER PAULINE'S TRIP TO Buy Buy Baby, she'd discovered the spot she'd vacated in the hospital's parking lot was still open, so she'd reclaimed it. Her arms laden with bags, she'd retraced her route through the lobby.

Her worst fear—that Therese would have drawn her final breath while Pauline was gone—wasn't realized. Nothing in the room had changed, except that Carlos had left.

"Pauline?" her mother said, getting to her feet as Pauline hurried into the room with the bags. "Where did you— What's all this?"

"I wanted to do something for her," Pauline whispered as she placed the bags on a table. She looked at her mother, willing her to understand. "I just . . . I wanted to make her happy . . ."

Her mother sat back down and watched as Pauline unloaded the CD player and CDs. She unwrapped the packaging on a CD, using her nails to tear apart the plastic, then inserted it into the disc holder and plugged in the machine. A sweet, acoustic version of "Mary Had a Little Lamb" filled the room.

Pauline found the soft pink teddy bear at the bottom of one of the bags and approached the bed. Had she ever touched her sister before? she wondered. She must have, but she couldn't recall a single instance. She'd always felt as if a glass wall was separating them. Now she lifted Therese's arm, surprised at how warm her skin felt, and carefully tucked the teddy bear beneath it.

She reached for the pink bottle of Johnson's baby lotion and squeezed some between her hands, then rubbed them together briskly to warm the lotion. She started with Therese's left arm, the one she had already touched. She rubbed gently, holding her sister's forearm with one hand and massaging in the lotion with the other. She hoped Therese could feel her touch and was comforted by it, but she wasn't sure: Therese didn't move or open her eyes.

Her skin was so perfect, Pauline thought. Of course, she had never burned it on a hot stove while cooking pasta or scratched it while falling off a bike. She'd never sunbathed on the beach with a group of girlfriends, giggling and confessing the names of their crushes.

Pauline heard a rustling noise behind her, and she looked back to see her mother moving aside a bag to get to the stack of blankets on the table. Her mother chose a pink, silky throw and untied the ribbon that made it look like a present.

"Here," her mother said, coming over to stand next to Pauline. "Let's cover her with this."

Together they removed the awful hospital blanket, and Pauline's mother tucked it in a corner of the room.

"Did you want to hang this up?" her mother said, walking back over to the table and holding up the mobile.

"If we can find a place," Pauline said.

"There," Pauline's mother said, pointing to the open bathroom door. "We can use the hook for the robes."

The little room felt so much nicer now, Pauline thought as

she straightened the line holding one of the mobile's dangling wooden animals. The colors, the music . . . It didn't matter whether Therese opened her eyes; she still deserved this.

Pauline walked back to the bed and reached for Therese's arm again. She looked up in surprise when her mother picked up the bottle of lotion Pauline had left at the foot of the bed and began working on Therese's other arm.

"I didn't know you went to see her last month," Pauline said after a moment. "I would have come with you."

Her mother smoothed the lotion up and down Therese's arm, her movements gentle and rhythmic.

"You and Dwight haven't been married that long . . . I felt you should be focusing on your new husband. That's why I didn't mention it."

"Did you visit her other times, too?" Pauline asked.

"Every week," her mother said. "More than that, lately."

"I should have, too," Pauline said. Her throat felt so tight it was hard to get out the words. She couldn't help feeling betrayed that her mother hadn't told her. "How hard would it have been? The facility's only a half hour drive away."

"Darling," her mother said. "This is exactly what I didn't want. For you to feel guilty or weighed down by responsibility."

"It's just . . . things have been so busy since I married Dwight," Pauline said. "Parties and charity balls and then there's the house to run . . ." Her voice trailed off. It sounded awful, when she put it like that.

"Pauline," her mother said, "you and Dwight have done so much for Therese."

"It's just money," Pauline said. She looked down at her sister again. "I didn't try to do anything else. I never even tried to *know* her."

There was a pause, then her mother said, "Yes, you did."

Pauline looked up. "What do you mean?"

"You did try to know her . . . back when we first told you about Therese. Darling, don't you remember?"

Pauline wrinkled her brow. "You and Dad sat me down on the couch in the living room and told me I had a sister . . . And afterward, we all went out to dinner at my favorite restaurant."

"No." Her mother shook her head. "We didn't go out to dinner that night."

"Really?" Pauline said. She remembered the talk so clearly, but her memory ended with her standing up from the couch. "What happened, then?"

"After we told you, you disappeared into your room. You didn't ask questions or show any interest. I assumed you were processing things in your own way. You were only a child, but such a serious one. You always seemed older than your years. But then you came out and you asked me to follow you back into your room. You had . . ."

Her mother dipped her head and swallowed hard before she continued. "You had made a little bed for Therese next to your own, with blankets and pillows. You told me she could come back and live with us . . . that you'd take care of her."

Pauline stared at her mother. "I did?"

"We had to give her up," her mother said. "You must know we couldn't have given her the kind of care she needed. Not without sacrificing your life."

"*Mine?*" Pauline asked. Her head spun; she'd thought her parents had chosen to send Therese away because they couldn't handle her. But her mother was saying they'd done it, at least partly, to protect Pauline.

"Think about what it would have been like," her mother said. "For her and for us . . . it was better this way."

Pauline nodded because her mother's sad eyes revealed her need for affirmation, but she couldn't help wishing she didn't feel as if her parents had chosen her over Therese. She knew that wasn't all of it; her parents would have been exhausted, trying to care for her sister. They would have needed a live-in nurse. And when friends or neighbors came over and saw Therese . . . well, Pauline couldn't pretend that she wouldn't have been embarrassed as a teenager. All of their lives would have been so different.

Therese began coughing again, and the raspy sound startled Pauline so much that she nearly dropped her sister's arm. Pauline's mother reached for the oxygen, but it didn't seem to help as much; the coughing continued for another thirty seconds, and the sound was different—harsher.

Pauline didn't realize she'd begun to sing until her mother's head jerked up to look at her.

"'Hush, little baby, don't say a word, Papa's gonna buy you a mockingbird,'" Pauline sang along with the CD. She sang about all the things one could buy that wouldn't make the slightest bit of difference to Therese. She kept singing for a long time, through the entire stack of CDs, while she rubbed Therese's legs and brushed her fine blond hair, and by the second song, her mother had joined in.

When Therese died in the dark, quiet hours just before dawn, her mother and sister were both holding her hands, whispering that they loved her.

Chapter Fifteen

Hellos

AHHHHHH, SAVANNAH THOUGHT AS she walked down the moonlit beach toward the staircase leading to the house. Her body was so loose-limbed and relaxed that she felt as if she were floating a few feet aboveground. Could that be due to the great sex, or to the fact that Mr. Red Bathing Suit had pulled out a ziplock bag and lit up a joint for them to share?

Jamaican pot was much more intense than the stuff she'd tried back home, Savannah reflected. She wasn't a regular smoker, but she never turned down a few puffs if it was offered at a party. Usually it made her feel giggly and sleepy, but this stuff was transformative. She felt boneless, like those chicken breasts she was always broiling for dinner because they were quick and low-calorie. She'd have to cook lots of boneless chicken when she got back home, to make up for all the rich food she was eating during this trip.

But boneless chicken were her kinfolk now, she thought as she began to climb the stairs. Could she, in all good conscience, cannibalize them?

Savannah giggled so hard that she missed a step and sprawled backward, onto the beach. She was pretty sure she'd twisted her ankle, but it didn't hurt a bit. Aha! Because there were no bones in it! She lay there in the soft sand, looking up at the sky. It was so beautiful. The wind was picking up, and the palm trees were dancing in unison, as if they were all taking a swing class.

She could stay here forever, she thought as she began to move her arms and legs to make a sand angel. Time didn't matter . . . Time wasn't real, anyway. It was just an invention of man, a way to try to exert control over what was essentially uncontrollable. The waves crashing behind her had been here long before the advent of time, and they would be afterward, too. Savannah wished she had a sheet of paper and pen to jot down her thoughts; they were so important.

She closed her eyes, but the sound of the waves made her realize she was thirsty. Cottonmouth, that's what they used to call it in college. Everyone got cottonmouth when they were high, usually followed by the munchies. Ooh, maybe there was some pie left at the house!

She pulled herself up and began climbing the stairs again. Jesus, had there been this many steps on the way down? They seemed to have multiplied. Maybe they'd been having sex, too; they should've used a condom, like she had. She began to count, "Three, four, five . . ." She almost slipped again, but she grabbed the rail. "'Five little monkeys, jumping on the bed! One fell off and bumped his head!'"

"Savannah?"

A dark figure appeared at the top of the stairs.

Savannah really wanted to finish her song. "'Mama called the doctor and the doctor said, "No more monkeys jumping on the bed . . ."' Oh, hi, Gary!"

"I was just going to come look for you," he said.

"Oh!" Savannah couldn't think of anything else to say, and she was terribly thirsty, so she walked past him, into the house.

All of her friends were in the kitchen, and they turned to stare at her, moving as one. Just like the palm trees. Maybe every single living thing on the planet was in sync right now, at this exact moment. What a beautiful thought.

"Savannah!" Tina said. "Did you see who's here?"

"Yup," Savannah said. She found a glass in the cabinet and filled it with water from the purifier built into the refrigerator, then gulped the entire thing down.

"Ah, so good!" she said as she filled the glass again.

"Savannah?" This time it was Allie who spoke. "Did you talk to Gary?"

"Savannah?" Gary had followed her into the kitchen.

"You all love my name, don't you?" Savannah said. "You keep saying it! Savannah, Shavannah, Shlavannah . . ."

Gio came closer to her and sniffed. "She's high." He burst into laughter. "Where'd you get the ganja, Van?"

"The guy from the boat," Savannah said. "The one who gave Stella her groove back."

"What guy?" Gary asked.

"Shhh!" Savannah lifted a finger to her lips. She reached into the pocket of her jean cutoffs and pulled out the ziplock bag. "I bought some from him. We can share!"

Tina was the first one to react. She hurried to Savannah's side, opened the bag, and inhaled. "Ooooh, I haven't gotten high in forever! Years! No, a decade!"

"Light one up, baby," Savannah said. "It's premium."

"Not in here, though," Tina said. "Should we go out to the pool?"

"Okay," Savannah said. "Just don't try to take off my pants again like last night."

"Who took off your pants?" Gary asked.

Tina laughed but didn't answer him. "Van? Seriously, stop molesting that pie and come on out. You joining us, Allie?"

"Nah," Allie said.

"She's a good girl," Savannah observed. "She's been yelling a lot on this trip, though."

"You have no filter right now, do you?" Ryan asked.

Tina snorted. "Like she ever did."

"You, I especially like right now," Savannah said, pointing to Tina. "You're fun again."

She began to walk out of the room, but as she passed Gary, she suddenly had a moment of clarity. She'd been scared, after her all-too-brief experience with her trainer, that she'd never find a man who could sexually satisfy her again. She knew the fear was ridiculous—plus she had a drawer full of vibrators, so it wasn't like she was going hungry in that department— but she and Gary had always meshed well physically and she'd wanted to know she could have that again. Now she knew she could. The crewman had been . . . insatiable. She'd come twice, her legs wrapped around his muscular waist, her cries drowned out by the sea.

Savannah could sense Gary registering the sand in her hair, and she licked her lips, feeling how swollen they had become from the rough kissing.

"Your shirt," Gary said. His mouth was a perfectly straight line, like something a little kid would draw on a stick figure.

Savannah looked down and realized she'd missed two buttons.

"Whoops," she said. But instead of fixing it, she walked by Gary without another word, hoping he picked up the scent of sex clinging to her along with the pot.

Allie couldn't believe how close they'd come to getting caught.

She and Dwight were hidden behind the copse of palm trees, but the bright headlights of a taxi had swing around the corner and suddenly illuminated them. For one jumbled, heart-stopping moment she'd thought someone was shining a spotlight on them, exposing their infidelity.

Luckily they were still fully clothed. Dwight's common sense had pulled them back from the brink a few minutes earlier. He'd tucked in his shirt and stepped back, breathing hard, and when Allie's hands had reached for him again, he'd squeezed them tightly in his own. "Let's slow down," he'd said. "The guys could come back at any second."

Allie hadn't wanted to slow down, though; even the mention of Ryan didn't conjure any guilt. She, who felt shamed when she kept out a book a day past the library's due date!

But Dwight had been prescient; moments later, the taxi had approached. Someone had gotten out, and then the cab had pulled away.

"It's Gary," Allie had whispered, watching him walk around the pool and go into the house. "I can't believe he's here!"

"He didn't see us," Dwight had said.

"I don't think so, either, but we need to go in," Allie had said. "But not together! I'll go now and you follow in a minute. If anyone asks where you were, just say you went for a walk on the beach to catch Gio and Ryan, but you didn't see them. I'll say I was at the pool." The story had slipped off her tongue as easily as if she'd been lying for her entire life.

"Okay," Dwight had said. Allie had smoothed back her hair as she hurried inside. But no one was around. She could hear Tina's and Gary's voices down the hall, by the bedrooms, so she'd slipped into the kitchen. When she'd come out a few moments later, she'd feigned surprise at seeing Gary.

Now Allie began tidying up the kitchen, glad that the pile of dishes and sudsy water gave her an excuse to avoid eye contact with Gary. He was just standing there, in the same spot, casting occasional glances toward the door where Savannah had exited.

"I thought she wanted to see me," he said. "She asked me to come."

No, Allie thought, scrubbing harder than necessary at a mixing bowl. *I'm not doing this!* Why did everyone come to her with their problems? She used to find it flattering, but not anymore. The new Allie couldn't fix everyone else's life; it was taking every ounce of her energy to hold the fragments of her own together. Besides, Gary didn't deserve sympathy. So he'd spent a little money and taken a day or so off work—big deal. He could afford it.

Gary reached for the wine bottle again and filled his glass, then sloshed more into Allie's. "Do you think I should go out there?" he asked. "You must know how she's feeling . . . Do you think she wants me to follow her?"

Allie dropped the scrubber back into the pan. Why was she the only one doing the dishes? Let someone else clean up.

She looked at Gary, letting her eyes rove over his fancy suit and his pretty-boy face. He'd skipped her thirty-fifth birthday party because he had to "work," but Allie knew he'd never made an effort with Van's friends. He'd never really tried to become part of the group. This was one of the few times she'd been in a one-on-one conversation with him, and that was only because he needed something.

The anger that had been building in her all week erupted in one clipped sentence. "I think you should've kept your dick in your pants," she said, relishing watching the shock spread across his face.

Then she walked out of the room.

Tina reached for the joint Savannah offered and inhaled deeply. "This is goooood stuff."

"You should've seen his other stuff." Savannah arched an eyebrow. "It was even more . . . effective." Tina reached over and gave her a high five.

"Watch it, woman," Gio growled as he came over to squeeze in next to Tina in the lounge chair. He kissed her neck. "Don't give her any ideas, Van. I don't want her running off with some eighteen-year-old."

"He was at least twenty," Tina joked as she passed the joint to Gio.

"Twenty inches, maybe," Savannah cracked, and Tina convulsed in laughter.

Tina leaned back against Gio's arm. By now Ryan had joined them, and Dwight, too. Allie was the only one not smoking, but she'd pulled over another lounge chair to form a circle with theirs. The night air felt swollen with the threat of rain, and the breeze was strong, but the house was blocking it.

Tina couldn't believe they'd all be boarding Dwight's plane again in a few days to go home. During this trip, the hours had seemed to pass slowly, but the week had rushed by. It was like motherhood, Tina mused. She'd always felt guilty when white-haired ladies approached her in the supermarket to exclaim over her children and say, "Oh, enjoy every minute! It goes by so fast!"

Really? Tina always wanted to respond as she tried unsuccessfully to keep her kids contained in the cart instead of tearing down the aisles and demanding sugary snacks. *Because I wish it would go by faster!*

And yet, when she looked back over the past eight years, they were a blur. If she could be granted one wish, it would be the ability to trade time in the present for time in the future. In twenty years, the requests for repeated readings of *Goodnight Moon* and the washing of soft little bodies in mounds of bubbles in the tub would seem like enchantments instead of burdens. Her house would be too quiet, her days too empty.

"Hi."

Tina looked up. Pauline was standing there, twisting her hands together.

"Hey, stranger," Tina said, feeling expansive from the weed. "Come join us."

Savannah drew up her legs, making space at the end of her chair, and patted it. Pauline walked over and sat down.

"Help yourself," Savannah said, handing her the joint. The tip glowed red as Pauline inhaled.

"You have no idea how much I needed that," Pauline said after she blew out the smoke.

"You are one surprise after another," Savannah said. "Hey, how's your mom?"

"She's . . . okay," Pauline said. "Better, I think."

There was a pause, then Pauline said, "You all are aware that there's a strange man in the kitchen, right?"

Everyone looked at her, then burst into laughter.

"It's Gary," Tina said through her giggles. "Savannah's husband. Ex-husband. Soon-to-be-ex-husband."

"That's what I thought," Pauline said.

"What's he doing, anyway?" Savannah asked, craning her neck to look back at the house.

"He was staring into a glass of wine when I walked by," Pauline said. "Is he staying?"

Tina glanced at Savannah and waited for her answer.

"I guess," Savannah said, shrugging. "I mean, we can't make him sleep on the beach. There's an extra room, right?"

Pauline nodded.

"I thought you were going to send him back to the airport," Tina said. "Send his butt packing."

"I will," Savannah said. "Tomorrow. It's probably too late for him to get on a flight tonight."

Lightning arced across the sky, causing everyone to look up.

"Did you see that?" Savannah asked. "Whoa—here it comes again!"

"That's amazing," Ryan said. "Usually you just get a few streaks. That thing lit up the whole sky like some kind of giant spiderweb."

"I'm thirsty. You need a beer, too, D-man?" Gio asked Dwight.

"Sure," Dwight said, and Gio jumped up to get it. Tina followed him with her eyes. He was still trying to make up for hurting Dwight on the basketball court, she knew.

"Here you go," Gio said, handing a Red Stripe to Dwight. He sat back down and popped his tab.

"So, Gio, are you going to teach me to surf tomorrow?" Allie asked, and Tina smiled. Allie hadn't spoken to Gio in the past few hours, but her question signaled everything between them was good again.

"Sure," he said. "The waves are getting fierce."

"Actually, about tomorrow," Pauline said. "I just got a call from the management company for the villa. They wanted to make sure we were prepared to evacuate, if it comes to that."

"Really?" Ryan asked. "They think we're scared of a little old hurricane?"

"They're sending someone to board up the windows and re-inforce the awnings tomorrow," Pauline said. "Just as a precaution."

"It would be kind of cool, to be in a hurricane," Gio said.

"Sure," Tina said. "Death and destruction is always a hoot."

Gio gave her a squeeze. "Not a big, bad hurricane. Just a little one. Like a Category Two."

"Someone's been watching the Weather Channel," Savannah said. "Listen to Meteorologist Gio Antonelli, tossing around fancy terms."

"Should we be concerned, though?" Allie asked.

For some reason, the formality of her words struck Tina as hilarious. She doubled over laughing.

"If we need to leave, we'll go inland," Pauline said. "If we get far enough away from the water, we should be fine."

"They've named the hurricane Betty," Ryan said. "You can't be scared by a hurricane named Betty."

"That's true," Savannah said. "Betty is just going to pinch your cheeks and tell you how big you've grown. She'll offer you cookies. She'd never rip the roof off your house."

"Whoa!" Tina yelled as lightning erupted in the sky again. "Betty doesn't like the way you're making fun of her!"

"If Betty turns on us . . . would we stay in a hotel inland?" Allie asked.

"I guess so," Pauline said, reaching for the joint again.

"You're exhibiting an admirable lack of planning," Savannah said. "Not that you were anal before. Whoops, did I say anal? I meant . . . focused. You were highly focused. Like a laser beam. A red, glowing, pointy—"

"Hold on," Allie said, lifting up a hand like a stop sign. "Is that a car I hear?"

"Maybe Gary called a cab again," Dwight said. "He could be leaving."

Allie stood up and looked toward the driveway. "It's definitely a car . . . it's stopping and someone's getting out. I can't see anything else, though. It's too dark."

"Probably the cabdriver," Tina said. She looked at Savannah, who stood up. "You're not going to say good-bye to him, are you?"

Savannah bit her lower lip. "What should I do? I mean, he came all this way and I didn't even talk to him."

"Oh, screw him!" Tina said. "He cheated on you. He dumped you! And now he suddenly wants you back just because he and his girlfriend broke up?"

"Well, when you put it like that," Savannah said, but she didn't sit back down. "You sure know how to make a girl feel special, Tina."

"Think about how I feel," Tina said. "I took off your pants and you never called me in the morning."

"It's kind of hot, the way you two keep talking about that," Gio said.

"You are so—" Tina cut her sentence off.

"Tina? What are you looking at?" Ryan turned around.

A policeman was standing there.

"Shit!" Savannah yelled. She looked down at the joint she was holding, then flung it into the pool.

The police officer walked over to the side of the pool and looked down.

"We weren't doing anything!" Tina cried—admittedly not a rousing defense, she thought.

"Smoking ganja is illegal in Jamaica," the officer said.

"Oh, man, we're sorry," Gio said. "It was one tiny joint."

"Still illegal," the officer said.

"Oh, my God," Tina cried. "You can't put us in jail. You can't!"

"Don't give him any ideas!" Savannah hissed.

"Excuse me, Officer." Everyone looked up at the sound of Gary's voice.

"I'd like to apologize on behalf of my friends," Gary said, walking over to stand between them and the policeman. "Someone they met on the beach gave them a tiny bit of marijuana. They're all upstanding citizens. They don't usually do things like this."

Tina held her breath and watched the officer weigh Gary's words. Suddenly Gary's formal manner and gray suit were an asset—they gave him a gravitas sorely needed in this situation. He looked like a lawyer.

"Just this one time," the officer said.

"We appreciate it, sir," Gary responded. Tina almost leapt up to hug the officer, then thought the better of it.

"Someone was mugged?" the officer said. "I'm here to take a report."

"That would be me," Ryan said. "But I got my watch back!" He stood up and walked over to the officer, who pulled out a little notebook.

"I hope he's sober enough to keep his story straight," Tina whispered to Gio.

"I just hope he can remember his own name," Gio whispered back, and Tina snorted. She snuggled closer to her husband, feeling the stubble on his jawline tickle her forehead.

"Can we spend a little time alone tomorrow morning?" she whispered. "Maybe have breakfast in bed?"

"Sure," he said. He kissed her on the temple, and she closed her eyes and smiled. In the early days of their marriage, she and Gio had always fallen asleep entwined around each other, but now a child—sometimes more than one child—climbed into their bed and wedged between them every night. On this trip, though, their bodies had fit back together as if no time had passed—her back pressed against his chest, his arm around her waist. She hadn't slept so well in ages.

Ryan and the officer were walking back over to the chairs, with Ryan seeming to make a special effort to put his feet down carefully.

"You're keeping an eye on the storm, right?" the police officer said. "You may have to evacuate."

"Yes," Gary said. "I've got the TV on now. Thank you for your concern."

The officer nodded, then walked away and got back into his car. Everyone was silent as he drove off, then Gio spoke up. "Nice job, man."

"Seriously, Gary, that cop scared me," Allie said. "I thought about offering him a bribe, then I wondered if it would make things worse. I didn't know what to do."

"It's okay," Gary said. He cleared his throat. "Savannah? I'd like it if we could talk now."

Tina watched as Savannah stood there, staring at Gary. He'd saved them from the cop, but he hadn't even said please to Savannah.

"Fine," Savannah finally said, and they went into the house together.

"Well, that's a bummer," Gio remarked.

"Why?" Ryan asked. "You don't think she should talk to him?"

"No." Gio shook his head. "She drowned our joint, and she's got the rest of the pot."

Chapter Sixteen

Thursday

PAULINE OPENED THE SLIDING door to her bedroom's balcony to let in the gentle breeze. It was another flawless day; you'd never believe a storm was coming.

"Good morning," Dwight said, walking up behind her.

"Hi," Pauline said. "When do they expect the hurricane to reach land?"

"Tonight," Dwight said. "At least, that's the best guess. But it's not going to hit us directly; it's still on course for Cuba."

"Still, with the wind and everything . . ." Pauline said. "Maybe we should go to a hotel. It could veer in our direction. They said that last night; I heard it on the television."

"Naw, let's stay," Dwight said. "The guys are already here putting up plywood just to be safe, and it's only going to be a Category Two."

"What does the hurricane scale go up to again—ten?" Pauline asked.

"Five," Dwight said. "But that's rare. Two is considered moderate."

"Right, I knew that," Pauline said. She'd seen it on the Weather Channel just yesterday, along with a diagram of the respective intensities of different-level hurricanes. A two wasn't supposed to be so horrible—trees would come down, but sturdy structures like houses shouldn't suffer much damage.

Her brain felt fuzzy, so she went into the bathroom and splashed cold water on her face. Usually she got up earlier than Dwight, but she'd woken late today—it was almost nine. She'd had trouble sleeping, and it wasn't just because of all the yelling coming from Savannah's room.

She tried to think if there was anything they needed to do to prepare to leave quickly. Maybe they should all pack, just in case. She went back into the bedroom and discovered Dwight still standing there, looking at her. He seemed to be waiting for something.

"Oh! Happy birthday," she said after a moment, realizing belatedly that her tone was flat. Last year she'd woken him with breakfast in bed—French toast and apple-smoked bacon and strawberries—and they'd ended the night at the chef's table in the kitchen at the legendary restaurant The Inn at Little Washington. She'd had a massage therapist come to the house after lunch, and there had been a pile of presents on Dwight's side of the bed when they returned from dinner.

She had some things for him tucked in the back of the closet here, and the chef had been planning a special dinner . . . But of course, Dwight had told her the chef had left because he was superstitious about the storm. She supposed she should do something else—make an effort—but she couldn't. Her usual energy had evaporated. Therese consumed all of her thoughts.

She recalled her phone call with her mother last night: They'd spoken right before Pauline had gone out to the pool to smoke weed with everyone, and it had been the discussion of funeral arrangements that had made Pauline crave pot—even though she'd smoked it only once before. But last night, she'd been desperate for oblivion. They'd decided to bury Therese in their family plot on Sunday, the day after Pauline and Dwight returned from Jamaica. Pauline would tell Dwight about her sister's death on the drive home from the airport, she'd decided.

Now she looked at her husband, standing there in his baggy Levi's and a shirt he'd picked up on his last business trip to New York. The shirt was an awful Hawaiian print, purple clashing with yellow, the sort of thing an older, color-blind man might choose. Dwight had probably bought it from a street vendor. Pauline hadn't had the heart to be honest when he'd modeled it for her, saying, "Won't this be perfect for Jamaica?"

Oh, Dwight, she thought. Why had she ever cared about his wardrobe—about the image he projected? Her husband was so kind and generous and good; he was the best person she knew. Maybe she never would have married him if it hadn't been for his money, but his money wasn't the only reason she stayed with him.

Suddenly she regretted pretending to be asleep last night when he'd begun to stroke her hip. She couldn't make love to him, not with images of Therese still so fresh in her mind. So she'd remained immobile, until she'd heard him sigh and roll away. She'd felt so terribly alone as she listened to him breathing in the darkness.

Now she felt the urge to spill out all her secrets: the abortion, her fears of not being able to get pregnant again, Therese's death. Dwight might be upset, but she thought—hoped—he'd forgive her.

She took a step toward him, feeling the words surge up inside her, suddenly desperate for the release of saying them aloud.

But just before she spoke his name, someone beat her to it. "Dwight?"

She turned to see Allie standing in the doorway.

"Oh, I'm sorry!" Allie said. "I just wanted to let you guys know breakfast is ready."

"Breakfast?" Pauline asked.

"Tina and I made it," Allie said. "And Dwight helped. The birthday boy mixed the eggs!"

"I can smell it from here," Dwight said. He began to walk away from Pauline.

Her disappointment mingled with relief. Maybe her impulse was a mistake. Maybe Dwight wouldn't be able to forgive her, after all.

"I'm just going to shower," Pauline called after them. "I'll be there in a minute."

But Dwight was already heading down the hallway, laughing at something Allie was saying. If he heard his wife, he didn't acknowledge her.

Savannah woke up with a familiar bedmate: a throbbing headache. She pulled herself to a standing position and headed toward the bathroom for Tylenol and a glass of water. Then she stopped, one foot held high in the air. She'd almost stepped on someone.

Gary was sleeping on the floor, rolled up like a burrito in a thin blanket.

He let out a faint snore, and Savannah smiled despite herself. He'd forgotten to pack something to sleep in—which he'd revealed after she came out of the bathroom and yelled at him awhile longer—so she'd tossed him the blanket from the end of the bed and told him to deal with it. Then she'd turned on the air-conditioning extra high and hunkered down under a cozy quilt.

When she'd imagined the possibility of Gary showing up—which she'd allowed herself to do exactly once—she'd envisioned telling him off, then watching him leave for the airport with his head hanging low. She'd anticipated feeling a sense of

vindication as she finally wrote the last chapter of the sad story
of her marriage.

But not only had she mispredicted Gary's actions, she'd mis-
judged her own response to him.

The icy, cutting woman who'd taunted Gary in the phone
call by the pool had disappeared last night. The pot and the
memories of long, lonely days without Gary—and worse, so
much worse, the nights—seemed to join forces against Savannah, clouding her mind and making her lose her bearings.
She'd fought her way out of the fog, powered by her fury. Her
hatred for Gary was so strong that she knew she hadn't stopped
loving him yet.

If Gary had acted arrogantly, or tossed off an inadequate apology, it would have been simpler. Maybe then she would've been
able to keep her composure. But there were tears in his eyes
when he told her he loved her, that he'd always loved her. He
didn't know what had come over him, but he'd do whatever she
wanted—go through counseling, take a break from their marriage, go away somewhere together . . . Savannah could set the
tone for everything that happened next. The only thing Gary
asked was that she call off the divorce.

"What makes you think I still love you?" she'd asked, hating
the way her voice broke on the word *love*.

"Hope," he'd said.

It would have been the perfect moment for her to deny it, to
order him to leave, but instead, she'd started to cry. He'd stood
up and put his arms around her, and for a few seconds, she'd
allowed herself to lean into him.

"I've missed you," he'd said, kissing her hair.

She'd smelled the citrusy cologne she'd given him for his last
birthday, two days before she discovered the BlackBerry messages.

"Don't touch me!" she'd yelled, whirling away. She'd wrapped her arms around herself and sunk down on the bed, feeling old wounds inside of her ripping open.

"I hate you!" she'd yelled. "Why did you have to come?"

"You asked me to," he'd said.

"I didn't *want* you to, though!" she'd cried. Seeing him again was awful. She didn't feel triumphant; she felt more vulnerable than ever before. It was even worse than the day Gary had left their home with his stupid, useless barbells.

She'd buried her face in her hands as she felt him sit down next to her, his movements so slow and careful that the bed had barely adjusted under his weight. He wasn't close enough to touch her, but she'd felt his presence.

For some reason, she'd thought of their wedding day.

It was silly, but she'd wanted a storybook wedding. Her desire for that one day to be perfect overrode her practicality, and she'd willingly overpaid for flowers, for champagne, and for a reception room in a fancy hotel. But Gary hadn't complained.

He'd bought her a beautiful ring—every other girl in her real estate office had envied it—and he'd let her spend a fortune on the reception. Gary had met her family. He understood what no one else could: that she wanted the first dance with her father while everyone watched, that she craved hearing toasts celebrating Gary's love for her. That she needed an album containing photographs with Savannah front and center.

Gary came from a broken family, too. It was why Savannah knew it was going to be impossible for her to forgive him. He'd committed the worst kind of cruelty; he'd dredged up her old hurts along with new pain when he abandoned her.

"I hate you," she'd said again, but this time her voice was worn and sad instead of angry.

"I know," Gary had said. He'd aged in the past few months, Savannah had thought, noticing the new threads of gray in his hair. He'd lost a little weight, too.

"Did you break up with her, or did she break up with you?" Savannah had asked.

"I did it," Gary had said.

"You're lying!" Savannah had shouted. "You're just saying that."

"No." Gary had shaken his head. "I left her. I moved into an apartment a few weeks ago."

Savannah had studied his face. "I had sex with someone else tonight," she'd said.

Gary had closed his eyes. "Okay," he'd said.

"You don't care that I screwed another man? He's much younger than you! And . . . and he's black!"

"Savannah," Gary had said. "I love you."

"Stop saying that!"

"Then tell me what to say!"

"Fine, you want to fix this?" she'd said. "It's simple. Become a famous inventor."

A furrow had formed between Gary's brows as he'd looked at her.

"Build a time machine," she'd said. "And go back, and un-cheat."

She'd walked into the bathroom and slammed the door so hard that for a brief, satisfying moment, she'd thought it might shatter like a mirror.

Allie's eyes flipped open at six a.m.

She felt, quite suddenly, as if she'd been electrified. What in the world had she been thinking? Not only was she acting unlike herself but it was as if a complete stranger had slipped inside her skin and taken over her life.

Allie couldn't believe she'd been debating whether it was better to know if she was going to develop ALS. Of course she had to know! There was no way she could live in limbo for the next few years, waiting to see if the disease would strike. She'd never been one to sit back and passively allow things to happen. The only reason she'd done so for these past weeks was that she was still reeling from the news. She'd counseled hundreds of people who were going through shock and anger and denial after a trauma—yet she hadn't recognized traveling through those symptoms herself.

She was going to call the genetic counselor this very morning. Suddenly, she was ravenous for information. She knew she was healthy—how could she not be?—yet she needed concrete answers.

She put on tan shorts and a spaghetti-strap tank top, then went into the bathroom to brush her teeth. She reached into her toiletries bag and found the folded rectangle of paper. She smoothed it out and stared at the ten digits she'd recorded in a pencil topped with an eraser shaped like a gingerbread man. She'd tucked a package of the erasers into Sasha's stocking last Christmas; Eva had gotten ones made to look like candy canes.

Allie smiled despite herself: If she had a doubt that she was making the right decision, the memory of those little rubber toys had erased it just as effectively as the gingerbread erasers had wiped out Sasha's incorrect arithmetic sums. She needed to know, not just for herself but for her daughters. She took in a deep breath, but the tears she'd anticipated didn't fall. She felt strong and resolute and optimistic—like the old Allie.

"Honey?" Through a crack in the bathroom door, she could see Ryan rolling over in bed. His voice was husky. "What are you doing up so early?"

She tucked the paper into her pocket and went back into the bedroom. "Sorry. Couldn't sleep."

"Come back to bed," Ryan said. He lifted up the covers by way of invitation. She stood there, looking at him in the dim light. His hair was too long around the ears; he needed a trim. His soft-looking stomach used to inspire tenderness in her, but the space in her heart that had been filled with love for Ryan just a few weeks ago seemed barren now.

I'm so angry with you, she thought. *Why can't you tell?*

She was falling apart in front of him, and he couldn't even see it.

"Als?" He was propped up on one elbow, a puzzled look on his face.

"Go back to sleep," she said. It was a test, maybe the most important one she'd ever given.

"Is everything okay?"

He was only asking about three weeks too late.

"It's fine," she said. She forced herself to summon a smile.

"Okay," he said, and then, as she'd known he would, he pulled the covers up to his shoulders and closed his eyes. And failed.

"Hey, babe," Gio said in Tina's ear. She felt him hesitate, and she remembered she'd ordered him never again to use that term of endearment.

"I was really pissed at you the other night, you know," Tina said. She rubbed the sleep out of her eyes and twisted around to look up at him.

"Yeah, I know," he said. He pulled her closer.

"It wasn't just that you flirted with my friend," she said. "The whole thing made me realize I haven't been happy lately. Or maybe it wasn't that I realized it, more that I finally admitted it to myself."

"You're not happy with me?" She could see hurt flare in Gio's eyes. She knew she had to be careful; her husband could be an unusual mix of overconfident and hypersensitive.

"I'm not happy with me," she said, reaching up to stroke his cheek and hoping it took the sting out of her words. "I love you. I love the kids. Having a big family is all I ever wanted, especially with my mom gone . . . but some days I feel really blue."

"Like, depressed?"

"It's not that bad," she said. "I mean, I can get out of bed and stuff, obviously. It's more feeling tired all the time, and overwhelmed. Do you know how long I've been meaning to clean out our medicine cabinet? Two years, Gio. We've got Advil in there that's older than Sammy. Stuff like that. A million stupid, silly things that overwhelm me every time I think about them. I feel like I'm never going to get caught up. I just get . . . farther and farther behind. In everything, really."

"Fuck the Advil," Gio said.

"But it's a symbol," Tina said. "I see these other moms at school, and they look so together. Their minivans are spotless and they're in exercise clothes and you just know they've knocked out an advanced Pilates class before whipping up chicken cacciatore, and I have no idea how they do it. It's like they're in this secret time-management club, and they're not letting me in. Or, who knows, maybe they're all just stealing their kids' Adderall."

"Seriously?"

"Some moms do," Tina said. "Or so I've heard. But you know the scary thing? When I heard that Adderall gives you tons of energy and focus, I was like, 'How can I get my hands on some of that?'"

"Babe, you don't need drugs," Gio said.

I need help, Tina thought. *I need a housekeeper to come once a month. I need more adult companionship. I need to feel young again . . .*

"Gio, remember that time when I left the kids?" Tina asked. "I still think about it a lot."

Gio was silent for a moment, and she wondered how often he

recalled it, too: Tina phoning him from the minivan, weeping, saying he needed to come home . . .

It had started as an ordinary day, which was to say that Tina was exhausted by the time she'd opened her eyes. While she'd been trying to find Sammy's shoes, the grilled cheese she was cooking for Paolo's lunch had gotten burned, so she'd thrown it into Caesar's dish, since they were out of dog food. But the sandwich had hit the edge of the dish, and blackened crumbs had scattered all over the kitchen floor. Then Jessica had announced that she needed to have forms signed or she wouldn't be able to go on the school field trip that day.

"What forms? Where?" Tina had barked, looking at the clock. The school bus would arrive in twelve minutes.

"I gave them to you!" Jessica had said, her face scrunching up.

Tina had dug through the pile of mail and bills on the counter, then she'd accidentally knocked everything to the floor.

At that moment, Sammy had unscrewed the lid from his sippy cup and spilled the entire thing all over the couch—deliberately.

"Damn it!" Tina had yelled, and Sammy had stuck out his lower lip and begun to cry.

"I'm sorry, baby," Tina had said. She'd grabbed a wad of paper towels and run to the couch.

"My forms!" Jessica had wailed. "I need them!"

Caesar had wandered over to his dish, sniffed, and rejected the burned sandwich.

"I'll get them, okay?" Tina had snapped. Her head had been pounding.

She'd been on her knees again, searching for the forms, when the school bus roared by their house on its way to the corner stop, six minutes early for the first time all year.

"Wait!" Tina had yelled. She'd leapt up, raced to the door, and waved frantically. "Please wait!"

Then she'd felt eyes on her from across the street, and she'd looked over to see two women from the neighborhood, each carrying a sleek stainless-steel travel mug of coffee, walking their calm, happy children to the bus. Tina was quite certain those mothers had turned in the field trip forms ahead of time.

She'd looked down and realized she was wearing only an old T-shirt of Gio's and a pair of mismatched socks she'd pulled out of the laundry basket because her feet had felt cold on the kitchen's linoleum floor.

"I missed the bus!" Jessica had sobbed.

"Mom! Come quick!" someone else had shouted, and Tina had reached out, slowly and deliberately, and slipped the mini-van's keys from the hook by the door. She'd walked outside and gotten in the van and driven two blocks away, then reached for the phone that she'd left in the vehicle the previous night. She was always forgetting her phone, and Gio was always nagging her about it, saying she was inviting a break-in.

"Come home!" Tina had shouted when Gio answered, then she'd burst into tears.

He'd been terrified that something had happened to one of the kids, and he'd arrived fifteen minutes later, squealing around the street corner and pulling into their driveway. By then Tina was sitting on the front steps of their brick rambler, still in his T-shirt and mismatched socks. Her tears had dried up, but she couldn't bring herself to go back inside.

"The kids," she'd said, waving him in. Gio had rushed through the door, his face stricken, then he'd come back out a minute later.

"Tina?" he'd said. "Everything's okay. The kids are fine."

"It's not okay," she'd said. "It's not. It's not."

"You're scaring me," he'd said.

"I never planted tulips in our yard like I wanted, and it's

too late now," Tina had said, and begun to cry again. Gio had moved next to her and put a tentative hand on her back, as if he was scared of her.

They'd stayed like that for a while, and then, because Jessica still needed her forms and a ride to school, and Paolo didn't have a lunch, she'd stood up and gone inside and splashed cold water on her face and gone through the motions of the day, feeling numb inside. She'd convinced Gio she was fine, and in an odd way, she was. But only because she couldn't afford a breakdown; she didn't have the time.

The memory of that morning shamed her almost every single day, partly because it wasn't an aberration. She still fought the urge to drive away, to *run* away, from the children she'd wanted to have so desperately.

"I live in yoga pants and I don't even do yoga," Tina said now. She swallowed hard, wondering why she was crying so much on the vacation of a lifetime. "Do you know Sammy once peed on me when he was sitting on my lap at the playground and I didn't even go home and change my clothes? I'd already gotten the other kids dressed and I'd packed up snacks and driven everyone there and it just . . . it didn't seem worth it, Gio! *I* didn't seem worth it. So I went around in smelly wet-pee pants all afternoon, and do you know what the worst part was? It didn't even bother me that much!"

She could feel Gio stroking her hair, and she sniffed and wiped her nose.

"What if we got that teenager who's helping with the kids this week to come babysit on Saturday nights?" he finally asked. "We could go out. Just us."

Later, when she looked back on this moment, Tina would be grateful that she hadn't uttered the first words that had sprung to her mind: *We can't afford it.*

She knew that sentence—an all-too-familiar one in their household, trotted out when the kids begged for a trip to Disney World or she and Gio lusted after new minivans that came with heated leather seats—would hurt her husband deeply. He worked so hard to provide for his family. She thought about their usual Saturday nights. She got into her pj's early along with the kids, and they made pizza for dinner out of the dough she bought at Trader Joe's. She was always asleep by nine-thirty. It was her favorite night of the week, since there was no school scramble the next morning and the kids always got donuts at church for breakfast, which meant no dishes or cooking, too.

"Just us?" she asked. "Every Saturday?"

It wouldn't be so expensive if they hired Lia for only two or three hours, and they didn't need to go anywhere fancy. They could still eat pizza with the kids, then go to a bar for drinks or to hear live music. But she could put up her hair, and wear perfume.

It wouldn't be enough, though, Tina realized. She still needed to find something—a new hobby or passion that could lift her out of her all-consuming role as a mother. Something that would let her be just Tina again.

"Yeah, every Saturday," Gio said.

He was really trying. She owed it to her marriage, and to herself, to meet him halfway.

"I'd like that so much," she said.

"And, babe?" Gio said. "You know I don't think about Savannah that way. She's a friend. It would be like you and . . . you and *Dwight* hooking up."

He burst into laughter and tightened his arm around her.

Tina felt a little smile play on her lips. For a moment, she was tempted to tell him about kissing Dwight so long ago.

Then she decided she was going to keep that little tidbit to herself.

"Should we get up?" she asked. "It's going to be an interesting day, with the storm. And I wonder if Gary's still here."

"I'm already up," Gio said, wiggling his eyebrows and pulling back the covers to show her exactly what he meant.

Chapter Seventeen

Storm Front

SAVANNAH HAD BEEN AWAKE for twenty minutes, and she was still sitting on the edge of her bed, her hands cupping her cheeks, as she studied Gary. She hadn't given him a pillow, but he must've snuck out to the couch to grab one at some point during the night.

Maybe they could become friends someday, she thought. But almost immediately, she scratched that idea. She couldn't imagine going to dinner with Gary five years in the future and meeting his new wife.

No, she and Gary couldn't be in contact again—ever. This trip was the last time she'd see him, other than in divorce court. Seven years of marriage, she thought. What a waste.

Savannah finally stood up from the bed and went into the bathroom to take a long, hot shower. She put on a robe and wrapped her hair in a towel turban before coming back into the bedroom. Gary was awake and already dressed in khaki shorts and a green knit shirt. He was sitting in a chair by the window, waiting for her.

"Hi," he said, fixing his eyes on her face. She knew he was trying to gauge her mood. She supposed she'd thrown him off balance by appearing nonplussed by his arrival, then announcing she'd just had sex with another man, before screaming at him, and finally crying until her throat felt raw.

"Morning," she said. Her emotions felt subdued, maybe because she'd released them so spectacularly the previous night. She wasn't angry at Gary right now. In fact, she didn't feel much of anything other than weary.

She crossed the room and opened the closet door, selecting a strapless blue-and-green-patterned sundress. She started to unwind the belt of her robe, then stopped and walked back into the bathroom. Old habits, she thought to herself. She'd never undress in front of Gary again. Never introduce him as her husband. Never fly to Australia with him like they'd been planning for their tenth anniversary.

"Savannah?" Gary's voice sounded close; he must have been standing on the other side of the closed bathroom door. "Do you want me to go?"

She got dressed and combed the tangles out of her hair before opening the door.

"I don't know," she said.

"I thought maybe I was making things worse."

Savannah gave a little laugh. "I don't mean this in a bitchy way, but I don't think you could make things worse, Gary," she said.

"Could I make them better?" he asked.

His hair looked completely ridiculous; it was sticking up on one side.

"I don't know," she repeated.

"So let's go have some coffee," he said.

She looked at him and wondered if this was Gary's Plan B: if he was hoping to hang around until she forgave him. Or maybe he hadn't gotten to Plan B yet. Maybe his backup plan was something else entirely—giving up on a reconciliation and moving ahead with a life that didn't include her.

"Sure," she said. She didn't bother with shoes or makeup, even though her eyes were a little puffy. But she'd had her eyelashes tinted black a few weeks ago, and they still looked fabulous—plus the dress was the most flattering one Savannah had packed. Then there was the fact that she'd brought the dress into the bathroom but hadn't carried in panties or a bra. Gary was very attuned to details, and she was sure he'd noticed.

She might not be able to forgive Gary, but she saw no harm in making him suffer a little more.

Pauline surveyed the basement shelf and found everything where the management company had promised it would be: electric lanterns with extra batteries, a dozen gallons of spring-water, a box of canned foods, and a portable radio. A representative from the company had phoned earlier, directing Pauline to the hurricane shelf, as she'd called it. Apparently the company kept one for each of its properties in Jamaica.

Pauline picked up a couple of lanterns and the radio and headed back upstairs to the game room, where everyone else was clustered around the big-screen TV. By now, the workers had finished covering the windows with plywood and the rooms felt strange and closed in and dark—it was like a completely different house. Still, Pauline was glad they'd decided to ride out the storm here. Their only other options would be to cut the vacation short, which no one wanted to do, or try to find hotel rooms in town. And who could say if they'd be any better off there? Betty could reach down anywhere she chose, and if she proved to be as unpredictable as just about every other hurricane in history, there was no way to outsmart her.

They'd be safe here, Pauline thought. All the pieces of out-door furniture had been tucked into storage so they couldn't turn into flying missiles. And the carefully tended landscaping around the villa was more than aesthetically pleasing—it was chosen with foresight. There were no big trees positioned close enough to crash onto the roof, and the thick shrubbery would provide a little protection against the winds. The only things they hadn't moved from the pool area were the enormous con-crete pots containing plants and flowers that rimmed the stone patio—but the pots were so heavy they wouldn't become air-borne.

"Anything new?" she asked as she sat down next to Dwight on the large sectional couch.

"Betty's shifting," he said, reaching for a handful of popcorn from the bowl on the coffee table. "She may hit us after all."

"Really?" Pauline asked.

"It's still unclear," Ryan said. "But it looks more likely now."

"I say we go down to the beach and do one last round of shots before the storm hits," Gio said. "Let's stare Betty in the face."

"Great idea," Ryan said.

"Tina?" Allie asked, twisting around to look at her friend, who was moving toward the door. "You coming?"

"I'm just going to mix up some shots," Tina said. "Lemon drops okay with everyone?"

"Sounds good," Savannah said.

A few minutes later, they were gathered by the front door. "Yeah, baby!" Gio shouted, pumping his fist at the sky. "Bring it on, Betty!"

Pauline looked up and felt a chill, even though the day was warm. The sky was a shade of pink she usually saw only dur-ing sunsets—but the sun wouldn't be setting for another few hours. The air was calm, but it seemed brimming with an uneasy electric power. Was she the only one who could sense it? The others were laughing and heading toward the stairs that led to the beach.

Pauline closed the front door and was enveloped by silence as rich and heavy as cream. She realized it was the first time during the entire trip that she'd been alone in the villa. She leaned back against the door, feeling exhaustion settle over her heavily.

After a moment she crossed the room and flicked a switch that turned on the gas fireplace, more for its light than for heat. She curled up on a couch and watched the blue and gold flames flicker and wondered how, when the trip ended, she'd find the right words to say to Dwight.

All around Allie on the beach, her friends were spreading out. Gio was jumping over the crashing waves while Tina set the bottle of vodka and bowl of sugar-dipped lemons down on the tiki bar, and Savannah was walking off to the left with Gary beside her. Ryan and Dwight were the only ones still near Allie, but she spun away from them.

She ran a few dozen yards down the beach, then abruptly turned and raced into the sea, feeling the shock of the cool water against her warm skin. She dove under a wave and silently screamed until all the air was gone from her lungs. She surfaced and threw out her arms and floated on her back, bouncing along with the waves. She felt as if the coming hurricane had materialized from somewhere inside of her and now it was absorbing her in turn, as if it was a physical manifestation of the tumult that was too big for her to hold in any longer.

Earlier today, while everyone else had been preoccupied with listening to a storm update, she'd slipped away to her bedroom to call the genetic counseling center. She'd expected to leave a message, but to her surprise, an actual counselor had answered.

At first, the woman hadn't wanted to answer any of Allie's questions over the phone. Only after Allie had pleaded, and agreed to schedule an appointment for the next week, did the woman relent. Or maybe it was the desperation in Allie's voice that had finally swayed her.

"Do you know if your biological father received genetic testing after his diagnosis?" the counselor had asked. She'd said her name was Ann, and she sounded like she was about Allie's age.

Allie had cradled the phone between her shoulder and ear and begun to fold and unfold the piece of paper in her hands. "I don't know. We've never even met. But if he knew he had the disease already, what would be the point?"

"For familial ALS, we can sometimes identify the gene that mutates and causes the symptoms. So if he was tested, and we could pinpoint the gene responsible, we could check your copy of that gene for a mutation," Ann had said.

"I can try to find out," Allie had said. She'd suddenly felt cold and shivered. "I heard he had three other children. Maybe he got tested for them. I doubt he would have done that just . . . for me."

"I see," the counselor had said. After a pause, she'd continued speaking. "You know, if he didn't get tested . . . in a way, it might be a blessing."

"A blessing?" Allie had held it together until then, but her voice had finally broken on that word. "How can *any* of this be a blessing?"

"The average age of onset for familial ALS is around forty-six," the counselor had said. Her voice was gentle and soothing—the same voice Allie used with traumatized clients. They were in the same general field, their names started with the same initial, they were probably around the same age . . . so why was Allie on the wrong side of this call? She was the one who counseled people through problems. She'd always been the one to find silver linings.

"Forty-six," Allie had said. "So, in about ten years." Eva would be seventeen; Sasha, nineteen . . .

"If you even have the gene," Ann had said. "You might not. But how would you feel if you knew you had it?"

Allie had just shaken her head. She couldn't answer the question; it was all she could do to breathe. Her earlier confidence had completely evaporated, and terror ballooned in the space it had left. Making this call had been a mistake!

"So try to live life like you don't have it," Ann had said. "Choose to believe you got that particular gene from your biological mother."

"Ten years," Allie had repeated. How many days was that? How many minutes?

"But your biological father must've been diagnosed later than forty-six," the counselor had said.

Allie had nodded eagerly, suddenly feeling as if she'd been grabbing at a tiny piece of hope. "He was fifty-two."

"In some families, it strikes later. There's a big range. And think of all the advances in medicine we're going to have in the next ten to fifteen years," Ann had said. "There was a huge breakthrough just recently at Northwestern University."

"Okay," Allie had whispered. "But what if I need to know?"

There was a long pause. "You could try to find out if he was tested," Ann had finally said. "Reach out to his family members."

"And then what? If he was tested?"

"You'd get some blood work done," the counselor had said. "But I don't think—"

Allie had cut her off. Who cared what the counselor thought? This was Allie's *life* hanging in the balance! "How long until I'd . . . know?"

"It would take six to eight weeks to get results," Ann had said.

"How accurate are they?" Allie had asked.

There was another pause. "Very accurate," Ann had said.

"Okay," Allie had said. She'd taken a deep, shuddering breath, then she'd said good-bye and hung up the phone.

She'd allowed herself one hard, fast cry, sitting on her bed and folding her arms over her knees and putting her head down while her body shook. Her fate would be determined by a spin of the roulette wheel—black meant she'd get ALS, red meant she wouldn't. She stood a perfectly even chance of living a normal life or enduring one of the worst things she could imagine.

Some time later—Allie didn't know if it was minutes or an hour—she'd woken up flopped over on the side of the bed, her arms still holding her knees to her chest. At first she couldn't believe she'd fallen asleep, but then she'd remembered that the mind had strange ways of protecting itself. She couldn't handle the news she'd received, so she'd simply shut down.

Her brain hadn't turned off, though, just gone to an altered state. Her dreams were filled with horrible images: the hurricane ripping off the roof of the villa; Allie getting hopelessly tangled in a vine underwater near the tropical reef they'd visited on the second day of the trip; a dealer at a gambling table turning over a card with a strange pattern and smiling, revealing a toothless hole of a mouth.

She'd heard knuckles against the door, then his voice: "Allie?"

But it had been the wrong voice.

"Hey, Ryan," she'd said, standing up.

"You okay?" he'd started to ask, but she'd brushed by him.

"Sure!" she'd said, flinching at the too-high note in her voice. "Just had to use the bathroom. Come on, let's go join the others!"

Now she flipped over and swam back to shore, fighting the

sea's strong undertow, and saw Dwight walking toward her. She felt her clothes plaster themselves to her body as she emerged from the water and went to meet him. She leaned up on her tiptoes to whisper into his ear. "Let's go back now."

He nodded. Allie glanced at the others and saw Tina watching them, an odd look on her face. Maybe Tina thought Allie was crazy for diving into the water with all her clothes on, or maybe she'd picked up on something else—whatever it was, Allie didn't care. She'd spent her entire life worrying about others and taking care of them. She was through being the good girl. Where had it gotten her anyway?

Still holding Tina's eye, Allie motioned to herself, then the stairs and waved good-bye. Tina nodded and turned back to look at the water.

Allie began walking up the stairs with Dwight a step behind her. She could feel another panic attack jabbing at the edges of her mind, and she tried to breathe the way Dwight had taught her.

But before she could push it back, a horrible thought burst free: Would it be worse to learn that her birth father had been tested, or to learn that he hadn't?

"That was a fantastic idea," Savannah said as she stepped into the house. "I've never seen anything like that pink sky!"

"It'll be a great story to tell the folks back home," Ryan agreed. He dropped his voice and mimicked a TV announcer: *"They walked through a hurricane . . . and lived to tell about it."*

"Technically it's not a hurricane yet," Gio said. "And it may not even hit us."

"But it will," Dwight said.

Savannah whipped around. "What do you mean?"

"It's going to hit Jamaica," he said.

"When did you hear that?" she asked.

"Five minutes ago," he said.

"So what do we do?" Tina asked. "Should we leave?"

"It's still just a Category Two," Dwight said. "It'll be fierce, but the house can stand it."

"Let's stay," Gio said. He reached out an arm and pulled Tina close. "I'll protect you, babe."

"Gio, come on!" she said. "You don't have to prove anything. We should go . . ."

"I'm staying," Allie said. Savannah looked at her and absently noted that Allie hadn't been around when they'd all done shots on the beach. Maybe she'd left while Savannah was walking in the direction of her encounter with Mr. Red Bathing Suit. She'd wanted to see that particular spot again, but if there had been any evidence of their tryst in the form of indentations in the sand or the condom wrapper that had blown out of her hand, the wind had erased them.

Still, she'd felt as if the score had been evened up just a bit. Gary knew she'd been with another man, and it hurt him; she'd read it on his face this morning, when he picked up a shirt off the floor of her bedroom. Initially, Savannah had smiled; during their marriage, Gary had forever been tidying up after her. Then she saw him staring down at the shirt, and Savannah realized it was the one she'd worn the night before and had misbuttoned.

"You really want to stay, Allie?" Tina was asking. "I figured you'd be the one telling us we should go."

"I don't want to leave," Allie said. "Besides, didn't you promise Dwight a superhero cake? Let's go make it."

"Okay," Tina said. "But should we see if Pauline wants to help? It's her husband, after all."

"Speaking of, where is Pauline?" Savannah asked, just as Pauline came in from the living room to rejoin the group.

"I'm going to fill some pots with water, just in case," Gio said.

"The bathtubs, too. Ryan, gather up whatever you can find. Candles, flashlights . . ."

"On it," Ryan said.

"Savannah?" Gary asked in a voice so low she was the only one who could hear it. "If you're not going to talk to me, I'll leave now. I can make it to a hotel before the storm hits."

She looked at him levelly. *I don't need you,* she thought. *I can be happy without you.*

It was what finally made her nod and say, "Fine. Let's talk."

The others left the room. The moment Savannah and Gary were alone, two things happened: First, Gary took a step toward her, his eyes intent, his mouth beginning to form a word.

Then all the lights went out.

Chapter Eighteen

Darkness

"I'M GETTING SCARED," TINA said. "Oh, my God, that sound . . . it's like someone is being tortured!"

"That's some serious wind," Gio said. He moved a few books off the top of a bookcase, clearing space for a fat candle in a glass holder. They were rationing the battery-powered lanterns, so just one was turned on, and the illumination didn't reach into the adjoining rooms. Only the game room, where they were all clustered, had enough light to see. Whenever people wanted to use the bathroom, they brought along a flashlight and hurried back as fast as they could.

"Betty sounds crazy," Savannah said. "She's almost human."

Tina wrapped her arms around herself, then flinched as a crash came from outside. "What was that? It's like a horror movie. We don't know what's happening out there!"

She could hear her voice growing shrill, but she didn't care. This was a stupid idea. They should have gotten off the island when they had a chance. People were routinely killed by hurricanes, and yet, they'd stayed—arrogantly assuming they'd be spared. She should've remembered the lesson she'd learned from her shifts in the ER: No one was immune from tragedy.

"It's a tree limb," Gio told her. "More will come down, so brace yourself for the noise." It seemed impossible that her husband was so calm. He was moving around the room now, thumping his knuckles against the walls and peering up at the ceiling.

"How long do hurricanes last, anyway?" Savannah asked.

"A couple hours," Gio said, lifting up an edge of a pinball machine to test its weight. "Ryan, help me move this to the far wall."

"A couple *hours*?" Tina shrieked.

"We're going to be fine, Tina."

Everyone turned in surprise as Pauline crossed the room to sit on the big sectional couch next to Tina. "This house was specifically built to withstand hurricanes," she said. "Everything is reinforced. It sounds horrible outside, and it's going to sound like that for a while, but we'll be perfectly safe."

Tina looked at Pauline and let out the breath she didn't realize she'd been holding. "Okay," she said. "Thanks."

"Is anyone else hungry?" Dwight asked.

Tina clapped a hand over her mouth, then exclaimed, "Your birthday dinner!" She looked at Dwight. "We were going to cook you something special . . . I'm sorry, Dwight. You gave us this incredible vacation and you don't even get a cake on your birthday!"

"Oh, yes he does," said a voice from the doorway. Tina looked up.

"Happy birthday to you . . ." Allie came in the room carrying a basket topped with a tall candle. She was holding the basket with one hand and steadying the candle with the other.

She put the basket down on the table in front of Dwight, and he closed his eyes and blew out the candle.

"Who says we need a boring old cake to celebrate a birthday?" Allie asked.

"Razzles!" Dwight said. He reached into the basket and pulled out Pop Rocks in three different flavors. "How'd you find all this?"

"I've got my ways," Allie joked. Tina glanced at Pauline, wondering if she minded Allie taking over the birthday celebration, but Pauline's face didn't betray any strong emotions.

Dwight poured some Pop Rocks into his mouth, then passed the package to Allie. "Man, I'd forgotten how good these are!"

"Candy for dinner?" Savannah laughed. "I love it. Someone give me a FireBall."

"Ooh, those things always burned my tongue," Tina said. "And whenever I had one I got impatient and tried to bite down and felt like I was cracking my teeth."

Tina reached for the Pop Rocks and let a few sizzle on her tongue. "It totally freaked me out when I heard Mikey died from eating Pop Rocks while drinking Coke," she said. "Remember Mikey? The kid from the Life cereal commercials? That might've been the first urban legend I ever heard."

"Mikey's an adult entertainer in Ohio now," Savannah said. "He specializes in bachelorette parties."

"Really?" Tina asked.

"Just wanted to see if I could start another urban legend," Savannah said. "I have no idea what Mikey's up to these days. I haven't been tracking the guy's career trajectory."

Tina laughed and welcomed the way some tension exited her body along with the sound. "Ooh, pass me the Hot Tamales," she said.

"So what did you wish for, Dwight?" Savannah asked.

"He can't tell us—then it won't come true," Allie cut in.

"It's okay," Dwight said. "I didn't make a wish. I feel like I have everything I want."

The radio announcer's voice fought through intermittent static: "Betty . . . in minutes . . . Seek shelter immediately . . .

away from trees . . . interior room . . . away from windows . . ."

"Tequila, anyone?" Gio suggested. He put a bottle on the table, along with a lemon with a knife stuck into it.

"Heck, yes," Tina said. She reached for the bottle and took a sip.

"Ah, tequila," Savannah said. She winked at Tina, then flicked her eyes toward Dwight. "Are you sure you should be drinking it?"

"It's fine," Tina said, glaring at Savannah.

"Do you mean because Tina has a low tolerance?" Ryan asked.

"Yes, that's precisely what I meant," Savannah said.

"I do not!" Tina protested. "I only got drunk the other night because I chugged so much during quarters. I can handle a shot of tequila."

"I'll have one, too, Tina," Allie said, grabbing the neck of the bottle. "To Dwight. Happy birthday!"

Everyone cheered: "To Dwight!"

"And thanks for being such a wonderful friend and host!" Allie continued. "You've given us the most amazing trip ever!"

Even in the dim light, it was easy to see his spectacular blush.

"Speech!" Gio shouted, and Ryan took up the chant: "Speech! Speech! Speech!"

Was she the only one who saw the hurt flicker across Pauline's face? Tina wondered. Sure, Dwight might've financed the trip, but it was obviously Pauline who'd done all the legwork. She'd even made sure there were vegetarian entrées at every meal for Allie. The whole thing had been Pauline's idea—Dwight had mentioned that at the very first dinner. Besides, shouldn't Allie have let Pauline toast her husband for his birthday first?

"And to Pauline!" Tina cried, raising her glass again. "The hostess with the mostess!"

Everyone cheered, and Pauline shot Tina a small smile. Usually Allie was the one who was attuned to everyone's feelings, Tina thought. Since when had they switched roles?

"Th-thanks for being such great friends," Dwight said. "This has been the best trip of my entire life!"

Better than your honeymoon? Tina thought. Something seemed off. She hadn't completely warmed up to Pauline, but she felt sorry for her. Pauline seemed to have shrunk away to the margins of the group ever since she'd come back from visiting her mother in the hospital. She'd stayed in the house today instead of coming to the beach with everyone else. Dwight hadn't seemed too concerned. He'd just been hanging out with Allie . . . like he was right now. The two of them were sharing a love seat, and Pauline and Ryan were across the room. Tina frowned. She'd convinced herself, despite their intimate body language, that Allie and Dwight were just casually chatting by the pool when she saw them in the middle of the night earlier in the week. There couldn't be anything going on between them. But they'd left the beach alone today . . . No! There couldn't.

Could there?

"I miss college sometimes," Savannah was saying. "I don't think we knew how good we had it back then. At least I didn't."

"No one did," Gio said.

"I wish I'd appreciated my classes more," Tina said, shaking off her thoughts. "For me, learning got in the way of fun. What I wouldn't give to be able to take any classes I wanted now! Like art history. Why didn't I learn about art when I had the chance?"

"I miss being in our dorm room in pj's, and wandering across the hall to talk to Van," Allie said. "Or knocking three times on the wall to tell Dwight to come over to study with me. Just always being together." She turned to look at Gary, who'd been sitting quietly next to Savannah. "Did you feel that way about college, Gary?" Allie asked.

He shook his head. "I worked every weekend in a sandwich shop," he said. "Friday and Saturday nights, and all day Sunday."

That was the last thing she'd have expected, Tina thought. She couldn't imagine Gary serving others.

"Gary hates sandwiches now," Savannah said. "Never eats them." She was holding the tequila bottle, and she accepted the lemon wedge that Tina handed her, then she took a swig. "Ahh, that burns!"

"I still have all the ingredients for the sandwiches engraved in my brain," Gary said, shaking his head as if to try to loosen the long-held information's grip on his mind. "The owner was crazy, and he held these impromptu quizzes. You had to reel off the ingredients of whatever sandwich he named in under ten seconds, or you'd lose your job."

"How many sandwiches were there?" Tina asked.

"Twenty-seven," Gary said. He reached for the bottle Savannah had set on the table and took a sip.

Tina started to ask Gary another question—this new information about him was intriguing, and she wondered if his parents didn't have money or just refused to help him with college expenses—but a huge crash drowned her out.

"Well hello, Betty," Gio said.

He stood up, walked over to the candle, and blew it out. "Just in case," he said. "We don't want a fire on top of everything else."

Something rammed into the side of the house with enough force to make the walls tremble. The noise of a spectacular crash carried into the room.

"That didn't sound good," Savannah observed. Her tone was light, but she'd moved closer to Gary on the big sectional couch. "It couldn't be a window, could it?"

"Nah," Gio said. "That plywood's thick. The wind probably

carried something to the patio and smashed it against the stone. We're going to find all sorts of stuff when we go out after the storm."

"I hope people got enough notice to get off the beach," Tina said. "They were saying on the Weather Channel that most deaths come from the storm surge . . ."

"They'll go inland," Gio assured her. "Jamaicans are savvy about hurricanes. They won't mess around."

Tina tried to ignore the horrible sounds coming from outside, but she couldn't. It was as if the hurricane had targeted their house specifically and was focusing all her rage on trying to tear it loose from its foundations, although Tina logically knew that wasn't true. She couldn't believe how violent and angry Betty sounded. She moaned and shrieked and thrashed and shook the house, like a giant in the middle of a tantrum.

Anxiety began to creep back into Tina's body. Could the house really withstand hours of this? Maybe Pauline was wrong; the contractors might've cut corners while building this place. Inferior materials could've been substituted for more costly ones to increase profits. That sort of thing happened all the time, according to Gio.

The house shook, and a bookcase in the corner crashed to the floor, its contents scattering. Tina couldn't help releasing a little scream at the sound.

I want to go home, she thought suddenly. Her heart jackhammered in her chest. She looked around, but the others had gone suddenly silent. Even Gio looked tense, which scared her more than anything else.

She closed her eyes, and the faces of her four children swam into her mind: Paolo, their oldest, named after Gio's deceased father. He was only eight, but his feet were almost as big as Gio's. Puppy feet, Tina called them. Angela was six, and she loved dogs and doing somersaults and shampoo that smelled of strawberries. She had big brown eyes and at night, just before falling asleep, she made the little cooing noises of a dove. Jessica was feisty and smart, and once she'd passed through the terrible twos, she'd developed a fantastic sense of humor— the kid could do a very credible Brooklyn accent. And sweet Sammy, with his skinny arms and big belly and soft kisses in the morning . . .

I miss you all so much, Tina thought.

She remembered how on the anniversary of her mother's death last year, she'd driven past a field of wildflowers and recalled how much her mother had loved flowers. She'd had to pull the minivan to the side of the road because she couldn't see through her tears. And then the high, worried voices began asking why she was sad . . . She'd told them the truth, that she missed her mom and the flowers had made Tina think of her. Then Angela had suggested they go smell the flowers and say a prayer for Grandma. Tina remembered the feel of their soft, small hands in her own, and the way Angela had danced in the field while Paolo had picked her a bouquet to take home . . . Oh, she loved those four small people so much it felt like a physical ache.

Her eyes snapped open.

Something had just happened to her, something important. She'd desperately needed something to cling to, and the thought of her children was what had given her solace.

She blinked back tears—again!—but this time they sprang from relief: She missed her babies. She couldn't wait to see them again. Her deepest fear—that something was wrong with her, that some vital mothering bone was broken inside of her— wasn't true. She had only needed a break. It was really that simple.

They'd get through tonight, and then on Friday they'd spend one last full day in Jamaica, taking in the aftermath of the storm and getting ready to leave. She'd be home Saturday night in time for pizza and pajamas and a family cuddle on the couch.

Betty shook the house again and roared, but this time, Tina didn't flinch. All week long, she'd felt as if she was back in college—and she'd jealously clung to that sensation, dreading the moment it would slip away. But right now she was a mother again, which also meant she was a warrior.

"Has it stopped?" Allie overheard Savannah ask.

Allie was on her way back from the bathroom, but she paused in the hallway. For the first time in almost two hours, she couldn't hear any noise from outside. Curious to see if there was any damage to the house, she turned and began walking in the other direction, then stopped short.

The living room, which had faced the brunt of the storm, looked like it had been ransacked. Knickknacks had fallen off shelves, smaller pieces of furniture had been shifted, and a glass statue lay on the wooden floor, broken into dozens of pieces. She stepped gingerly through the mess, moving toward the coffee table books that had slid onto the floor. She found the one with the pictures of waterfalls on the cover and opened it, holding her breath. Her gift to Dwight was still there, hidden between the pages.

Allie reached for the slim rectangular package, which was wrapped in a sheet of newspaper comic strips—the only thing she could find that resembled wrapping paper. But she knew Dwight would love it; he'd once told her he still read the comics first, before the business page and main news section.

It wasn't the most elaborate present she'd ever given anyone, but it might be the most meaningful. She'd taken photos of Dwight on the catamaran on the second day of the trip, and, after she'd discovered a little nook of an office in the house containing a computer and printer and fax, had managed to print out a decent copy of the best one. It wasn't framed yet, but she'd sandwiched it between two pieces of cardboard to keep it from becoming creased. She'd left it here because she didn't want Ryan to find it in their bedroom.

Allie wanted to give it to Dwight tonight so he'd know how he looked through her eyes: In the photo, he was leaning against the rail of the boat, the breeze blowing back his dark brown hair. He wasn't smiling, but he looked thoughtful and a little mysterious, and the blue-green water mirrored the tints in his hazel eyes. It was a wonderful picture.

Allie could hear Ryan's voice calling her name as he came toward the room. She clutched the package to her chest. Where could she hide it? If the others began putting the room back together, they might discover her gift, and it was for Dwight's eyes alone.

She could hear Ryan's footsteps. He was almost here. She glanced wildly around, realizing she'd be trapped if she went into the kitchen; then she unlocked the front door and slipped out, closing it silently behind her.

The air felt clean, and it was light enough that Allie could see the pool area was remarkably unscathed. A lot of tree limbs had blown into the area—mostly small ones, but a few that were thicker than her wrist—but since all of the furniture had been put into storage, there wasn't any real damage.

Allie cast a glance behind her to make sure no one was coming, then walked around to the copse of palm trees on the far side of the pool, thinking she could tuck her gift there, then hurry back inside. Later, she could bring Dwight back to the place she now thought of as theirs. She knelt by the trees and found the perfect hiding spot between two close-together trunks. She was reaching for a rock to anchor the package when the world exploded.

There was a long, loud shriek—the only warning Betty gave—then wind smacked into her like a brick wall, wrenching the package out of her hands and sending it swirling upward.

"No!" Allie shouted. She reached up, trying to catch it, but it swooped farther away as a dark gray fog rushed in to envelop her.

The rain pelted down and up and sideways, and her wet hair slapped into her eyes. She pushed it out of her face just in time to see a branch fly by, far too close to her head.

The hurricane wasn't over, she suddenly remembered. Every elementary school student learned about the structure of storms, and she was no exception. But she'd completely forgotten that every hurricane had a brief window of calm called an eye.

Get back to the house, she told herself. She staggered a few feet forward, but the wind was gaining strength as fast as Allie was losing it. It kept pushing her over, like a playground bully. The house was about twenty yards ahead and a bit to her right, Allie thought as she dropped to her knees. But what if she was wrong? She couldn't see that far in front of her. She reached around the base of a tree and locked her fingers together.

"Help!" she yelled, even though she knew no one could hear her over Betty's howling. Already, she could feel the strength in her arms ebbing away. Another branch smacked down a half dozen yards away, and she began to cry.

She'd been so consumed by her possible ALS diagnosis that she'd never considered the fact that there were so many other ways to die. Hurricanes routinely killed people in Jamaica. Maybe she'd become another statistic, the foolish tourist who'd forgotten about the eye of the storm and had ventured outside at the worst possible moment.

She bowed her head and cried harder, feeling the bark of the tree scratch her arms and cheek as the wind clawed at her. When her hands finally lost their grip, Betty would lift her up and throw her into something—another tree, one of the huge concrete pots by the pool, the house itself. She'd break bones, probably hit her head. She'd lose consciousness, and then it would truly be all over; she'd be a rag doll in a washing machine.

She lifted her head and gathered all the strength she had left, funneling it into a yell that seemed to emerge from her core: "Ryan!"

He couldn't possibly hear her, but calling his name released something inside of Allie that had been tightly clenched. The anger she'd felt toward her husband was ripping away, revealing the abyss of terror that had always lain just beneath.

Maybe she hadn't ever been angry at Ryan after all; maybe he was just a safe target for the fury she felt at everything else: her jerk of a birth father and his crappy genes, her birth mother and the thoughtless way she'd unleashed the news like a bomb into Allie's life, ALS itself. The unfairness of it all.

Her fingers were almost completely numb. The wind was pulling at them, trying to wrench them loose. She couldn't last much longer.

"Allie!"

Somehow she heard his yell—or maybe she'd just sensed it, the way her mother, Louise, always said she'd sensed Allie's cry the moment Allie was born.

She tried to call out to Ryan again as he stood in the doorway, holding a lantern that seemed like the only spot of light in the world, but her voice was gone. Then the light disappeared.

Ryan probably hadn't been able to see her, or if he had, by some miracle, then he'd gone to get help. But Allie couldn't help feeling as if he'd deserted her. She deserved it, though. She'd deserted him first.

Hold on, she ordered herself, clenching her teeth and steeling her body. Enduring this was harder than making it through the wall she'd hit during the twenty-third mile of the marathon she'd run last year, harder than the pain of childbirth, harder than anything she'd ever known. Her muscles screamed and her skin felt raw. She prayed for Ryan to . . . to what? Not to come out here; he'd be risking his own life!

Earlier on this trip, she'd wanted him to become a different kind of man. But now, amid her terror, she saw not her own life but Ryan's flash before her eyes, and she realized how wrong she'd been. She saw her husband reaching for her hand and slow-dancing with her, to no music, in their hotel room on their wedding night; then Ryan was feeding her ice chips with his fingertips and strength with his eyes while she panted through labor. She saw him as a father, straining his back as he carried their sleeping children out of the minivan and up two flights of stairs because he didn't want to wake them; she saw him making up silly jingles to get their daughters to put on their shoes when they were defiant two-year-olds.

She needed Ryan to be safe, to stay around to raise their girls. No one could do as good a job.

She lifted her head to whisper a prayer and saw the light again. Ryan had attached the lantern to his belt and was down on his belly, inching toward her, hooking his fingers around the ridges of the stones on the patio to gain traction. He looked like a rock climber who was moving horizontally instead of vertically as he felt around for the next crack between the rocks.

Somehow, he'd known where to find her. Renewed strength flooded into her arms.

She lost sight of him for a few agonizing minutes, then he reappeared just yards away, rounding the edge of the pool.

"Here!" she screamed. "I'm here!"

Thank God for those huge concrete pots—he was bracing his feet against them, then using them to push off, like a swimmer doing a flip turn. His feet were bare, and she could see blood on them, but he kept relentlessly inching forward in a small circle of light.

She could see all the tendons in his arm stand out as he battled the wind. He must be exhausted; Allie knew she was, and she was only kneeling in place and had the tree for support.

"I'm sorry!" Allie cried when he finally reached her and collapsed on top of her, wrapping his arms around both her and the tree. He was violently shaking. "I'm so, so sorry."

Either he didn't hear her or he couldn't spare the effort it would take to answer. Their tree was bending now, yielding to the wind, and Allie was terrified it would snap.

Ryan was signaling for her to lie flat on the ground, and then he pointed in the direction of the house—or at least what Allie assumed was the direction of the house. She squinted and realized he was fumbling with something tied around his belt, next to the lantern. He'd gotten all the stretchy resistance bands from the gym and had linked them together to form a makeshift rope, she realized. He must have attached one end to the house so they'd be able to find it in the darkness.

Ryan's lips moved, but his words were lost in the wind.

Was he telling her to start for the house? It wasn't far away, but they'd have to take a circuitous route around the pool, which doubled the length.

Allie began to crawl, but Ryan stopped her by putting a hand on her shoulder. He wrapped his legs around the tree to anchor himself, then pulled off his T-shirt and twisted it around Allie's left arm and his right one, tying the ends into a knot. The fleeting thought crossed Allie's mind that it was good Ryan had been a Boy Scout. He took off his watch and fastened it around the knot, securing it even tighter. Linking their fates together.

"Now," he shouted, his mouth close to her ear.

Away from the protection the copse of trees had provided, the wind hit her from every angle. Small twigs and clusters of leaves slammed into her face and arms, and the rain felt like tiny knives jabbing her exposed skin.

She could feel Ryan's bulk beside her as she crawled and pulled and fought her way forward. Sometimes he almost dragged her along, and the shirt was cutting off the circulation in her arm, but she knew without him, Betty would've overpowered her. They finally reached the first potted plant by the pool, and took refuge against it for a moment, breathing hard.

"Almost there!" Ryan shouted above the wind.

It was a lie—they weren't even halfway there. Allie moved another inch forward, then screamed as a thick branch cracked down onto the patio a few feet in front of them.

A gust scooped a big wave out of the pool, and it crashed down over Allie and Ryan. She was so startled she lost her grip and started to roll over, but Ryan counterbalanced and tugged her back. She felt nausea rise in her throat. They might not make it. Her stupidity could cause both of their deaths, leave their girls orphans. She bowed her head and tried to force her legs and arms to move forward, to keep fighting. But she had nothing left.

Then something jerked them forward a few inches. Allie squinted and saw a light coming from the doorway again. Gio was there now, yanking on the other end of the resistance bands, adding his strength to theirs. As Allie watched, Tina and Gary and Savannah and Dwight and Pauline joined in the tug-of-war against Betty.

Allie and Ryan scrabbled along over the remaining distance to the house. One big pull from her friends dragged Allie along the stone patio and skinned her knees, and the shirt was biting deeply into her arm, but she didn't even register the pain.

And then they were at the doorway, and hands were pulling them inside, and the guys were throwing their weight against the door as they fought to close it. Papers had been flying around the room, but they fluttered to the floor like confetti when the door cut off the storm.

"Oh, my God, Allie!" Tina cried. She enveloped Allie and Ryan in an embrace. "What were you doing? Why did you go out there?"

Allie was panting so hard she could hardly speak. She reached to release the shirt around her arm, but Tina was already working on the tight, wet knot. "I just . . . I thought the storm was over."

"Ryan went to look for you," Tina said. "You were taking so long in the bathroom and I thought you were just feeling sick from the tequila, but he went anyway . . ."

Ryan was bent over, hands on his knees, sucking in air. Allie put her hand on his back and saw blood drip onto his shirt. It was coming from her arm, she realized—the shirt had rubbed off the top layer of skin.

"We need to get some Neosporin and gauze on that," Tina said. "And on Ryan's feet, too."

"Good thing you found your watch," Gio said, handing it back to Ryan. "It came in handy."

"I had to find it," Ryan said. He shrugged. "It was a present from Allie."

Allie felt her knees buckle.

"Whoa, girl, let's get you somewhere you can sit down," Savannah said, catching her by her uninjured arm.

"We should go back to the game room," Gio said. He gestured to Ryan. "Come on, buddy. Lean on me. Dwight, give Allie a hand."

"No!" Allie said. Dwight had been walking toward her, but he stopped when she spoke, and confusion flitted over his features. Allie lowered her eyes, feeling her cheeks burn from the wind and her shame. "I mean, I can walk."

"I think this calls for more shots of tequila," Savannah said.

Her words were light, but her voice shook. She gave a little laugh and enveloped Allie in a hug. "You know, you've really livened up this vacation, girlfriend."

Allie rested her head against Savannah's shoulder. "I may need some help walking after all. My legs are like Jell-O."

"I've got you," Ryan said. He shrugged off Gio's arm and moved to Allie's side. Outside, Betty was shrieking and smashing things, her rage reaching a fevered pitch. Allie shuddered and leaned into Ryan.

He hadn't gone after the watch to prove anything. He'd done it out of love, she thought. She'd been so wrong.

"How did you know where to find me?" she asked. He looked down at her. *Those eyes,* she thought. *I've always adored those eyes.*

"I'm not sure." He shrugged. "I just knew."

Chapter Nineteen

Change

THEY'D BEEN STUCK IN the same room for four hours—well, other than that bit of excitement when they'd hauled in Ryan and Allie like half-drowned kittens, Savannah thought. But somehow, it had turned into one of the best nights of the trip. It was safe and cozy here, with two lanterns casting a soft glow and the squashy sectional couch providing enough seating for all eight of them. Pauline had found a stack of extra blankets in a closet, and everyone was snuggled under one. The tequila had made its rounds more than a few times, which probably accounted for why everyone was feeling more relaxed about the storm, and the candy was almost gone.

It was Savannah's turn to ask a question. "Favorite movie," she said. Everyone scribbled on scraps of paper, then folded them and put them in front of Savannah, who mixed them up in her hands.

She picked one and opened it. *"Anchorman: Ron Burgundy,"* she said. "That's got to be Ryan's or Gio's."

"Mine," they said in unison. They leaned toward each other and high-fived as everyone laughed.

Savannah unfolded another square of paper. *"Titanic.* Hmm . . .

well, it's a given it's one of the women. No guys would pick it; they're too threatened by the hotness that is Leo DiCaprio. Tina!"

"Nope." Tina shook her head.

"Allie?" Savannah asked.

"Not me," Allie said.

"It's my favorite," Pauline said.

"Oh, that's interesting," Savannah said. "I would've guessed you'd pick something artsy. Maybe a black-and-white film. Why *Titanic*?"

Pauline shrugged. "I guess I'm a sucker for a good love story."

Savannah squinted at the level of tequila in the glass bottle, wondering exactly how much Pauline had consumed. The woman sitting across from her wearing a sweat suit with her blond hair tangled around her shoulders barely resembled the prim hostess who'd welcomed them all to Jamaica almost a week ago. True, her sweat suit was obviously a designer brand that was never meant to be sullied by perspiration, but the woman inside of it was different. She truly seemed not to care what anyone thought of her, which made Savannah realize how very much she must've cared before.

Savannah unfolded another answer. *"When Harry Met Sally."* She crumpled up the paper in her hand.

"Aren't you going to guess?" Tina asked.

"It's Gary's," she said.

"Kind of a chick flick, isn't it?" Gio teased, but Gary didn't answer.

"Okay, who's next?" Allie said. "Pick another one, Van."

But Savannah just tilted her head back on the couch and closed her eyes. "Someone else take a turn," she said. She heard nothing for a moment, then Tina said, "Okay, I'm up. Favorite guilty pleasure!"

There were a few laughs, and Gio cracked a joke, but the

noise the others made seemed low and muted to her because Savannah was deep in the grip of a memory.

She'd been filing a ragged fingernail when he called to invite her to a movie. "Which one?" she'd asked, cradling the phone between her shoulder and ear while she shaped the nail into a perfect oval.

"*When Harry Met Sally,*" he'd said. "It's a matinee at three o'clock."

"How can that even be in a theater?" she'd asked. "It's so old!"

"They're having this—this revival," he'd said. Later she'd think back and remember the hesitation in his voice as he answered, but at the time, she'd assumed he was distracted.

"Sure," she'd said. She'd always liked that movie. But he'd driven to the winery instead, and as the sun had begun to set, he'd reached for her hand.

"Savannah," Gary had said. "Will you marry me?"

She'd looked at him for a long moment, then she'd smiled.

"Ask me again," she'd said. "After you get down on one knee."

He'd done it, and she'd cried out, "Yes!" and had flung her arms around his neck, and then everyone around them had broken out in applause. Gary had slid the ring onto her finger, and as she sat there gaping at it, the winery's owner had come by with a bottle of their best vintage. Then they'd driven home, and Gary had surprised her again, with two plane tickets for a long weekend in Montreal . . . She'd moved in with him the next week.

"Savannah?"

Tina's voice brought her back to the present. "You need to write down your favorite guilty pleasure."

Savannah looked at the blank piece of paper in front of her. She was furious with Gary for ambushing her with that memory.

These past few days had taught her what her new life would look like, if she and Gary stayed separated: sex with hot younger men, nights out dancing with her girlfriends, a renewed appreciation for adventure . . . It didn't sound so bad, after all. Jamaica had shown her that she didn't need Gary and his shameless attempt to manipulate her.

She scribbled *Sex on the beach in Jamaica,* then handed her paper to Tina.

There was another loud crash from outside, and Savannah reflexively glanced up. Gary was in her line of view, and he was staring at her. The expression in his eyes made her catch her breath. He looked so sad.

Her fury drained away as she stared back at him.

She wondered what he'd been about to say to her when the lights had gone out. Then her thoughts of just a moment earlier came rushing back to her: *If she and Gary stayed separated . . . If.* At what point had her certainty turned into such a tiny word so filled with possibility?

"Wait!" Savannah cried. She reached over and snatched the papers out of Tina's hand and began frantically unfolding them, searching for the awful message she'd intended for Gary, the one that would make him stand up and walk away from her, perhaps forever.

She crumpled it in her hand, then shoved it into her pocket. The silence in the room made her realize everyone was staring at her.

"Well, you kind of killed that round, Van," Ryan said.

"Sorry," she said. "I changed my mind."

Chapter Twenty

Friday

THEY'D MADE IT THROUGH Hurricane Betty, Pauline thought as she opened her eyes and took in the stillness. Everyone had divided up the flashlights and lanterns and had gone to bed around one a.m., carrying bottled water for teeth brushing, since the purity of the tap water was iffy. There wasn't any power—there probably wouldn't be for weeks on the island—and it had been far too dark to venture outside. They'd take stock of their surroundings later.

Dwight had been reading the Steve Jobs biography when Pauline succumbed to exhaustion and rolled over. But now, as she glanced at her iPhone, she realized she'd slept for only a little more than an hour.

As she got out of bed, she realized Dwight was missing. She wasn't concerned; he'd always been a night owl. He'd probably gone to read in the living room so he wouldn't disturb her. Since he'd taken the lantern, she reached for her iPhone, which had a tiny bit of life left, and walked soundlessly toward the center of the house, guided by the weak light of her phone's screen. But Dwight wasn't sprawled on one of the couches, or rummaging for a snack in the kitchen.

Pauline smiled. He'd probably gone back to the game room. She hoped he was still awake; it would be nice to have company. Maybe they could read together for a while.

She was a half dozen steps away from the room when her phone died and blackness enveloped her. She trailed one hand along the wall to guide her as she closed the distance to the doorway. She could see a faint light coming from it, and just as she opened her mouth to speak Dwight's name, she heard Allie's voice.

"I don't know how it happened," Allie was saying in a voice just above a whisper. She sounded . . . desolate.

Pauline stopped moving even before she heard the voice of the other person in the conversation.

"You had to have known I was in love with you back in college," Dwight said. "I guess I kind of . . . fell into those feelings again when we got here. Us all being together again. It felt like college, in a way."

"I didn't know," Allie said. "You were in love with me?"

"Crazy in love," Dwight said.

Pauline felt certain they must've heard her sharp intake of breath, but there wasn't a lull in their conversation.

"But . . . how did it *happen*?" Allie was asking, and her voice broke on the last word. "We weren't thinking clearly. We must not have been thinking at all!"

Run, Pauline's mind said, but she moved quietly and deliberately as she retraced her footsteps back to her suite. She climbed the stairs and passed the bedroom next to hers.

The bedroom she'd specifically assigned Allie because Allie wasn't a threat like Savannah.

As she closed the door behind her and climbed into bed, Pauline finally let out her breath, feeling as if her lungs were trembling along with the rest of her. She pulled the covers up to her neck and faced the wall. She was cold, so cold that she felt numb. She couldn't cry. She couldn't speak. She waited a long time, and was beginning to think he wouldn't come to bed at all, when she finally heard his tread in the hallway. Their bed creaked as he sat down, then he got under the sheet and light comforter and flopped his head onto a pillow. After a moment, he sighed and turned away from her.

Pauline stayed frozen in place, staring into the darkness. Had there been any signs? she wondered. She thought over the past week, searching through her memories to see if there had been private looks, or times that Allie and Dwight had disappeared together. But she couldn't recall a single instance.

She closed her eyes and traveled back to Allie's thirty-fifth birthday party. She saw the bright paper streamers taped to the ceiling, smelled the sweet-sharp aroma of chili bubbling on the stove, and watched the group lift glasses high into the air. Dwight was standing on the periphery, and the look on his face—the one that transformed it; the one Pauline had never seen before—was of pure joy.

She'd thought being within his circle of friends was the reason for his happiness. That inclusion in a group was a vital, missing piece in the life of the man who always seemed to be an outsider.

But now, for the first time, she drew in her focus more tightly. She tracked Dwight's point of view. He was standing by her as everyone hooted and laughed and cheered. Savannah was next to them, too. Tina and Gio were nearby. But Dwight wasn't looking at any of them. What was he staring at when that smile broke out on his face?

Two little girls were bringing in a cake, and Allie was closing her eyes to make a wish as she smiled . . .

Allie.

Pauline felt as if someone had punched her in the stomach. He'd been watching Allie the whole time.

Her husband was in love with another woman. Maybe he always had been. She'd tried to give him this trip as a gift, as a way to fill a hole in his life, but he hadn't needed it.

He'd only needed Allie.

"Did you hear something?" Allie asked, glancing toward the door of the game room.

Dwight got up, holding the lantern. He peered down the hallway, twisting his head in both directions. "Nope," he said. He walked back over to Allie and sat down again. But this time, he put a little more space between them.

"Ryan and I were having problems," Allie began. Her body sagged against the couch. "It started when I learned about the ALS. I felt like—"

Dwight interrupted her. "He loves you," he said. "When I saw him dragging you back to the house . . . that look on his face, Allie. He wasn't going to let anything happen to you."

Allie was too ashamed to respond. She hadn't explained things well. She and Ryan weren't having problems; she'd created a problem for them. Not a problem, a catastrophe.

Dwight leaned his head back against the couch. "I was saying how in college I was in love with you— I still can't believe you never noticed—but . . ."

"But?" Allie echoed when his voice trailed off.

"But now I love you as a friend. You're the best friend I've ever had."

Dwight was ending it, Allie realized. And even though she knew it was the right thing to do, even though she wanted to stay with Ryan, a tremble of fear ran through her body.

"I meant what I said on the beach," Dwight told her. He reached for her hand. Hers must've been cold, because his was so warm. "I will always take care of you and your family. If you ever need anything, I'll be there. Faster than you can imagine."

Allie was crying now, tears streaming down her cheeks. Sweet Dwight, with his pants legs tucked into his socks and his understanding of fear so powerful it turned into panic, didn't blame her. Even though she'd instigated what had happened: She'd led him up to the cluster of palm trees while everyone else had stayed on the beach to do lemon drop shots and confront Betty.

"Are you sure?" Dwight had asked when she'd reached for the zipper on his shorts. But instead of answering, she'd kissed him, cutting off any chance of conversation. She hadn't even looked into his eyes—she'd just tried to lose herself in the sensations. It hadn't worked; the sex had felt mechanical and frantic instead of soulful. Afterward, they'd pulled apart quickly and Dwight had looked as stunned as she'd felt. Now he regretted it; she could tell.

My fault, she thought. *I did this.* She despised the person she'd become on this trip.

"It's okay, Allie," Dwight said. He squeezed her hand.

"I'm so scared," she sobbed. "Just . . . please don't hate me, okay?"

"It's okay," he repeated. "Shhh . . ."

They stayed that way for a while; then, because she knew she didn't deserve his comfort, Allie slid her hand out of Dwight's. She stood up and leaned over to kiss him on the forehead.

"I've always loved you, too," she whispered, wishing it didn't feel like a good-bye. "I always will."

Chapter Twenty-One

Aftermath

THE SUN SHONE IN a soft blue sky and the wind had disappeared. If it wasn't for the fact that the shoreline had been completely transformed, it would seem as if Betty had never existed.

Getting down to the beach had been a challenge; Betty had ripped out two of the stairs, damaged others, and the railing was in tatters. But they'd all wanted to come here. Everyone except Pauline; Dwight reported that she had a horrible headache and needed to rest.

"It's so sad," Tina said as she looked out over the beach. "Look at this."

She swept out her arms to encompass jagged pieces of wood mingled with some trash, heaps of seaweed, and what looked like the rusted engine of a powerboat. Their tiki bar was a pile of demolished wood, and Betty had taken a huge bite out of the midsection of the floating dock.

All around her, the others were walking down the beach or picking up branches and tossing them into the fire pit in preparation for a bonfire. Savannah had brought down a big pot and some instant coffee she'd discovered in the pantry, and they were planning to brew Sanka over the flame. Ryan had

had the good sense to fill a cooler with plenty of ice and hot dogs and veggie burgers before the storm struck, which meant they could cook lunch and dinner on the beach tonight. All of the other food—the tins of caviar and homemade sorbet and good cheeses and fresh crab cakes that no one had noticed until they were cleaning out the refrigerator—had been lost to the storm.

Cowboy coffee and hot dogs, Tina thought, smiling. What a far cry from the lobster bisque and champagne at the beginning of their trip.

Tina leaned over to stretch her back, then glanced at Allie, who was slumped on the trunk of a downed tree.

"You okay?" she asked.

Allie shook her head. She seemed steeped in misery.

Tina studied her oldest friend, then walked over to Gio. "I'm going to take a little walk with Allie down the beach," she said.

"I'll come with you," he said.

"Actually"—Tina glanced back at Allie—"I think Allie needs to get something off her chest. Do you mind? We won't be long."

"Don't go past the bend where Ryan was mugged," Gio said. "Stay in sight."

Tina agreed, then walked back over to Allie and extended her hand. "C'mon," she said.

They walked silently for a moment, still holding hands and choosing their steps carefully to avoid a patch of broken glass.

"Talk to me about Dwight," Tina said when they were safely out of earshot.

After a pause, Allie asked, "Is it that obvious?"

"To me. I doubt to anyone else. I saw you both in the middle of the night by the pool, or I might not have noticed."

"I slept with him," Allie said.

Tina stopped walking. "Oh, my God! Allie!"

"I know," Allie said. She gave a half laugh that ended up

sounding more like a sob. "I don't know what came over me. It was completely insane."

"Has it been going on for long?" Tina asked. She felt a bit dizzy and sat down, releasing Allie's hand.

"No! Just this trip," Allie said. She sank down onto the sand next to Tina. "We only . . ." She dropped her head into her hands. "God, I can barely even say it. We only did it once."

"When?" Tina asked.

"Yesterday," Allie said in a nearly inaudible voice. "You guys were down on the beach right before the hurricane and we . . . came back early."

"Allie," Tina said slowly. "Pauline was in the house then."

"Oh, God," Allie said. Her head jerked up, and she stared at Tina. "But no—she couldn't have seen us! We were outside, way back behind some trees . . . and it just happened so fast. I don't even know why I did it, Tina. And it *was* me. Dwight didn't instigate it—I did. It's almost like it happened to someone else. It doesn't seem real!"

Tina nodded, even though she didn't understand. None of this made sense! Allie and Ryan seemed like the ideal couple—they rarely fought, and they were devoted to each other and to their children. They'd celebrated an anniversary a few months ago, and Ryan had bought Allie swing dancing classes as a present. Tina had always noticed the way Allie filled up Ryan's coffee cup in the morning, before he even asked—it was just one of the small, considerate gestures that made them such an enviable couple. If their marriage was this fragile, then whose was safe?

"I don't know what to say," Tina said. She felt nauseated.

She loved Allie, but she adored Ryan, too. She'd stood by their side during their wedding. She'd come to the hospital twice to see Ryan staring down at a swaddled infant with an expression that mingled love and awe, topped off with a healthy dash of terror. They'd shared countless dinners—times when Allie and Ryan had brought by pizzas and Tina had opened wine and made salad and all of the kids had romped in the backyard on warm nights. Ryan always made Tina laugh, and he listened when she talked—really listened. He was the male version of Allie!

They were family. Both of them.

"Are you going to leave Ryan?" Tina finally asked.

"No!" Allie said. "And it's never going to happen again. Tina, please don't look at me like that!"

Tina shook her head. "I'm just . . . stunned." And mad, but she wasn't going to tell Allie, not yet.

"Me, too," Allie said. "I don't know what happened." She wasn't crying, which made her words seem almost worse, Tina thought. Allie looked awful—all of them did, since they hadn't been able to shower—but Allie's skin seemed drawn and her eyes were shattered.

"I felt like something was going on with you during this trip," Tina said slowly. "You kept getting angry, which is so unlike you . . . and you got really intense about us all going away together next year. It's hard to explain, but you just weren't yourself."

"I was mad at Ryan for not noticing that," Allie said.

"Mad?" Tina barked out a laugh. "That's what you do when you're mad at him?"

"That wasn't the only reason!" Allie protested. She finally looked at Tina. "There's . . . other stuff going on."

"So tell me," Tina said.

"I'm so scared," Allie whispered. "I've messed up my whole life. What if Ryan finds out and he leaves me?"

Tina looked out at the water and didn't say anything. She thought back to how furious she'd been when Gio and Savannah had flirted. She might leave, in Ryan's place.

"There's more. I just found out that ALS runs in my biological family," Allie finally said.

Tina's head whipped around. "Lou Gehrig's disease?"

Allie nodded. "I've got a fifty-fifty chance of getting it."

"No!" The word erupted out of Tina, and she launched herself toward Allie. "You won't! You can't!"

She could feel Allie finally begin to cry, and Tina held her friend tightly.

"You're going to be okay, Allie," Tina said. "Listen to me! You're the healthiest person I know!"

"That doesn't make any difference," Allie said. She wiped her eyes with the bottom of her shirt.

"When did you find out?" Tina asked. Her heart was pounding, but she tried to keep her voice calm.

"Right before the trip," Allie said. "I think that's why I did it. Dwight offered to take care of me—"

"Wait, you told him before you told me?" Tina said before she could stop herself.

"I didn't want to ruin the vacation for you. Or Ryan," Allie said. "But that night in the helicopter, after I freaked out, Dwight and I talked on the beach . . . It just slipped out. I guess I had to tell someone. And then he said he'd take care of everything—my medical care, the girls' college—and I felt this surge of love for him . . . It was like, once I told him, he and I were in our own private world. As long as I stayed close to him, I was safe."

"Why did you tell him and not Ryan?" Tina asked. "Was it really just about not wanting to ruin the trip?"

Allie shrugged. "Maybe because it wouldn't destroy Dwight's world like it would Ryan's. God, Tina, I don't even know. I can't think straight. I'm so messed up right now. But I didn't sleep with Dwight because I fell in love with him. It was more of an . . . escape."

"Have you talked to a doctor?" Tina asked. "I want to be there, Allie. I'll go with you to the appointment."

"I know you will," Allie said. She massaged her forehead with one hand. "I always felt like I was too lucky, you know? Like I'd grabbed a bigger share of the pie than I deserved. Great kids, great husband, great friends, great job. Great life. Nothing ever really went wrong for me. I was waiting for something like this to happen."

"Why?" The word burst out of Tina. "Why shouldn't you deserve to have everything be wonderful for the rest of your life?"

"Because it doesn't work that way," Allie said. "I see it all the time in my job. Sweet kids get ripped apart because their parents use them as weapons in a divorce. Men beat up good women. Families lose their homes because there aren't enough jobs to go around. I always felt like I could make a little bit of a difference, you know? If I just tried hard enough to help—cared enough—it would offset some of the problems in the world."

"And it did," Tina said. "You made a difference for those people!"

Allie didn't seem to hear her. "And now I have to figure out how to tell Ryan, 'Oh, hey—I might die on you. And by the way, I slept with our friend.'"

"Don't tell him yet," Tina said. She tried to come up with some advice to give her friend, but she was too overwhelmed to think clearly. "Let's take this one step at a time, okay?"

Allie nodded. A big wave came toward them, then broke, sending white foam rushing up the beach to touch their legs. Tina reached down and traced designs in the rough, wet sand with her fingertips.

"I don't know if I can live with myself if I don't tell him," Allie said. "The guilt. I couldn't sleep last night. I went downstairs so I wouldn't wake up Ryan, and I guess Dwight heard me. He followed me, and we started talking. He wishes it had never happened, Tina. I could tell."

Tina squeezed her eyes shut. What a mess.

"I'm like a human version of Betty. I'm destroying everything in my path," Allie said.

"Stop it!" Tina's tone surprised them both.

She took a breath and softened her voice. "You got some devastating news. You thought you might die. Do you know what the opposite of death is?"

"Life," Allie said.

"Not exactly," Tina said. "It's sex, which creates life. That's why people do weird things like hooking up at funerals."

"Please don't try to excuse what I did," Allie said.

"You made a mistake," Tina said.

"It was more than a mistake!"

"A big mistake. You're not a bad person, though. There's a difference."

"You know what the worst part is?" Allie said. "If there's a worst part; it's all so awful."

"What?"

"Knowing Ryan, when I tell him everything, he'll stay with me because he'll be worried about the ALS. He'll want to make sure he doesn't desert me in case I start to die, even if he doesn't love me anymore. I don't deserve him."

"Allie," Tina said firmly. "You do deserve him. And you deserve to live a long, happy life. And you will."

Allie seemed not to hear her. "Please just tell me how to get through the next day and a half," she begged. "Being here, on this trip . . . I thought it would be a good thing. I tried to pretend I wouldn't think about that horrible gene running through my birth family. But now everything is so much worse. I've made it worse."

Tina watched a few more waves crash down while she thought about what to say.

"You were the one who told me to take it moment by moment when I didn't want the trip to end," she finally said. "I think you should do the same thing now. We'll stay here and talk. Then we'll go back to the others and get some coffee. That's all you have to do for now."

Allie nodded. "Tina?" she said. "Could I ask you something?"

"Anything," Tina said.

"Stay close to me today, okay?" Allie said. Her tears started up again.

"Not just today," Tina said. She tilted her head so it touched Allie's. "Always."

"Hello!"

Savannah was the closest to the stairs, so she heard the shout. She turned and shaded her eyes with her hand as she looked up. He was wearing shorts and a T-shirt instead of his chef whites, so it took her a moment to recognize Patrick.

She waved, and he slowly made his way down the stairs, moving in a zigzag pattern to avoid the broken ones.

"You're all safe?" he asked when he reached them.

"Yep," Savannah said. "We can't say the same for the bottle of tequila we opened last night—it met an untimely end—but we're still standing."

By now Allie and Tina had come to join them. "How's your family?" Allie asked.

"Everyone is good," Patrick said. "No loss of life in this storm."

"If that was just a Category Two, I never want to see a Category Five," Tina said, shuddering. "It was awful."

"What are the roads like?" Savannah asked. "I'm surprised you made it here."

"I have a motorbike," he said. "No way can a car get through. Trees are down everywhere."

"But we're supposed to leave tomorrow!" Allie cried.

"That's what I came to tell you," Patrick said. "If you need to get to the airstrip, all of my cousins have motorcycles. We can give you lifts."

"Let's do it," Tina said. "We can just carry essential stuff and have our suitcases shipped later. Or we can leave it all. I'm not really caring about stuff right now, you know?"

"I'm ready to go home, too," Allie said. "I really want to see my kids. Thank you, Patrick."

He inclined his head.

"Is your home okay?" Tina asked.

He shrugged. "Lots of damage. Shingles came off the roof, mostly. We've got leaks."

"Oh, no!" Savannah said. "What are you going to do?"

He smiled broadly. "Rebuild," he said. "It's what Jamaicans do."

"Patrick, my man!" Gio wandered over and slapped Patrick's palm with his own. "What's in the bag?"

Patrick opened the white sack he was clutching. "Biscuits with ham and cheese," he said, passing out the foil-wrapped packages. "I made them yesterday before the storm hit and kept them on ice, then I heated them over the fire before I came. Just cheese for the lady," he said to Allie as he gave her one.

"They smell incredible," Tina said. "And they're still warm. Thank you!"

Patrick frowned. "There were seven of you, so I brought seven . . . but now you're eight?"

Savannah could feel the others turn to her.

"Yes," she said. "My"—she cleared her throat—"husband joined us at the last minute."

She looked at Gary. He'd taken off his shoes and was wading

up to his knees in the water. As vacations went, this one probably wouldn't top his list of favorites: He'd slept on the floor, been denied a shower or shave, and now he'd get nothing but Sanka and some bruised fruit for breakfast. Yet he'd come all the way here, not knowing what awaited him.

Savannah looked down at the biscuit in her hands, then broke it in half.

"Gary!" she called. "Breakfast!"

Could she ever trust him again? she wondered. She'd always be tempted to check his BlackBerry, and she'd need to know if The Nurse was working the same shift every time he left for the hospital. And what if Gary left her again—five, ten, twenty years down the line, when her face was wrinkled and her body had gone soft? When her window of being beautiful had passed, and no young crewman would ever flirt with her again?

Rebuilding was more difficult than Patrick made it sound. It always took longer, and ended up being more costly than you expected. Savannah wondered if she had it in her to do it.

She watched as Gary came toward her. She knew the answer wouldn't be simple.

Everyone turned toward Allie at the sudden, sharp sound.

"Oh!" she said, reaching into her pocket. "I'm getting cell phone reception! How is that possible?"

"I guess Betty wasn't strong enough to knock out the cell towers," Gio said.

"Aren't you going to get it, Allie?" Ryan asked.

The others could hear her say, "Hello?" And then she walked away, down the beach.

Chapter Twenty-Two

Roulette

"HEY, IT'S DEBBY."

Allie rolled her eyes. Her birth mother's timing was exquisite.

"I'm going to have to call you back later," Allie said. She kicked up a cloud of white sand with her toes, then watched it scatter down.

"Hang on a sec," Debby said.

"I'm in Jamaica now," Allie started to explain, then she stopped herself. Why was she being so polite? "I've got to go."

"No, don't hang up! It's . . . important."

"What is it?"

Allie could hear the sound of a match striking, then Debby's quick, fierce inhalation.

"Look, if you need to borrow money again, this is a horrible—" Allie began.

"It's nothing like that," Debby interrupted. "So, all that stuff with Hank and the Lou Gehrig's disease?"

That stuff? Allie thought.

"I, ah, keep thinking about how upset you sounded when I told you," Debby said.

"Well, *yeah*," Allie said. "There's a fifty-fifty chance I got his gene. I've been a little upset!"

She took a breath and erased the sarcasm from her voice. "I appreciate you calling. But there isn't anything you can do—"

"If you'd just let me get in a word edgewise!" Debby almost snapped. "This isn't easy, okay?"

Allie almost laughed. Not easy for whom?

"Hank and I were together junior year," Debby said. Allie could hear her sucking in more nicotine. "Just for a few months. I told you all that. But there was this other guy . . ."

"Another guy?"

"I was, ah, with him a few times, too."

Allie collapsed to her knees. "Oh, my God," she breathed.

"Look, I figured it was Hank who got me pregnant because I was with him more, and besides, what did it matter? It's not like either of them wanted to marry me."

"Who was the other guy?" Allie asked in a voice that didn't sound like her own.

"Some dude a year ahead of me. He fought in Iraq, I heard."

"I need his name," Allie said. "Debby, you've got to give me his name!"

"Jason. Jason Phillips."

Allie closed her eyes. "Jason Phillips. Do you know where he is now?"

"Naw," Debby said. "I told you everything."

"You have to tell me more, Debby. Do you have any idea which one was my father?"

"If I had to guess?" Debby said, and Allie held her breath. "I'd say it's fifty-fifty. You don't look like either of them."

Those exact odds again, Allie thought. Her life was a tiny silver ball whirling around a roulette wheel, slipping into a red slot, then bouncing out and landing in a black one, then spinning out again.

"I wasn't a slut or anything," Debby said, her voice making the statement into an argument. "I only slept with those two guys all year!"

"I never— I don't . . . Debby, I don't care about any of that!" Allie said.

"Anyway, I thought you should know," Debby said.

"Thank you," Allie said.

"Look, you're not going to hold this against me, are you?" Debby asked. "For not telling you the truth?"

"Debby, right now all I want to do is hug you," Allie said. Maybe later she'd be angry that her birth mother hadn't admitted it from the beginning—or at least when Allie learned about Hank's death—but now there wasn't room for anything in her but relief.

She ended the call and stayed on her knees, feeling the sand biting into her skin as she stared out at the water.

She didn't deserve this possible reprieve. Other people should've gotten this piece of luck instead.

"Thank you," she said aloud.

She looked up at the sun in the perfect, seamless sky, then out at the water again, feeling as if she were seeing it for the first time on this trip. All the colors! The sea was green and turquoise, sapphire and indigo. Songbirds called to one another over the sound of the gently breaking waves, and a larger bird arced toward the water, hoping to find breakfast. Jamaica was battered, but her beauty still shone through.

"Thank you," she repeated, her voice rising with every repetition. "Thank you, thank you, thank you!"

She breathed in the warm, salty air and got to her feet, walking close enough to the water to feel the spray on her face. Then she turned back around. Tina was coming toward her, a worried look on her face, and Allie smiled to reassure her as she began heading back to her friends.

In the distance, Allie could see the others still talking to Patrick. Then Ryan twisted around and held her eyes with his own, and she was reminded of coming toward him on their wedding day, feeling as if she were brimming over with joy. But now Dwight was turning around and staring at her, too.

Allie's eyes flitted back and forth between them, and she made a vow, just as she had on that long-ago day. This time, though, it was a silent one, and it was to both men: *I promise to spend the rest of my life making it up to you.*

Chapter Twenty-Three

Friday Night

"IS PAULINE STILL SICK?" Savannah asked.

Dwight nodded. "It's a bad headache."

"Does she get them often?" Tina asked. "Migraines are the worst."

"I don't think she's ever had one before," Dwight said. "Not like this, anyway. I brought her some Tylenol right before we came down here, but she said she just wants to rest."

They were sitting around the fire pit, watching orange and gold flames reach toward the sky. The night air felt velvety soft. Patrick had come back a few hours earlier, carrying a bulging backpack down to the beach. As everyone had gathered to watch, he'd pulled out two coconuts, put them atop a rock, and used a machete to break them open. Then he'd served everyone a fresh slice topped with brown sugar.

"I've never tasted anything so good!" Tina had squealed, but she corrected herself a little while later, after Patrick had pulled out a frying pan and a tin of his cornmeal dumplings and cooked them over the fire.

Now the chef was gone, but he'd left behind a quart of fresh coconut juice, and everyone was drinking it along with a healthy dose of rum. It tasted like a little bit of heaven, Savannah had said, and they'd all agreed.

"Can we do anything for Pauline?" Tina asked now. "I feel like she has missed so much of the trip. First when she went to go help her mother, and now this . . ."

"I'll bring her a plate," Savannah said. She stood up and brushed the sand off her legs. "I'm sure she doesn't want a hot dog, but I'll get her some bottled water and fruit."

"I'll help," Allie said, jumping up.

"Me, too," Tina said.

"Oh, great, the three of us in the kitchen? You know that's never a good scene," Savannah said.

"You going to take off each other's pants again?" Gio asked.

"Seriously!" Tina said, rolling her eyes. "You're a father of four. A churchgoing father of four!"

Ryan poked at the bonfire with a stick, sending up a shower of sparks. "Check the pantry for marshmallows before you come back," he said.

"Ooh, good idea," Tina said. "Don't you guys feel like we're in camp? Toasted marshmallows would be the perfect touch."

"S'mores would be even better," said Ryan. "Isn't it funny how you never hear anyone ask for s'less?"

Tina laughed and linked her arm through Allie's. "Let's go," she said. "It's still light enough to see on the steps, but we should bring the lanterns when we come back."

"Definitely," Allie said, shuddering. "I've used up all my good luck for today. I don't want any of us to trip on those stairs."

"You've got a lot of luck left," Tina said, squeezing Allie's arm. "Trust me."

"Why do I feel like you two are talking in code?" Ryan asked.

"I always feel that way around women," Gio said. "Hey, Dwight, will you beer me?"

Dwight reached into the cooler and tossed him a Red Stripe,

then opened one of his own as the women began to climb the stairs.

"What do you think Pauline would like?" Allie asked once they reached the kitchen. "Maybe toast? Oh, wait, we can't toast the bread without electricity. Plain bread?" She wrinkled her nose. "That doesn't sound so appetizing."

"Probably just water," Savannah said. "And maybe one of those bananas. I'll ask her if she wants something else."

"Should we all take it in there?" Tina asked.

"Nah," Savannah said, tucking the bottle of water under her arm as she reached for the banana. "I've got this one."

"Well, that was odd," Tina said as Savannah's footsteps echoed down the hallway. "She's not usually the Florence Nightingale type."

"Maybe she's just grateful for everything Pauline has done this week," Allie said. "Being here made it possible for Gary to make a grand gesture. It wouldn't have been so effective if he'd just driven a few blocks across town."

Tina laughed and slung her arm around Allie's shoulder to give her a minihug. "I can't stop thinking about what Debby told you," she said. She'd been struck speechless at the news, and she'd made Allie repeat it twice. She hadn't even begun to wrap her mind around the fact that Allie might be diagnosed with ALS at some point, and now here was a possible reprieve.

"I know," Allie said. "Me, too. I keep hearing her voice in my mind, telling me another man might be my father."

"Does it . . . change anything?" Tina asked. "In terms of what you're going to do?"

Allie nodded. "Yeah," she said. "It does. I've made a decision. I'm not going to try to find out."

"You mean which one's your biological father?"

"Any of it," Allie said. She leaned back against the counter, and Tina was struck by the fact that for the first time on this vacation, Allie looked at peace.

"I'd have to track down Jason, and convince him to take a paternity test, then wait for the results . . . then if I wasn't his, I'd have to see if Hank got genetic testing, then maybe go through testing myself . . . Tina, it would consume my life. And I might not even get any answers."

"So you're just going to hope you don't have it?" Tina asked.

Allie nodded. "The counselor said something to me that sounded crazy at the time, but now it kind of makes sense. She said I should choose to believe I don't have ALS. That's what I'm going to do, Tina. I don't have it. I really feel like I don't."

"I *know* you don't," Tina said.

"And as for Ryan . . ." Allie took in a deep breath. "I can't tell him about Dwight. I won't do that to him, to either of them. I'm going to talk to him about the ALS possibility, of course, but I can't lay all of this on him."

"I don't think you should, either," Tina said. "You might feel less guilty, but he'd be devastated."

"I'm going to live with the guilt, every single day," Allie said. "That's my punishment. I'm going to know every time I look at Ryan that he risked his life to save me and that I don't deserve him."

"Please stop saying that," Tina said. "Look, Gio and I have done stuff to each other—not this, but we've hurt one another. Said awful things. There have been times I've almost hated him. No marriage is perfect, Al."

Allie knew Tina was trying to help, but she didn't want to be absolved. She welcomed the guilt, even though she knew it would haunt her every time she heard the word *vacation,* or listened to one of their college songs, or tasted a piece of candy. It would torment her in all of the spaces between those times, too. Maybe she was making a kind of unconscious trade-off—she'd wear a heavy, lonely cloak of guilt, just so long as she didn't get ALS—but it didn't matter.

"Should we go back to the guys?" Tina asked. She grabbed one of the lanterns from the kitchen counter and handed Allie a flashlight.

"You're forgetting something," Allie said. She smiled, opened the pantry door, and reached inside. "Look what I found," she said, holding up a full bag of marshmallows.

"See?" Tina said. "You're lucky. I told you so."

They stepped outside, pausing to admire the setting sun. Allie glanced over at the tree she'd clung to during the hurricane and shuddered. It was just steps away from where she and Dwight had had their awful, rushed bout of sex. She remembered Tina's earlier words about the close link between death and sex. Here was physical proof of that.

"Marriages are so complicated, aren't they?" Tina said. "I mean, look at Savannah and Gary."

"Do you think she's going to take him back?" Allie asked.

"Yup," Tina said. "I kind of knew it the first night, when she didn't send him away like she'd talked about. Don't you think?"

Allie nodded. "I can see her softening toward him. Earlier on the beach he whispered something to her, and I saw her laughing. But I'm worried."

"You mean that it might happen again?" Tina asked.

Allie nodded. "I hate to say it. But I've never trusted Gary. I still don't."

"Me, too. I've never liked him, either, even though it was pretty cool of him to stand up for us with the cop," Tina said. "But Savannah can take care of herself. I doubt she'd give him another chance if he messed up again."

"Do you think Gary knows that?"

Tina thought for a long moment. "I have no idea," she finally said. "I hope so, though, for Van's sake. I really do."

Savannah knocked and waited for Pauline's voice to grant her entrance, but instead, the door swung open.

"Hi," Savannah said. The windows' gauzy white curtains were pulled back, and just enough light came into the room for her to see that Pauline had returned to normal. Her hair was in a sleek ponytail, and she wore designer jeans and a midnight-blue, silky halter top. Savannah knew none of them had been able to shower because the water supply was tainted, but you'd never guess it by looking at Pauline. She couldn't possibly have washed her hair with Evian, could she? Savannah wondered.

"I brought you water and a banana," she said, holding up her offerings and suddenly feeling ridiculous.

"Thanks," Pauline replied. She accepted the water, but not the fruit.

"So, if your headache's gone, we're all hanging out down on the beach," Savannah said. She leaned closer and lifted her eyebrows. "And I've got one more joint, just in case you're interested."

Pauline nodded. "Dwight's there? And . . . everyone else? Allie, too?"

"Actually, Allie and Tina were in the kitchen a minute ago," Savannah said. "They may have gone back down. I'm not sure."

"I'm going to stay here," Pauline said. "But thank you for the invitation."

She started to close the door, but at the last second, Savannah reached out to stop her. Unfortunately, she reached out with the hand holding the banana, which got squished between the door and the frame.

"I guess you really don't want this now," Savannah said, looking down at it. "You know, this reminds me of a guy I once dated." She couldn't help laughing, but Pauline didn't join in.

"Was there something else?" Pauline asked.

This was the hostess Savannah remembered—Ms. Stick Up Her Butt. Still, Savannah wanted to say what she'd come to tell Pauline.

"Just, thank you," Savannah said.

Savannah knew she'd gotten on Pauline's nerves a few times, like during that dinner when she'd said she only turned her phone off during sex. She'd done it deliberately; passive-aggressive, repressed people like Pauline drove her crazy. She'd been trying to get a rise out of Pauline—some genuine show of emotion. Today, though, she was feeling magnanimous and wanted to end things on a positive note.

"It's been a great vacation," Savannah said. She sighed. "I really needed one, too."

"It's been our pleasure," Pauline said, a clear note of dismissal in her voice.

"Okay then," Savannah said, stung. Her good intentions evaporated; this was the real Pauline, not the woman who'd shared a joint with them two nights earlier.

"We'll certainly miss you tonight," Savannah said, her voice ringing with a deliberate falseness.

Did that bitch really just mock her?

Pauline watched Savannah disappear down the hallway with her mangled banana. That did it; she was sick of this selfish, ungrateful group. They ate the dinners she'd so thoughtfully arranged and belched at her table. They insulted her. And one of them had screwed her husband!

Pauline threw the bottle of water on the floor and stormed

out of the room. Allie was in the kitchen, Savannah had said. *Good,* Pauline thought as she hurried in that direction. But when she arrived, it was empty. She stepped into the living room, but no one was there, either, so she went out onto the stone patio. She could hear laughter filtering up from the beach.

Glad you're all having fun, Pauline thought as her fingernails bit into her palms. If she saw Allie right now, she'd walk up to her and slap her. Spit on her. Demand that she leave.

Then a traitorous thought wormed into Pauline's brain: And if Dwight came to Allie's defense?

Pauline's rage was instantly erased, leaving in its place a sorrow so deep and raw that she felt gutted. She fell into a lounge chair and stared out at the dusky purple sky.

She knew why she'd married Dwight. His money had sparked the initial appeal, true, but she'd also grown to love him in a comfortable, steady way. She'd imagined being with Dwight forever; he was a constant whenever she envisioned the future.

She wondered why Dwight had married her, though. Was it because Allie was already taken, and Pauline happened to be there, like the last, dusty bottle of soda in a vending machine?

She considered her options. She could still storm down to the beach and confront Allie, letting everyone know Allie's sweet, innocent exterior was fake. Or she could start walking the ten miles to the airstrip where Dwight's plane waited. Maybe that's what she should do. She never should have returned to Jamaica after Therese's death. She should have stayed with her mother and helped arrange for the funeral. She didn't belong with this group.

Maybe she didn't belong with Dwight, either.

She laid her head back on the soft white cushion, listening to the high, sweet chirping of insects, feeling a profound heaviness in her limbs.

She'd replayed Dwight's and Allie's words a hundred times in her mind. *How did it happen?* Allie had asked. That didn't sound as if the affair had been going on a long time, and the pain in Allie's voice hinted she wanted it over. Pauline had needed to get away, to amass distance between herself and the horror of her discovery, but now she wished she'd stayed to overhear Dwight's answer. If their dalliance was brief, and it had already ended . . . well, then she might be able to ignore what had happened, and never bring it up to Dwight. She could learn to live with being second best, even if it broke her heart.

The only other option she could think of was to try talking to Dwight.

She'd come so close to telling him about Therese's death on his birthday. To telling him everything. She had no idea what his response would have been, which was precisely why she hadn't tried to bring it up again. She'd always stepped so carefully with Dwight—with everyone! She'd tried her hardest to make this trip flawless, but her efforts had exploded: The chef had left, the hurricane had struck, her husband had cheated . . .

Damn it, she thought, remembering how she'd agonized over the menus, planned the helicopter tour, even brought along extra sunscreen in case someone had forgotten it. What had been the point?

Something caught the corner of her eye, and she looked to her right to see a black and white butterfly land on a flower in the giant concrete pot next to her. She watched its wings flutter once, twice, and then the butterfly took off again. Pauline reached over and touched the petals of the pink flower it had alighted upon, then dug her fingers into the soil, patting it more securely around the plants that had been wrenched askew by Betty. The dirt was still damp from the storm. She lifted a pinch to her nose and inhaled the wonderful, rich scent. She never gardened; she hired people to do one of the things she loved most in this world. In college Pauline had thought, briefly, about a career as a landscape architect, but then she'd dismissed it. It didn't fit in with her life plan.

Her life suddenly seemed full of such missed opportunities. She could trace the points where she'd veered in the safest directions, away from risks and possibilities; they stood out as sharply as the angles of the constellations in the clear sky above her head.

Once a young artist had come into the Georgetown gallery where Pauline had worked until she met Dwight. Pauline had been transfixed by the woman's art; her paintings were bold and original and reminded Pauline a bit of Georgia O'Keeffe, except they featured eyes instead of flowers. All different eyes, with different expressions . . . Pauline never knew eyes *could* have so many expressions. But the gallery owner didn't consider walk-ins, and Pauline had turned the young woman away, watching as she zipped up her portfolio and headed back onto the street. What she wouldn't give for a painting of those eyes now; they'd haunted her for more than a decade. She should have bought one, and maybe helped the woman get a show, become her mentor . . .

Pauline let the soil slip through her fingers as the day's last bit of light disappeared. Still she didn't move. Indecision weighted her down so heavily that she felt as if she could've stayed on the lounge chair forever, until she crumbled into nothingness.

She heard a noise and turned in its direction.

If she'd needed a sign about what to do, maybe one had arrived: Dwight was walking toward her.

"Hey," he said. He put his lantern on the side table and sat down in the chair next to hers. "I was just coming to find you, to see if you were feeling any better."

She looked at him steadily, wondering if he'd really left because it was too painful for him to be around Allie and Ryan together.

"How's your headache?" Dwight asked.

Pauline kept looking at him instead of answering.

"I hate escargots," she finally said. "I always have. They're horrible. Slimy. Repulsive little creatures."

Dwight blinked. "Okay," he said. He folded his arms behind his head and looked at her.

"And I know you slept with Allie."

It was a bluff of sorts; it was impossible for Pauline to know how far things had gone between them.

He flinched, then closed his eyes. "Oh, Pauline," he said, and his tone told her she'd hit on the truth.

"Do you love her? Do you want to be with her?" She remained perfectly still, feeling as if she were a passenger in a speeding car that was about to crash head-on into a stone wall. Pain and devastation were rushing toward her, and she was powerless to prevent it.

"No," Dwight said. "It's—it's over!"

"It is not over. You slept with another woman, on the vacation I tried so hard to make nice for you," she said, leaving a tiny pause after every carefully enunciated word, so her accusation felt like a series of flutter punches.

"I'm so sorry," he said. He started to reach for her, then pulled back, rightly assuming that she couldn't bear for him to touch her.

"How many times did it happen?" she asked.

"Once," he said. "And never again." She looked at him, and to her surprise, she believed him. Dwight's emotions had always been transparent on his face, and he'd never before lied to her. At least not to her knowledge.

"But you were in love with her in college!" Pauline cried. "You've always been in love with her! Why did you even marry me? Because you couldn't have Allie?"

"That sound outside the door," Dwight said. "Was that

you? . . . Pauline, did you hear me tell her I didn't love her any-more?"

"You told her that?" Pauline said.

"Yes," Dwight said.

"Then why?" Pauline whispered. *Why did you do this to me?*

"I keep asking myself that, too," Dwight said. He sighed. "She's worried she might get sick, Pauline. Really sick. And she came to me for help."

"For help?" Pauline bit off the words. She wasn't numb, not anymore; now her body felt like it was on fire. "So you decided to help her by screwing her?"

The rough words tasted alien in Pauline's mouth. She never talked like this to anyone. But it felt strangely good.

"No, no, it wasn't like that," Dwight said. "I'm not trying to make excuses, I promise. I just want to explain. P-please."

"So explain," Pauline said. She crossed her arms.

"It made me feel, I don't know . . . like a man!" Dwight said. "That I could help her. That I could help *anyone,* Pauline. No one's ever needed me to do that before."

"I've needed it!" Pauline shouted.

"No," Dwight said, and there was a new note in his voice, one Pauline couldn't easily identify. "You haven't needed me for anything."

Pauline felt unease claw at her belly; what was happening? Why did she feel as if Dwight was talking about something else entirely? She tried to think of something to say, to get their con-versation back on track, but it was too late.

"You never want to sleep with me," Dwight said. "Not any-more."

"That's not true!" Pauline said.

"We haven't had sex once on this trip," he said. "You've al-ways got some excuse, or you pretend to be asleep."

She cringed; he'd known she'd been faking, but he'd misunderstood the reason. She thought of him reaching to pull her into the shower at the beginning of the trip, and saw herself twisting away. There were so many similar moments before that, too—times he'd started kissing her, and she'd moved out of his grasp or slipped under the covers to give him a quick blow job. She hadn't known he'd felt rejected; she'd only thought about the reprieve she'd granted herself from failing to get pregnant again.

Was that part of the reason why he'd turned to Allie? Because he thought Pauline didn't want him anymore?

"And I thought you didn't want me to see your sister because of *me*," Dwight was saying, now looking straight ahead, into the darkness, instead of at her. "Because you thought I wouldn't know what to do. That maybe I'd make her uncomfortable. I know sometimes I don't . . . whatever. Fit in."

"No," she said. Dwight had blamed himself? She'd never imagined that; she didn't realize he'd even thought about Therese. "It wasn't that, Dwight. Never that."

"So I thought I could research things. Figure out how to act," he continued. "You said she had something like Down syndrome. I decided to read a little more about it. You never told me exactly what she had." He gave a little laugh. "But if there's one thing I'm good at, it's computer research. You know that."

"I didn't— I just—" Pauline felt panicked. What was happening? She was the injured party here; she was the one who'd been dealt a body blow. So why did Dwight look so upset?

"I looked into the facility, too," he said. "My accountant pointed out the name to me a while ago. He thought it looked like an unusual expense, and he always shows me those."

"It wasn't that much money!" Pauline said. "Not in the grand scheme of things . . . I just—"

"Pauline," Dwight said. "Do you really think that's what I care about? The money?"

She fell silent.

"Why didn't you tell me the truth?" he asked.

Excuses swam through her mind, but she couldn't grab hold of any of them.

"I was scared," she finally said.

"That I couldn't handle it?" he asked.

"Maybe," she said. Pauline squeezed her eyes shut. *The truth.* "No, that I couldn't."

"I wish you'd told me," he said. He sighed deeply. "And I wish I'd never cheated on you."

It's too late for that, Pauline thought.

"I'd really like to visit Therese with you," he said.

Too late, Pauline thought again.

She let her eyes drift back to the sky. She'd learned long ago that only a fraction of the constellations were visible at any given time; the overhead landscape was constantly changing. So many stars were glowing in distant places now, even without anyone to bear witness.

She took a deep breath.

"Her favorite song was 'You Are My Sunshine,'" she began. "Therese's. Therese's favorite song. And she liked . . . for her arms and legs to be massaged."

Dwight didn't say anything, but he was watching her carefully again. Had he caught her use of the past tense? Pauline wondered.

"There's a question I need to ask you," she said. "What are your thoughts on adoption?"

"Adoption?" Dwight echoed. He shook his head, but he wasn't giving a negative answer; he seemed to be trying to clear it. "Pauline—I mean, I think it's great."

"What about a child with special needs?" she asked. "Would you ever adopt one?"

"I . . . guess so," he said. "I'd have to think about it. I mean, sure, maybe."

"I think I might want to," Pauline said.

It didn't matter if she and Dwight could bear children; this was what she needed to do. She'd been surprised that he had been receptive so quickly. But now she remembered: Allie was adopted. It would be something else to link them, another shared experience.

Maybe she wouldn't ever be able to escape from Allie's shadow.

"I kept waiting for you to tell me about Therese," Dwight said. "But you never did. You just gave off these signals of not wanting to talk about her. Just like you gave off signals of not wanting to sleep with me. Pauline, I didn't know what to do."

She nodded slowly.

"I— So I hired someone last year," Dwight was saying. "A private aide. To check on your sister every few days and give her extra care."

Of all the things he'd said tonight that had shocked her, nothing had come close to this. Pauline couldn't breathe for a moment.

"It's a good facility, but nurses are stretched thin everywhere," Dwight said. "He's really excellent, Pauline—I had him checked out first. So this aide comes to, you know, read to her. Things like that."

To paint her fingernails. To sing to her, she thought. *Carlos.*

He violated my trust, Pauline thought, *but what I did was even worse. I never truly trusted him in the first place.*

"Pauline?" Dwight said. "Please don't cry. I'm so sorry."

She knew he thought it was because of Allie, but she couldn't explain, not now. Her throat was too tight for her to speak. But she could do something else. She could get up, and climb into Dwight's lap, and feel him hold her while she sobbed.

Maybe it isn't too late, she thought as she held on to his shirt tightly with both hands. *Maybe, for once, our timing is exactly right.*

Chapter Twenty-Four

The Last Day

TINA ZIPPED HER SUITCASE shut and walked over to the private balcony off the sitting area of their bedroom.

She stepped outside and spun in a slow half circle, trying to soak everything in for the last time. She wanted to absorb the sweet-salty smell of Jamaica, feel its warmth on her skin, and hear the unhurried rhythm of its waves.

"Do you think that kid down the street drank all my beer?"

Tina smiled but didn't turn around.

"Definitely," she said. "He probably had a few parties at the house, too."

"That's what I would've done at his age," Gio said. "As long as they didn't break the TV."

He came up behind her and wrapped his arms around her, kissing the back of her neck.

"Actually, I guarantee we drank more on this trip than any teenagers," Tina said, leaning into him. "It's going to take me a few weeks to dry out from all that alcohol!"

"Ready to go?" Gio asked.

Tina was looking out at the exact spot where the sky blended into the water. She could stare at that shade of blue forever, she thought. If only she could fix the hue in her mind. Maybe she'd try to match it and paint her bedroom that color someday.

"Just give me five minutes," she said.

"Okay," Gio said. She could hear the bedroom door shut behind him, as if he knew she needed solitude.

She sat down on a big wooden chair and tilted her face up to the sun. She needed to hold on to this feeling, she thought. On those days when she was bleary-eyed from lack of sleep and couldn't find matching clean socks for the kids and had to dig through the laundry basket, searching for the least smelly ones, she'd need to remember Jamaica's lesson: Everything would get easier in time. Paolo would grow into his puppy feet and Angela would change to a fancy new shampoo instead of one with a cartoon character on the bottle, and Jessica would eventually get a cell phone and Sammy would step onto the school bus with a brand-new lunch box for kindergarten while she stood on the sidewalk, hiding her tears as she waved good-bye.

It seemed impossibly far away, but she knew that day was rushing toward her, as inexorably as the waves.

She reached into her pocket for the perfect shell she'd discovered on the beach yesterday. It was creamy white and crescent-shaped, with a mother-of-pearl sheen on the inside. She was going to turn it into a key chain fob so she'd see it every day. Maybe this talisman would help her remember.

But first, she thought as she ran her fingers over the shell, she was going to sit here and do absolutely nothing but breathe for the next three hundred seconds.

Chapter Twenty-Five

Departures

"CALEB?" PAULINE SPOKE INTO the phone. "We're over the Atlantic now. We'll be landing in half an hour."

"The cars are ready," the house manager said. "They're at the airport—one for every couple except Savannah and Gary. I checked ten minutes ago, and their connecting flight to North Carolina is scheduled to depart on time. Gate A-Twenty-Three. Is there anything else, Ms. Glass?"

"No, thank you. See you in a bit." Pauline hung up the phone and watched as the steward cleared away the platters of cheeses and summer sausages and strawberries from the main cabin. The group was much more subdued than they'd been on the trip down, she thought.

Her eyes slowly traveled over the couples. Allie was reaching for Ryan's hand, and Ryan was smiling and brushing a strand of hair out of Allie's eyes . . . and now Allie was leaning back and Pauline could see her lips tremble before she pressed them tightly together. Would Allie ever tell Ryan what had happened with Dwight? Pauline wondered. She supposed she should hate Allie, but for some reason, she didn't, not any longer.

Pauline looked across the aisle, at Tina dozing against her

seat's headrest. Gio was reading something on his BlackBerry and frowning, but his other hand was resting on Tina's knee. Just looking at them, you could tell they were going to make it. They'd be the type of couple who slow-danced at their fiftieth wedding anniversary while their grandchildren cheered.

Then there was Savannah, sitting across from Gary in yet another too-short skirt. Did she buy them in the teen departments of stores? Pauline wondered. Gary was lifting up his glass of wine, and offering it to Savannah because her glass was empty and the steward was busy with the dishes from the snacks. Pauline watched as Savannah looked at Gary for a long moment. She didn't smile, or thank him, but she finally reached over and drank from his glass.

The only one left was Pauline's husband, sitting alone in a big leather chair. He was apart from the others, and his chair was tilted toward the window, facing away from Allie.

It still hurt to know what had happened with Allie—it hurt more than Pauline thought possible. She'd imagined that she was the one who brought grace and beauty into his life, that she was the only one he thought about when he closed his eyes at night.

But then again, didn't all marriages carry thousands of hurts? Didn't husbands and wives injure each other all the time, leaving wounds both big and small, with snapped words or forgotten anniversaries or emotional buttons deliberately pushed? But thousands of kindnesses existed in marriages, too. The important thing was that the kindnesses triumphed over the hurts.

She'd hurt Dwight, too.

She walked back down the aisle and sat next to him, feeling exhausted. It had been such a very long week.

Tonight she'd tell Dwight more about Therese. She'd bring him a glass of scotch, and ask him to sit with her on the couch.

She'd tell him everything. About rushing to the hospital. About holding Therese's soft hand as she died. She'd lay bare every single secret she'd ever kept from him.

"I love you," she whispered, so quietly she wasn't sure if he could hear her.

She waited, tears brimming behind her closed eyelids, until she heard her husband repeat the words in answer.

Those three small words could contain so many different meanings—an apology, an implicit promise, an answer to an unspoken question, a good-bye . . .

But as she felt his arm reach around her shoulders and pull her close, she knew, beyond the shadow of a doubt, that they also held the strength to carry her and Dwight through, into a new future.

Acknowledgments

I'm beyond lucky to get to work with Victoria Sanders and Greer Hendricks, the agent and editor of my dreams. This book is dedicated to them for their invaluable guidance and constant support. I cherish our friendship and look forward to many more books together.

Atria Books is a wonderful home for authors, a nurturing publishing house that's committed to building the careers of writers. In the publishing world, it's a rare and special place indeed. I'm so grateful to be a part of the Atria family. Publisher Judith Curr is a class act as well as a visionary, and the rest of her team—Paul Olsewski, Chris Lloreda, Lisa Sciambra, Lisa Keim, Carole Schwindeller, Hillary Tisman, Anne Spieth, and Yona Deshommes—are a pleasure to collaborate with. I remain ever grateful to the amazing Sarah Cantin for her constant help and kindness, and I'm thrilled to be working with the dynamo publicist Cristina Suarez.

Superpublicists Marcy Engelman and Emily Gambir have worked magic on my novels—I'm proud to be your client, and in awe of what you've done! Thank you, thank you.

At Victoria Sanders & Associates, Bernadette Baker-Baughman and Chris Kepner are on top of every last detail, always with patience and good humor. And my foreign rights agent, Chandler Crawford, continues to bring my novels to new countries, which is always a thrill. My thanks to Chandler and to my publishers overseas, especially Simon & Schuster Australia for all their support.

Anna Dorfman creates gorgeous, distinctive covers for my books, and the sharp-eyed copy editor Susan M. S. Brown continues to catch my errors and save me from embarrassment (her best catch on this book—I had a character covering her hand with her mouth. Whoops.).

Helping me get some critical hurricane-related details right were Dr. Will Drennan of the University of Miami. And Lisa Kinsley, certified genetic counselor, also generously gave of her time and expertise. Any errors, however, are mine alone.

Rachel Baker and Michelle Subaran helped me recall the beauty and power of Jamaica (it has been a while since I've visited!), and I'm so grateful for their expertise and their patient answers to all my questions. Thank you, wonderful friends!

And to all the amazing book bloggers who have taken the time to read and review my novels, and to the booksellers and librarians who have recommended them—your support means everything. A special shout-out to Kathy Roberts and Jen Karsbaek for doing an early read of *The Best of Us*.

I'm so happy that readers have taken the time to find me on Facebook and Twitter. I love hearing from you and sharing the publication process with you! You've helped me name characters, come up with titles, and inspired me on days when the words refused to show up on the page. Thank you doesn't begin to cover it. For any readers who would like to connect on social media, please come find me—I'm waiting for you!

My parents, John and Lynn Pekkanen, and our "Alvie"— Olivia Cortez—help keep my kids happy when I'm on deadline and help keep me sane (at least somewhat). My love to you all.

And to Glenn and our boys, Jack, Will, and Dylan. The only thing better than writing books is getting to have you as my family.

The Best of Us

SARAH PEKKANEN

A Readers Club Guide

Questions and Topics for Discussion

1. Which of the women in *The Best of Us* did you most identify with, and why?

2. Discuss the four marriages that are depicted in *The Best of Us*. What kinds of adjectives would you use to describe each of them? Do any of your past or current relationships have similarities to one or more of these marriages? Which marriage seems the strongest and the most appealing to you?

3. What do you think each woman learns from her time in Jamaica? How does the trip change each of them?

4. At several points in the novel, Gio makes jabs at Dwight and the way that his financial success is on display during the vacation. Allie suggests that Gio's ability to provide for his family might be a sensitive point for him, saying, *"Everyone has different emotional triggers, and even if they don't make sense to the rest of us, it's important to respect them"* (p. 109). What is this moment in the novel saying about both Allie and Gio? And do you agree with Allie's assessment?

5. Savannah has many, many witty lines over the course of the novel. Did you have a favorite? She also doesn't hesitate to say exactly what she is thinking, which contrasts with the personalities of "peacemakers" like Allie. Which woman are you more like, and has there ever been a time when you've slipped into the other's role?

6. As Allie faces the possibility of a fatal illness, she begins to second-guess many aspects of her life, including her relationship with Ryan. She wonders: *"Had she been mistaking her husband's passivity for agreeableness all these years?"* (p. 171). How did you interpret Ryan's easygoing

nature? What do you think this quote is saying about the behavior patterns that couples fall into over time?

7. Tina is devastated when she realizes she forgot to call her kids on the first night they all arrive in Jamaica— and then wonders why Gio hadn't remembered, either. How are their parenting styles shown to differ throughout the novel? How do you think one's role as a parent affects one's role in a marriage?

8. There are many characters in *The Best of Us* who look for forgiveness at some point during the narrative. What do you think the novel is saying about the role of second chances in marriages and close friendships? Should they be freely given? And can romantic or platonic love ever truly be unconditional?

9. Which aspect of the trip to Jamaica sounded the most appealing to you? However, as relaxing as a vacation can be, *The Best of Us* illustrates that it can also be an occasion for stress. Did this resonate with you? Why do you think this happens?

10. Since Savannah, Allie, and Tina were all close friends in college, Pauline is less comfortable with them, and sometimes appears to be standoffish. Did your opinion of Pauline change over the course of the novel?

11. After learning that Dwight has cheated on her, Pauline thinks, *"He violated my trust, but what I did was even worse. I never truly trusted him in the first place"* (p. 329). Do you agree with this?

12. *"Didn't all marriages carry thousands of hurts? Didn't husbands and wives injure each other all the time, leaving wounds both big and small, with snapped words or forgotten anniversaries or emotional buttons deliberately pushed? But thousands of kindnesses existed in marriages, too. The important thing was that the kindnesses triumphed over the hurts"* (p. 334). Do you agree with this assessment of marriage?

If you had to pick one mantra or saying that defined a successful romantic relationship to you, what would it be?

Enhance Your Reading Group

1. Savannah makes a playlist of songs from their college years to bring along on the trip to Jamaica. If you were to make a playlist of the hits from your college years, what would be on it? Share your compilation with the group.
2. If you haven't already, read Sarah Pekkanen's *Skipping a Beat* as a group. Compare and contrast the portrayal of marriage in each book.
3. In many ways, the trip to Jamaica that Pauline and Dwight plan for their friends sounds like a dream vacation. What does your dream vacation look like? Where would you travel to, and what kinds of activities would you ideally do there? Would you want to travel with family or friends—or even go by yourself? Share your imaginings with the group.

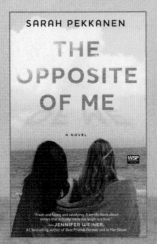